KM77 $7.00

A BRIGHT TRAGIC THING

*Signed for Kegan
Hope you enjoy
the story
Best Wishes

HHClark
December 2008*

A BRIGHT TRAGIC THING
A Tale of Civil War Texas

L. D. CLARK

CINCO PUNTOS PRESS   EL PASO, TEXAS

A *Bright Tragic Thing*. Copyright ©1992 by L.D. Clark. Printed in the United States of America. All rights reserved. No part of this book may be used or reproduced in any manner whatsoever without written consent from the publisher, except for brief quotations for reviews. For further information, write Cinco Puntos Press, 2709 Louisville, El Paso, TX 79930; or call 1-915-566-9072.

ISBN 0-938317-17-2, Paper $14.95
ISBN 0-938317-18-0, Cloth $24.95
ISBN 13: 978-0-938317-17-3
Library of Congress Catalog Card Number 91-078329

Cover photo: The only known portrait of Nathaniel Miles Clark, the great grandfather of L.D. Clark. It was made about 1860, just two years before Nathaniel was executed in the Great Hanging at Gainesville, Texas.

Photograph of L.D. Clark ©1992 by LaVerne Harrell Clark of Tucson, Arizona

Cover and book design
by Vicki Trego Hill of El Paso, Texas

Typesetting by TypeGraphics of Texas, Tyler, Texas

Special thanks to Suzan Kern

Printed on acid free paper by
McNaughton-Gunn, Inc., of Saline, Michigan

∞

Glory is that bright tragic thing
That for an instant
Means Dominion

– EMILY DICKINSON

Foreword

THIS NOVEL RE-CREATES a Civil War tragedy known as the Great Hanging at Gainesville, Texas. The chief material source is *Civil War Recollections of James Lemuel Clark*, ed. L. D. Clark. Texas A&M University Press: College Station, 1984. Other elements are drawn from Thomas Barrett, *The Great Hanging at Gainesville, Cooke County, Texas: October, A. D. 1862*. Gainesville, 1885, (reprinted by the Texas State Historical Association, 1961); and from "George Washington Diamond's Account of the Great Hanging at Gainesville, 1862," ed. Sam Acheson and Julia Ann Hudson O'Connell. *Southwestern Historical Quarterly*, LXVI, #3, January 1963, pp. 331-414. In keeping with the time-honored freedom of the story-teller's art, truth to the spirit of the event in this narrative takes precedence over a strict adherence to history.

I

OH YES, it was only one out of the many local turmoils that so intensified the national calamity of the Civil War, and it happened so long ago that few are left alive today who suffered through it. But I, for one, will carry fresh to my grave the memory of those harrowing weeks here in Milcourt, Texas: weeks that I began as a boy of eighteen and ended having gone through tribulation enough to mature ten boys like me. All of a sudden, as the oldest son, I became head of the family, thrust into making decisions for Ma and Sis and my three brothers—for Pap himself, too, snatched away from us and locked up as he was. Every hour of those weeks found me agonizing over some choice demanded by one frightful incident after another that swept us along as fast as perdition could spew them out. And yet, for all my entanglement and confusion, those events occupied from the start a unique sphere outside the world of the common self that exists from one breath to the next, and though all the while this self struggled to keep pace with those events, it never could. Running their course swift and terrible, they created in me a being that has not overtaken my earthly, time-ridden self to this day. Drawn up in wrinkles my face may be these days, as I go around Milcourt and the countryside hiding behind a white beard and peering out through faded eyes, limping with a cane when I can walk at all—but I still picture myself in the image of that bewildered boy who thrashed out in horror and delirium against forces threatening to annihilate him as well as the family he was suddenly responsible for. As a result, I never will be a man who advanced through the ordinary stages of life to reach what I pass for today: Grandpa Todd Blair—grandfather to everybody and nobody, childless, my wife dead for years—but will remain a solitary creature forever living over my youth in that special realm where this story lies.

At the center of this tale is Pap. Today I'm older by far than he was back then, yet I see him still as truly the old man—a father in desperate need of help from a son who strains and strains to break through from youth to manhood and save him. Sometimes I think of our predicament as an unrelenting dream where the sun stands still above the two of us, all motion gone out of time—. And that tree, that giant tree undying in memory, rearing up as a mighty web of trunk and branches blackening the sky, the whole world gone murky from the shadow of it. And Pap I see as falling, falling, through the dark sky and the great greenish mesh of that tree, while I stand reaching out with the power draining swiftly from my hands ever to grasp and lift him up to safety.

On that order I dreamed our dilemma for years after the catastrophe. Now and then I still do—more often of late, in fact: which is why I have put myself to telling this story.

The spot on earth to go with these happenings never old is right here in the Cross Timbers of north Texas, where Pap brought our whole family so long ago. A strange thing it is we're still here, I suppose—myself and a great many more descended from Pap through my sister and my brothers—when what occurred could just as well have sent the Blair family migrating to the ends of the earth. But then there was Pap's great love of the Cross Timbers, right from the time when he first heard about it, and on to the bitter end too. And though it was agony for me to live through what this region finally brought him to, yet the land became so much a part of him in memory that I would not have felt right about leaving it after the tragedy was over. And Ma thought the same, as she would never have told me outright—and never had to.

And so time went on, after the blow fell and all that came in its wake, and that horrifying hour I still re-live—of Pap falling, falling, and me forever helpless to rescue him—began to edge away from the other hours and days of my life, and these brightened more and more with what I had grown to love about the Cross Timbers for its own sake. Until in due course, in my time-bound existence as well as in that sphere of marvels, I came truly to belong to this corner of the earth, and it came to belong to me.

Mutual acceptance between the other inhabitants of the Cross Timbers and my family was another matter, an accommodation of twists and turns best understood through the laying out of a complete account starting with the sort of people who settled here when the country first opened up. By and large they were as fine as any folks in the world. But then a few among them, when public affairs did not go to suit their beliefs, undertook to exert control over the majority—and would have called on the help of the devil himself to do it, if need be. That was when the Civil War was brewing up. Most of us in this part of the country were strong in opposition to seceding from the Union: wrenching the nation apart, as we saw it, just to uphold slavery—which we did not support anyhow, some on principle, though most of us because all the land we ever expected to own we and our children could work for ourselves. So what came about was a situation of the majority pulling for the Union while a few men in high places and the numerous breed subject to rabble-rousing were determined to carry our region in the other direction, come what might. During the ensuing four years of carnage it did often look, to be sure, as if the rebels would be triumphant: our region swept with the rest of Texas into a Confederate States of America once and for all. Of course, we know long since how ruin overtook that cause instead. And I'm sure one reason I can offer for still living here is knowing that my side won, that we kept the state and the nation like we wanted it—a knowledge that helped when neighbors who did leave the Cross Timbers begged me to join them in Kansas: said Texas was fit for nothing but rebels and Indians. But then I never could see it like that. Outside of a few hotheads—and at first they were bad enough, I must admit—no one after the war ever gave me any great trouble. Nowadays we live together peaceably enough, victorious Unionist and defeated Confederate alike, with the conflict and all its tumult sliding far into the past: to a point where I can now look on from a distance, in sorrow and never in anger, when the Confederate veterans of this county, old and dwindling in number year by year, gather in the Milcourt city park for their annual reunion. Though I must say, from the way they act, that with each passing year the event looks more like a celebration of victory than a commemoration of defeat.

—Is that always true: that any youthful episode in retrospect takes on the color of triumph? Do all defeats turn at last to victories, if you live long enough?

—Oh no. Not so. The other way around, if anything holds without fail. So illusion then, and illusion let it be: to trump up victory out of defeat. Recognizing the deception of looking back makes the past no less precious: at least that is so of the illusions I have to sustain me. So I'd be the last to wish to see taken away those of the graybeard Confederates reminiscing under the big pecan trees in the park about defeat made golden and indistinguishable from victory by the passage of years. And some of these men, I've found, have forgotten their grudges too, against me and the few other Unionists who still live in this county. Because a man about my age that I hardly know came up to me on the street a couple of years back and invited me to attend what he just called the veterans' reunion. Well, he'd forgotten, I thought, which side I fought on. But when I reminded him, he shook his head: no, the time had come, he said—and here he laughed—to bury the hatchet for good and all. It was the history of the thing that mattered now, that we never wanted to lose while we drew breath, he said, and we could guard it better together than apart. It was heartfelt for me to say how much I agreed with him and how greatly I appreciated the invitation. At the moment I dodged the issue, would not accept or decline. But in the end I stayed away. Not all the former Confederate soldiers felt as he did—far from it. In some the old wounds were still too subject to pain to risk touching them—and who knows, maybe on such an occasion I would have had a relapse too. For one thing, to this day the Milcourt city park is a place I avoid when I can, a spot with its own unsettling memories of the old tragedy. Or at least, in a congregation of veterans there would be the obsessive talk of old-timers on subjects bound to clash, and I had long since learned that in order to occupy the same community, faded blue and faded gray had to abide by one unspoken accord: which subjects to bring up and which ones not to when in company together.

Now if all this adds up to some sort of justification for not heading on to new territory after the war, yet it's not the only one, or even the most telling. What has held me here above all is simply the land itself, the land the way God made it. I caught the pulse of this place the moment we arrived: with all the more power because I was young. And not even the rampage of killing fools who caused all the disturbances later on could ever lessen that. Never to this day have I lost the sense of that beating pulse. It touches me closest in certain moments: like when a few sprinkles of rain on the cabin roof used to surprise me awake some black midnight, and there awakening with me was that pulse thumping: thrilling yet in its way fearful, awesome. Or take a low reaching of sun-glow, with dusk already dimming it—how it softens the green of the pasture sloping down to the branch-bottom below the house, and beyond that throws a last flare across the distant edge of the timber. And there it comes again, that pulse beating. It can tick to life in a cricket chirping; it can underlie that spangling of fire when the rising sun hits needles of frost on a railfence; it can pound in thunder; it can vibrate in a streak of lightning. Even in the ordinary routine of life, during the dullest of the passing hours, that pulse hovers at the far borders of consciousness, not invading my blood for days or weeks at a time. But it's always there: a cadence, a rhythm, the rise and fall of life in this place, this land itself.

—So here I am, and here I'll stay, for what's left of my life. And as long as I like the sound of my thinking and telling, I'll try to lay out the why's and wherefore's of what that boy in me experienced long ago and never stopped reliving. And in order to make sense of my story, I must go back to the beginning, to what first put us on to the Cross Timbers and how eventually we came to settle here.

2

AS MA ALWAYS TOLD IT, from the day when she and Pap became engaged, long ago in Kentucky, he talked about going to Texas, going to Texas. From my earliest recall, anyhow, that was a recurring subject of his. We lived in Missouri at that time, where Ma and Pap landed first in moving west from Kentucky and where I was born. Mahuldah—that is to say, Sis—also entered this world in Missouri; and after her, Montecristo. We did call him that, too, because Ma would not have it any other way, and this is how it came about. She had to stay in bed a great deal while she was carrying him, and a schoolteacher friend who boarded in the neighborhood often sat by Ma's bedside and read aloud from a book with that name in the title. Ma got so wound up in the story that she firmly believed listening to it had helped bring her and the baby through. So she gave him that name and was downright superstitious about hearing him called by anything else.

But then nothing like that was true of the next child, for sure, the last one born in Missouri. The Jenkins he was given from an old family name on Pap's side was soon cut down to Jenk....

Texas. I remember how Pap used to sit with the palms of his hands outspread side by side before him, as though a fabulous map of that part of the world was traced in them, and say what a fine place Texas must be, a new state abounding in everything and begging for settlers. But then the years passed, and nothing about Texas went forward only Pap's repeated dreaming speculation. What pulled him out of that and finally put us on the road in the right direction came about by coincidence. On a trip to St. Louis he happened to fall in with three fellows on their way to Texas, one of whom had a little book full of wonderful words about how rich the land was down there, plenty of it available to be patented, and much of it already improved and selling for a song. This man read some of the best passages from his book aloud to Pap, who came home all excited and repeated to us every word he could remember. For another thing, this man had a description of a region in Texas known as the Cross Timbers that he'd taken out of a report by an exploring party, and Pap got so enthused over it he sat down and made himself a copy....

I can see him yet, seated by the fireplace the night he came home from St. Louis, bent forward to be near a candle, reading from a page covered slantwise with his big old scrawly handwriting, stopping often to spell out a word before pronouncing it—for Pap had so little schooling he could barely read his own writing after it got cold. I was at that age when you can't yet read but you can listen and remember better than you ever will again. Some of what Pap read that night went so deep I can find it there to this day. That the Cross Timbers was "fashioned by the Great Creator of all things" sounded to me as if that creation had taken place only yesterday, and yet at the beginning of time. I did my best to picture what were described as bands of oak-timbered hills with little glades spotted on them, and between the hills the heavy-grown bottoms along clear streams fed by bubbling springs. The writer of that report said Spanish explorers had named the Cross Timbers "El Monte Grande," and the French had called it "La Grande Forêt": words that Pap stumbled over the best he could, in syllables that fell on my ears like an incantation. But the best phrases of all for that far-off country were "border of the immense western prairies," and, as it went on to say, lying next to the pristine "home of the Red Man." I could just see us living out there in a snug place looking west over great broad expanses of grassland where wild Indians roamed. Oh, in my mind I knew well enough that such Indians meant danger, but in my childish heart all I could feel was the wonder and adventure.

And so, with Pap's fresh resolve urging us on, early one spring we did at last set out in our ox-wagon for Texas. But then right away delays intervened. We came to so many creeks and rivers on the rise that we made but little headway. When the biggest river yet brought us to a standstill, Pap decided we ought to call a halt and make a crop, our money and supplies being none too plentiful. So we rented a farm with a cabin in fair shape on it and began planting, late in the spring though it was by now. And then of course we had to stay through harvest that fall, and then the weather got cold early, and so the upshot was, that first year we didn't even make it out of Missouri.

And that's how it went, in fact, for a few years to come: move on a little at the beginning of winter, rent a place when the weather went against us, stay and put in our crop in the spring—lay it by, gather it in the fall, round up everything and make ready to go. At last we'd pick up our journey, but then before we'd covered much ground behind those old slow oxen, it would turn off too cold to travel. So we'd find us another cabin with a couple of fields around it—half the time that cabin would have scrawled on it GTT, for "Gone to Texas"—inquire who to rent the place from, and settle in for the winter. We'd never seen so many cold ones in a row, either. And then on top of all that here would come spring and high water, and time to plant again or go hungry. Once we finally did leave Missouri behind us at that rate, we strung out in the same fashion across Arkansas for a few more years.

Well, by and by Pap got enough of it. Late one summer he declared, "If we don't get a move on, we won't make it to Texas by doomsday."

So what he did was go out and locate a man who bought our crop in the field for a fair price. Then we loaded the wagon and yoked up the oxen and headed out once more. That was three or four years before the war—I was fourteen, I think. We crossed a corner of the Indian Nation, came on down to a fine spot on Red River where we'd been told there was a ferry boat operated by a Chickasaw Indian.

Here we crossed, and now, at long last, we really had come to Texas, and early enough still in the fall to get fixed up before winter set in. As we inched along south of the river we passed through one rich bottom after another, some of them laid out in plantations, with slaves in the fields picking cotton. Pap kept on sending uneasy looks in their direction, with a deep frown on his face, as if he could not believe what he saw: that Texas, so far, was no different from Missouri. That was when I first became aware of a reason I hadn't heard much about as to why Pap wanted to leave Missouri. It was too near to what people called "bleeding Kansas," and to the quarrel over slavery territory building every day towards a fight. From the woeful little Pap had known about the situation, the Texas frontier must have appeared out of reach of such turmoil. Certainly the glossy words we'd seen applied to the Cross Timbers made it seem like a region for small farmers, not plantation country at all.

As we angled away from the river we began to pass through open country, largely grassland, with just enough patches of timber for a good supply of firewood, and the whole stretch of it barely scattered with settlers. We also made long treks now and again over high prairie not suited for anything maybe but grazing, though Pap and I did scratch into the soil and found it to be blackland heavy and rich under a thick matting of grass. But there were no springs in the draws, and you would have had to dig no telling how deep to strike water for a well, besides the wrestle you'd have had with the turf to break it up and put it in cultivation.

So then that first day in Texas we kept on going till camping time. And on the bright, cool second day, after we'd tangled around for a good while among thick stands of timber, in country now sandy and now yellow clay, we came to a rise where a big incline of prairie stretched down and away in front of us. Far off to the west, just before the land rose again, we could make out a heavy line of timber marking a creekbed, or maybe a river, from the size of the wooded bottom. Somewhere behind we had gotten off the main trail, but now we picked it up again and it led us on over swags and ridges toward the stream course. After a while we saw ahead what looked like the beginnings of a town sprawled out close against the timber of the big stream.

"That ought to be Milcourt," said Pap—because the Indian at the ferry had told us about a town of that name, the last one on the frontier in this direction.

"Must be," I said.

As we rolled on and the distance lessened, we made out the curving line of a small tributary creek we'd have to ford to reach the eastern edge of the town—it gave me unaccountable pleasure to think of the town as lying between two converging streams. We then passed a scattering of willows and a few big pecan trees, and there before us lay a sloping bank into the channel of the little stream. The oxen braced against the yoke to ease the wagon downhill to a gravel crossing over a shallow rippling current. Upstream a ways from the crossing the water came curling around a bend, water so clear that any bit of light falling on it set off a sparkle and a dance. The oxen gouged in their hooves and lifted their necks against the yoke to pull us across, while the water bubbled and swirled and splashed. That current flowing so brightly under us, and the glitter and dazzle around the curve upstream filled me with a surge of bounding joy. As did a massive elm tree some twenty yards downstream from the ford, the biggest and fullest tree we'd come across since we left the river, the leaves of it shot through with the first yellowing of fall. The tree leaned a fraction toward the water, and to balance the great bulk of it an enormous limb pointed straight away from the channel over a wide grassy plot:

Just like a tree
That's planted by the water

From the old hymn those words came back to me, and the tune went vibrating in silence through my vocal cords.

Coming up out of the creekbed we began to pass log cabins strung out wide apart along the rutted main street, no people closeby, a few figures in movement a distance away. Then all at once came two men on horseback, materializing from opposite directions, apparently unaware of each other till they met in recognition on the main street, then proceeding together in our direction. Approaching, they separated as if to pass on either side of us, but when Pap pulled up they did likewise, one on the left of our wagon and one on the right.

Pap sang out in his cheery hello voice, "If I'm not mighty mistaken, this is Milcourt."

"You ain't lost," said the man on the left. "Milcourt it is—the little there is to it."

With his deep blue eyes roving around then fixing suddenly on you, plus the thickest black whiskers I'd ever seen, he made even the air around him seem warm and friendly. None of that could be seen in the other man though. He was tall and gaunt with a hard-featured reddish complexion. Yet at first glance you might have thought he would be easily amused, seeing a trace of a smile on his lips—till you caught his eyes, blue as well but paler than those of Black Whiskers, with a bulge like they might pop out of his head if you crossed him. He took his time, in silence, about looking us over, as if he had some natural right to judge what he expected to catch you doing. Pap sat and gazed at him: puzzled, resentful.

"Y'all going fur?" this man finally asked, his voice hard and dry.

"Well, we ain't altogether decided yet," Pap answered, pleasant enough, relieved. "We've heard a whole lot about the Cross Timbers. Concluded we'd come and have a look at them. Oh, my name's Nathaniel Blair."

On Pap's side of the wagon Black Whiskers leaned in the saddle and stuck out his hand: "Monk Harper. Pleased to meet you. Y'all too." And his eyes swept beaming over the rest of us.

Bug Eyes took it for granted he was out of reach of a handshake, so he only touched the brim of his hat.

"Harley Dexter," was all he had to say.

A pause, a bare moment of words arrested, then Harley Dexter with a wave of his hand was riding away, dismissing us. Monk Harper's wide blue eyes could not hide his embarrassment: "Don't judge everbody in these parts by him. Not a bad feller, in his way—when you get to know him."

Pap offered no comment. I decided to take the opportunity to ask the way to a wagonyard, which I did, and Monk Harper looked happy to change the subject and tell us. Then his big awkward hand extended itself again: as though maybe two handshakes from him would make up for none from Harley Dexter.

Soon, then, we were on our way down the street once more, past other log cabins, a couple of frame buildings too—though the county courthouse, centered in a square too big for it, was made of logs. Pap liked what he saw, I could tell, and so did I. Ma and Sis were taking it all in, looking pleased and curious. Montecristo and Jenk had been tired out, and drowsy, but now they perked up and gawked with the rest of us. We drove on steady till we came to a wagonyard, west of the square a ways, and there we staked out for the night.

Next morning, after Pap had made a few inquiries, we started out down the east bank of the big stream, though swinging away from it for a distance now and again to ford branches running into it. This was the Elm Fork of the Trinity River, we'd learned, though everybody we talked with in Milcourt cut the name down to just "Elem." One man told us how at the Head of Elem, as he called it, about thirty miles to the west, some big springs gushed out of the ground to form the beginning of this fork of the river. In Milcourt and as far as we stayed with it, the stream was wide and clear, a shallow current rippling over a sand and gravel bottom.

The river had turned south at Milcourt, so now for the first time since we'd left Missouri we were not traveling southwest anymore. And this day, like a few others just past, was perfect for the road: the sky clean of any clouds, the sun flashing pure, the leaves shot through with the first turning of fall, the green dying out of the grass, and a slight breeze touching you cool— altogether the right kind of a day to choose a place and call it home.

By the middle of the afternoon we had passed only three cabins, and met nobody at all on the trail. But you could not have imagined a country more to delight in—all that the descriptions Pap saw had claimed and more. Down through the woods it looked like a picnic ground: no underbrush, just a sweep as far as the eye could gaze of ruffled leaf-tan ground under big postoaks and blackjacks standing evenly spaced as though planted that way. And here and yonder glades like the ones we'd read about opened out smooth, grassy and fertile, just waiting to be turned into fields. Then if you should happen to lift your eyes toward the high bald prairie west of the river—"home of the Red Man"—that opening to the faraway made the land over here seem more enclosing, more nurturing.

"So this is what the Cross Timbers turns out to be," Pap would say from time to time as we rocked and jolted along. He kept on cocking his eye to the sun, too, to judge how much farther we could travel before pitching camp. I said next to nothing, too much occupied with taking it all in. Sis and the boys were also quiet. Ma too. And she was certainly satisfied with the country—Ma was rarely talkative, but you could read a lot in the quality of the silence around her.

A while later in the afternoon the trail curved east away from the river and crooked around through deep woods. No openings now, and when I could glimpse the sun through the trees I estimated it was an hour or less away from setting. We could easily have retraced our way to a spring about a mile behind us and stayed there overnight, but we were all reluctant, I thought, to give in to turning back. The right place might still be far off, but then it might be near at hand, and that joining of doubt and hope drew us on in direct and immediate search.

After a little while we began climbing a long wooded slope, surely the last stretch we could manage before nightfall. Then luckily at the top of the rise the timber drew back, and what we saw stopped us cold, and kept us there gazing and gazing.

On the right hand was a strip of woods holding to the curve of the rise and coming to an end a short way off at the edge of a big double circle of prairie glade. The near circle also ran along smooth to the north, in front and on our left, bending around the base of an abrupt hill thick with timber then fanning out into a marvelous bottom partly open, partly thickets, with a beaver pond here and there. And yonder on the best open swell of ground above the bottom stood a big double log cabin. You could sweep your eye past that cabin to the east and south for a mile or more, over another low swell with a straggling of trees, and on into the south oval of the glade. By the thickness of the vegetation you could count at least three spring branches running through the territory you held in your gaze.

By the time our eyes were good and full it was nearly sundown. And so we headed out in the direction of the cabin. The folks there saw us coming long before we drove up, for a man came walking out to meet us. From far off you could tell he carried a rifle, but you could soon see he let it swing loose at his side, as if he was half-embarrassed to be armed. The closer he came the taller he looked, a towering man. He waved at us first, and we waved back, and when he came up to the wagon, with a sociable smile on his big ruddy face, Ma and Pap and I all shook his hand and returned his greeting. Rufus Hackett was his name, and right from the start he and Pap launched into a big acquaintance. Mainly because as the two of them walked along beside the wagon over toward the spring next to the cabin, Mr Hackett added to a remark of his, "As old Mr Gideon Blair used to say," and Pap struck in, "Well I swear. You know him? That's my uncle. I bet you're from Missouri, from Cedar County, sure as the world." And it turned out he was, and knew or else knew about a great many of our relatives.

I saw right then how that put the cap on the matter. Around here closeby we were bound to settle.

Now of course the Hacketts wouldn't hear of us not coming in for supper, and making our camp beside their cabin. The whole family outdid themselves to make us welcome. Just as with most pioneer cabins, theirs was teeming with people. Besides a great-aunt who lived with them, and a man of some kin who had stopped by for a visit on his way west, there were two sons and two daughters, and Mrs Hackett was pregnant with another child ready to enter this world any minute. The biggest boy—nicknamed Brother—was a couple of years older than me, while the other one, Willun, was a year younger. He and I hit it off at once, just as Pap and Mr Hackett had.

That night after supper, all of us sitting out in the yard till bedtime, the chatter that broke out when we arrived was still in progress. Gradually the pace slowed, with most of the talk now coming from Pap and Mr Hackett, and more than ever it seemed like the Blairs and the Hacketts would be fast friends. The only sour note came when Ma piped up unexpectedly at a passing mention of slavery—that and how the Union fared being on everybody's lips in those days—and said we could have brought a slave to Texas with us if she and Pap had only accepted him as a gift. Ma had the habit of dropping that remark to new acquaintances just to let them know we were not any of your ordinary drifters but had gentry back yonder behind us—at least on her side of the family. Often enough the people she told were uncertain how to take what she said, since she acted just as proud of being offered the slave as she did of having turned him down. As I'd heard it told a many a time, when she and Pap got married, her father had offered them a slave as a wedding present—he had fifty or more on his plantation, they said: I never had seen it. Pap refused the offer, and Ma supported him in it, even though their attitude angered her father and soured the few contacts we had with Ma's family after that. I'd heard Pap say time and again, in private, that no member of his family, except for a few who landed in Virginia in the earliest days, had ever owned slaves, and that he'd about as soon starve to death as break that record.

The Hacketts' visitor—I've long since forgotten his name—spoke up quick: "By grab, if it'd'a been me I'd'a taken him. You could'a sold him when you got here if nothing else. Why, up yonder in the Red River bottoms they're setting up plantations acoming and agoing, and slaves're going up in price ever day of the world."

What Mr Hackett added was non-committal: "Worth their weight in gold, as the old feller says."

Now you could see Pap wished Ma had kept quiet about that. Clearly he didn't want to come right out and say why he'd refused the gift of the slave. Because as nice as the Hacketts were treating us, it wouldn't do to risk a quarrel over slavery or the Union. That's how it was in that day and time. If a man wanted to avoid argument, he could not open his mouth on those two topics without first sounding out how the men around him felt. I wouldn't have blamed Pap a bit if he'd worked around the subject with something like 'Niggers're too trifling to own'—a common remark from men who had no money to buy them—or another one on the same order, like: 'Niggers're more trouble than they're worth if you ain't fixed up to own and control a big bunch of them.' So I watched Pap close. Nearly always he could shy away from trouble without circling far from the truth. This time he sat there in the dark a minute like he was deep in thought, then he said, "Well sir, it sure don't look to me like you'd need any slaves to make good in this strip of country. I don't believe I ever saw any prettier lay-out."

Now that kind of talk being right up Mr Hackett's alley, he was more than willing to change the subject. So he lit into talking about how rich his land was, and how pure and good the water from the spring. The only drawback, he went on to say, was that he'd bought more land than he and his family were able to work, though not enough to support any slave operation: said the land agent he bought from had actually warned him not to go in for as much acreage as he had, but it was just so danged cheap he couldn't help hisself—as the old feller said, which he threw in almost every time he got ready to close his mouth. Pap had an answer ready for him, and from then till bedtime they went on with that land talk that farmers never get too much of.

Now not long after sunup the next morning, when they'd both had the opportunity to sleep on it, Mr Hackett and Pap made a trade. We were to buy the south half of the big piece of land Mr Hackett owned—the other loop of the double glade—where there were two gushing springs and a fine branch bottom, even a small lake: in short, everything a family could want. A week or so later, as soon as we'd taken possession of the land, a merchant in Milcourt agreed to sell Pap a great deal of stuff on the credit. With Mr Hackett and his boys to help, plus a couple of neighbors from a mile or two off, we got busy on a cabin and a barn. We began clearing land too, cutting down timber and breaking up that part of the glade where the turf wasn't too heavy. We all went about our work feeling assured that when spring came we'd have fields better than any we'd ever dreamed of....

Oh, what I wouldn't give to bring back one fourth of all there was to life in those days. That fall the weather stayed beautiful for week after week, Indian summer days stretching on and on, all still and smoky across the hills. Early in the morning a ragged mist might hang tree-high in the bottom, till the sun burned it away. Later on a few big clouds would puff out white and gray, and float here and yonder, with fringes ravelled out gold in a warm hazy sky. The leaves went on turning and shrivelling till the countryside lay a rich brown with bursts of red and gold as far as you could cast your eye. By now it was the time of the year for the passenger pigeons to fly through. At night flocks of them bunched up to roost in the trees, sometimes crowded so close together that a limb would break under them. And then came the geese winging south, staying high up in tiny dark lines, honking as they went till the whole landscape rang. Around the countryside nearly anywhere was all the game you could ask for. Prairie chickens would burst into the air from under your very feet. You might jump a deer out of any thicket.

Once in a while we even saw buffalo strays from the great herds on the prairie. And with plenty of wild cattle roaming the country too, fresh meat was always plentiful.

So no, I could not have been happier. Only for one thing. I could not forget that we had no more than crossed Red River when we saw those slaves. And then, right away, those old fearful subjects of slavery and the Union had come up, on the first night we'd spent in this country that we'd been so long about looking for. Not that any problem ever arose with Mr Hackett. It soon became clear that he had no strong views about slavery; but as for the Union, yes, like Pap, he was devoted to it, caring with such a deep anxiety that he seldom talked about it, and when he did he concealed that anxiety by putting on his bluff and careless manner. As for me, I began to feel that first night at the Hackett place, just before I dropped off to sleep, that a great danger had tracked us all the way down from Missouri, a danger you could not escape, wherever you went. It made me uneasy that the big slaveholders had got their hand in the game this early, for as few of them as there were in the county that had just been set up, it turned out they had charge already of too many public affairs.

But then we had much else to occupy our minds just now besides slavery and the Union: everything that went with establishing the farm, of course, but that wasn't all. Border between the White Man and the Red Man indeed! Which was one thing when set up in persuasive words in a book and fed to a boy too green to grasp the reality, and another thing entirely when you came to that border itself: to the wild country where the Indians did not always roam on their own side of the Cross Timbers boundary. The Kiowas and the Comanches would slip into the settlements on a raid once in a while, the worst ones taking place during light nights of the moon. But then even here, so far, luck was with us. At the time we arrived people assured us there had not been a raid in this part of the country for a long while. But it was a hard matter to keep that in mind, after we discovered about a half-mile from our homestead the cinderpile of a cabin the Indians had burned a few years earlier, killing and scalping the man, carrying away the woman and the children. On a moonlit night when sleep would not come, I could all but see fierce Indians crossing past those cabin ruins and stealing on straight for our place.

But anyhow, time went by with no raids occurring anywhere near us. And the country began settling up at a fair pace now: more and more sod plowed, more and more timber cut or burnt off. Inside of three or four years we had several neighbors closeby. A bigger family too, for another little brother—Scooter—joined us a couple of years after we'd settled in. So with seven of us in all to fill a home, we built another box of a log cabin set away a little from the original one, floored and roofed the opening between to make an open hallway—a dogrun, we called it. Not long afterwards, when lumber became easier to get and went down in price, Pap and I built a shedroom onto the back of the main cabin.

As for livestock, having only the one yoke of oxen when we arrived, in time we accumulated all else we needed: a couple of milk-cows, a span of mules, two saddlehorses—. I take it back: one of these I have to call more than a saddlehorse. No such common name will do for him.

First we bought Old Prince—he was a saddlehorse. Some time afterwards, when Pap came riding home from Milcourt one afternoon leading another animal, I took one look and broke out laughing. Pap waited up there in the saddle, that solemn smile of his just showing through his beard. When I stopped for breath he said, "You want him? Or reckon we ought just to shoot him and be done with it."

"Well, all I can say is that no uglier critter called a horse was ever born."

With me shaking my head and Pap still gravely smiling, we both looked a while at that pony: hammer-headed, churn-legged, a rusty bay color making his shape look worse than it was by nature, a long rumpled black mane with a tuft of it hanging over his eyes.

—Then Pap was saying, "John Hanks, that trader from the Territory, all but give him to me. Says he was captured from the Comanches and ain't fit for nothing."

"If it was more than a dollar you paid for him," I said, "why John Hanks still skinned you in the deal."

But then let me tell you, I soon found out how wrong we were. Comanche, I named that horse, and my first surprise came when he accepted a saddle without moving a muscle.

"Waiting, huh?" I said to him. "All you want is to lure me onto your back." And as long as I could put off mounting him, I did.

But of course the time came when I had to face it. So in order to slow his pitching and soften my landing, I led him out into the middle of a patch of thick grass. Then holding my breath, up in the saddle I climbed.

And I want you to know that again nothing happened. While I sat there in the saddle all huddled and tense, Comanche just stood quiet—but as much as to say, 'So? You know how to ride a horse or don't you?'

Well, but I still wasn't convinced. My next thought was that he'd prove to be a runaway. But when I finally twitched the reins he just began walking away as pretty as you please.

But even yet, for a few days after that I took it slow riding him around the place, wary still that he might explode into an outlaw when I least expected it—and all the more suspicious because he acted so tame and obedient. Why, no horse alive could have been easier to handle, more responsive to a heel touch, a flick of the reins, or even just a word.

Then one day—partly because I'd taken a good look under that hank of mane into his smart and shining eyes—I began to feel that Comanche must have a poor opinion of me, and had given in to just playing me along—him training me, so to speak, and not the other way around.

"All right," I said to him. "All right then. Here goes."

So the next day I rode him out into the widest part of the big glade. I stopped, I bent over his neck, I braced in the stirrups and let out a "Yeee-haaa"—the best I could imagine as to how an Indian warrior might sound. And it must have come out close enough, for let me tell you, that Comanche shot away so fast I thought my body had been snapped like a whip. That horse, I mean to tell you, could run like the striking of a blue norther, rushing on so smooth and fast I'd swear he left the sound of his hoofbeats behind. He had his head now, and I let him keep it, out of pure wonder and excitement. And so along we raced—that is, till I happened to raise my eyes and saw the edge of the timber coming at us too swift to believe.

'Now he'll do it,' ran through my mind. 'He's sprung his trap this time for sure. Into the woods we go, and under a low tree limb that'll take care of me for good.'

But no. Nothing of the kind. I gave a slight pull on the reins and that pony halted so nearly in his tracks that I all but kept on going. And the miracle was, he didn't seem to be at all winded.

Just the same, I walked him back to the corral, and after unsaddling gave him a good rubdown. The best thing I could think of to say to him was, "Comanche, you are one devil of a horse."

Then I lifted his forelock and we looked at each other. Comanche seemed as pleased as any devil whatever—with both of us.

And so, after that, when I was on Comanche's back was maybe when

I felt most at home in the world—and I spent a lot of time on his back.

Too soon afterwards, though, came what tore me and everybody else loose from feeling at home in the world.

The war broke out and dashed everything to pieces.

3

THE FIRST DAY of those weeks of outrage comes before me as plain as yesterday: if not more so, since in the scale of time remaining for an old man, a day from long ago may stand closer than one just past....

I see myself in the image of the boy I was, hacking at stumps with a grubbing hoe in a newground field. I have been there since early in the morning, under a hot October sun now beginning to dull for evening. Most of my thoughts, though, are not on the work at hand but rather on the expectation that Pap will soon be coming home from Milcourt: I am so anxious to see him that I can almost project the sight of him riding up to our cabin on the opposite slope a distance away, see myself hurrying to meet him, eager to know what is happening in town yet afraid of what I may hear. I have just glanced at the sun to estimate the time before nightfall....

Now it was for Pap himself that I was most concerned, though also a little for myself, in the midst of this war that had torn our world apart. First had come the turmoil over Texas seceding from the Union, when, even though in our county and several others nearby a loud voice was raised against secession, the local slaveholders thrust their own delegates on a willing convention in Austin and stifled our support for the Union. Next, after the statewide referendum in which our region voted as heavily against secession as most of the rest of Texas did in favor of it, there arose a clamor for the Red River counties to withdraw from the Confederacy, to form a new state and rejoin the Union, as we'd heard West Virginia was doing. But a noise that soon died down was all it ever came to, chiefly because many a mile of rebel ground, not to mention wilderness and Indians, cut us off from loyal territory.

And besides, the war soon caught up in its fever many who had opposed it at the outset. Thousands of men from the Cross Timbers flocked in to join regiments that local leaders organized, and marched away to fight. With so many men avid for battle to fill the ranks, the determined Unionists, if they held their tongues, could so far go their way unmolested.

But that could not last, and we knew it. As the war pursued its deadly course, with one Confederate victory after another, hopes of complete success ran high in the South. But then so did the need for more soldiers, while the supply of volunteers dwindled. And so military conscription—a thing till now unheard of in American history—was imposed: with me at precisely the right age to be caught. Among the few exemptions in the draft law was one of which the Union men could say, 'Oh yes, we knew. We could have guessed it all beforehand': the provision that an owner of ten or more slaves was excused from military service. The argument that the South depended on agriculture—which meant slaves, which in turn meant masters present to control them—carried no conviction for us. All we saw was that the very men who had brought on the war could sit back while others fought it. Over this the Union men in our county finally spoke up: a hundred or more, Pap included, signed a petition of protest to the Confederate Congress. That was not all either. Here lately Pap had often been gone from home till late at night. All I could see as the cause was secret meetings of some sort, though he volunteered no explanations, and I did not dare to ask for any....

Yes, I had just glanced at the sun to estimate the time remaining before nightfall, then for the hundredth time toward the cabin: to see with surprise a tiny figure in jerky motion—it could not be Pap—a single fragment of speed across a still landscape. By the time I realized that it was a little boy running, and that it must be my brother Jenk, I was walking toward him, curious. Then the urgency I could see in his sprinting headlong put me also into a run. He reached the branchcourse before I did, where he stopped, out of breath, ready to drop, but still trying to yell something that came out only in squeaks and screeches. I ran up and stopped on the bank across from him.

"What's the matter, Jenk? What is it?"

He went on panting and gasping till he finally found the wind to say,

"It's Pap, Todd. It's Pap. They got Pap locked up."

"Locked up! Pap? What in the name of God are you talking about? Who said so? And stop that screeching."

"They have! Him and a big bunch more. The ones that signed their names. That's what Mr Hackett said: the ones that signed their names. He was in town. He saw it. He just now come by to tell us."

"Good Godamighty, that petition!"

So I jumped the branch and tore out for home at a dead run, with Jenk trailing, but falling behind and squealing at the top of his voice for me not to go so fast. But right now I couldn't bother about him. He knew the way home, for sure.

I was thinking, 'Comanche, where is he? What part of the pasture? Get him saddled up quick.'

And yes. All right. Ma and Sis had had forethought enough to know what I'd be intending to do. For there they waited, Ma standing in the cabin door, Sis below the steps holding the bridle reins—saddled, yes.

Oh hell, Old Prince. Of course. Of all the damned luck. Because it had slipped my mind that I'd lent Comanche to Pap for the trip to Milcourt this morning.

As I came charging up Ma sang out loud and clear: "Yes, I know you're aiming to go to town. So get in yonder and put you on some clean clothes. They're all laid out and waiting."

"Damnation on any clean clothes! Just let me at that horse."

"Here!" says Ma. "You hold on to that tongue of yores, young man."

I paid her no heed. I took the reins Sis handed me. At the last second I remembered to check the saddle girth: for once Ma and Sis had cinched it up almost tight enough. Strapping it just one more notch, I swung into the saddle and rode off, twisting around to yell back, "Don't y'all worry. I'll set them damned rebels straight"—taking no account of how foolish that sounded till it was out of my mouth.

But right at once I had to turn my attention to the horse, wishing more than ever for Comanche, because Old Prince refused to get a move on, though I gouged his flanks with my heels, and as soon as I was out of Ma's hearing I lit in to cussing him besides. All to no effect. So I left off kicking and cussing and wearing myself to a nub for nothing. But what do you know, once he'd proved his independence, Old Prince decided on his own that he wouldn't mind a sort of a canter. Which would do.

The sun had just gone down when I reached the edge of Milcourt.

I didn't let up till I came to the courthouse square, which was spilling over with people. The bulk of the crowd was packed in between a two-story building on the east side of the square—the Dayton Building—and the courthouse across the street to the west: a two-story frame building itself, put up just the year before to replace the one of logs. In the main the crowd was made up of women and children, though I did pick out some boys among them as big as men. There they all stood, gathered in knots and struck dumb. Next to the Dayton Building and along the east side of the courthouse where the main door was, a heavy guard of men was ranked, holding rifles and shotguns like they meant business, some of them in whatever pieces of militia uniform they owned, a good many in ordinary dress. I recognized Harley Dexter and Carlton Dawes and Richard Goss and several others I knew to be hot for the rebel cause—with old Harley Dexter, as you might guess, having put himself up as the ringleader. No one had to tell me, now, that all the Union men that crew could round up—the hundred that signed the petition and probably more—must be prisoners in one of those buildings.

But why? For signing the petition? Or being sympathetic to the Union? Only something like that? A chill ran over me....

Now nobody was being let into either building except a few community bigwigs, county officers for the most part, and large slaveholders to a man. I saw the two county commissioners from the river precincts enter the courthouse as I swung down and tied Old Prince to a hitching rail. Then I made out Colonel Oldham, a plantation owner on Red River, coming out of the same door, the militia making the crowd give back for him. I was standing where I'd dismounted, a hand gripping the hitching rail: that at least was firm. Not that I was dizzy, just in need of something steady, something fixed, to begin from. Because I meant to find out what this was all about—though who knew how? The sight of that crowd hanging back, with some boys my age or even older among them, made me clench my teeth. Like cattle, herded, milling. What had come over that bunch of people anyhow?—And that wasn't the first time I'd noticed it either, since the war began: how a mass of people would allow themselves to be dragged into anything by their self-appointed leaders.

Now I saw my chance. Yes! I headed straight for Colonel Oldham. Not that I'd ever said a word to him in my life, only knew him by sight. But then I'd always heard Pap speak well of him, no matter if they did stand opposite on secession and slavery. He would know, he could tell me—if he would.

"Hey!" called out one militiaman from behind me, then another. And then two more stepped up and barred my way. I veered off at an angle to intercept Colonel Oldham, or try to, who by this time had mounted and was guiding his horse through the crowd outside the ring of guards. But as I approached him a thronging of people pressed back against me, to let him pass, obstructing any way through for me.

"Wait!" I yelled out, "Colonel Oldham. Sir! Wait a second."

But he rode on, either unhearing or unheeding.

I whirled around, a fury rising in me now. I wanted and needed to steady myself before plowing on, but no time for that—not when I saw where Harley Dexter was standing, which only made me madder. From that day when we first met him to this, Pap and I never had liked him worth a damn, and he despised us right back. And besides a natural detestation from both sides, he and Pap had had a row over a strip of land it turned out neither one of them owned.

So what good would it do to hit him up? Yet, if I could only hold on to my temper....

So I threaded my way back through the clusters of people, till finally I ducked around three militiamen busy pushing aside some inquisitive onlookers, and edged along till I was at Harley Dexter's side: him perched on the rock steps of the courthouse with that old rifle of his he was always bragging and blowing about planted beside him, leaning on the outslanted barrel, a self-important sneer on his face and his eyes bugging out over the crowd. Big shitass of a patriot—thought he'd founded and could uphold the Confederacy all by himself. Tingling all over, fighting my own muscles to keep them from quivering, I growled up at him: "Harley Dexter, what did you have to do with throwing Pap in jail?"

He jerked his old head around and looked down. I saw his teeth clamp shut and his lips draw back when he recognized me: "Boy, what business you think you got of being here? This ain't for brats to meddle with. Now you scat on out of here before you get hurt."

I gave him a straight cold stare and held my ground. For the time being, anyhow, I could see I had him buffaloed. He wouldn't want to admit he needed help, and he knew if he made a move to lift that rifle I'd be all over him like a wildcat. Oh, that would've been a fright, now wouldn't it? if big old Harley Dexter had to drop his great powerful rifle and fight off a boy. He'd have had his hands full too, for I was nearly as tall as he was, strong for my age, and about to foam at the mouth, I was so mad.

I kept my hands clawed at my sides though, my voice almost steady: "Come on. Out with it. What's this all about?"

A couple of militiamen had caught sight of me and slipped up through the crowd. Before I was aware of their presence, they had me pinned by the arms.

So then of course Old Shit-and-Blather took on a high and mighty tone: "Put him back out yonder but don't hurt him. He's just a boy so tore up he don't know what he's doing. Thinks he knows something about *treason* and such, I reckon."

"I'll make you think 'treason.' And I'll make you think 'boy,' you bug-eyed sonofabitch, if any harm comes to Pap."

With that, one of the militiamen gave my arm a twist. "Keep your mouth shut now," he said. Then he and his partner jerked me back through the ring of guards and pitched me out with my legs so tangled I fell over a woman and two children. In the middle of the commotion that caused, I got to my feet and began brushing off the dust. The woman, who turned out to be Mrs Ellery Smith—Hannah—didn't complain, rather she patted me on the elbow and helped me with brushing off my back, shushing her two little girls all the while, who were scared and whimpering but not actually hurt.

With no one else to ask, I broke out questioning her: "What is it? Why are all these men under guard? And what do they mean, 'treason'? To what? The damned Confederacy?"

All of that I blurted out before I became horrified remembering that about a year ago her husband had died fighting for the Confederacy, the first man from our county killed in action. But her kind and pretty eyes were just amazed, as mine must have been, and her voice shook: "They say a man, a spy, worked his way into secret meetings of the Union men. And he swears they meant to seize the ammunition depot in Grandville and terrorize the country. And murder women and children."

"Well, tarnation, m'am, it's all a blank lie! Whoever heard of the like? My father murder women and children!"

"Yes, I know, Todd. Who could believe such as that about any of them? Why, two of them men in there are my close neighbors, and they've give me no end of help here lately."

"Well, listen here, I'll find out what's behind all this if I have to break down that courthouse door. Thank you, ma'm. Thank you."

So I rushed away, but I might as well have been running in circles, for I was still at a complete loss about what to do. So I cooled myself down some, and for a while all I did was just weave in and out among the crowd: just movement to keep me from another outburst, and to give me time to think, to think.

Pretty soon I looked up to see a new detachment of soldiers come marching into the square, not militiamen this time but all dressed up in regular Confederate uniforms. My heart caught a notch when I recognized their commander: none other than Colonel Ticknor, who owned more slaves than Colonel Oldham did, who had made the most noise around here to pull Texas out of the Union, and who had the notoriety of stopping at nothing to get his way.

—Now the only glimpses I'd had of the prisoners themselves came once in a while when two guards would lead one of them over to the outhouse on the corner of the square. The one slim hope I had, so far, of seeing Pap was that he might be escorted out, and maybe that would give me the opportunity to slip up and exchange a few words with him.

But as I kept on pacing to and fro, still there was no sign of him.

I was yet in a quandary, and it was night entirely by now, when the guards began to conduct a few men at a time out of the courthouse and across to the Dayton Building where, as word soon circulated, the prisoners were being fed supper. At least with this development, I had only to wait and see whether they brought Pap over, not even knowing up to now which building they were holding him in. With that one little thought I saw, too, how much of a strain I was under, because hope and fear combined all but wrung the breath out of me. My knees suddenly went weak.

Then luck turned my way on one score anyhow: from where I happened to be standing I looked up and saw Comanche tied to a hitching rail nearby. As I walked over he tossed his head in recognition. A lump rose in my throat. Whispering "Hello, Comanche," I turned and leaned my back against his shoulder. He twitched his hide under my touch.

Over and back now the men went, six or seven at a time. Finally, when I had decided that Pap must be in the Dayton Building already, three more prisoners—the last, as it turned out—emerged from the courthouse. One of them was Pap. It took all the strength I could muster, as he slowly crossed the street, not to shout 'Pap' and run over to him. And then the effort to get a grip on myself seemed, with a frightening suddenness, to distort my vision: as though I stared at and through a fragile scene in danger of shattering before my eyes. The pit of my stomach began to sink away as if never to stop, and Pap appeared to be a long way off—Pap, who had been within my reach almost every moment since I was born, all at once at a great distance, as only miles in a dream can be distant. Tears filled my eyes that I could not fight back, and although I cursed myself in silence for a weakling, and made my body rigid, my whole being, yet still the tears came.

But then when Pap had disappeared into the Dayton Building, a great fright seized me that he might never leave it, and that fright dried the tears, though it left a deep hurting instead.

At last, a half hour later, Pap did come out and retrace the way to the courthouse and go in. I could watch more quietly now, but only for the space of a few deep intakes and explosions of breath, before the gnawing desperation over what to do next returned....

"They got a bunch of them herded together in that west room on the second floor." —I looked around toward the sound of the man's voice, words directed not at me but at a companion. The courthouse, he must have meant, because he stood gazing up at it.

Then instantly and completely I knew what to do, and it came to me with another rush of fright as much as of eagerness. Not even stopping to think further about it, I ducked around to the west side of the courthouse and stopped to lean against a hitching post: a pause to gather my wits, to watch.

From what I could tell, all the troops were around on the east side of the square. As there was no door over here on the west, apparently they hadn't thought to suspect interference from this direction. The only openings in this wall of the building were three narrow windows facing my way on the second story, showing a vague light and a flickering confusion of shadows.

Now I knew I could do it—yes, when the right moment came. So I kept a sharp eye in every direction. To see more people all the while collecting in the square and the branching side streets: horses, wagons, buggies packing in; lanterns and candles winking; fires here and yonder on the ground—whole families camped out and waiting. And with its growth the crowd had now begun to drift, to mill, if sluggishly. The night was not dark, the moon standing by now halfway above the eastern horizon. But close in beside the west wall of the courthouse, I was overjoyed to see, the moon shadow was deep, and the commotion of the crowd would obliterate a view of anything else beyond a few feet.

So I began inching across toward the courthouse, drifting with the eddies of the crowd. If anyone I brushed against recognized me, I saw no sign of it. In a little while I had reached the place where I must be: in the shadow of the courthouse wall just where the roof of an attached buggy shed slanted down from beneath the row of windows.

I stood for a second calculating the right footholds for climbing, took a last glance around, and skinned up on that roof in one bat of an eye. The first instant I could, I flattened out on my belly and lay still. No sound from below to suggest I'd been discovered, and from what I could see by peeking over the roof edge, the same ceaseless milling went on as before. So then I slithered up to the middle window, the one giving off the most light, and rose to my knees at the sill, peering in.

Twenty or thirty men sat or stood thick-packed in the room, with a pair of guards at the door. One lantern burned, and half a dozen candles. Pap it took me a fraction of a minute to single out, because he stood by the door with his back to me, facing one of the guards, trying to reason with him maybe, because the guard, whose face I could see but not identify, kept on shaking his head. And for all the crowding, not a one of the prisoners was close to the window. I lay down prone again, to let matters take their course for a while.

Unexpected it came. No warning. Scared to death, that was why—. For suddenly I wanted to piss so bad I just had to let loose somehow. So I scooted over to the edge of the roof next to the wall, checked to make sure no one was standing directly below, then let it pour. An instant later, glancing down again, I saw what I was doing to the leather upholstery of a buggy parked halfway under the shed. I came near to bursting out laughing to think that buggy might belong to one of the rebel bigwigs inside the courthouse even now scheming against Pap—small revenge, maybe, but at least a chuckle as one defense against panic.

Back at my window I lay low, except to peek inside occasionally. No one, still no one, near enough to signal. But dang. Dang! What was the matter with that bunch of men in there, especially with Pap in the bunch? Dumbfounded, like so many of the crowd? But only two guards! Why not jump them, tie and gag them, and be out of these windows and gone before the soldiers downstairs knew what was up? That or any wild scheme whatever looked worth it to me, as time went by and I lay there itching for action—though I knew I was scared desperate, and maybe not able to think straight. And mad. Madder than I'd ever been before in my life. And burning all over by now with impatience. Why, why couldn't I attract Pap's attention! Why were his eyes always in another direction? A time or two I stared in at him, risking my face against the window glass, as though he might feel my eyes on him and turn.

At long last he sat down, far across the room, his face for the first time toward me, but a wavering of candlelight between us must have blinded him to the window. Then, as in the street before, all of a sudden the distance across the room seemed vast. And Pap, with his long black hair and his full black beard, half in the dark as he was, loomed all at once bigger than life, again like someone far off who came from long ago. It terrified me, this certainty that I was losing Pap to an immensity of time never to be crossed....

It took a couple of agonizing minutes for me to struggle back to where I could hold him in present life again; and then came wonder and admiration at how straight in the chair, how calm he sat, his eyes roaming over the guards, as if he could not believe that his neighbors held him prisoner, with guns ready.

Yet I could see, and my heart surged, that he was not dumbfounded, after all: not afraid or angry, or nearly out of his senses, as I was.

'Let it steady you, the way he looks,' I told myself.

Then another man crossed the flickering between Pap and me, headed toward the window, stopped a little ways off, a man I vaguely recognized, then all at once knew well: Monk Harper. This recognition came to me with a flash of memory at once torn across: that day when we first drove into Milcourt, with burly, laughing Monk Harper beside our wagon, while on the other side hung the grim, sour face of Harley Dexter—as though what had to be good and what had to be bad about this place had come out to meet us simultaneously.

Now Monk Harper stepped closer, happened to face the window. I took a big chance. I flattened my palm against the pane, and held it there for an instant. He saw. And yes, he had the presence of mind not to let on. He turned around slow, eyed the guards, paced back and forth, picked up a chair, placed it unconcerned close to the window, sat down with his back to me.

By luck one of the windowlights had a good-sized chip out of a corner, a hole somebody had stuffed a rag in to keep out the wind. I worked the rag loose and pulled it out, which gave me an opening a couple of inches from the back of Monk Harper's head.

I spoke in a forced whisper: "Get Pap. Get Mr Nathaniel Blair to trade places with you."

And so he did that: by standing up, pacing some more, stopping as if by chance next to Pap, hardly bending to speak a few words before moving on. Pap understood, for he too soon rose, and in a minute ambled over and eased himself into the empty chair. I could have reached a finger through the hole in the glass and touched the back of his head. At that the very thought of someone doing harm to Pap swelled in me so hideous that I hardly had the strength to choke back the sobs convulsing my throat. I tightened my chest till I thought the muscles would snap, then at last feeling my breath relax, I put my mouth to the windowhole and heard my own voice grate out, "Why don't y'all make a break for it? You ain't got but two guards."

Pap heard me well, for he slowly shook his head.

I couldn't contain myself. A husky straining of whisper escaped my throat. Oh, too loud. "Then let me ride home and pick up the rifle and the musket and the pistol. I'll be back here in a shake, and we'll give these coots a run for their money."

—Rushing on against a determination not to rush on, my voice threatening to give me away after all my caution.

Again Pap heard, and again he shook his head. But he meant to answer: that was in the set of his shoulders. He began turning in his chair, half-profile to me. Then a shadow passed over him, at which my heart plummeted. My God, caught! For the standing form of a man had entered the left border of my vision. But in almost the same instant I saw that it wasn't a guard. No. Monk Harper again. He stood looking down at Pap as though expecting a reply to some remark he had just addressed to him. By now I knew that word of my presence had been passed along to every prisoner in the room, from the way they kept up a mutter of conversation to cover Pap's voice. And while he spoke to me, he directed his words to Monk Harper. Still, with my ear to the windowhole, I could pick up everything he said:

"No, son. You'd only make matters worse by doing such a thing. You listen to me, now. I want you to climb down off of that roof and head on home, and reassure Ma and the kids, because everything is going to work out all right. Now climb down, and be quick about it—please!—because somebody's liable to see you up there and take a shot at you."

But I couldn't bear the idea of leaving, just crawling away, after all the obstacles overcome in getting here. I pressed my mouth to the window again—the broken glass, the care to avoid it, as though not just my lips but my words, too, could be gashed:

"But listen, Pap, there must be *something* I can do. What is it? Just tell me."

"Keep a cool head, son. That's what I want you to do. And don't despair, now. Because listen. Colonel Oldham was here late this evening. I spoke with him, me and a couple more did. We told him about the meetings the Union men have had; I let him know that some of the talk there was pretty wild, but up to now it hadn't come to nothing only talk. He stopped me then, said just to be fair he didn't want to know too much about our defense ahead of time. But you see, they ain't nothing really against us only signing that petition and a few meetings, and Colonel Oldham come right out and said if that's all, he didn't have no doubt but what we'll come clear. He's on his way right now to call a council of the river planters. He thinks they'll want to get up a jury, but he'll try to supervise it hisself, and he'll bring the slavery men around to reason, you watch and see. And he'll put a quietus to the hothead talk from that bunch of the farmers, too. You can bet on it. Now I'm begging you, son, go on home, before you get hurt."

Before I could answer he had to let the matter drop, with the bustle of two new guards entering the room to relieve the ones on duty. Pap got up and walked away with Monk Harper, and then came a great deal of shifting before a general settling down again, with Pap back in his place and Monk Harper facing him now in a chair he'd brought over, as if they meant to take up their conversation where they'd left off.

"Son, I hope you're not still out there."

"Yes Pap, I am." And again the sobs nearly caught me unawares.

"Well, get down and go on home now. Please! Just go on home."

"All right, Pap. All right. I'll do like you tell me."

Then, more frustrated than ever, just as I was about to lower my body to slip away, a suspicion came to mind. I put my lips back to the glass.

"Pap," I whispered, maybe too loud again, "I want you to tell me one thing anyhow. Who was it laid hands on you and throwed you in here?"

For a few seconds he was silent. Plain enough he didn't want to tell me.

"Who was it? Was it Harley Dexter?"

"It was, yes," he breathed out low. "He seen me riding into town and come over, him and some more militiamen, and what he called put me under arrest."

"That bastard'll pay for this."

"No! Don't you run onto him. And don't talk rash. And for God's sake, do get out of here. —And take Comanche home with you."

"Yes, of course I will. But listen now, Pap. Listen. No, I won't do anything foolhardy. But I will do something. As yet I don't know what, but I'll find a way somehow."

And with that I slipped away at once, lest he forbid me to make any effort at all—lest I start sobbing too, close as I found myself again to doing that.

I did not look back. I wormed along on my belly to the roof-edge, stopped to check—no, no one too near—and slid quickly to the ground. Then I merged at once with the crowd, because a couple of men did catch a glimpse of me climbing down and looked up, suspicious. I could only hope they would not recognize or report me.

But even so, I could not yet bring myself to leave: I just could not. I hated more than anything I'd ever done to go away and leave Pap locked up in there. And I couldn't get out of my mind that pistol lying primed and ready on the mantelpiece at home, and the rifle on the deerhorns above, and the musket leaning in a corner of the front room....

No no. That, in any case, Pap had forbidden. Besides, really, three weapons: what would they amount to against so many men, mob and soldiers together? Think, that was what I must do. But how? Towards doing what? Even Pap....

Now then never before in my life had I seen a time when I didn't take it for granted that Pap would always know best what to do in any emergency. But this time I had to face up to it: I could not make myself believe he was right. I'd heard what Harley Dexter had to say: treason. Even before a jury was called—and what kind of a jury would it be anyhow! Of course put up by himself next to Colonel Oldham, Harley Dexter didn't amount to a fart in a whirlwind. But just to think how many others like him we had in this county. And then to add on several of the big plantation owners, not one of them by a long shot the man Colonel Oldham was. Colonel Ticknor, for instance—and him commanding officer of a big unit of Confederate troops. He and his kind hated the anti-secession men bad enough to kill every one of them, and maybe if he was hesitant to come right out and use his troops to do that, scoundrels like Harley Dexter needed little enough prodding to rouse the mob to a fury and carry out the dirty work....

During this time I had untied Old Prince and led him over to

Comanche, and untied him too, and was making ready to climb in the saddle when a voice from behind me barked out, "Hold on. You can't take that horse. It belongs to one of the prisoners. It's been seized."

I swung around. It was a kid about my age in a half of a militia get-up: Will Judd's boy.

It crossed my mind that all at once neighbors had become enemies—.

"Seized, in a pig's ass. This is *my* horse. The militia ain't turned horsethieves along with the rest of it, have they?"

'Oh yeah, sure,' I thought. 'Blaring out before you think, like you always do. Calling a man with a gun a horsethief, and you unarmed!'

I stood my ground, though, and kept on looking him in the eye, my anger against all this nonsense storming inside me. His face went beet-red, and a mad scowl came with it, but he couldn't hide a look of guilt and shame over what he was supposed to be doing as a militiaman. So after a tense moment he just spun on his heel and walked away.

I went ahead and mounted up, quickly, and rode off. Nobody else approached me before I left the crowd behind, and soon the town as well.

On my way home I let Comanche take his own time: a slow walk, a soothing rhythm. For nothing in this world can turn so bad that being on a fine horse at an easy gait won't improve it. Yet even that could not help much this time, what with more trouble staring me in the face than I'd ever encountered before in my life. I could not even begin to sort it all out so as to make a beginning on what to do next. It seemed I could do nothing, for the time being, except wish—like a kid. I wished Pap had never signed that cussed paper. I wished he'd been more careful about joining in on the meetings of the Union men. I wished he hadn't laid himself open to danger from the rebels by riding into town in broad daylight. Pap was too trusting, that was his trouble. If he'd been as wary as he ought to have been, keeping whenever he could out of the rebels' way, when the rounding up began he could maybe have taken to the brush and given them the slip: as we later found out several other men had done.

Now after what I'd been through tonight, this kind of wishing came so easy, as compared to thinking ahead, that I just kept at it: going back, back to the beginning of it all. I wished we'd never come to the Cross Timbers in the first place, especially when I recalled how Pap had looked on this part of the world: his notion of settling in a frontier place out of the way of secession and slavery troubles—and how I'd suspected from the start, that night at the Hackett place, that those troubles could track you down in the Cross Timbers as well as the next place.

As I rode along, one hand lying on Comanche's neck, I could feel the dark hills rising ahead of me and falling behind as I passed, under a moon high up now, the luster of it blanking out all but the brightest stars. Comanche's hooves beneath me, and Old Prince's behind me, clopped along steady and sharp on the road, through this country I'd ridden over so many times within the peace of that sound, only to have it contending now with the rhythm of despair. And still I wished, and still I wondered, why Pap and the rest of us had ever delivered ourselves years ago to this disaster. Before long what came to the foreground of my mind was that piece of writing Pap had discovered in St. Louis: that fine and glowing description that was the first we ever knew of the Cross Timbers. And now my heart sank to its deepest: only to think how at this instant I rode in fear and misery through the very band of country that had been made to sound so magnificent in that description.

"Let's see now, how did it go?" I said aloud to the night.

And from not so deep inside came words remembered from that page: 'fashioned by the Great Creator of all things'—though what purpose it was supposed to be fashioned for I'd forgotten. 'Land rich and fertile' did it say?—not quite that, surely. 'Border of the immense western prairie.' Oh yes, and 'home of the Red Man.' No more than those phrases could I remember, but they were enough to embitter everything. Here it was now that this said-to-be wonderful country was swarmed over by a pack of mad-dog rebels worse than any wild Indians could ever have been—.

Right at that moment I should have put a stop to the turbulence of my thoughts, before they left the bounds of reason, which they soon did. In a minute I actually set in to blaming the man in St. Louis who had given Pap that description of the Cross Timbers; and, worse yet, the man from the exploring party who wrote the report: blaming them for our predicament, men whose very names I could not remember, if I'd ever known them. I was that hard up for someone to accuse: just as if those two had worked hand in glove to make us out a passel of fools. Why, if I could have laid my hands on either one of those men at that moment, I would have kicked his ass ten ways from Sunday. But then not having them in reach, the next best thing I could do was light in to cussing them. So I blustered and raged and swore like I didn't have a lick of sense in the world. I threw out on the darkness all the cusswords I'd ever learned—not that many in those days—and when they didn't suffice, I invented some more. I raked those two men over the coals for a good half hour, knowing all the while that what I did had no rhyme nor reason to it, and yet unable to quieten myself down.

—Till all of a sudden, in the middle of a long string of cuss-words, I burst out crying, sobbing. And then I couldn't control that anymore than I had the cursing. Nobody around to see or hear me along the deserted road: that much was a blessing. And by the time the tears had rolled free for a while, I began to feel better. And before I'd wiped my eyes for the last time, I was already shaping in my head something I might be able to do, after all, to help rectify matters—considering things like a man now, because I could not permit myself to remain a boy any longer.

What I would do was this: first thing tomorrow morning I'd head for Red River, seek out Colonel Oldham. By leaving early and riding hard, I might arrive in time to see him before the river men gathered. Or if they had, maybe so much the better. Why not try reasoning with all of them? I could lay Pap's case before them. How could they fail to understand that Pap could never be guilty of anything so monstrous as murdering women and children...!

That night the wind rose sharply before I made it home, a wind that came down unexpected from the northwest, from straight behind me, and felt as though it was sweeping me and Comanche and Old Prince along. That was the first norther we had that fall: a light dry one, as it turned out. And since the wind struck right after I'd made my decision for tomorrow, I took that for a good omen—maybe just because all my life I've always loved a moonlit night when the wind blows.

4

AND SO as I came near home that night, a stirring of hope grew as though in the cool wind around me. I took a deep breath to be ready to play up that hope to Ma and the rest of the family by making as light as I could of the bad tidings I carried: to be ready besides for a clamor of questions that I expected to greet me before I got out of the saddle.

I was surprised, then, when once in sight of the cabin, to find it dark and silent—until I noticed two dim shapes huddled under the big postoak near the front door. When I had come close enough to be seen in motion against the background of timber, the forms lengthened, rising: Ma and Sis stood up from the ground and came hurrying out to meet me.

Still the first words out of Ma's mouth were, "You must be about starved to death, son. I've got a bite waiting."

Sure—because if you were condemned to be shot in the next five minutes, Ma would see to it you died on a full stomach.

So shaking Sis by the elbow to keep her quiet, Ma led the way inside, with me deepening my voice, unwittingly, to call out after them: "I reckon I'll unsaddle first."

Once I'd done that, and entered the cabin, I found the whole space filled with the small light and flapping shadows of two candles. Ma was busy stirring up and dishing out beside the fireplace. Sis was seated—or more like crouched—at the dining table next to one of the candles, eyes already intent on the chair I'd be occupying across from her. As I dropped into that seat Ma arrived with a huge plate of beans, a hunk of cornbread, a sliced raw onion, and with that a tall glass of fresh-churned buttermilk—set all this before me, made another trip for the candle by the hearth, placed it on one end of the table, slid the other candle to the far end, sat down close beside Sis.

—It was all I could bear to steady my eyes on the waiting faces I loved. And hungry as I was I couldn't for the time being lift a bite to my mouth. And my whole insides clutched when I saw Montecristo and Jenk coming out of the shedroom in their night-clothes and stealing up close behind Ma—that left only Scooter, still under two years old, asleep in Ma and Pap's room across the dogrun: if he'd woke up and begun to cry I was certain I'd have broken down again myself.

But Scooter slept on, and I held myself in check, barely, by beginning to eat, slowly, and by talking in a voice as bass as I could make it. Once started I told them a lot, and then when no one interrupted, more yet. Only two things did I hold back—.

Turmoil of questions, nothing! Not a peep. Because of Ma's look, I realized: a wordless command for silence that Sis did not dare to disobey. The corners of Ma's mouth were drawn down tight and grim, but that wasn't what tore at me: it was those clear-shining dark eyes from her side of the family that could pull you in to the torture at work inside, and stop your tongue.

But anyhow Sis it was who first threw off the spell. She jumped up, already talking a blue streak, circled the dining table, the candle flames throwing off a violent dance of shadows. At one second she declared that no men in this county could ever stoop low enough to accuse their neighbors like this; and then in the next breath she swore they had it in them to do worse.

I let her go on for a while, Ma still silent, then I stood up and took Sis by the shoulders and brought her down gentle into her chair again, and went back to my supper.

Montecristo and Jenk were knelt on the floor in shadow now, huddled up together like a tornado was about to blow the cabin away.

"But how can they do that?" Sis stormed out from where she sat. "How can they accuse and imprison people just because they stand up for their rights? How can they do that?"

Ma's voice, sudden and raucous, jarred me: "Accused. Yes. Of what? No more than of signing a paper to Congress?"

—That was one of the things I hadn't spelled out—maybe if I had just let Sis rave on, we could have put this off, at least until tomorrow.

"A man named Channing—a spy—worked his way in among the

Union bunch, went to a meeting of theirs. Then he run to the Confederate military swearing the Union men were plotting to seize that Grandville ammunition depot and start a rebellion of their own—."

"And I suppose murder women and children," Ma added, with scorn. "That just naturally goes with such accusations."

"They're saying that"—I didn't, and wouldn't, add the "treason" charge till I had to.

"But how can they say that? How can they? Just tell me!" Sis's voice was becoming shrill.

But Ma just looked grimmer than ever. And when she wouldn't comment, and I wouldn't either, Sis let out two or three frustrated sobs, till a hard stare from Ma quietened her.

Then this occurred to Sis: "Meetings? What meetings?"

I did not answer that either, nor did Ma, although it was clear that she knew about the meetings. And our silence was such that in a little bit Sis understood this was not the time to discuss that question.

But was now a good time—maybe—to launch into the second thing I hadn't brought up: my plan to visit Colonel Oldham?

I decided it was, so I began to explain, and Sis was soon taking it all in eager and breathless, which fired my own hopes more than ever. Only it did trouble me that Ma appeared not to share a whit of our enthusiasm. About all I could get out of her was that anyhow maybe it was worth a try. It dawned on me then that Ma had long known better, as I had not, than to rely ultimately on Pap's trusting nature—and from that not to put too much faith in his optimistic opinion of what Colonel Oldham would do.

It was a long while later before we all went to bed: nearly midnight it must have been. But I for one lay wide-eyed for hours to come. For already, in the pounding of my heart, I was riding toward the river, try as I might to drag myself back and gather in the sleep I needed before actually riding tomorrow. Sometime away in the afterpart of the night I did drop off, but only to strike dreams that ran fast, far and wild....

—What brought me out of those dreams, still deep in darkness, was a sound like a voice calling my name, and each time the syllable came it threatened to shatter the whole world and bury me alive. I fought off the covers—when finally I recognized they were the ordinary covers—and scrambled out of bed groping around on my knees for the pistol, which I'd laid on the floor just below my head. And I scrabbled even harder to find that pistol when I caught instead of a voice a clumping of hooves at a slow walk—a rider, for certain, and not just one of the horses astir near the barn. Then, the pistol now gripped in one fist, I gimped along at a crawl out of the shedroom, then across the floor to the front door, skittery enough to bust loose shooting any second.

Unwilling to speak and wake up the household, I stood with my free hand on the door-bar, waiting. Came the rustle and creak of the rider dismounting, then a loud straining whisper: "Todd. You in there? It's me. Willun."

I'd never been so glad to hear his voice.

"Hold on," I whispered back, "I'll be out in a second."

Whispers, maybe, but enough to bring the whole family to life. Sis bolted upright from her bed in a corner of the front room, Montecristo and Jenk came bouncing out and met me head-on in the doorway of the shedroom. By the time I'd gone in and put on my clothes and shoes, Ma had lit a spill from the coals and then a candle. Some noise or other woke up Scooter and set him to bawling at the top of his voice.

I slipped out quickly through the front door.

Willun Hackett stood there by his horse beyond the big postoak in the first paling of night, bridle reins in one hand, in the other a big muzzle-loader looking longer than he was tall.

Now happy as I was to see him, I still wanted Willun to speak up first, not sure where anyone, even Mr Hackett, might stand these days: all the more leery since he'd been in Milcourt yesterday too and hadn't been arrested.

But Willun wiped away all suspicion right at once, as soon as we'd walked off toward the corral where we could talk undisturbed. He said: "Deddy's done on his way to town, so's to learn whatever more he can find out. They won't suspicion him, he thinks, because he's kept a mighty close counsel on his leanings, and so nobody really knows what a strong Union man he is. But let me tell you" —his voice shook with excitement— "a big bunch of the Union men're fixing to meet tonight in that deep holler on Jeb Grantley's place—you know where it is, right out east of town. They figure on a couple of hundred at the very least—."

"That many!" I burst out. And my heart began to hammer with gladness. "Why, that'd be enough to pull off a rescue of the prisoners—."

"Yes! Yes! That's the scheme. Sure we can. Anyway, that's the idey."

His voice had fallen.

"What's the matter then?" I asked.

"Oh, nothing atall really, I guess. So you see, if Deddy's safe from capture, as they all think, then like I say, maybe he can find out a whole lot of what's going on. Late this evening he'll leave town on the quiet and meet up with y'all tonight in Grantley Holler, bringing what he's learned to help lay the plans for the rescue...."

"Y'all?" I said.

"Oh yaow," Willun said, his voice low and disgusted. "Deddy put his foot down on me taking part. Brother'll be there though. He's going to drift up in that direction during the day, leaving it up to me to look after Mammy and all of them. Which ain't no more'n good sense, Deddy says, and I reckon he's right. But lands, I sure do hate to miss out on storming them rebels with y'all."

"And what does Mr Hackett want for me to do between now and night?"—I could hardly keep up with all that was running through my mind: that I'd best put off consulting Colonel Oldham, feeling relieved and excited, too, that a big body of grown men were now taking over, men bound to know better than I did what to do: and had made it evident by their decision to fight that they had no faith in an appeal like the one I'd planned—.

"Just lay low, Deddy says, nothing but lay low till about night, and it better be out in the woods where you can keep an eye on the house. Deddy says nobody knows where this rounding up of suspects is gonna end. They could even come after you, your pa being so deep in this thing and all, and you being—."

"Oh yeah, go ahead and say it: I just turned the age for their *conscription*, that big word they use for sending you off to be killed in their interest. Why yes, I reckon—lock up my daddy and then throw me in their army—oh yes, I reckon...."

"Yaow. So Deddy says when you leave here, late this evening, to stay in the timber the best you can all the way to Grantley Holler—. Now then, I got to be getting back, before there's too much stir. No telling what'll come off today, and I don't want to be grabbed up myself."

"Willun, I sure do wish you could be with us."

"Shore you do. Like I say though, I guess Deddy's right about it. No more'n good sense."

He mounted up in a hurry and rode off, while I stood and watched him through the dawn and let what lay ahead of me sort itself out in my mind—as well as it could, that is....

When I went up to the house, now, for breakfast, I broke the news at once—about the rescue scheme. Since I couldn't risk hiding it from them, better to play it up than play it down, and that's how I went at it. We'd catch the rebels by surprise, I claimed. We'd move in so fast we could hope to free the prisoners without any bloodshed at all—with the big force of us that was gathering, maybe up to three hundred—. Easy to excuse to myself claiming that number: I didn't actually know how many, did I? So better to make it high rather than low.

During all my talk Ma had as little to say as usual—but she put little trust in our plan, you could see. And her silence again made Sis hesitate to open her mouth.

By a little after sunup I was ready to take to the brush. I went and hid out in a thicket that reached in close to the west side of the barn, sitting on a stump or else making it a backrest when I slumped on the ground, with the cap-and-ball pistol stuck in my belt and the saddle musket close at hand that Pap had given me as soon as I was old enough to shoot. I'd left the rifle at the cabin: there would be no long-range shooting in my present situation, and that also meant that Ma and Sis would have a weapon if worse came to worst.

Now never in my life did I put in a longer day, waiting and fretting and not knowing. Sis carried grub out to me twice during the day, refilling my canteen on the second trip, and both times sat with me while I ate. We didn't dare to talk much, or to look at each other too closely, we were both so wrought up. During a couple of my quick glances in her direction I saw tears standing out in Sis's eyes. Each time after she left me I had a lonesome hour of it, I tell you. Her going away seemed to cut me off from my whole family, with a distance widening like the dreadful space I had experienced the night before between Pap and me. And him too—I tried not to think about him, and failed of course, for it only meant that he hovered all the while in the back of my mind. And the rescue—no, I was not afraid to go, to face gunfights probably. No, I was eager to be rushing in. But the uncertainty of it all. How many men, truly, could we count on? And what if today, let alone tonight, was already too late? What if that jury spoken of was already made up, and already trying and convicting? Or what if the mob had taken matters in their own hands and were at this very minute shooting or hanging men right and left? Worries like that attacking me would now and then drive me to pacing in a circle around my stump, as if I was on a leash, till I wore out a trail.

Around the middle of the afternoon, during one of my pacing spells, yonder came three men riding along the road—first the sound of their horses and then their voices alerted me. I quick lay down in the thickest brush at hand and trained the musket in their direction—.

But they rode on by, talking unconcerned, clopping down the road toward Harper's Knob. As well as I could distinguish at a distance, when I jumped up to peer out after them, I wasn't acquainted with any of them.

Finally, finally, after long hours when I thought the day would never end, the shadows began to creep longer across the pasture below my hiding place: time now for me to pull out. We'd arranged that Sis would saddle Comanche and bring him to me just before sundown. I looked out of my thicket. I saw—a strange woman! No. Rather, yes. It was Sis, all right, with Comanche at her shoulder. It was Sis, and yet it wasn't. She had on her black taffeta skirt and her new white shirt-waist. Her fine blonde hair with darker tones—sunlight and cinnamon, they'd always brought to mind—was plaited and rolled in a bun on top of her head. And there was her pert face coming near.

I looked away, my vision all at once blurred.

So maybe, when she walked up, she thought I was ignoring her: while she handed me the reins, while I hung the musket and the canteen on the saddle horn, while I tied the slicker and the blanket behind the saddle, while I tucked this and that into the saddlebags: a lunch of cold biscuits and bacon with the rest.

But then she may have known that I didn't really need to turn in that direction to see her, with the shock of her new presence keeping her planted constantly before my eyes, even if they had been shut: this young woman who like me was yesterday a child, today grown up, both of us driven across a dividing line that yesterday we hardly knew existed—.

('I'll be so glad when you two kids grow up,' I could hear Ma's voice repeating. 'You've fought and scratched since the day you were born.')

When I could take no longer preparing to ride, I slowly began to turn toward Sis, but she grabbed me by the shoulders to swing me around and into the tightest hug we'd ever given each other in our lives. Her face felt taut enough to burst behind the hard kiss she held and held against my cheek. I was as near to crying as I knew her to be, though not a tear did either of us shed. Neither did we utter a word. For my part, I could not say even to myself so much as 'Sis.' To form that silent but all-meaning word, or any other in reference to her, would have put me to weeping never to stop. I said goodbye with just a long kiss on her forehead. Yet as soon as I had swung into the saddle and was hurrying away from her, 'Sis, my sister, my only sister' went coursing through my heart in joy and sorrow without the interference of tears.

And then—all the same never daring to look back—I was across the road and heading for the timber to the north.

As I was a little ahead of time, and glad to have the ordeal of saying goodbye over with, I loitered along, letting night come. The moon hung low and magnified above the eastern hills, a white blot with a tattered rim: so one more night, then, till full moon. In fields golden with sunset light now and again visible through gaps in the timber, I saw people still at work or just taking out for the day, going about their affairs as if nothing out of the ordinary had occurred, or ever would. Was it only for a handful of us that the world was falling to pieces, and no one else was touched, or even needed to know about it?

Once in a great while, too, I would glimpse a rider a good distance off, but I succeeded in keeping out of everybody's way, taking trails I knew well through the deepest of the woods, which in those days was still unbroken in great stretches.

As I rode on, the sun burned down to its last behind the ridges in the west and the moon floated up to turn creamy and whole. By the time dusk settled in, I had reached a spot I recognized as near my destination, and from there let Comanche pick his way up a draw and then along the top of a rocky ridge timbered thick enough to hide us. It led to where I'd figured it would, to a slope above the head of Grantley Hollow.

From there Comanche and I wove our way down, and once our route led between clay bluffs in the soft sand of the ravine bed, we barely crept along, as I paused often to listen: for how did I know but what the rebels had got wind of our intentions and laid a trap for us?

The farther down the draw we went the slower we moved. Night had closed in altogether by now, with the moon high enough above the eastern horizon to send a dim light down to my level, obscured as it was by a long narrow skiff of cloud that hung unmoving. Soon I began seeing the shape of a man at every turn: in what always materialized as a rock, a bush or a log. And then, when I had got over the worst of my skittishness and was ready to believe that the whole hollow was empty except for me, a sudden movement out of a huge dark blotch of shadow stopped me in cold terror: truly a man rising to his feet, and in an instant the shape beside him became a horse. I laid my hand on the pistol in my belt and held my breath.

"Ho," came his low voice—familiar, maybe.

"Evening," I answered, and did manage to keep my voice from quivering.

"Good evening," he answered—and yes, I did know the voice, and now also the approaching form: it was Peg Madill. My chest ungripped. I let out the deep breath I didn't even know I'd taken.

I got down, we shook hands, I led Comanche into a clump of brush beside Peg's horse, and then he and I sat down cross-legged on a low bank with a dense and for now moonless shadow at our backs. Nothing more was said: it did not seem to me a time for words, and Peg Madill in the most sociable of circumstances was not a talkative man.

In a little while the cloud bank still forming a second horizon above the opposite shoulder of the wash kindled gold along the rim, and slowly the moon lifted out of it, into the deep clarity of a sky renewed by yesterday's norther. The sand of the wash glowed pale while shadows cast by the brightening moon went darker than ever.

All of a sudden I was caught up, gazing as though to absorb the moon, or to be absorbed by it, the awe of this night taking on the wonder, the splendor, of that great burning globe. I was afraid to look, yet I could not escape from looking. When in time I did pull my eyes away, shut them and bowed my head, in an instant I had to open them again, and to fix them once more on the moon—because Pap's face had flashed on my inward vision: not for the first time today, not for the hundredth, but now in warning of another terror I could feel closing in. The moment I dared, I looked around to know how to flee from this terror—or to seize and suppress it—searching frantically as well for what maybe could never be visible to eyes wide open. And yet it did prove to be: for I glanced and found it, a few feet away, in the facial outline of Peg Madill, whose features I knew so well that their image came to me in the obscurity as distinct as in daylight: nose long and straight, bushy sandy eyebrows, skin ruddy and deep-wrinkled for his age. But the unnerving vision was not in Peg's face alone. I saw peopling the darkness other faces collected around his. None of them resembled Peg's except in this small feature or that tint of complexion, or in nothing at all—beyond what was everything: the kinship of ancestry, of race; the profiles of men in my own isolated community gathered from the far-flowing human stream of those who had left the villages of

Britain and landed on wilderness shores to migrate west, west, west. It was the face of my people, but suddenly the face worn by friend and foe alike—and that was the terror. Never till now had anything of this sort troubled me, or even so much as crossed my mind: nor, that night, could I have put it into words, as I can at least attempt to do after so many years of meditating. But what I could not say at the time I could feel just that much stronger: I was out to kill men of my own blood, and they were out to kill me. I saw the faces of Carlton Dawes, of Richard Goss, of Will Judd's boy, of Colonel Oldham, and most perplexing of all, the face of Harley Dexter: the faces of men I liked, and of men— anyhow one man—that I hated. I had never thought of killing Harley Dexter, of shooting him down, let alone any of the others. Just the hint of killing another man in cold blood chilled me to the core. Of my own death, of being not the killer but the victim, I hardly thought at all. Today I know it was not courage that closed my mind to that fear. In the fullness of life at eighteen, while I could imagine a bullet entering, tearing my flesh, and even wince at the prospect of pain, I could not conceive of a fatal wound, of death dealt to my immortal self—.

Yet, if only from excitement, I was quivering all over, and I could not master that quivering. I jumped up, to walk it off. Peg jerked his head erect, startled. He must have thought I had made that sudden move for a different reason, because just then came the first sound of horses easing up the draw, a sifting of hooves in the deep sand. Peg's horse nickered softly. Comanche barely wagged his head. I whispered to him, "I know."

There I stood, not shaking now—for a blessing—but with my veins hot from the marvel of watching as dark forms rounded a bend and Peg too stood up, giving that low deep-voiced "Ho," and receiving the same in reply from two men.

As they dismounted I peered into the darkness, but I could not identify either one of them. Before I had time to think much further about it, or ask, more riders came drifting in, two or three at a time. The first one I picked out for certain was Brother Hackett, and I hurried over and clapped him on the shoulder, never more eager to see anybody, as he was the only person here close to my age. But steadily now, from up and down the draw and the slopes around me they came, twenty or thirty men in a few minutes' time. My heart leaped at the thought that I was one of many arriving ready to fight, that out yonder beyond, the night must be full of brave men resolved to carry out the attack that would save Pap and all the other prisoners.

What was left of the norther breathed around us, light and cool. The moon stood brilliant above—a perfect night for tactics like ours: plenty of light to maneuver by, darkness enough for spreading confusion in a surprise attack.

My eagerness swelled, with no tinge of fear now, until I was near bursting to see the attack unleashed at once: as if we could all just sail into Milcourt and brush aside everything in our path, an invincible force.

Time went by, maybe more than I was aware of, as I stood dying to speak out but could not bring myself to do so, lest I be taken for a kid too brash to keep his mouth shut. I was certain too that the quietness of these men must be good, and that I must struggle to emulate it.

I had lost count of time, really, when a dark figure appeared at a distance, creeping along on foot up the bed of the draw, coming like a shadow over the pale sand.

"That's my daddy," Brother Hackett whispered.

The same "Ho's" went back and forth, and in a moment we all gathered in close around Rufus Hackett, breathless to hear what he'd learned, my impatience nearly getting the best of my resolution to keep quiet. But then his first words came out as a question: "How many of us here so far?"

I looked around. Now that we were all clustered in one spot I saw with a sudden empty feeling how few we actually were, no more than say fifty men: and so the night was not filled with courageous men anymore. The silence that was the only answer to Mr Hackett's question brought me back to earth again. And what he went on to report was sufficient to crush all my bounding hopes.

As we learned straightaway, the fire-eaters had a throttle-hold on Milcourt. Colonel Oldham had brought the river planters to town that morning, but right away these neighbors of his had joined forces with the "citizens"—a soft word for the hotheads. What happened after that went so slick that manipulation must have been involved. Colonel Oldham was elected chairman of the assembly by acclaim, and immediately empowered to choose a committee of three men, who were in turn to select a jury of twelve, constituting what passed for a "citizens' court." Colonel Oldham had turned out either to be as ruthless as the others or else easily deceived, since he was prevailed upon to appoint all slaveholders to the committee of three, which of course insured that the planters would be heavily represented on the jury—.

My glimmering hopes of arousing a sense of justice in Colonel Oldham all but went out.

A questioning murmur that arose among us found a voice in someone who said, "Now what's this about appointing a jury in a manner no one ever heard of? If somebody's broke the law, the fall term of court's about to begin, ain't it? We have a county judge that can empower a grand jury, don't we?"

"Oh no. I mean yes, but no," said Mr Hackett, "Too much emergency, they say, for the regular process of law. And that's not the worst of it: the county judge is one of the committee of three"—at which a heavy silence fell—. "Why, as the old feller says, any fool with half sense and one good eye can see what's taking place. One man appoints three, and then they pick out twelve to decide all cases just like the leaders want them decided. Barely pretending to hide their scheme, I call it. But just enough, I guess, to fool Colonel Oldham, who I believe to my soul wants to be fair and just, and thinks he is being. What he don't know, what we knew before—and if we didn't, we know it beyond the shadow of a doubt now—is that once the fire-eaters get in charge they'll go full blast at taking revenge on any Union man they can grab and run through a so-called trial before their so-called jury."

A voice from near me: "Revenge. Yes, for certain. Nothing short of it." —That was Peg Madill speaking, as I now recognized.

"And if you ain't heard enough already," said Mr Hackett, "why here's more: that jury aims to decide by majority vote, and if I ain't mistaken, they made that up among theirselves after Colonel Oldham left town—. Now ain't that something for a *jury*? And you might as well top it all off with this: the way I see it, if any man slips through the clutches of the jury, why the citizens, as they call theirselves, will be ready to take care of him without no trial. Because who's around to keep them from it? Nobody but Colonel Ticknor, that's who, and him in command of the militia plus two companies of Confederate soldiers. As the devil'd have it, General Dudley's out of the county and not to be reached. —And still I have to keep agoing: for Colonel Oldham, like I said, went home. Had a sick spell right during the proceedings today and had to be carried back to the river in a buggy. He's home on sick leave from that regiment he commands because of his health anyhow, as you may've heard—."

"And so what charges're they bringing again them?" Jeb Grantley it was—I hadn't known he was here till now.

"Conspiracy, treason and insurrection."

"Whyn't they throw in disturbing the peace while they was at it," Jeb growled.

Nobody laughed.

A man I didn't recognize who had just ridden up and got out of the saddle put the question we feared most of all to hear the answer to: "How many rebels there, soldiers and the rest?"

Mr Hackett didn't hold back: "I magine upwards of four, five hundred men—including the *citizens*."

For a little bit everybody in that draw must have quit breathing. I veered my eyes back to the moon. It seemed remote and alien now. And just as far off lay any hope of saving Pap.

Guilt? The guilt I'd felt before to think I might have to shoot men of my own kind? In an instant I was raging inside to kill them all, to annihilate anyone standing between Pap and freedom—.

"And, fellers, setting up that big joke of a jury ain't all they done today—even yet," said the man just arrived. "Not as I heard tell right before I left home. And if you're in no rush to pass it on to us, Rufus, I don't blame you."

"No, it ain't all they done, like you say," said Mr Hackett. "They put two men on trial a while before sundown: Dr Henry Carlisle and his brother Webb, them knowing the doctor to be a big voice among us Union supporters. Yes, and he's the very one that give the show away too: to that snake Channing, that wormed his way into Dr Carlisle's confidence, and got among us, and then went to Colonel Ticknor swearing we had a plot to rise up right at once again the Confederacy. Oh yes, and murder women and children—they been throwing that in regular. And I don't know what else besides." —Mr Hackett's mind wouldn't stop running on that, I could see—.

"So the jury tried 'em. Tried 'em! They didn't even have no lawyer to defend them—went through the motions, as the old feller says, and in one hour brought in a verdict. Guilty! And" —he struck his open palm twice with his fist— "to be hung. Sentenced them to be hung, I swear to God!"

That stunned us one and all—and the shock was worse for me because of the inkling I'd had earlier in the day of some such atrocity.

Mr Hackett now became agitated by his own words, and walked out of the center of the group. For an instant I thought he meant to go away and leave us; instead of which he stepped over to the low bank where

Peg Madill and I had waited and sank down, elbows on his knees and face buried in his hands. To a man we followed, and gathered into a silent half-circle before him.

He lifted his face, baffled: as much as to say, 'Why? Who put me in charge?'

But he said nothing aloud, nor did anyone, till Peg Madill tried to sound matter of fact with, "How many of us altogether have the rebels run in? I've heerd different reports."

"Better'n a hundred, by the best guess making the rounds."

"Well then," said Jeb Grantley harshly, "besides the ones of us already here, there ought to be another hundred or above it on the loose."

"That's what I figure too," came some voice I did not know from behind me, and after it a few mumbles of agreement.

"Then by God, why ain't they here!" Jeb Grantley barked out. "We swore a oath to come to one another's assistance again the rebels. With a hundred and fifty in a bunch we might have a show of pulling this thing off."

Mr Hackett all at once stood up straight and drew back his shoulders. "All right. Yes. I know. Plain enough we'll need a lot more men than we've got right now before we can make any headway atall. But let's don't give up. Let's just grip our fist and hold on to our patience. It's early enough yet for a good many more to slip in, careful as they have to be. And all of you know, I reckon, the later in the night we set the ball arolling the better"—only his voice did not sound as assured as his words implied.

So wait we did—a long time and then longer yet. Every now and again a couple more men would drift in. But as the moon was approaching the top of the sky, they quit coming. I could see them all grouped into the wash now. At an outside guess we had sixty men armed and ready to go, but that was a handful when you thought of the odds we'd have to face. Even jumping the rebels by surprise could not come near to offering enough advantage, outnumbered as we'd be. And anyway, there was no surprise to be hoped for, because another thing Mr Hackett told us was that Colonel Ticknor had posted a heavy guard in a double ring all around Milcourt, for fear the Union men might attempt just what we meant to undertake.

Midnight had come, to judge by the moon, before we forced ourselves to admit it: we'd all be killed or captured, and nothing gained, if we sprung a raid with no more men than we had. You could feel it in the air: the tension of failure building, till what finally broke the spell was one man walking over to his horse, swinging up without a word and turning to leave—.

"Where you think you're going!" snapped out Jeb Grantley.

The man reined in his horse. "Well, Jeb," he said in a mild voice, "I may be the first one to make a move, but I'll bet I'm not the only one to think this thing's knocked in the head. We just ain't got the men, and we ain't gonna have the men, not if we set around here till sunup—."

"You're blessed right," came another voice. "And I'm gonna follow suit and draw off on my part of it too."

"'I God, your blood's turning to skim milk, that's what!" Jeb roared out, "I don't know about the rest of you, but my *brother's* one of them prisoners."

Mr Hackett rose to his feet. "Now, now, Jeb. Hold on."

He then slowly and deliberately pulled out his watch, bent and slanted the face of it to the moonlight. "Do y'all realize it's purt near one o'clock." He said it evenly, for all the world like he was suggesting bedtime to his family after a long day working in the field.

To that sort of approach even Jeb Grantley had nothing to reply.

"Yes, we just have to face up to it, fellers," said Mr Hackett. "Much as I hate to be the one to say so. You might as well all go home, or wherever you judge best. And I don't know what else to add to that, only for to say, that from this on it's ever man for himself."

Peg Madill climbed into his saddle now, where he said loud enough for everybody to hear: "Boys, speaking for myself, I'm certain sure if I go home that militia'll be out after me by sunup—may be laying out there waiting right this minute. So I for one am heading for the river brakes to hide out, like a passel of others have already done, and join up with some of them if I can. And if any of youinses feel like it, why come on with me."

By the time he'd sat for a minute, four or five more had mounted up to join him, then they all reined around and trooped off down the draw.

How could they keep from coming to a bad end in the river brakes? I was wondering. The miles of thick brush up there furnished hideouts for every sort imaginable: honest-to-God Union men on the run, deserters from both sides, downright outlaws loyal to nobody who rode out to attack and plunder whenever and wherever they could—.

Along with that kind of thinking it came to me that I was right back where I'd been the night before: and what else did I have in prospect only to head for the river myself, danger or no danger, for although Colonel Oldham might be sick, still maybe, maybe—if I could only persuade him—he might yet carry weight in the right direction....

As I was standing there in thought, I heard Mr Hackett exchange a few quiet words with Brother, who then got on his horse and left. Then stepping over to me, Mr Hackett said, "Todd, could I have a few words with you before we part company?"

"Yes sir."

The last of the men were riding away, even Jeb Grantley, as silent now as the rest. Mr Hackett and I stood in the middle of the wash, all at once alone.

"I don't know what you're aiming to do—" he began.

"I do," I broke in. "I'm intending to take up where I left off this morning when Willun come to tell me about the rescue plan. That is, I figure to hunt up Colonel Oldham and lay Pap's case before him—case of some others too, the best I can. Sick or well, Colonel Oldham's got plenty of say among that rebel bunch, if he can just be woke up on how to use it—for if he's been fooled like you say—."

"Well, I judge he has been, but he was looking too puny to do much of anything when he left town this morning in the buggy. So I don't know....I just don't know. It's about got to where anything's worth a try though. But anyway, if that's yore idey, all the more reason for me to pass on to you what I've been studying about to tell you."

Then he stopped, like he was at a loss about how to go on....

Next time his voice sounded I felt a jarring from head to foot. I'd been leaning against Comanche with one arm thrown straight across the pommel of the saddle, and for a moment I'd gone to sleep on my feet—.

"I'm the one that set it agoing, you see—the Union League, as we called it." He stopped, sighed.

"You!"

"Oh yes. I hit up the Carlisle brothers to begin with, and right after that yore pa joined up. At first it was no more'n a matter of swearing that oath Jeb mentioned: to help one another if the rebels got after us, and also to work towards bringing back the Union—."

So that was how astute and cautious Mr Hackett had been: first among the Union men, and his sympathies not known to the rebels even yet. If only Pap had been as careful as that....

And now Mr Hackett seemed to take up what I was thinking: "All day in town I was nervous one of the prisoners'd put the finger on me: to save his own skin, maybe. Shows just how fine a bunch of men they are——." His voice broke. "But anyhow, I wanted you in particular to be told all there is to know about this business. It looked real good at the outset. Absolutely a sure thing. And as time went on, we rose to as much as two hundred and fifty strong. In just a little while too. And still growing by leaps and bounds when they come down on us. Oh, if only we could all have kept our mouth shut, made secret contacts up and down the river counties—why I'm satisfied we could have doubled or tripled in size inside of a month or two. Too powerful to stop, we might have been. I was opposed to signing that infernal petition, making so many of our names public: just like walking up and informing the rebels the Union men was organizing, the way I seen it. But I was overruled. Couldn't do nothing only refuse to sign it myself, which I done. Lay low. Lay low. Not open your mouth to any man before making dead certain he was willing to throw in with us: that's what I kept harping on. And then looks like them Carlisle boys got to where they figured they could recruit anybody simply for the asking. Why, Dr Carlisle was plumb fooled in a minute by that Channing sonofabitch. Let him take the oath right straight, mind you. Brought him to a meeting, for God's sake: one I didn't happen to be at, I can be thankful. But your pa was there. Soon as they told me about Channing I had terrible suspicions. Why, it's public knowing he was a colonel in the Confederate army from the jump-go, and got wounded in a skirmish and was sent home to recuperate. Oh, he let on like he'd had enough of it. Disgusted with the Confederacy. Ready to turn Union, he swore. And for Carlisle to be convinced by no more'n that!

"But then never mind. Too late for regrets now. So anyhow, the Carlisle brothers persuaded a bunch of us—not me, though—to cook up a raid on the Grandville ammunition depot—they said it was Union property the rebels had seized, which most of it really is. That galled them, you see. Taken away their judgment, I'd call it. Because they meant to go over there, fool-like, and just ask for that ammunition. And then, they said, be ready to fight if the rebels didn't hand it over. Talk about thoughtless! Me and your pa and a few more come out strong again that idey. At least, we said, put it off till we'd gained about twice the strength we had. And we did finally get the jumpy ones to agree to that much. And then be damned if Henry Carlisle didn't turn right around and commence putting out blanket invitations——."

"But y'all hadn't done nothing as yet only sign the petition? —I mean the ones that did. Was that the way of it?"

"That was the way of it. Oh now, we did aim to take up arms, I admit that. So naturally you can't expect the Confederate government to pass over us easy, now that they've found out about us. But this jury, as it calls itself, why they ain't no telling where they'll stop. Just label you a Union man and make that a hanging offense, it looks like."

He fell into thought, into weariness too, and stood as if he might never come back to himself....

After a bit I spoke up and said, "Mr Hackett, I'm greatly obliged to you. Pap kept all of this from me. Didn't want me to get implicated. But now, if it's all right with you, I reckon I'll be moving on. It's a good long ways to the river—."

He sort of jumped. "River! You ain't gonna try to make that trip tonight, surely. Not by yourself."

"Yes sir, I do aim to. Comanche's the finest kind of a night horse. By sunup or a little after I can be in the neighborhood of Colonel Oldham's."

"Well, yes. And you'll have the moon with you till nearly morning. But don't you forget there's liable to be bands of armed men out there just about anywhere. Militia. And no telling what kind of rough customers when you hit the river brakes."

I was wishing now that I'd gone on with Peg Madill and the others. But then again four or five men were more likely to be spotted by patrols than one.

"I'll take it cautious," I said. "And now I'd appreciate it if you'd just let Ma know—."

"Oh, I ain't going home neither. I got the jump on the rebels now, and I mean to keep it if I can. I told the woman and kids this morning that if the rescue didn't come off I'd be heading north. That's how come I sent Brother home just now."

"North, you say?"

"Yes indeed. North. Can't be all that fur, I don't imagine, to country the Union's got in hand. Like the northeast part of the Indian Nation. Or right across into Kansas, I know for a fact. Fort Scott, that is."

"But then—." Maybe I just didn't understand.

"Yes, I know what you went to say: I'll be heading for the river too, so why not travel together. I'll be crossing Red River, of course. But I aim to take out in another direction first. And well, the truth is—now

I ain't fixing to tell you any more'n I have to, as the old feller says—there's two other men waiting to join up with me, that don't want their names known to nobody: two that never seen any chance of getting up a rescue."

Well now, that nettled me, to learn those two men had failed us. Though on second thought, they'd just seen before the rest of us how pointless it all was—. Yes, but then besides, there was something else in Mr Hackett's tone....

"Mr Hackett, tell me, did *you* believe enough of us'd show up to bust in on that rebel outfit and carry out a rescue?"

"Well no. Really I didn't, son. I felt like I owed it to yore pa and all the rest of them that's prisoner to give it a try. But volunteering for a thing like that—well, when it comes down to real danger, and whose skin comes first—. Well, you can see for yourself how it's turned out. No more'n natural, I reckon."

So wait. Mr Hackett wasn't so much holding me up from starting out for the river as I was delaying him—or rather, he was delaying himself, to make me understand. And every minute he tarried put him that much closer to the risk of being nabbed.

So I held out my hand, and he took it and gripped it in both of his, hard and steady. We said nothing more. With the handshake done, we turned away from one another. By the time I was in the saddle, Mr Hackett was a good piece down the draw, walking: headed, I knew, for where the other two men were waiting with the horses. Then, having ridden halfway up a sloping bank on the north side of the hollow, I caught a glimpse of him as a dim blot drifting east along the opposite ridge.

—And that was the last I ever saw of Rufus Hackett. Nor did his family ever learn what happened to him, even though they never gave up hoping, after the war, that one day he'd come home.

Awareness that the last of tonight's companions had disappeared—all the brave men gone—put me into a growing anxiety. Alone now. Nobody but myself and Comanche to rely on, with me not sure of my way and him not knowing where I wanted to go. I couldn't help being overwhelmed at how many miles of woods and thickets and creekbeds and steep jumpoffs and sudden rocky ground lay between me and Colonel Oldham's. Through any of those obstacles as such I knew Comanche could carry me safely. Only it was up to me, with no other guidance than the moon, again a glad if lonely presence, to keep us going in the right direction. And since patrols might be out even this three miles or so from Milcourt, I had to swing away into a big circle around the town, and still just creep along, keeping out of the open when possible: had to accept covering twice the distance to travel if I could have made straight for Colonel Oldham's. Which had me wondering whether after all I could reach the vicinity of his plantation before sunup. And then besides, I was so near exhaustion, with consequently less control over the sources of fear. Although the moon gave off its essential light, soon it was also twisting every shadow of anything big enough to cast a shadow into a man on horseback, a man lying in ambush, a man suddenly near at hand with a rifle trained on me, or else a band of men some ways off under a stand of trees. That procession of menacing shadows went on till I was keyed up tight enough to snap—though I thought, 'Well, at least, if I'm that scared I won't go to sleep and fall out of the saddle.'

But even that consolation did not hold. For one time when I'd hurried across a big glade I couldn't avoid and made it into the woods, I slid down and stood to piss, and damned if I didn't fall asleep on my feet, and would have collapsed, for sure, if Comanche had not tossed his head, knowing something was wrong, and the jerk of the reins in my hand brought me to.

As the night went on, I rode through fewer terrifying shadows, and most of my drowsiness in time passed. I pushed on faster then, hurrying all I dared to make the most of the light I had before the moon set.

5

For all the distance I rode that night, I never met a soul, as many times as I did scare myself into seeing bushwhackers in moon shadows and the dim figures of patrols along nearby ridges. The hours crawled by, and the moon wheeled west, and still we pushed on, Comanche and I. A couple of miles after we crossed Wolf Ridge, where the water flowing to Red River divides from what flows to the Trinity, I pulled up to take a look at the huge dark swag ahead marking the course of the Red, and decided against tackling those brakes at night. Besides, the moon was already near setting, about to leave me in the dark for as much as an hour before dawn.

So I swung aside and dipped into the head notch of a creek that had a little spring to start it off—which was a blessing, as Comanche and I were both about to pant from thirst. After we'd drunk our fill, I unsaddled and staked him out on a horsehair lariat I always carried, to where he could reach a fair circle of grass—not that he would ever have run away, but he might stray to the crown of one of the ridges and be seen by no telling who. Next I sat down under a big hackberry and rested my back against the trunk and ate the lunch Sis had fixed. Again I wanted to cry, thinking of her, and the pain deepened when remembering her brought the rest of the family to mind. But I scowled myself out of it all as best I could, then stretched out rolled up in my blanket, facing east, toward where I judged the first rays of the rising sun would strike my eyes.

But then I turned over in my sleep, and I was so worn out I did not wake up till the cool of the morning was gone and the sun on my back had turned hot enough to pop out the sweat.

When I did come alive I sat up like I'd been shot at.

Nothing astir. Comanche stood nearby, his head drooped and one hoof propped, fast asleep, but jerking awake the second after I did.

Absolute quiet. The low grassy hills surrounding me, the slashes of timber in the draws between, the river brakes in the distance below—all these could have been affirming what I felt as I gazed around: that I was the only person on the face of the earth, but not lonely, not even—as before—lonely for home. All my life, off and on, I have found myself in some strange place where I sense, if only for a little while, that the land itself understands my solitary presence, and that a silence out of the earth responds to a silence in me—.

Yet I did wish that I had a better idea of where I was. Out of the few spots I could have recognized in the river country, this was not one of them. The best I could gather, I must be a ways upstream from Ticknor Bend—that is, Colonel Ticknor's plantation—and I did know that Colonel Oldham's place was west of his.

So I set out, and it was mighty slow going, riding along taking care not to show myself on high ground any more than absolutely necessary, and making a halt every few yards to listen. I did that out of the need to remind myself constantly that this was dangerous territory, let it be ever so peaceful to look at. After about an hour of inching along like that, deep now in the brakes, I came unexpectedly upon a wagon road cut through the brush and paralleling the river: surprising in what was little more than wilderness. But this had to be the way between Ticknor's and Oldham's, didn't it? Or again, not necessarily. Come to think of it, a couple of pioneer homesteads did lie upriver from Oldham's, so in fact his place might be to the right, after all, and not the left. Still, on a general feeling, I took the road west, keeping a sharp lookout before and behind, ready to duck into the brush if I had to. Once in a while the view was open on my right down to the river channel, where the current was low and winding among a lot of sandbars.

My greatest fright came when once I heard several horses splashing across from the Indian Territory side. I reined quick into the brakes, in case they should come my way. But then once on the near bank, they turned east and rode on out of hearing. I wondered if it could be Peg Madill's bunch, but I didn't dare risk being seen in trying to find out.

Noon was not far off when I struck the edge of a broad open space bordering the river and drew rein in utter dismay. Upslope to my left, looking down on fields and pastures and facing the stream, was a house that had to be Colonel Oldham's—it was common knowledge that he lived in the last two-story house going west on Red River, before the prairie took over. But this dwelling was much more than that: it was a plantation manor-house, the like of which I had not seen since leaving Missouri. Oblong, four rooms you could guess on each floor, deep front porches on the front above and below, a big shed-built extension at the back—so two more rooms: the whole building weatherboarded and painted dazzling white from eave to underpinning. Greatest of all to see, two white fluted columns flanked the long steps leading down from the front entrance. Yes, an honest-to-God plantation mansion out here on the wild rim of Indian country.

As I sat staring, an impulse flickered in me beyond surprise, some recognition of that house besides resemblance to others seen in the passing distance from an ox-wagon: a memory, a dream. Neither, and both. When it came clear to me I grew uneasy: this house recalled one in Kentucky I'd never seen, only heard Ma describe, the house where she was born and spent her girlhood.

As I began to advance across the well-trimmed grounds and swept my gaze through a larger scope, I became aware really for the first time, behind the house a good space away, of two rows of log cabins for the slaves. And I had barely ridden into the yard proper when two fierce dogs came out in a rush and created an uproar, tearing around me in a circle barking and snarling but staying clear of Comanche's hooves.

"I would if I was you," I said. "Or he'll send you to dog hell with one swipe."

Just as I approached the front gate a boy about my age appeared on the porch and came down the steps between the columns and then along a walk bordered by two rows of flowers, with a pistol pointed at me from the waist.

"Stop and state your business," he yelled.

I pulled up at once, but before I could get out a word Colonel Oldham emerged onto the front porch: tall, stooped, seeming none too steady on his feet but still prepared to take hold of any situation that arose.

"Hold back, Bill," he called out gruffly.

I wasted no time.

"I'm Todd Blair, Nathaniel Blair's son."

Hearing that, Bill Oldham seemed to tense up his pistol hand, and glowered back at his father, as if to say, 'See there!' Colonel Oldham halted, scowling. The three of us might have been planted there, from the length of those seconds of silence. My heart began to pound like a stampede.

The colonel was the first to regain his presence of mind. He motioned for his son to come back, stepping to the edge of the porch and speaking out in a friendly if assertive voice, "Get down and come into the house, Todd. You're quite welcome."

Another glare from Bill, before he called off the dogs and then shouted for a slave—a grizzled but powerful-looking old man who now came in sight around a corner of the house and took charge of Comanche. I had to let him, though I did not like for any stranger to handle my horse. And Colonel Oldham and Bill both gave me puzzled glances when I said, "Yes, go on, Comanche. It's all right."

Till I stood on the ground I hadn't been conscious of how shaky my legs were, so that mastering them took the whole time of walking over and up the steps to the porch, with Bill Oldham following, and reaching out to accept the handshake that Colonel Oldham offered. Next Bill and I shook hands too, by no means because either of us wanted to. And the sizing up of each other that went with the handshake was cold and suspicious on both sides.

Already Colonel Oldham was leading the way into the parlor, where I had some notion of what was coming and made ready to hold my own against it as well as I could. And sure enough, here came Mrs Oldham out of the back part of the house all smiles and motherly-like, and could hardly hear who I was from her husband before she began: "Why how do you do, young man. We're just about to sit down to dinner, and we'd be very pleased if you'd come in and join us."

To hear her talk, I might have been the company they'd been expecting and dying to see for a month. Bill had slipped into a side room so as not to be involved in any exchange of courtesies. Colonel Oldham nodded a time or two, as much as to say that he was of the same mind as his wife, and even stood aside and waited to let me enter the dining room ahead of him.

Now under the circumstances nobody but a damfool would have offered 'I done et, thank you, ma'm' or some such excuse. And so not knowing what else to do only take them up on the offer—not counting that I was hungry enough to chew up a steer alive—I laid my hat down on the first thing at hand: which happened to be the lacy pillow of a davenport, and preceded Colonel Oldham into the dining room with a "Thank you, sir."

By this time I had my backbone stiffened up enough, I thought, to take whatever they came out with in the way of etiquette, and to give back equal to what I got. But then no way on earth could I have been prepared for what happened next. The minute I set foot in that dining room, three girls came sailing in through the back door, taking my breath away and giving my legs the weak trembles again. Mrs Oldham gushed out their names, but I was so bashful and confused I missed hearing what they were, catching only that two of the girls were her and the colonel's daughters.

Now bad enough all this would have been if they'd been wearing ordinary clothes, but all three were decked out ready for a high-society ball, in silk or satin bright-colored and full of pleats and furbelows—I thought of poor Sis in her cotton shirtwaist. The two Oldham girls were dark-headed, with rippling long black hair as glossy as a flock of blackbirds in the sun. The other one had long shining brown hair thrown back over her shoulders and giving off sudden little gleams of light every move her head made. The two with black hair, the younger one still almost a little girl but sure putting on to be a woman, had round delicate faces and very dark eyes, all four of those eyes set on me, and the smiles to go with them. The brunette girl's face was longer-shaped, and her hazel eyes, golden flecks and all, gazed straight at me too, with no batting. She had full cheeks the color of wild plums turned rich-ripe. I was so paralyzed by those three pairs of eyes that I could have sunk into the floor, or just as well have taken off to fly—. Or I might just have stayed frozen there for a week, if Colonel and Mrs Oldham hadn't both asked me most politely to sit down to dinner.

Which I did. And as I recall it to this day, I never had a more terrible trial in getting through a mealtime. I moved my hands around over the table as though everything I touched was made of thin glass—and a great deal of it was. I did my best to eat slowly and methodically, and to remember the table manners Ma had tried to teach me—wishing I'd paid more attention to her than I had. Oh, but I could have accomplished just that part of it well enough—if only those girls had not given me such bold and inquiring looks so often. With each one of those my stomach felt like doing a somersault, and my heart began hammering fit to break loose from my rib cage. During the whole course of that meal I never got out a word except "Yes, m'am" and "Yes, sir" to the older folks a time or two. If anybody had touched me just once, my head would have gone through the ceiling—or at the very least I'd have sprung up with my plate and run to the backyard to eat with the slaves.

The one thing that did operate to hold me under control was Bill Oldham, who sat two chairs away, never looking at me, and me only sidelong at him: enough to note his deep frown and his eyes glowering on the near distance before him.

'Yaow, you,' I thought. 'Yaow, what about you?'

When that dinner was finally over with, Colonel Oldham had a slavewoman to carry two cane-bottom rockers to a shadetree in the front yard. Then leading the way out there, he invited me with all the courtesy you could ask for to please sit down. I did, and I was more than glad when Bill Oldham did not come out to join us. But then his father must have seen to that.

As soon as I was settled and got my first level look at him under these conditions, I was struck to see that Colonel Oldham's eyes were the same color as his daughters', only his were as steadfast as a rock under bushy gray-black brows: eyes kindly enough to look into but letting you know that any great disagreement with him was probably nonsense that he would not stand for. Sick to some extent he may have been, but his jaw cut square and broad announced that he meant for it to take far worse health than this to weaken his constitution or incline him to give up authority—.

"What can I do for you, my boy?"

My throat felt like it had a ton of dry weight on it. To get out the first words was the worst obstacle yet.

I heard them coming weakly out of my throat: "I'm here about Pap, sir. And...and what I have to say is, he's not guilty of any crime."

"Well now, if he's not, what comes out in the trial'll show him to be innocent."

"Well sir, not to dispute your word. And I don't claim to know a thing about the law. But then how could a proper jury in less than an hour hear enough evidence, whatever it was, to sentence two men to be hung? And that, mind you, with no lawyer to defend them."

Before I was halfway through saying this I saw a different Colonel Oldham suddenly visible in the face before me, a man in the first shock of fear that if he does not take action immediately, events may pass him by. The stern eyes grew troubled. His hands rose and lay fisted on the arms of his rocking chair, with a slight quiver he could not control running through them.

"No defense lawyer? Why yes. You must be mistaken. We decided as part of the procedure that anyone accused would be represented by counsel. And anyhow, what two men are you referring to?"

"Dr Henry Carlisle and his brother Webb, that's who. Tried yesterday evening late and sentenced to be hung. An eyewitness told me all about it, so it's straight. He declared they didn't have any lawyer to defend them."

"Where's Bill?" The colonel snapped out so quick my stomach convulsed. "Hey. One of you niggers. Go tell Marse Bill to come here. Right at once."

But then Bill's own voice answered: "Yes, Pa. What is it you want?"

The colonel glared at him. For be damned if that skunk hadn't been just around a corner of the house within earshot the whole time we'd been talking.

"Did that company of Carson's bring some word from town this morning that you kept from me?"

"Keep it from you? Why no." He hung back till the colonel gestured sharply for him to come forward. "You see, Pa, you'd just gone upstairs to rest when they stopped by. And then this kid here showed up right after they left. And then we had all the womenfolks there at the dinner table—."

"Never mind. Just tell me straight out right now. What's taken place?"

"Why, what they did was—just what the kid says. Sentenced the Carlisle brothers to be hung. And no, no lawyer to argue their case. They didn't have a case. So what did they need with a lawyer—."

"No need! On trial for their lives and no need for a lawyer?"

"Well sir, they confessed to being members of that league. Purpose of the league was treason, conspiracy and insurrection. Murder, too. So it was open and shut, you see. They surely deserve the penalty for what they admit to."

With no more than a side view of Colonel Oldham, I could tell that his eyes bore down on his son as if to pierce to the core of him.

I judged it was the right time to put in a word: "It's not like they're acting as a regular jury would neither, Colonel Oldham. They're deciding cases by majority rule."

His hands were not poised now on the rocking-chair arms, they were gripping them, white-knuckled. I had not noticed before how much older his hands looked than his eyes.

"That's so, I suppose," the colonel hissed at Bill.

"It is so. And no disrespect, sir," that sonofabitch answered, "but you appointed the leading citizens of the county to select that jury, and you well know they'd pick men who'd come to a reasonable and necessary conclusion under the present circumstances. You said yourself this situation calls for drastic action."

You could hear the colonel was near to choking, and sicker than he'd let on, as I had to admit for the first time. My heart went hollow.

"You go on away and be quiet about that," said the colonel in a stern if weakening voice.

And so with a nasty set to his jaw and a leer at me, Bill wheeled around and left. A little more out of him and I couldn't have prevented myself from wrenching that jaw crossways on his face.

The colonel had such suffering and dismay in his eyes when he turned them back to me that I was hard put to meet his gaze.

"You realize, Todd, that nobody had told me any of these things."

"Yes sir, I realize that."

He caught in a deep breath, a gasp. Along with his hands, his head was trembling now too, as an old man's will. Yet his voice was firm again: "You know a good deal more than most of us about this affair, don't you?"

"Yes sir, I do."

The way he slowed his voice I knew he meant to avoid putting me on the spot: "You tell me whatever you can without implicating anyone too deep. It'll go no further than right here, of that I give you my word as a gentleman."

I knew I'd be repeating a lot of what Pap had told him, but he could not guess that I knew....

"Well sir, you know what a strong stand a great lot of men in the river counties took against secession. A while back they went and made up a league sworn to work for bringing back the Union. I don't deny that. I don't deny that Pap was one of them. I don't deny, neither, that they did mean to rise up: that is, to gather in a body when they'd won over enough men to their side, and—uh—go seize back the Grandville arms depot."

"That appears like a whole lot to be guilty of to me. Doesn't it to you?"

"It would be, of course, but as yet they hadn't carried out a bit of it. Only signed that petition. Some of them not even that. And I know for certain that when the reckless ones argued for making that arms depot raid, Pap was dead set against it. And him and some more men talked them out of it."

But Colonel Oldham had ceased to follow my words: "Just a second. 'Seize back'? Did I hear you say that?"

"Seize back, yes sir. You see, the way the league has it down, the reb—the Confederates confiscated that stuff from the Union to start out with and—well, they hated to see United States weapons used against the United States."

"You're forgetting something, my boy. The Union was a partnership. When we withdrew, we were entitled to take our share of the common property with us. In addition, the Confederate States of America, like any other nation, has the right to defend itself by any means found within its territory—."

He was trying to keep his voice kind but it grated in his throat: "The Confederate States of America is now on equal footing with what's left of the United States, and is proving it every day on the battlefield."

I thought his spine went a little stiffer for an instant: "Now we want to make it—*I* want to make it—as easy as humanly possible for all of us in the South to pull together. To have this war over with. To make peace. To go back to normal living in our own land, with no Yankees to tell us what we can do and what we can't. And what we can own and what we can't."

"Begging your pardon, sir, but Pap and me don't feel like that's how it'll turn out—."

I bit off the words: 'Oh God, no. Don't argue politics when lives—when Pap's life is at stake.'

"But then," I went on, "supposing the Confederacy does come out of this war independent. Its government is supposed to be based on justice: you believe that, I know. But that jury—. Now how could you say it's operating according to any notion of justice? You take even the way it all started. That was an overwrought—crowd (mob, I thought) that voted you in as chairman. Then you appointed three plantation men for a committee and asked them to choose a jury. That ain't no legal way to go about it, now is it? Still, at that, seeing as how they claim to be a jury, why don't they at least *act* enough like one to do what juries have been doing since time out of mind: that is to say, deciding unanimous. No way in the world can they claim that a majority vote's legal. And on top of that to bring in a verdict in under an hour on some mighty quick strung together evidence that ain't even open to question by a defending lawyer. That kind of thing never happened under the United States...."

"You're absolutely right. No question!" the colonel's voice ground out, as he pounded an arm of his rocker with an unsteady fist. "These trials must be carried out as I—or rather as the committee—intended, acting on the authority vested by the people, vested first in me and then by me in the committee. And majority rule! Why, we gave no such instructions as that—."

"Well sir, did you tell them at all how to carry on their work?"

"We did not. No. We assumed...well...but I'll tell you this. That committee must be reconvened. Just as soon as I can get to Milcourt. And this, too. The Carlisle brothers must have a new trial. No more of this majority rule business. The jury will be instructed to bring in a unanimous decision, in their case and all the others. Just as you say. Just as juries have always done. Each man must be tried fairly, and what each man is guilty of, he will be punished for, according to his crime—. Or cleared, if that happens to be the verdict. I'll see to all this. You can take my word for it."

Oh, but he was weak and panting, for all the forced power in his voice. And didn't his words say that even he, apparently in spite of himself, had concluded that all league members, with maybe a few exceptions, must be guilty of great crimes?

"Sir, I hope you won't think I'm overstepping myself, or take offense in any way, but why did there have to be a special—I guess citizens' court is what you're calling it—set up for this purpose, when the fall term of regular court begins in a few weeks?"

"No sir. No sir. We discussed that. Too slow. Under wartime conditions emergency measures are proper. And certain rights are properly suspended. Habeas corpus for one, if you know the term. Believe me, I know the law on this. The public safety at such a time calls for swift decision, swift justice—."

But he could not control the panting. It nearly smothered his voice. Yet a terrible sound his closing words had: 'swift justice.'

"Well, colonel, yes, I know it's justice we're after...."

For a moment now, he was free of the breathlessness, and maybe he did not speak because he did not trust the flow of his weakening energy. For whatever reason, the only real resolution I could make out was in his eyes, in the fierceness of his stare.

"All right, sir," I sort of mumbled. "I know your word's as good as your bond—Pap always says it is."

A little color of pride showed in his pallid cheeks.

An idea I'd carried in the back of my mind all along—desperate? Maybe. But try, try: "With your permission, Colonel Oldham, I'd like to speak a little on another point"—not quite the private talk with the slavery men that I'd had in mind, which I now saw would be useless, but—"Since, as you say, I know something about this thing, could you persuade the jury to call me as a witness in Pap's trial?"

He cocked his head as though listening to his own inner counsel. Then "Oh no. That—that couldn't be done. A family member. A son—?"

"Or if not for Pap's trial, then for one or more of the other men. Because you see, I know them all so well—."

He knew what I was driving at: if I could help clear some man or men close to Pap, the benefit might flow over to him.

"No, I can't intervene for that. I don't know that it'd be wise. Fact is, I'm sure it wouldn't."

"Well sir, you see, all you'd have to do is mention it to the jury, or to the prosecutor, or whoever's in charge."

"That would be the president of the jury, as we've designated him. Well, all right then. Yes. Ask, yes. Though don't forget, as you seem to—as you're maybe too young to realize—that we can't grant special privileges to one or two. We must be even-handed and fair to all."

What did he mean, really? And why the fist now pumping the air for emphasis, the scowl more savage than ever? Better not to ask, not to confuse the issue any further. But how could he think I was trying to pull something dishonest in asking to testify, not even for my father but only for a neighbor? And maybe I was too young to—what? Too young to understand a gent's honor—was that it? Planter's honor. That rankled me. And didn't he mean no special privileges for the dirt farmers? Oh sure, see they all suffer the same.

For a little while he said no more. As we sat there eyeing one another, I put every effort I could call up into hiding my disappointment. I knew he liked me, and was ashamed of his eavesdropping son—that wasn't gent's honor, by any means. I knew he would do what he could to be fair, if only he could be sure any longer what that was, having as he did to fight his own prejudice and convictions, and more than that to oppose the hotheads, who, as I knew and he suspected, had used him and then pushed him aside to run headlong as they chose—.

What caused our gazes to separate was disconcerting to me, coming unexpected as it did: the voices of the three girls, and in a moment their appearance from around a back corner of the house. In other dresses than earlier they were now, fine at that but not fancy—one pale green, one dull red, one bright gray: snug bodices, long sweeping skirts, each girl with a white parasol tilted above her head. The pit of my stomach contracted. I shut back a groan in my throat, for fear they might walk our way, and let my breath ease when they strolled away from us toward the river.

Colonel Oldham might as well have been reading my mind: "So they've changed out of those dresses, I see," he chuckled. "Just couldn't wait to try them on—you know, the ones they came to the dinner table in." —Did I know! Boy and howdy!— "Gowns for a ball, they were supposed to be," he was saying. "Just arrived. Surprised me dresses like that could even be had, away out here in wartime and all. But that new dressmaker in Milcourt actually located the goods for them. Oh, those girls were eager, let me tell you, for that ball Colonel Ticknor was planning. A chance, of course, for them to meet the young officers from Confederate units in the neighborhood—. Oh, but that was before all this turmoil came up, you understand."

The look he threw me, was it apologetic that he'd referred to such frivolity in these terrible days? Or was it resentful that a gang of Union-loving clodhoppers had upset the social order of his world? In an instant, anyhow, his eyes veered back to the girls, as mine did, each of us caught up in his own way by the meaning enacted in the scene centered on the girls: meanings in which I sensed the whole purpose of this visit slipping away. Here we sat, a young man and an old man, enthralled by three young ladies on what passed for a fashionable stroll. In me the grace and rhythm of those three figures withdrawing across the landscape reawakened the throb and the fever I'd undergone during their recent presence in the dining room, with a new thrilling of dread from what must have been evident as well to Colonel Oldham: that what we were truly contending about lay framed in the picture before us, in the setting and the manner of the girls in walking through it—a world sustained by the fine tall house behind us, with its fluted columns and its cluster of slave cabins in the rear, and spreading out from it around us and the girls the outbuildings and the tended fields: a smokehouse, a blacksmith shop, corncribs, hogpens, a big barn with a hayloft, stables, horse corral, cowlots; then the teeming fall garden and the orchards beyond the barn. On ground farther away, the corn had been gathered, and two fieldhands slowly advancing behind mule teams were plowing under the stalks. Late cotton-picking was in full swing, a scattering of slaves bending and inching forward through wide fields. In pastures spaced between the fields were cows, sheep, horses, mules.

And all of this was summed up in the manner of the girls walking through that picture. Their steps were those of ladies, even in the girl as yet a child. It was the scene they were born for, born out of: it existed for them, and they for it. Colonel Oldham was well aware, as I became in those culminating moments of my few hours on this plantation, that everything lying before our eyes in the scene completed by the girls walking through it was at stake in what was going on this moment in Milcourt, and beyond that in what was ripping the nation to pieces.

As the girls turned and came strolling back in our direction, a thought trembled through me: that once my mother had belonged to surroundings like these, and that the man beside me could not be very different from what my grandfather had been....

Then came a vivid recollection of the time when we'd passed the plantations on first crossing Red River into Texas. Likewise, I remembered the outcry of an abolitionist who a year or so before the war had spoken on the courthouse square in Milcourt—that is, until he left town ahead of a mob: declaring that no matter how rich and fine a plantation might appear, any social structure with slavery at the bottom of it lay under a curse, and like the house built on the sand that structure would fall, and great would be the fall of it—.

Pap had stood with me listening to the man speak....

At the thought of Pap I sprang out of my chair like I was stung. In that instant came an aching to jump on Comanche and make for town at a dead run, wild-eyed to do something—anything. Yet a small voice of caution began telling me not to go so fast, not to give in to panic. But all the steadiness I could call up was only enough to keep me standing there trembling.

The girls had circled now, and so I had that dread to suffer too: that they might yet drift over to us. They still did not, although they came near enough for me to hear what flattened me just as their presence would have. The two older girls burst out laughing, teasing the youngest one, goading her away from her womanly role into screeching out to the brunette like the little girl she was: "Jenny Ticknor, you hush up your mouth! You hear me!"

Ticknor? *His* daughter? Good God alive!

—But then of course. Why not? Visiting a neighbor just up the river. Everything as far down as my belly sank into my legs and turned them to lead.

Maybe Colonel Oldham thought I was just waiting for parting words from him. When they came, they sounded weary: "I'll go to town this evening, if I can. And I'll go there for certain tomorrow morning. I'll do all in my power, son, I promise you that. I'll see that the accused get lawyers, and I'll put a stop to this majority rule business."

All I could do was thank him, express confidence in him—only wishing I could make it ring truer than it did. If he was ever able to go to Milcourt—if it all came to a showdown—if—if—. Seeing him in the midst of this plantation world he shared with most of the jury, I could not make myself believe that he'd actually champion the small farmers against his own kind—.

He was looking away again now, as if at the blank distance, forgetful of me, shaking his head with the helpless dreariness of an old man.

"Colonel, I got to be going now. I'm—I can't do anything only go to Milcourt myself. And see. And wait."

He stood up, sighing, and responded dutifully to the handshake I offered. In a moment I was hurrying away to the barn. Remembering his manners, Colonel Oldham called out to the old slave who had tended Comanche earlier, "Cabus, go and saddle Marse Todd's horse."

Cabus looked up from some task he was puttering around at near the smokehouse, in no hurry to obey, for I got to the corral well ahead of him, to find my saddle hanging over a top rail and Comanche snuffling over the last few oats in a feedtrough. I swung up over the fence, had the saddle on and was cinching it down when Cabus came trudging along. And he was by no means feeble.

"What you want to do is wait," he said. "The colonel give orders for me to saddle that hoss."

It was how little he sounded like a slave that made me glance sharply at his grizzled and humorous face.

"I'm in a fair big hurry," I said. "And besides, I'm used to taking care of myself. Ain't discovered as yet that I need no slave to wait on me."

"I spect you ain't, coming like you do out of folks don't have a dime to their name." And he gave a chuckle as though it was comical that I didn't have a slave of my own.

Now that was the limit. I drew the cinch tight, and as I mounted I snapped out: "See if you can open that gate"—and be damned if my voice didn't sound too much like Bill Oldham's might have in my place.

Cabus took his own time about opening the gate, all the same, and I sat there and let him, a long way from being as cool as I acted, thinking, 'So it's free the slaves, is it, Mr Lincoln? And then a person runs across something like this.'

—Just at the second the pole gate swung back, I saw the girls again, saw them walking out from among the trees of a big orchard and dallying along toward the house. And they caught sight of me at about the same time I did of them.

All at once I felt ready to explode. So I gouged my heels into Comanche's flanks as hard as I could dig, taking him clean by surprise. But then a split second was all that horse ever needed to catch on. He snorted and sprang and tore out through that gateway like he'd been launched from a catapult. As we busted across the plantation grounds, I half-turned in the saddle and grabbed off my hat and swung it in a wide circle over my head. The three girls suddenly forgot to be stylish and began waving back with those ruffly parasols for all they were worth. And Jenny—good God alive, *his* daughter!—pulled out a lacy filmy white handkerchief and tossed it into the air.

It wafted and settled gently to the ground.

6

OH SURE, it was a great thing to be showing off before three pretty girls. And the headiness of it lasted for all of five minutes: till I reached the edge of the plantation grounds, where slowing Comanche to a walk I had such a collapse of spirit that I could have swung to the ground and pounded my head senseless against the nearest tree—that's how changes had been coming over me, sudden and violent, since Pap's arrest. Just how—I lashed out at myself—could I have been lured so far out of my element as to go flirting with high-toned young ladies while my father lay imprisoned in danger of his life?

And further, that strutting for the girls was in fact only the final stage in a crisis I'd gone through during these last couple of hours, in that alien world of the plantation where dealing with any person had been so strange to me that I was now driven to the verge of losing faith in myself. The manners of that Oldham household: the refinement and unsettling beauty of the girls, the instant enmity between the son and me, and, of all things, the superior airs of a slave—it was too much to have thrown at me in so short a time.

Yet, for all that, maybe I could claim one achievement: Colonel Oldham, not even bothering to hide that he saw in me certain traits he wished for in his son, had treated me with frankness and respect, man to man, giving me reason to believe that he could and would help to save Pap's life—which was what I'd come all this way for, wasn't it? So how could anything else really matter?

Yet—again—I must not lose sight of what I had to fear even there: that Colonel Oldham, no matter what course he took, would never be able to undo what he'd allowed to be done. The mere recall of his quivering head and hands now put the thought I'd been carrying into blunt words: He's an old man who's been used and shoved aside.

Or if he had any power left—again—would his own nature permit him to use it in the way he'd promised? Even if we'd still been a community where a Colonel Oldham could raise his voice and set things right, could I have trusted his word?—that word of honor that plantation gentlemen like him professed never to break. However that might be, one thing now appeared certain: when the war erupted, truth and honor had deserted this country, leaving us all to the ruthlessness of the Colonel Ticknors and Harley Dexters, who meant to rule by sentencing to death any man who opposed them. For a Colonel Oldham to hold to his word under such conditions was sure to come down to challenging his own kind, consequently to risking all he had: his plantation, his slaves—not to mention the welfare of his frilly daughters. I'd seen it in his eyes, heard it in his hoarse and weakening voice: when the showdown came—word given or not—Colonel Oldham would all too likely throw in with Ticknor and the rest of the plantation men, not with a passel of frontier hicks—.

And what else? More yet! Everything agonized by a haunting impression I could not confront, yet not deny: the face, the hair, the gaze of hazel eyes resting on me: Jenny Ticknor—but oh good God alive! *his* daughter—.

With no guiding to speak of from me since our dash across the plantation grounds, Comanche had taken up a fast walk, making steadily for home, retracing the route we'd come that morning; though I hardly noticed, I'd been so deep in thought, till a sudden tiny noise lifted me out of my sorry mood. I drew up. But no perking of Comanche's ears, so no danger: nothing after all but a light gust of wind brushing a thicket. Then it registered on me that we'd almost arrived at the foot of the line of grassy hills marking the limit of the river bottom.

Again I gave Comanche his head, and sank back into my troubles, taking no precautions now along this trail where I'd been so wary a few hours earlier. By now I was too discouraged to bother about who might be lurking in the wilds of Red River.

My mind was in such a whir that it took a new sense of space to alert me: the openness of a bald slope we reached a while later on, with Comanche still homeward bound, now at an even faster clip.

I reined up, took a deep breath, relaxed in the saddle, sat there immersed in the warm sunlight, eyes absorbed by the lumpy little clouds that sailed along in the faultless blue overhead and lulled me down till the sleep I'd lost the night before overtook me....

Drooping in the saddle. Snapped awake. Comanche skittered.

There was Wolf Ridge ahead, a long swell of prairie from whose crest Milcourt would be visible. The hell of what was going on in that town flashed through me as it had at Colonel Oldham's, and so suddenly that by reflex my heels again dug into Comanche's flanks. He gave a sidestep, unwound and levelled out at full gallop, with me bent low over his neck and the drumming of hooves sending a tremble of wonder and distress through me. The skyline of Wolf Ridge came rushing at us. We topped it. I reined in again.

There it lay: Milcourt. A mere town: a few buildings seen across treeless rises and bands of timber in the draws, a scene peaceful as the sky above, no motion in it but a shimmer of heat. Yet the name of Milcourt repeating itself in my struggling consciousness gave me the shivers.

Then, lo and behold, what did I spot crossing the landscape a half mile away but a lone rider. I shifted the pistol in my belt, touched the musket hanging from the saddlehorn.

The rider had covered half the distance between us before he noticed me and stopped. I waved. He waved back, came on my way. Before he was much closer I recognized him: Afton Thatcher. Nobody else alive could look that much like a scarecrow on a horse.

Afton was a big talker, too, so it was odd—ominous—that he uttered not a word till he'd ridden up beside me and we shook hands. Maybe he wanted the expression on his face to prepare me for the worst, as woebegone as he looked.

The pressure became too great, he blurted it out: "They hung them Carlisle brothers this morning."

I tried to swallow, my throat stuck. I fought the hysteria rising in my guts—.

"But wait now, Afton. Wait. Surely.... Why, they sentenced them just yesterday. Now surely to God they have to allow some delay—for appeal, I guess—before"—finally I did swallow—"before hanging them."

"Why no. That's just it, you see. They sentence whoever they please and hang them when they want to. Why, that ain't no jury, Todd. No jury to it. Lynching, that's all they're after. And it's got to be squelched, I tell you."

"But why, Afton? Tell me why, if you can. Tell me what this is all about. Why hang them in such a hurry?"

Afton stared at me as if he had just told me, and found me deaf: "I—I can't tell you, Todd—. I mean to say, all I can report's what I heard. People say the Confederate outfit's afraid the Union men still on the loose'll get up a rescue, and so they're hanging these two men right at once to show they mean business."

Our aborted rescue plan last night....

"But for Christ's sake, Afton! This is liable to turn the Union men desperate. Start bloodshed back and forth till the last man in this county's dead."

"That's what I know. That's why I'm out to stop it. But then it ain't only the jury, you see—I mean this hanging the men as soon as they're convicted ain't—ain't really the jury. Or I mean to say, that's not all of it."

"Who then?—Oh yeah, I know. Harley Dexter, for one."

"Well yes, him. Eager enough, you bet. But Colonel Ticknor, I mean. He's the main one, he's the kingpin. Hand in glove of course with the slavery men on the jury. Why, in their decision they didn't fix it so he'd have to wait for their permission to carry it out. Nor nothing. Just let him go right ahead this morning and jerk them Carlisle boys out of jail and string them up."

My voice could barely squeeze out of my throat: "Any more? I mean, are they trying more men today?"

"Oh yes. They are....Oh now, I don't know about your pa, Todd. Monk Harper and Rufus Reed was before the jury when I left town—so I heard. Militia's still rounding up people too. They brought in Jess Larkin and that boy of his'n this morning."

"His boy! Why, he ain't more'n fifteen years old."

"That's what I mean. Them hotheads've got to be stopped. And even so our town'll never be the same again. Why, you just take that tree—oh, I wouldn't go watch the hanging done, though lots did. But how can I ever go near that tree for the rest of my born days? And how's a person gonna avoid it, if you go to town at all, that tree standing where it does? And even supposing you was to cut it down, the place where it stood could never be took away."

A tree? That hadn't entered my mind, but of course—.

"What tree they using?"

"Why, that big old elem on Walnut Creek at the east end of Main."

—First tree we saw the day we hit Milcourt, after that long trek from Missouri—Pap driving our wagon across the stream by that tree. That welcoming tree:

> *Just like a tree*
> *That's planted by the water....*

Now, as then, the line from the hymn: *Just like a tree....*

I plucked my thoughts away from that: "Afton, where you headed? If it's any of my business—seeing as how you don't live up this way."

"Out to see Colonel Oldham, that's where I'm headed. If any soul on earth can halt this rampage, it's him. Oh, he set up that so-called jury and started this thing arolling, I know that. But then they ain't adoing it like he told them to. Oh no, they ain't. And he'll bring them to taw. Mind what I tell you. I only hope to God he ain't terrible sick, like one story I heard said he was. —Now I got to be getting along, Todd. No time to lose."

"I hate to tell you this, Afton, but that's where I just come from: talking to Colonel Oldham."

"Oh, you have! Looky here, I'm glad to hear that. Wha'd he say? What's he gonna do? He's not real sick, is he?"

"Not what you'd call real sick, no. Up and around. Promised he'd try to help, and all like that."

"By diggedy, I knowed it!" Afton slapped his leg. "He'll get in there and set them people straight."

"Yeah. Well, the fact is, Afton, looks like they just used him and shoved him aside."

"Shove Colonel Oldham aside! Pshaw, Todd, you don't know him like I do."

"Well—?"

"You'll see. And I got to be going, I tell you. Go add my voice to yore'n. And don't you ever doubt it. He'll *do* something, Colonel Oldham will."

So I let him ride on without saying another word. I just sat there stupefied. Ever since the news of the hanging, I'd felt like somebody had punched me in the wind and left me struggling for breath. I discovered too how tired one fist was, gripped, as I now noticed, around the bridle reins. Next I tried ordering myself to settle down, but that only sent a spasm through my body, and a sudden void, as though some vital part of me had been absent for the time I talked with Afton: gone in search of a way around the lunacy that had seized the world, wandering to the room where Pap was a prisoner, wandering to the hanging tree.

Then all at once I went into near panic again. Pap! What might be happening to him while I drifted here, halfway out of myself. A heel touch this time sent Comanche into a lope that put the distance behind us fast.

But then by the time we'd climbed the next rise, I began to hesitate again about rushing hell for leather to Milcourt, and into no telling what. What was to prevent Ticknor or Dexter from locking me up as they had Jess Larkin's boy?

With that I slowed Comanche to a brisk walk, and for the hundredth time tried to envision a course of action—and met as always with frustration, any direction I turned. All it came down to now was a terrible need to see Pap, if only to say I'd gone to consult Colonel Oldham as I'd promised—though so far nothing had come of it, and the outlook was grim that anything ever would.

Meanwhile I kept riding across the prairie toward Milcourt, slower now, till I struck the Trinity River upstream from town. There I stopped and dismounted, sat down on a fallen willow, gazed out over the shallow rippling water still fresh and clear from the gushing springs thirty miles to the west.

Maybe it was the water that freed my thoughts. They gathered quickly and swept along faster than the current. But no purity about them. Ugly thoughts. Never more so, and never more compelling. The figure at the center of them, standing out in horrifying clarity, was Colonel Ticknor. Harley Dexter? What was he after all but a flunkey? Ticknor! He was the man to blame: the man who would order Pap killed—and soon, the way things were headed. From that I was driven by a terrible logic to what seemed the inevitable conclusion: to kill Colonel Ticknor before he killed my father. But *her* father, *her* father.

But wait, what had I just said to Afton Thatcher? One killing leads to another, on and on, multiplied without end. Besides, some other man as vengeful as Ticknor would fill his shoes right off, and they'd hang Pap just the same. And me with him, if they caught me.

Yet, in the next breath, that reasoning was wiped out by words driving home the opposite: 'No, you fool! You can't let a man live who means to murder your father! And don't you see?' intervened a tempting voice. 'You have to have another step ready to take if Colonel Oldham can't or won't help. And to kill Colonel Ticknor, of course that's it.'

On and on went my mind, in a murky turmoil. And my body seemed to taunt me, thrust at me, driving me into motion, into the saddle. So I mounted up and hurried on till I came to a gravel ford, and once across the stream picked up the main street of Milcourt and went clopping along toward the courthouse square.

Along the way I passed a bustling of people apparently going about their ordinary business—just like out in the fields yesterday. How in the name of God could people do that! When other citizens of this town were taking the lives of their neighbors just up the street. And this keeping of a routine till hell froze over was all the more disturbing to see, going on as it did among the other people I saw in another mood: those who drifted on the verge of hysteria up and down the streets or gathered in little patches, eyes haunted by the incredible: the tragic knowledge of death threatening someone they loved written on their faces.

The closer I came to the courthouse the more soldiers I saw. Mr Hackett had been right. We'd have ridden into certain destruction if we'd made that raid last night. The fear of being arrested today still gnawed at me, too, as I rode along. But seeing others moving on horseback in both directions, I could only hope that I was not too conspicuous.

When I came in view of the courthouse I drew up. And sat there, staring at my perch of night before last—only night before last—on the roof of the buggy shed, where above all hovered the image of Pap sitting with his back to the window while I knelt on the roof outside and whispered to him through the hole in the window pane—an image almost taking shape in the window glass. And then a terrible yearning to see Pap with my own eyes: see him, talk with him, or only to enjoy one long gaze into his face in this hour of great decision: the face I'd always looked to as the source and solace of hard choices. Without that support, how could I make this maybe foolhardy, this surely most dangerous decision of my life: whether to kill a man in the doubly desperate hope of getting away with it and saving Pap's life. Not to divulge, not even to hint at the plan, if I saw him. No! Only to see his face—certain though I was already that he would never himself make the decision to kill.

But visit him—how? Since the trial of Monk Harper and Rufus Reed must still be in progress on the second floor of the courthouse, in a room near where they were holding Pap, the refusal of entry to members of the prisoners' families was sure to be stricter than ever. For that matter, even staying where I was any longer might attract the wrong attention.

So I flicked the reins, angling into a side street to swing wide around the courthouse. Mainly soldiers in the quarter I now entered, some making cartridges, some lounging, idle, glancing at me—paying me no great attention, but still I grew uneasy and at the first opportunity I rounded a couple of corners and made my way back to the main street.

At least the square was a good distance behind me now, the east outskirts of town not far off: which brought to the surface another concern I'd so far avoided thinking about openly. Straight down this street was the ghastly place itself, the fatal tree. *Just like a tree....*

But why go to it? Why record with my own eyes the horror of it?

I stopped, I closed my eyes, stared into the wavering darkness—.

At first I could have sworn the voice I heard rose from the inner darkness itself. I opened my eyes wide and glanced down: at two young boys who now lifted their faces to stare at me—we were directly in front of the log post office.

The one that was cotton-headed and squinch-eyed, I spoke to him: "Did I hear you right? The tree, you said?"

He squinted more than ever: "You a stranger that just rode in? You ain't heard about'm hanging the men on that big old tree?"

I recognized him now: "Aw, you know me, Tommy Evans. Todd Blair."

"Todd! Sure enough. 'Scuse me, Todd—." And he took off at a run, the other boy—his cousin Randy—bolting behind him.

What! Really? Afraid to be seen associating with me.

Gore Estes—I hadn't noticed him till now—spoke up from where he stood by the post office hitching rail: "You know the tree. That elem down yonder on the creek bank." He jabbed a finger in that direction.

Him too? That hostile voice. I'd never till now thought of Gore Estes as much of a rebel.

"Much obliged." I said, and twitched Comanche's reins to head on.

"Welcome."

Slowly, slowly I rode: as if the tree drew me while I fought its power. Before I'd gone any great distance, another boy came tearing across my path so close and heedless I had to pull Comanche to a halt. The boy ran on to a wagon parked in front of Stanley's Feedstore, scrambled up into the wagonbed next to another boy crouched behind a woman in a huge bonnet. Every word pouring from the boy's mouth came to me distinctly.

"You just orta seen it, Jake. They stood these here men one at a time on the tailgate of a wagon. Then Mr Alec Dunbar tied the rope around their necks. Like this"—he made motions circling the other kid's neck. "They had this nigger driving the wagon, see. And when Mr Dunbar got down and give the sign, that nigger popped them mules with a whip and jerked that wagon right out from under that man. And there he swung akicking. And then the nigger turned and come back, and him and another nigger cut the body down and loaded it in the wagon and druv off. Jake, you never seen the like. Come on, lemme show you."

They jumped to the ground and ran, ignoring the calls of the woman in the bonnet to come back.

There I sat, in the middle of the street, huddled over Comanche's neck, a darkness once more closing in on my brain. No escape now, if ever there had been. Nothing would do but to ride on to that tree.

—I came in sight of it. At first glance it was the same as always: huge, spreading, leaves once more tinging for fall—just as when I'd first laid eyes on it. Only this was different: a scattering of people formed a half-circle a little way back from it. Some came and went—I saw the two boys leaving, stealthily, creeping as if caught in a forbidden act—but a great many stood rooted, looks fastened on the tree as if they'd never seen one before.

I'd ridden in closer than I intended. My eyes resisted focusing; I forced them, stared at the huge outreaching limb that balanced the trunk leaning on the opposite side toward the stream. In horror I saw that a ring of bark on the upper surface of the limb had been rubbed off, baring the white wood—. I got a quick picture of a rope wearing a groove in the limb, deepening and deepening as body after body dangled back and forth beneath.

I reached out with my right hand to clench the barrel of the musket hanging from the saddlehorn: I squeezed it till I nearly cracked my knuckles.

—Now if I had stayed there ten seconds after what happened next, I'd have lost my wits. The evening had turned off warm, the sun blazing prickly enough to bring out the sweat, the air breathless and still, sultry. Till out of nowhere came a little whipping of breeze. The touch I got of it made me lift my face.

Down the near bank of the creek to the right was a field of dry cornstalks. The wisp of breeze that passed me must have struck another one coming opposite. A dust devil formed, whirling and rattling dead stalks, and skimming trash through the air as it bore straight down on the hanging tree—.

I fought with all my heart not to see the whirlwind strike the tree. Yet any swerving and the whirlwind might head for me, and that I feared just as much.

I swung Comanche toward the creek. To cross, only to cross. As if the whirlwind could not pursue me over the stream.

Comanche sprang into action, down the low bank and across in a great splashing. A few yards beyond the stream I drew him in, wheeled.

—I could breathe again: the whirlwind was nowhere to be seen.

Shall reap the whirlwind.

Why did my right hand feel stiff and cold? My eyes sought it out: I'd forgotten I still had a tight grip on the musket barrel. Then came words from deep inside, as if demanding to be communicated to the musket, words not to be gainsaid: 'Kill Colonel Ticknor! Kill him! If Colonel Oldham fails—and he will—*kill* Colonel Ticknor.'

7

THAT VOICE WOUND ME UP so tight I had to let go in some direction. I kept myself collected just long enough to decide that the direction ought to be back into town, in danger of being nabbed or not, so as to spy out what I could toward putting into action the desperate recourse of assassinating Colonel Ticknor. And so recrossing the creek, I let Comanche amble back along the main street, laying down the law to myself as I went to keep cool, to sharpen my wits, to mark out a spot for ambush and an escape route. All along the way I looked over one building after another, pondering the layout of Milcourt as I never had before. Just a hiding place to shoot from would not be enough. It had to be a point from which I could hope to disappear before anybody discovered where the shot had come from.

Yet what place? Where? Never before had the town looked so wide open: just cabins and a few frame buildings scattered over barren ground cut by wagontracks and horsetrails. No alleys to duck into except around the courthouse square, and these so few that you'd be trapped in one of them in no time.

Which brought on another knot of thinking to be untangled. Right on the square, yes, naturally that was where I'd be likely to find Colonel Ticknor the biggest part of the time. And as a commanding officer he would nearly always be in the midst of a body of men, shielded by them. Still, one shot. Yes, I could count on that. And had no fear I'd miss, if only I could separate him as a target. Surely that chance would come, if only I could find the patience to wait for it;

and I was growing more assured that I could. So, what then? Back to the hardest problem. How could I hope to escape if the right alley could not be found? How expect not to be gunned down myself a minute later?

Wait now. Wait. Colonel Ticknor couldn't be in the square all the time. Where did he sleep, for instance? Not out here with his soldiers, you could bet. In some house: such as a friend's place on the outskirts of town, that he might sometimes leave or approach alone, maybe in the dark of night.

Or a window, what about that? A candle or two lighting him as he stood near them in some room. Bushes or tree shadows to conceal me. My one shot, and then gone. Comanche hid in a thicket. Me halfway home or mingling with the crowd in the square before the disturbance cleared and a search could begin.

—All of which began to jell in my thoughts as the feasible plan.

Very well, suppose I did get away with killing Colonel Ticknor, then what? Would that only lash the rebels into such a fury they'd hang all the prisoners out of pure cold-blooded revenge?—

'You said yourself, Todd Blair, to Afton Thatcher, this very morning, that murder on one side is always answered by murder on the other, on and on—.'

'Yes, yes, but the rebels mean to hang all the prisoners anyhow. So go on! Get to the man directing the killing before he gets to us—that makes sense, right?'

And then a weak tremor of hope that Colonel Oldham might—.

Around and around in my head such arguments spun, and whatever turn they took I'd see a flash over and over of what was in store for Pap in any case: a noose around his neck, a wagon driven out from under his feet, his thrashing and kicking in the air till he strangled to death.

By this time I had reached the courthouse square again, picked my way through the crowd and pulled up finally on the west side of the courthouse, in view for the second time today of the windows over the buggy shed. And only now did I take full account that what had brought me back this way was not only surveying the town for an ambush spot but also the hope even yet of glimpsing Pap's shadow through a windowpane, a hope more intense than ever for just that much of a sign to guide my instincts on whether or not to kill Colonel Ticknor. Going in circles indeed.

But the light on the windowpanes kept a hard and undisturbed sheen, with deep shadows behind. *Through a glass darkly.*

For a good half hour I sat there in the saddle, till I was forced to admit that I could never draw myself away unless I made the attempt—at least that—to see Pap. No way could I go on without it.

At a deliberate pace, then, I rode around to the east side of the square, got down in front of the Dayton Building, looped the reins around a hitching rail. For a minute I stood motionless, resting my hand on Comanche's mane, catching a twitch and quiver along his neck that I thought reminded both of us that something risky was afoot.

I said to Comanche, "Yes. Sure enough." And all the while I eyed the second floor of the courthouse, or else the front door.

One piece of luck, it looked like. On guard at the main door was Wint Crigley, an old acquaintance that lived not a half-mile from our place. Oh, I had to swallow my wrath to see him standing there as one of Pap's jailers. But that I could do. And with it I made up my mind to treat Wint Crigley like he was just as important as old Jefferson Davis himself—if that was what it took for him to let me through to see my father. I inched my way across the street, then, over to where Wint stood cradling a beat-up old musket in the crook of one arm—on the very step where I'd accosted Harley Dexter night before last.

I got my request to Wint out of my mouth soft and easy, so as not to scare him. But not pleading. For an answer he slid his eyes around in every direction but mine, with that big Adam's apple of his bouncing up and down his neck. Finally, after I'd cocked my head this way and that till I plain forced him to catch my eye, he spoke up, but so hoarsely I could barely catch his words:

"'I gannies, all right, Todd. Five minutes, now. And no more'n five minutes to save your blessed soul."

Be damned! Of all the luck! Because crossing the street in our direction, though Wint hadn't seen him yet, here came Harley Dexter. And no way for me to slip inside the courthouse so quick he'd have to come in after me, for he was already closing in.

"What's this all about?" he snapped out.

Wint jumped, then put on a hangdog look: "Oh, just letting Todd see his pa for a second, that's all. I know—."

Harley snorted and cut him short: "Ain't no family members get in to see the prisoners, Wint Crigley. You know that as well as I do. That's orders."

Then he gave me a twist of a grin and mouthed out, "See your old daddy, is it? You fool with me and you'll see him all right—straight in there locked up with him. Beats me why you're still running around on the loose anyway. If it was up to me, you wouldn't be."

At least, then, somebody had put the clamps on Harley and his gang arresting whoever they pleased—. Jess Larkin's boy was released that afternoon, as I later learned.

But immediately another idea struck Harley Dexter, because you could see in his eyes that he figured he had me cornered from some other angle. And I wasn't long in finding out what it was:

"You got a gun?" he growled. "Nobody but the militia allowed to have firearms on the square. Orders from Colonel Ticknor."

I could thank my stars I'd just for convenience slipped the pistol into a saddlebag before riding into town, but that musket—man oh man, how I could have kicked myself. Had little enough sense to leave that musket hanging on my saddlehorn, when any fool—.

"You see one on me?" I answered.

"Oh, I don't mean *on* you." Then he barked out, "Where's your horse?"

All I did was glare at him, for whatever good that did. Easy enough for him to glance around and spot Comanche—for everybody in the county knew my horse.

"All right," he said, "I see it—I see that musket too. Now I'm going to ask you to step over there and hand it to me peaceable—or don't, then, if that's what you wanta do. Just go right ahead and give me a good reason to run you in."

I turned around and took my time walking in Comanche's direction, wary, taut, calm, not looking back: yet not sure, controlled as I felt at this moment, that I could maintain this composure when the second came for my hands to touch that musket, remembering how I'd clutched it down by the hanging tree. And here was one man I'd now, at this moment, gladly kill. I had just enough presence of mind left to stop a foot from Comanche and turn around slow. Harley had followed close behind, stood with his rifle levelled at me from the hip.

I gave it a stare, I gave him a stare, I waited.

He saw. He changed his mind about how he'd disarm me.

"I reckon I'll take that gun off'n the saddle myself. You move back."

Nothing else I could do, so step back I did. Felt relieved, in a way. Not the time for gunplay yet. Spoke to Comanche too, or else his teeth might've taken a chunk out of old Harley's butt. By now I was in a sweat, too, that Harley might decide to go through my saddlebags while he was at it. My stomach would not stop crawling till he'd stepped back in possession of the musket.

Sonofabitch looked ready to crow:

"You won't get unruly now, I reckon. So go on about your business. For the time being."

Then he turned his back on me and strode off.

I had kept back till now the gasping that broke out of me, and after that a sudden dizziness hit me, and I reeled. Somewhere, but where?—that calm, that wariness of a little while ago must still be in my make-up. I had to find that steadiness again, had to: for today, for tomorrow, for oh God how long?

Then as usual—and a blessing it was—the necessity of making the next move took over from immediate distress. I'd run enough risks for one day, hadn't I. Best thing would be to make Harley Dexter believe I was backing down. So let me get out of town straightaway. On the road home, too, I could search out a place to—why yes, to be sure: go home, pick up the rifle, have that place in mind to hide it till I had need of it. And strange to say, that decision took the pressure off my breath. Because if and when the hour came to kill Colonel Ticknor, I'd have the right gun in the right place. And besides, another worry was nagging at me. I'd been assuming Ma and Sis would conclude that I had indeed just gone on to Colonel Oldham's place, when they learned from Brother Hackett that the rescue raid had fallen through. But by now in any case they'd be wondering their hearts out over what had become of me.

So I headed out. Came close to forgetting I'd pass the hanging tree if I followed Main Street. Decided to swing a good ways to the south and pick up the road home well out of town. That's what I was about, with the square far behind me and following a crooked lane that angled off toward Walnut Creek a good piece below the hanging tree—when all of a sudden I heard hooves thumping behind me. I jerked Comanche's head around and got in position on one side of the lane, my hand on the butt of the pistol inside the saddlebag.

Turned out it was nobody but Flem Nugent, as harmless as any man alive. But he was in a great rush to get somewhere, so much so that he'd have thundered right on past me on his old roan nag without knowing I was there if I hadn't hollered him down:

"Flem, hold up. What's the matter?"

It took some distance for him to rein up and turn back, and then he began in a loud and desperate voice before he'd come up beside me: "What's the matter? Why it's Monk Harper and Rufus Reed, that's what the matter is. Both of them sentenced to be hung. I'm on my way out to tell Rufus's wife and littl'uns. Nobody else to do it. He ain't got no folks around here, did you know that? Come off down here from Missouri by theirselves. I don't know why they done it, but—."

Must be he was grabbing at any straw to avoid that horrible main topic, was why he began on how the Reeds came to Texas.

"But for Christ' sake, Flem, that trial ain't been going on no time!"—then the recollection of the fate of the Carlisle brothers jarred me at the very moment Flem was saying, "Time enough for that jury. And a little more time, I reckon, than they give the Carlisle boys. And if they're shoving them through two at once now, who knows when they'll commence scooping them up by the dozen. Anyway Monk and Rufus're to go to the killing tree first thing tomorrow morning."

All at once he clamped his mouth shut and his face went red, plainly because it had slipped his mind about Pap. "Todd"—he sounded like it was a funeral already—"I'm shore sorry, awful sorry, about your pa being in there. Oh, them men, Ticknor and all of them. Oh, they ort *not* to be adoing this. Where's it gonna end?"

It was either burst out crying or else cursing, so I snarled, "Natural-born sonsabitches may ride on top for a while, but they'll be brought down."

"Oh, but you watch your business, son. Watch out. Watch out. Ticknor's hard as ary rock. No mercy on nothing or nobody. And I don't have to tell you about Harley Dexter and his pack of blackguards afrothing at the mouth to clean out whoever's left in this county that favors the Union. And their murdering kind call it 'patriotism,' 'standing up for the Confederacy,' and all like that."

That word had hit me the wrong way one time too many.

"Confederacy!" I bellowed out. "What in the hell does the Confederacy amount to only a bunch of hotheaded bastards out to destroy the Union. And that Stars and Farts rag of theirs! The glorious Conflubbacy! And all of it just for the sake of slavery, no matter how loud they mealy-mouth it about the right to this and the right to that. And on top of it all hollering treason and conspiracy. Why goddam it, they're the traitors. They're the ones that ought to be swinging on that tree."

"Oh son, now son, you oughtn't to cuss and swear and carry on like that. Oh no, that won't help none."

When I saw the horrified look on Flem's face—as bad as when he'd ridden up and announced the hangings—I felt ashamed, recalling as I did that Flem taught a Sunday School anytime he could gather a few people to listen somewhere in the neighborhood....

Right then it crossed my mind: Confederacy. Justice. Jury. Now why was it I'd never yet inquired about exactly who was serving on the jury: dumb as it made me look to myself. —Well, I'd been in too much of a rush to ask Mr Hackett, and I reckon wouldn't have asked Colonel Oldham if I'd thought of it. —In the next instant the question was out of my mouth to Flem.

And so one by one he gave me their names. As he ticked them off I stopped him after each one and repeated that name aloud, making up my eternal list of mortal enemies but nearly swamped by a helpless rage all the time, for what could I ever expect to do against so many of the biggest men in this part of the country? And if I could not stop them from hanging my father, how could I ever expect to kill them, either?

Flem went quiet now, and so did I, my thoughts straying.

"Looky here," said Flem. "I hate to go off and leave you, Todd, but I can't stay another second. Rufus's place is a good ways off."

And with that he raised his hand good-bye and took off at a lope.

Coming back to myself, I touched Comanche's flanks to put him to walking along steady. From there on home I kept my head down and rode, just that. And all the while the names of those jury members, now one by one, now all in a jumble, went coursing through my head. What got to me most of all was that I knew most of those men well, every one except three, and taking my cue mainly from Pap I had never had a thing against a single one of them.

With the agitation over the jurors swirling through my head, at least I kept at bay the worry of facing Ma and Sis when I got home. Though that too flooded over me when I came in sight of the cabin, and the peace that lay all around it only made matters worse.

The weather had warmed up little by little since noontime, and the mild evening was now turning into a sundown as red as flame. The few clouds of earlier in the day had filled out heavy in the west and built up into thunderheads here and yonder, all bold and black except around the edges where the low-sinking sun set them on fire. The whole branch bottom down the gentle slope south of the cabin was alive with the singing of insects. We could have been back in the middle of August.

I crept in so quiet the women did not see me, not even while I lingered at the barn stabling Comanche and piling his feed trough high with ears of corn. Bye and bye, when I couldn't delay heading for the house any longer, I went toward it, every step I took like dragging a weight. When I came to the big lone postoak that had decided us more than anything else on where to build the cabin, all of a sudden I could not move a foot farther. I sat down—or dropped was more like it—into the little plank swing Pap had put up for the kids. Weary to the bottom of my soul, I gazed up into the branches. A couple of tree-frogs had begun that little high-pitched singing I'd always loved so well to listen to at night—and again it was like late summer....

Oh but I sprang up then like I'd been jabbed. My eye had caught the two ropes by which the swing was suspended: had seen how they circled a big limb up there—.

It was a good thing that for now I had no more time to think about being at the end of a hanging rope. Luckily, Ma and Sis had finally seen me, and out in a flurry they came, with the boys right behind them.

While I told them everything I'd done and everything I'd found out, I was able to control myself better than I'd feared, though with a catch in my voice again and again. While I was in the middle of my report we all went on inside and congregated around the dining-table, just as we'd done night before last: Ma and me in chairs, Sis on the bench now, the boys on the floor. What I hated most of all to tell them I kept back till the last: the names of the jurymen.

The beanpot was steaming over the fireplace. Ma had interrupted herself in the middle of fixing flapjacks, and in a little bit she got up and went back to it. Sis then sliced off some bacon. The sight of all this ought to have made me hungry, since I hadn't had a mouthful for many an hour. But all it did was turn me so weak I felt ready to collapse.

So now I was finished with telling them, and there I sat like a lump, in no condition to notice anything. And so it did not register for a few minutes that Ma was crying. That ought not to have surprised me, seeing that no one could've had more reason to shed tears, but then Ma had never been as quick at that as a great many women are. The tears had just come of their own accord, and were coursing down her cheeks before she seemed to realize they were there. For when she did, she gave up. She sank onto the bench and drooped her head, leaving the flapjacks to burn if Sis hadn't stepped in. What Ma did next gave me a terrible fright, lifting her apron not just to cover her face but flinging it over her head and ducking into the crooks of her elbows placed on the table, hugging her head as if trying to crawl into her arms and hide. Now I'd seen Indian women do that, but never anyone else. Sometimes it slipped my mind for a long time that Ma was a quarter Indian: because she was just Ma, and she never talked much about her background. But in that instant it hit me straight in the heart. As if her sorrowing went deep not only within herself but into the wailing of women far back in time beyond counting, even to the first grief that ever came to a woman on earth.

Sis could not hold back for long either. Nearly dropping the last flapjack as she forked it onto a plate, and leaving the meat to sizzle in the frying pan, she leaned against the wall by the hearth and broke out in sobs fit to tear her throat apart.

I couldn't stand it, I rushed for the door. As I was passing the fireplace I snatched the rifle from its rack above the mantel. Then I was out under the postoak, rushing. I stumbled, grabbed one rope of the swing and sent the whole contraption into a wild tossing. And did not look back. And did not stop till I had come to the barnlot fence, where I leaned my elbows on the top rail with the rifle clenched in both hands and thrust out crossways before me, as I might've lifted it up for an offering to—who knew what? Yet still in the right position to swing the butt instantly to my shoulder and draw a bead. And then I could not choke back unshed tears any longer: I sobbed, I bellowed, and the tears gushed.

The swimming of my vision was cut across by the last thin rim of light running along the skyline to the west, where clouds low in the sky had burned down to coals at the bottom and higher up were packing in darker all the time.

Finally I quit crying, had to, wrung dry. Leaned the rifle against the middle rail. Wiped my face a couple of times with my shirt sleeve. Scowled and clenched my fists and began beating at the air on both sides of me, fighting whatever was there. Then began to sway back and forth. Glared at where the sun had gone down, twisted my head away, twisted it back to glare once more—. "I'll kill you, Ticknor! I'll kill you, Dexter! I'll kill *all* of you murdering bastards—." And then one by one I bawled out names till I'd gone through the whole of the jury. Then I repeated them, louder. This time my voice rose to a scream and went echoing in waves to lose itself in the surrounding woods.

While I was pacing up and down at this, the sky thickened into total night. I came to a halt. Fool-like I doubled up one fist and made a swipe at the top rail of the fence—and ran a big splinter under the skin along one knuckle. I stood working around with the nails of my thumb and forefinger to get a pinch on the end of the splinter. The pain was a help, good to have, along with the urge deep and burning to be loping back to Milcourt, with the rifle in my hands, this very second. To kill Ticknor, to kill Harley Dexter, both, tonight. Then to go on, at once, to killing members of the jury.

Just as I jerked the splinter free, and clenched my teeth against the hurt, I felt rather than saw a dazzle from the western horizon.

The first stab of lightning....

8

On no other night could a rainstorm have been more welcome. 'Let it be a gully washer,' I thought. For as anyone living on and by the land will reflect from second nature, even in the midst of a massacre, I reminded myself of how little rain we'd had that fall, and so how much we needed a soaker to season the ground for spring planting.

Darkness came on complete now, and still I stood there by the barnlot fence, waiting for each far-off spear of lightning and never disappointed for long, for now they flickered here and yonder across a wide band of sky from west to north. A big rain was on the way for certain, with a norther behind it, and not to be long in coming. For another norther to hit so soon after the first one two days back was odd, but the weather in north Texas was as unpredictable as weather could be anywhere.

'Better see about the womenfolks.'

And that thought sent me creeping back up to the cabin, where I paused at the door listening, and caught no sound coming from inside. Then nudging the door open and stepping softly in, when my eyes lost the glare of the lightning I made out only one figure in the glow of the room: Ma still sitting on the bench where I'd left her. Now, I was thankful to see, she'd taken the apron from over her head, had it gripped in a crumple against her breast, sitting reared back poker-stiff and grim-faced, eyes dry and big as saucers, the glint of the candle flame in them, staring into that flame as if it held some terrible significance she was helpless to fathom.

I leaned the rifle in a corner of the room close to the door, eased over and sat down next to her and slipped my arm around her waist.

Motionless still, she began to whisper in a paper-dry voice: "Son...," and then trailed off into a moan deep in her throat, uttering not a word more. We both sat and stared at the candle flame as if in a trance. Several minutes passed before I ventured to remark, "Don't you reckon we better get to bed, Ma. I expect you need sleep as bad as I do."

She sucked in a deep breath like it was the first one she'd drawn all day. And her voice surprised me, coming out now clear and strong: "Tell me their names again, the *gentlemen* of the jury."

How could I say, No, please. And I shuddered, those names yet ringing in my ears from my shouting them against the woods. But I went ahead, made my voice as reassuring as I could, repeated each name smoothly, huskily, without taking my eyes away from the candle flame, terrified that a glance in her direction would cause her to break down again, and send me scurrying once more into the night.

When I had gone through all twelve names, Ma took another deep breath and said between her teeth, "So they've got a preacher as one of their number, have they? *Brother* Harry Tillman—."

"The *Reverend* Harry Tillman—you might even say 'Reverend *Doctor*,' seeing as how he's a sawbones along with it."

"He's taken dinner in this house a many a Sunday."

To which I could have made no reply except in words I never used in Ma's presence.

Then all at once she gasped and jumped up from the bench: "Why Todd! Precious, you've still not had a bite to eat."

"I ain't a particle hungry, Ma."

But she got busy anyhow: warmed up the flapjacks, sliced and fried some bacon to replace what Sis had let burn to a crisp, and dished me out a steaming bowl of beans. She had fresh buttermilk for me too, having churned that day. The smell of all that grub was enough to rouse a faint appetite. So I took a couple of mouthfuls. Then when I least expected it the hunger came. I dug in. I made that first helping disappear, followed by another that Ma was quick to serve. And all the time, when she was not bringing me food, she sat in a chair across the table and never took her eyes off me.

As I was shaking my head to decline the offer of a third plateful, she broke out suddenly: "Todd, why did you take the rifle out to the barn with you?"

Now of course I hadn't opened my mouth about the possibility of killing anyone, well aware what Ma's response would have been if I had.

I shifted my gaze involuntarily from the candle to the fading coals in the fireplace: "Well, I ain't getting nowhere going about it peaceful, am I? And something's downright gotta be done if Colonel Oldham fails to come through, don't it?"

"Something has, yes. But not that. Not yet—if ever. Who'd you have in mind?"

I drew in and let out a deep breath:

"Maybe Colonel Ticknor. Maybe Harley Dexter. Maybe both."

"You know better'n that, Todd. Start any of that gunplay and Pap'll be a goner for certain. And no telling how many more along with him."

"No telling any of that as it is."

I pushed back my plate. Ma stood up and carried it over to add to the stack in the dishpan.

—Anything to change the subject: "I'll go to the spring after a bucket of water."

She stopped me before I could get to my feet: "The dishes'll wait till morning."

I tried going back to an earlier suggestion, still dodging: "Let's go to bed then. Like I say, I magine you need sleep as much as I know I do."

"Todd, promise me you won't shoot nobody till you've run out of all else that can be done."

"Well—. Let me say it like this: I'll put it off if I can see any better direction to go—. But listen now, Ma, I'll have to be the judge of when to do what."

—Like I was the man of the house now, the one to decide the big issues. Like she could rest assured I knew what I was up to. When of course I didn't, and she wasn't fool enough to believe I did. She turned away in silence, was all. To swing the beanpot out from over the coals and put a lid on it; to rake ashes into a heap to guard the coals till morning. As she went about these and other before-bedtime chores, she trudged around like she was sagging in her tracks.

I looked away.

Then Ma surprised me by leaving the room without another word passing between us. —Couldn't be she was giving in by silent consent to my big claim on decision-making: more like disapproval she might not express but could never be talked out of—.

I stepped outside to take a leak, stood under pitch-black heavens.

After a moment a lightning bolt split the sky halfway down in the west and thunder hurled itself across overhead. As I closed the cabin door behind me going back inside, there came another streak of lightning, with even heavier thunder passing from one horizon to the other—.

The Lord will pass over the door, and will not suffer the destroyer to come in unto your houses to smite you.

"Oh Lord, if you will, if only you will," I said under my breath.

So all except me were in bed now, maybe Sis and the boys long asleep—anyhow, long silent they'd been. No sooner had I groped my way into the shed room, slipped out of my shoes and clothes, and crept into bed, than the forces of the sky began to clash in earnest. Came a closing in of lightning flash and thunder crack, one on top of the other. I lay and listened, carried away by all this tumult, but impatient, impatient.

'Come on, rain. Come on. Soak the ground. Make us ready for a crop next year,' ran through my mind again and again.

Which simply brought grief down to crush me once again: Pap might not be alive next year. I knew it, and I feared it, and yet it still did not seem possible. Putting in a crop in the spring: as far back as I could remember that had always been the new beginning. And how could it ever come about again without Pap?

—Suddenly I saw him as if standing in the middle of a fresh-plowed field under a bright spring sky. At the same time my emotions said that I could never plow a field for planting without him, never bear to look out over a newly furrowed earth, though an awful need for a vision of how to be whole in his absence penetrated like a wound the darkness of my head—.

Pow! A lightning bolt struck nearby, wrenching me body and soul out of the torpor I'd sunk into. For a moment I lay stunned, gathering my wits to restore consciousness to the waking night.

Then on impulse I did a quick flip over on my stomach and dug my face into the pillow. Just in time. Maybe I could not prevent myself from crying, could only hope the pillow would muffle the sound from reaching anyone else's ears.

—That second another whipcrack of lightning popped so nearby that I could hear the sizzle of it, and then thunder crashed like a mountain falling, followed by a mighty rush through the timber that for the time being gave me power to hold back the sobbing: a distant rushing that might be wind, might be rain. In my soul I longed more than ever for rain, rain, rain: a blessed unleashing of flood.

An instant later I knew that what I heard was truly rain. On it came, as I welcomed it, exhilarated: a drenching rain indeed, a thrumming on the roof punctuated by sharp pings of hail, and now and again by a heavy thump of scattered raindrops massive among the lesser ones. Then would come another searing of lightning, with thunder unfurling across the sky roll by roll. Not much wind yet, but as I was puzzling why that was so, a gale slung in out of the storm like it meant to sweep cabin and all to Kingdom Come.

Yet the wind held back this side of destruction, while on went the downpour, a great abundance of water approaching flood.

Not a peep did I hear out of anybody. All asleep? Or all staring wide awake maybe, each one in anguish alone, huddled up and frightened to death—. A silent prayer went through me for the blessing of deep and peaceful sleep on each head within these walls: my family, for whom it could well turn out that they had nobody but me to guide them through long years of loss and torment—.

The storm still kept me from weeping. But scarcely.

On and on went the rain and the wind, till I thought they would never stop, till finally they did reach a slackening, as if the worst might be over. The noise of the rain lulled enough now for me to hear the branch on the rise in the bottom, though not a monstrous overflow, from the sound of it. Still, it was a mercy that all crops in the bottom fields had been gathered, so that the water could swamp the soil, spread out to saturate the earth for—. I struggled to head my thoughts away from this reminder of next year's crops....

Now what about the wind though? Bound to veer to the north, turn the weather cold. I lay suspended in wait for that, but as yet caught no noise of it.

Now all along through the storm—not that I quit listening to it in the meantime—the names of the jurymen had kept coming back to me as though out of the elements. I spoke those names to myself, whispered them over and over, sure that a darkness in my mind was hiding something about them: I just could not grope to the right opening for the meaning of it to emerge.

Suddenly a powerful clap of thunder lunged out of nowhere, even after the rain had diminished to sprinkling and the darkness had gone still: a blast of thunder with no lightning first as a warning. At that sound my body convulsed, and I did a flip again, this time off my belly onto my back.

'Hey! For God's sake! Why yes, I reckon so! Damn it all!'

Words came now in tumult: 'Just count up—count up—why didn't you do that before?—too addled—too stupid—. Why see here, Todd Blair, *seven* out of them twelve men're slaveholders—seven! And they're pulling together, that's what they're doing, in deciding by simple majority. How can they miss?—no wonder every man they drag before them ends up on the hanging tree—. Oh yes, I know. Mr Hackett did refer in some way to who all was on the jury, as I remember now. But that just plumb slipped my mind. To count up, I mean. Treason and conspiracy, my sacred ass!—it's no more than a plot to wipe out every man with a Union look in his eye. It's that simple. I knew that, of course. Yes, yes, really I did. But the plain and simple gall of how they're doing it. I mean—.

'Here! Here!'—I sat up in bed and clutched at the edge of a quilt till I nearly tore it—. 'All right now. This is the way to go at it. If I can just work it around so's to talk to the other five men, the ones with no slaves. If even two or three of them could argue for doing away with that infernal majority rule.... Why damn it to hell, like I been shouting to the world, a jury's supposed to decide unanimous. And that perditious outfit at least *calls* itself a jury. Ain't they got at least enough legality about them to be shamed into passing sentence the way it's always been done?'

—On and on like that, my mind in a whir. Till at length I simply ran down. And maybe also because a rain always freshens up the worst of things—by now the scent of it had filled the cabin. Anyhow, once again, as on the first night of the troubles, with that dry norther pushing me gently home, I looked again on a change in the weather as a heartening sign. And in no time I began to feel even more encouraged about it all, having come to what seemed the natural choice of the first juror to hit up—a man who might be sympathetic, who might instigate a push for a change in the jury's decision rules. Who else but Preacher Tillman? I knew him far better than the others, because he was our preacher, more or less, and had put his feet so often under our dinner table.

Who'd have thought I could ever grab a wink of sleep, keyed up with anxiety like a high-tuned fiddle string as I was, and casting around for arguments to present to Preacher Tillman. Oh, how voluble I was there in the dark of night with words that I could only pray to retain and to utter tomorrow.

Yet for all that I slid unawares into sleep.

—To encounter another dream, long and contorted and leading me to the hanging tree. And to that dust devil I'd seen sweeping past the tree. And into a horrific current of alarm as I watched a multitude pulled by a power unseen to that tree to be hanged. Who they were was hard to tell. Pap was not singled out from among that host of men. Some had the faces of the prisoners, and some, beyond reason, the faces of the jurymen, though most had the faces of strangers. The rifle that I suddenly discovered clutched to my chest was useless, for I could not move it. Another realization, soon the most terrifying of all, was that I could not make out for certain whether the tree that claimed the lives of these men was the big elm on the creek bank or the postoak in our yard. I could not distinguish between the ropes from which dangled a misty childhood swing and other ropes coiled not only around the necks of the men but enmeshing their whole bodies and binding them to the killing tree. In my terror of not knowing the tree of death from the tree for play, it came over me in my dream that in this time of chaos and atrocity all the trees in the world might be transformed into hanging trees....

9

MORNING CAME with a brilliant clarity of stars and a chilling, gusty wind from the northwest. Not cold enough to bring the first freeze of autumn though, in spite of last night's bluster. Curious, since a norther ushered in by a heavy thunderstorm usually brought frigid weather.

I was so eager to start for Milcourt that day that now and again I shook all over while I waited for Ma to stir me up a bite of breakfast. Knowing her so well, I was pretty sure she'd say no more about my scheming to kill someone—nor dodge the issue by declaring that I was leaving her and Sis without a weapon when I went over to lay the powderhorn and a buckskin pouch of bullets by the rifle still standing in the corner where I'd left it last night—but rather would do just what she did: give me sorrowing looks worse than a torrent of begging. I couldn't plan anything in any direction till I'd made my escape from those eyes. So the first moment I could, still before dawn, I saddled Comanche and left.

If I took aim to kill a man this day or any other, how could I see past those pleading eyes?

Outside of town a ways I found a good hiding place in a thicket, wrapped the rifle in a fragment of wagonsheet I'd brought along and buried it, handy for when I might decide to make use of it. And risky though it was to go on carrying the pistol in the saddlebag, I had to do it, trusting that if Harley Dexter hadn't thought to search me yesterday for a hidden weapon, he'd overlook doing it today as well. And I just might be in danger from men that Harley didn't dare to challenge about the guns they carried openly, though no more members of the militia than I was. Among them were fiery rebels who knew where I stood and had already sent looks of hatred my way.

Just as I rode into Milcourt the sun came up, the sky clear and the wind still gusty.

The thing now was to locate Preacher Tillman as quickly as I could, before the time came for the jury to convene. Yet what to say to him I could not this morning begin to formulate—the words from last night having evaporated. Each time I tried to push my mind to shape an effective phrase, what it gave me instead was echoes of the threats I'd hurled out last night against each member of the jury, and thoughts about how weird and infuriating it was that this very one of them—Preacher Tillman—might end up being as responsible for the death of my father as any firebrand rebel sitting next to him. What had thrown the world into such madness that I must harbor killing thoughts even against Harry Tillman: a well-respected preacher, a long-established friend?

Now in those days no church buildings had as yet been built out in the country. What served the purpose was the one-room log schoolhouses that the various denominations took turns holding services in. A minister was any man who felt inspired and could persuade a few others to think so too. Our family did not belong to any of the denominations, so we went to this service or that, just as the notion struck us. But to Brother Tillman's more often than any other, though I'd never quite known why. To me he seemed to assume self-importance too easily. He called himself a medical doctor too—which also in those days could mean anyone who believed he had the power to heal and convinced a few others that he did. As a doctor we had never tried him out, which may have been because we did not believe in him all that strongly as a preacher. Still, he was better than the rest at making Sunday different from the other days of the week when we wanted it that way. As often as not he would come home with us for dinner. His wife was sickly, never came to church, and he was so much the preacher who could tuck away fried chicken that we suspected she never cooked a decent meal either. After dinner he and Pap would talk, most of it coming from Brother Tillman, with Pap as the kind of listener who can make even a moderate talker open up.

—And now to have Preacher Tillman hovering over Pap in judgment of life or death.

Now Brother Tillman lived on a homestead farm a distance east of town, far enough out that in order to be near for the sake of his jury duty he might be staying with kinfolks of his who I knew lived in the north part of Milcourt. So I hurried there.

Their small white house stood near a pecan tree from which the norther was plucking a few early-shrivelled leaves. A sudden gust of the wind nearly lifted Preacher Tillman's derby hat off his head as he came hurrying out the front door, just as I was riding up and climbing down by the yardgate. When he saw who it was, one foot hung in the air above a porch step for an instant, then holding his hat against the wind, he came tramping on hellbent. His nerve gave out just as he reached the gate. He faltered, stood with one hand clutching the latch, the gate still closed between us. His face was by now strained red and taut, his breath raucous. For my part, I could hardly breathe at all, my teeth were clamped so tight—and as I later discovered, one of my fists was clenched.

No words I could think of—still—were of any use, nor apparently any that he could think of either. From the look on his face, it may have been the first time in his life he'd been at a loss for something to say.

He recovered before I did:

"I can see you don't know, Todd. I was in hopes you might've heard. Some have, I know, and spread the news—."

With those remarks came a lifting of the chin that took me back to Sunday mornings when the same motion of his head had introduced a sermon.

I shivered—.

"Understand, Todd. And if you inquire around, a good many will bear me out in this. I'm in that jury room to save lives, not to take them—."

If I'd had words ready, that line of talk would've driven them out of my head. No opportunity anyhow to open my mouth—.

"I've argued myself blue in the face for clearing every man that's yet come to trial. I'm doing it at the risk of my own safety, Todd. Because the mob fever's running so high that any word you utter in favor of the accused men can be interpreted as treason itself—. And I can't stay and talk, Todd, much as I'd like to. The jury's convening just as soon as we can all get there."

With that I found my tongue: "Hold on a second, Brother Tillman"—last thing I felt like calling him, but if I didn't walk soft no use starting out: "You positive it makes any difference how loud you argue for innocence? That so-called jury decides by majority vote, and I'd lay ten to one the seven slavery men make up the majority time and again when it comes to passing sentence."

That hit him direct. He pursed his lips and puckered his forehead—that quirk of his too I'd noticed in church, but never as now with despair eating at my insides. I swallowed hard to fill the void. I did my utmost to gaze steadily at this Preacher Tillman who stood playing himself as a public man given to making weighty decisions, who would fasten on that same look whether he was pleading to save your soul or persuading you to take a dose of medicine—or deciding on your death sentence.

His tone of voice contained all that: "I'm not at liberty, you must understand, to discuss the proceedings of the jury."

The words almost escaped my lips, 'You old fool.' Only I had just enough forethought to remember that I might have him and no one but him to depend on—.

"All the same," I said, "you know what I'm telling you's so. Argue yourself blue in the face, or black in the face, and still the slavery men'll vote together and run the show, just like they have from the start of the whole secession hullaballou."

Brother Tillman began fumbling in his pockets for who knew what—for an answer he couldn't find elsewhere maybe. What he came up with was a little pearl-handled knife, and opened it with a kind of flourish, and began scraping under his fingernails, which already looked clean enough to me. Evidently he was on the run. So it was not the time to let up now:

"You keep on with that majority vote rigamarole and you'll see. The slave owners'll do away with everybody that breathes the name of 'Union.' And when they run out of the ones under guard they'll go out and corral some more. You surely don't reckon it was any accident the jury ended up seven to five in favor of big slavery men, do you? And then they, the majority, went and voted theirselves the power to make all the decisions. You don't truly reckon the situation was any different from that, do you?"

He'd given thought to that, plenty of it, but there he stood looking as if he wished such a thing had not occurred to anybody else.

—He snapped the knife shut and fixed his eyes on me: "Oh, if you could only know how long and hard I've argued against hanging a one of those men," he croaked out, and his eyes moistened. But he couldn't help himself: his voice carried that preacher sound, a wheedling tone, and a touch of overbearing in it—.

"You ain't saved none yet, as we been saying." That came grinding out between my teeth in spite of me.

His voice went mournful, and building on that preacher-like swing he intoned: "No, I haven't. No, Todd, I haven't. But I've got to stay on that jury and fight against what's happening the best way I can. Let me tell you a thing you don't know, that I promised myself never to breathe to a soul. But you have a right to hear it—. I quit that jury when they condemned the first man—or that is, I tried to. I swear I did. Then some of the rest of them—not the plantation men—begged me to come on back. And for the very reason I'm asking you to accept. You've got to believe me. If I leave that jury, twice as many men or more will die. I can't discuss the hows, whys and wherefores, but it's beginning to work. I declare to you, it's the God's truth. I'm a minister of the Gospel, son."

"I'm not disputing your word. But whatever you do or don't do, I can't believe it'll work any better than it has before. Now listen to me, Brother Tillman"—to go on throwing in the good manners was the only way I could keep my head—"just listen now. Surely to God *somebody* on that jury on the hothead side still wants you there, or you'd have been let go. And so you ought to be able to raise some small voice to shame them into acting like a regular jury. A jury is supposed to decide unanimous. Any fool knows that. I mean, 'treason,' 'conspiracy,' 'insurrection'! Why damn it all, man"—a slip, be careful—. "And the accused men were supposed to have a lawyer to defend them too. Whatever happened to that?"

—This might be just the moment to insert that thorny business—and then if Colonel Oldham did come through as he'd promised—.

Preacher Tillman's eyes widened. How did I know about the failed provision for defense?

For an answer he clutched the brim of his hat, as if a gust of wind had caught at it again—which it hadn't. The trouble in his gaze was so intense now that I began to think better of him. And to feel a tingle of reassurance besides. If only he could lose that preaching attitude.

Which he did not: "I'm a public man and a doctor and a minister of the Gospel, son, so you might try to realize that with so much more experience in the world than you could have, I've given all that you say much thought, and another thing besides—I've mulled it over and over in my heart. But then even I can only go so far. Myself, and the others on the jury that vote counter to the majority, we suspect that—well, if we're not mighty careful how we tread, we could go to that hanging tree ourselves."

The little respect I'd worked up for him fell apart. It was all I could do not to say it aloud: 'What you mean is, if you don't deliver men for the mob to hang they might hang you—.'

I had to put a stop to such thoughts. And hold my temper. I reached inward to get a grip on myself. I did that. But it didn't last. I heard myself rapping out before I could hold my tongue: "You could try. You could try. You could try—."

I was on the brink of cuss words too. Those however I did succeed in holding back, though what I broke out with was little better: "If you don't at least make the effort to change that jury's way of doing, you ain't no public man, you ain't no doctor, you ain't no *minister* of the Gospel."

—Words succeeded quickly by the thought, 'Oh what have I done now.' —To have come so far, and to lose it all!

I whirled around—momentum I had no control over—and put my foot in the stirrup and swung up so hard I all but went off on the other side of Comanche. When I looked down at Preacher Tillman he was standing there with his mouth open as if his jaws had locked that way, his hat off now and the brim gripped in both hands. The stream of words at his command anytime he was playing hard at being the public man or the doctor or the preacher had all at once dried up and left him standing there empty.

But he was not long in digging down another layer to discover another small flow. What came out nearly choked him, though mild and sorrowful, just as I was yawing Comanche's head around to ride away:

"I don't know, Todd. Oh Lord, I just don't know. All I can tell you is this: I'm following my duty the way I see it. I'll continue to do all I humanly can. Do all I can, yes. But right at this minute I just don't see clear what that'll be."

I bobbed my head, as much as to say, So long. But then just as Comanche began to move off, Preacher Tillman called out, "Wait, Todd. Hold on a minute."

I drew back on the reins and half turned in the saddle to look at him.

He came out of the yard slowly, awkwardly, the hat now clamped on his head tight and square. He stepped up to me and laid a hand on the saddlehorn: "Todd, I'll tell you what I'll do. It's been on my mind for some time. And I want you to listen to it carefully. On my soul, I don't believe there's any way I can ever persuade that court to act on a unanimous basis. But let me tell you what's running through my mind. I'll admit I may have been wrong not to bring it up, not to press it, before now—."

He let his voice drop as if we were hatching a plot:

"I've thought long and hard about this, and I've prayed earnestly about it too. I've thought I'd lay it on the line: either act according to the customary way of juries or I'll resign. And not be talked out of it this time. That would make it a showdown. And yes, it might put me in danger myself. But no—on second thought I believe you're right. I'll start pressing it today. I won't force it to the showdown right away. I'll lead up to that. But I'll make a beginning—."

On what? I thought. One sentence running into another was all I heard. How could he make a beginning on a showdown without it *being* a showdown? That voice of his was emphatic and hollow in the same breath—the worst of a preacher expounding: words that might sound great coming out of a pulpit, when there was nothing at stake but talk....

I sat there beating my brains, wondering. Had I already said too much, or was I really pinning him down? At least my temper subsided.

"Make a beginning how? What do you mean?"

He answered in a hoarse whisper: "I ought not to confide this even in you. But all right, I will. Under your hat, now. Under your hat." He pinched the brim of his own between thumb and forefingers. "I've had another thought. I see I'll have to share that with you too, so as to make myself clear. A two-thirds majority, that's what I'll reach for. That much I might be able to put across."

—Was he really and truly standing there offering that as some great scheme? I wanted to lash out at him. With words. Even with the bridle reins.

Alarm showed in his face: "You don't understand. Remember what you said about the jury: seven slavery men. A swing of one vote might make all the difference, you see. Eight, not seven. Understand?"

Well yes, I did. All of a sudden I did. And immediately—while I was calling myself stupid for not catching on sooner—Preacher Tillman began to look like not such a fool after all, and to rise in my estimation.

"That could be," I admitted—which did not seem enough, his look told me, so I tacked on: "Because, as you say, you know the jury better than I do."

A look of tremendous relief came over his face. He stood nodding quickly, benignly. Till it occurred to him he was already late for the convening of the jury.

"Todd, see here. I have to be on my way. Trust me. Please do trust me. And...and, let me say this. This much I know. Your daddy won't be coming up for trial today."

It was such an unexpected twist that I felt let down, my voice turning frosty in spite of me: "Today or tomorrow or day after tomorrow, or next week—." Then in the next breath I tried to make up for it: "I do appreciate you telling me. And yes, I will trust you."

His voice was eager now: "I'll make every effort. Just keep that before you as a consolation. For you see, if I succeed, then the ones in on this plot no deeper that your daddy is will be easy to exonerate."

Already he was turning, was rushing away, as little willing to receive a reply as I was prepared to give it. And he couldn't help himself, that irksome preacher tone was back in his voice: a few words of consolation to a faithful church member. Bland, blind optimism could not have sounded worse, and how could he ever hope to succeed if he fell so easily into one of his conventional poses?

So what to think now? What to do next?

By reflex, with a flick of the reins, I turned Comanche's head to ride away.

10

But I had not ridden twenty yards before I drew up and turned in the saddle to watch Preacher Tillman out of sight, groping to fix at some constant point my wavering trust in him. He withdrew at a fast walk, arms and legs flinging out excess motion, with every appearance of floundering along except for the set of the derby hat, level and firm, that bore him forward as balance and guide.

And so here I sat left behind by events, at the sudden end of a determined course of action with no assurance I'd made any advance whatever. I carried the burden of that disappointment with me as I rode on again, making for the center of town under the premonition that Colonel Oldham, whether from illness or failure of will, would not appear in Milcourt today, would never intervene; that the maybe-so with Preacher Tillman would come to nothing; and that the only alternatives left were to kill or do nothing. Which brought to mind again the need to search out a hiding place to fire from: at least I could do that—though it might be no more than an exercise in frustration—while I waited for the outcome of Preacher Tillman's efforts with the jury. To ride around town inspecting every building, then—but slowly, slowly, so as not to arouse suspicion.

With that purpose in mind, I rode toward the middle of town at a slow pace, down Industry Street, as they called the main stem north and south. But before I'd gone far, I came upon a sight that brought me to a halt, because at first I did not know what to make of it.

Wasn't that the old Stockton house? That banker?

Sure it was. The first house in Milcourt put up out of dressed lumber—so people said—vacant since the owner's death some years before. Or rather, the house had never actually been lived in at all, for Stockton dropped dead the very day it was finished and ready to occupy. A tale had even spread that it was haunted, that his ghost anyhow had moved in.

So being torn down. But why? Piles of lumber scattered here and yonder over the wide grounds of the place. Two slaves at work ripping down the last of the walls. One of them I recognized: Slick, belonging to Jacob Reasoner, who was one of the jury. Funny time to be salvaging lumber, for a new house or whatever, with a killing spree going on just down the street. Same as the routine I'd seen in the fields the other day, and on the streets just yesterday: revelations of how little most people cared about anything except their own affairs—.

But all this line of thought went askew, then shattered, from the shock I got on glancing at a far corner of the property and spotting two other slaves busy slapping together boxes out of the scrap lumber.

Boxes!—Coffins! Three or four already built and standing open in a row.

I wheeled Comanche aside into a lane to erase that sight from my eyes, clenching my teeth till the jaw muscles began to throb.

Yet ducking aside did not matter much at that. Any direction I turned there it all was, if not with me or before me then close behind—Pap's life running out for certain and the same old agonies of impotence gnawing at me, magnified now by the sight of the coffins. With those on this end of town and the death tree on the other, how could I skirt around either one as I went through the streets seeking out a place of ambush?

Only one consolation appeared in the midst of all this turbulence: Pap was not to come up for trial today. Though how, as a matter of fact, could Preacher Tillman be sure of that? But if so, then I had one more day to maneuver, even though that day would fly past in a hurry.

Now I left the last cabin behind, as the lane I was following narrowed to a trail hemmed in by tall waving grass. Like all the other ways leading west out of Milcourt, this one struck the banks of the Trinity, thick with bushes at this point. I rounded a thicket to an opening and pulled up to rest my eyes on the clear-sliding water. Almost as soon as I'd done that I caught a movement going on a distance to my left.

Men digging? Good God, no! Not digging. Three slaves under some trees on the river bank were pitching the last shovelfuls of dirt on what appeared to be the mounding of a grave.

I pulled Comanche's head around and trotted over to them.

My voice came out dry and shaky: "Why're you burying somebody down here?"

A tall lean slave looked up at me as at someone asking a foolish question, but with restless trouble in his eyes too, and spoke in a measured voice: "Why, you say? Cause we was told to."

"Who is it?"

"The nigger driving the dead wagon told me his name's Rufus Reed."

"Why, he's got a family. Why in the name of hell is he being pitched into the ground like a dead dog!"

"Suh, I don't know nothing about it. Why you expect me to? You know good and well I just has to do whatever they put me at."

I settled myself down: "Of course you do."

He began packing dirt into a mound with the flat of his shovel, carefully, with a peremptory motion for the other slaves to help him, and they all went about rounding the grave over in neat fashion. As he worked, the lean slave broke out talking as though to himself: "They didn't give me no board with his name on it to put at his head. They didn't give me nothing." And when the mound was finished he stood erect, planted his shovel before him, fixed his eyes on the grave and said, "Rufus Reed."

A strange conviction came over me that the way he spoke the name set it forever, as an epitaph, between the living man and the dead man.

I thought of something: "You know Flem Nugent?"

"I do. Seen him a little while ago. And you know what?"—he stabbed the ground with the shovel blade—. "He ast for this man's body, Mr Flem Nugent did. He pled for it. And they wouldn't let him have it!"

"Why? Who's 'they'?"

"Captain Dexter, mainly."

"*Captain* Dexter? Old Harley Dexter?"

"That's the gennelman."

"Well, I'll be a double-dyed sonofabitch!"

"How's that?"

"Harley Dexter wouldn't make a wart on a captain's ass."

"What I know about it? You tell *him* that."

I thought, 'Hell, he's right. If the best you can do is spout off to a nigger slave—.'

And so feeling cold, hard, and yet on the verge of ripping apart whatever came within my reach, I turned and rode off, back up through the river bottom again toward the main part of town. Smooth grass where I was riding along now, under spreading pecan trees: this being the very plot donated for a city park to be built one of these days when we had expected to have a town fine and dandy. Civic spirit, that's what the widow who gave the land said she wanted to promote.

Oh yaow. Civic spirit. A graveyard for men murdered in civic spirit by leading citizens of the county.

Later on I learned that some families were afraid to claim the bodies of the men they lost, for fear if they came to town they'd be arrested themselves. So the order had gone out that if no family member picked up the body at once, away it went to the new-made graveyard. In this case it stood to reason why Rufus's widow would send flem, as a good friend, to take charge of her husband's corpse. Then lo and behold, Harley Dexter would not turn it over to him. Other horrors were to come, too, in the disposal of bodies. Some families buried their men in secret places, fearing desecration of the bodies—as did happen in one case, when certain rebels dug into a victim's grave far back in the woods in order to turn the body from facing east to facing north, to them the direction of Yankees and hell. Worst of all, the shallow graves made in haste in the would-be park on the river bank failed to put bodies beyond the reach of scavengers. Later on I heard that a hog was seen dragging a man's arm along Industry Street.

(But even the unmolested graves on the river bank were lost inside of a few years, and this plot did in time become the city park. I used to wonder how many of the Confederate veterans attending their reunion were aware of that park's history.)

—Soon back among the town buildings that Saturday morning, I rode on till I came into the square, and stopped, struck by how little noise arose from the crowd assembled around the courthouse. What I picked up most in stray words drifting my way was a curious repetition of "he." "He" would be coming out any second, one man said. Precisely who this was I had not yet caught, but the simple word sounded eerie. Not till I had made my way around to where I could see along the street between the courthouse and the Dayton Building did it all become clear: the death-wagon stood waiting.

The world went reeling, I clutched the saddlehorn. Someone, in the next instant, was to be sent to the hanging tree—and who could that be, this morning, but Monk Harper. Came a burning recall, once more, of our wagon stopped in the street that first day in Milcourt, Harley Dexter on one side, Monk Harper with his wide blue eyes on the other, and Pap sitting puzzled between....

A shifting of figures around the courthouse entrance broke the image. Then out through the door, a heavy guard of soldiers packed in around him, came Monk Harper: big and thick-chested, beard black as a crow's wing. I was only too glad to be so far away I could not see his blue eyes.

The soldiers created a wedge to open a way through the crowd. Monk did his best to walk strong and steady across the space carved out for his passage, but his feet in spite of him angled off this way and that, the soldiers always having to steer him right again. There was the wagon waiting: the mules, the slave sitting high in the spring-seat, a stillness in man and animals like a total unconcern with the approaching figure. Monk now saw the wagon directly before him, halted as though surprised by its presence, lifted one foot with great effort, thrust it at the wagonstep, missed, crumpled and fell. Three soldiers caught him before he hit the ground. Every muscle in his body was now out of control, jerking, gyrating. It took four soldiers to lift him bodily into the wagonbed.

My breath went shallow, my shoulders twitched, tears blurred my eyes—all from wrestling not to think what I could not help thinking: what if this were Pap taking the same last walk? And it *would* be Pap. And soon.... Could I watch? How could I not watch?

Why, oh why did I have to catch sight of Colonel Ticknor just then? —not forty feet away, giving orders to some officer, planted ramrod stiff and pointing with his thumb toward the wagon now moving off with Monk Harper.

Why! No rifle necessary. Just reach down a couple of inches, lift a leather flap, draw out the pistol, level it and lay Colonel Ticknor dead in the flick of an eyelid. So powerful was the urge that to suppress it I all but had to grab my right hand with my left. I tried shutting my eyes against the temptation, only to see myself going ahead in a fantasy that supplied its own justification, senseless though it was. How could I know what lay hidden in this silent crowd? my obsession whispered to me. What if a hundred men—two hundred—likewise had concealed weapons, and would spring into action behind the man with the boldness to step forth, to lead?

It seemed a fearful long time before the unreason of any such belief burst through my compulsion to act, accompanied by the same old frustration of being driven to the wall along a blind alley....

Still, in that dark impasse, while I did not recognize the true nature of it at the outset, was the glimmer of a way ahead. At first it was a face, the one I'd grown to expect in the wake of any thought about Colonel Ticknor: Jenny's face, clear and close as a living dream. And inexorably the voices that went with it, the little girl screeching, 'Jenny Ticknor, you hush!' And again: 'For Christ's sake, that's her *daddy*.'

I groaned aloud. At that my eyes, shut for so long, flicked open: to wipe away that face, that echo, that sickening thought. The wetness of tears cooled my lashes, while my eyeballs felt scalded.

—To my great relief, Colonel Ticknor had stepped out of sight among the soldiers.

The last I saw of Monk Harper he was sitting huddled on the floor of the wagonbed, hugging his knees, head sunk between them.

I'd had all I could take for now. I guided Comanche away, going opposite to the route of the death-wagon, breasting the crowd as it thronged in to follow to the hanging tree. Many people were craning their necks, could not tear their eyes away from Monk Harper. Some men gave me hostile glares anytime Comanche and I momentarily cut off their view in Monk's direction.

I drew up only when I had gone as far as I could from the hanging tree and still be in Milcourt—away northwest beyond the house where Preacher Tillman was staying....

But now when the thought of Jenny Ticknor circled back to me, the faint hope that I'd sensed earlier grew bright enough to express itself in words. Surely to God a blooming young woman like her, who looked around her as though she loved the whole world and was certain it loved her in return, could not be in favor of stringing up innocent men on a tree. And the crucial accompanying thought: Colonel Ticknor's heart might be as cold as an axe blade on a frosty morning, but surely he did have a heart somewhere, and if anybody in creation could reach it, that ought to be his beautiful daughter....

From this my thoughts ran on again with a sense of purpose—hurried on even as I cautioned myself not to jump to conclusions, not to clutch at hope just to resist the horror of having seen a man go to the same death that awaited my father.

Because yes, think ahead. Colonel Oldham, what had become of him? Preacher Tillman might bring off, against all probability, a change in jury policy to reverse the fatal progression of one death sentence after another. Yet even then Harley Dexter and his evil crew could be waiting for Pap or any other prisoner who walked out free, and none to save them—if anyone could—but Colonel Ticknor. Of course, from all that was said about him, it was best to assume that he would not forbid the mob—not unless a dent could be made in his hatred of the Union men. And there was just a chance that an appeal from his daughter might achieve that.

So here I was all at once confronted by a reversal of thinking, and I could only trust that the enormous relief it brought was not leading me astray. Far now from wishing and scheming for Colonel Ticknor's death, I must instead see him as maybe the final hope for ending the executions.

By the time all that had halfway streamed through my head, I was already on my way out of town. And once I'd struck the prairie to the north, I gave Comanche the right signal and we lit out for the river bottom. Exactly how I'd go about talking with Jenny Ticknor alone— and it would have to be alone—that I'd figure out along the way.

Or so I thought. But then, in the lurch, I couldn't come up with a plan, though I probed hard into my mind: only to feel awkward and stupid, realizing that at the clip I was going I'd soon be there, and everything still a blank. All that I could dig up in fact just got in the way of being sensible: a sort of smugness I wasn't used to feeling and hated to find at work in myself. Thinking: 'The way she cut her eyes at me, I wouldn't be a bit surprised if—oh sure, sure, don't you know she could just turn plumb crazy about you in no time: her brought up a like a doll among all that finery, slaves to wait on her hand and foot, young men from the plantations panting around her—and you straight out of a log cabin, as homespun as they come.

'And besides, you blame fool, what do you know about courting girls anyhow—nothing but a hick, that's what you amount to. Can't even get within ten feet of a girl from the next cabin over the rise without turning beet-red and stammering your head off—.

'Shut up—listen—get some sense in your head. Think how you can draw her aside and lay this situation out sensible. But remember now, that means getting around Colonel Oldham. And that mean-eyed boy of his. To say nothing of the other girls.'

Or—first things first—what was I going to say to Colonel Oldham if he was still at home? He'd sworn to go to Milcourt today at the latest, to do all in his power to see that the accused men got fair trials. Yet I was certain he'd still be at home. So——. Well no. Not what was I to say to him. Better put to ask what he'd have to say to me?

Could be tactful, though. Claim I'd heard he was awful sick and was coming to check up on him. Could help by that line of talk to save him embarrassment, placate him in case he still might come in handy.

But any attention to Colonel Oldham only hindered what kept hammering at my brain underneath: how to approach Jenny. Yet time went by, and I'd hit the river bottom, and still I had no more of a plan than when I'd first started out. One consolation: on this trip I knew where I was headed. In jig time I found the wagon road and went along it toward Colonel Oldham's. Then I had to set myself a limit: 'If I don't think up a scheme by the time I come to the last bend before the Oldham place, I'll plant myself right down in a thicket and stay there till I *do* come up with something definite——.'

—But just then voices startled me out of my thoughts: first voices from behind me at a distance, difficult to locate precisely, and a moment later two more voices from up the road ahead of me.

Caught. Trapped. Quick!

I reined into the brush.

The voices behind—two men—sounded cautious, stealthy. Now I realized they were on the opposite bank of the river. Intending to cross? Yes—for soon there came a splashing of hooves through the water.

Rufus Hackett crossed my mind. No. Far up into the Territory by now——. Or Peg Madill and some of his bunch? A terrible longing to see any of them came over me——.

Then flashing through me came the need to consider the voices from ahead—two voices also, and no caution in them. A woman's voice. A man's.

So I kept quiet, suspended, knowing I could see the road but not be seen myself.

Then I got a glimpse. My heart turned ice-cold and yet flared. I saw Jenny Ticknor riding along sidesaddle on a fine bay horse. Beside her, on a mule, a slave—oh yes, Cabus, who'd made fun of me yesterday for not being able to afford a slave myself. Jenny was rattling on unconcerned as a girl in high spirits will; the old man was chuckling and putting in a couple of words when he could. If she had not been white, and he black, they could have been a girl and her grandfather.

At the rate Jenny was talking, neither of them had heard the other riders, who all of a sudden went quiet. Then just as Jenny and Cabus came up from the left nearly even with my hiding place, two men broke out of a thicket on the river side of the road a little ways to my right. All the riders came to a dead stop, two facing two some twenty steps apart.

The two men were hard-looking customers, strangers to me.

I slipped the pistol out of the saddlebag.

Jenny tried, in a faltering voice: "Good morning."

—And got no answer. Cabus looked around like he wanted desperately to do something, but what?

One man nodded to the other, and both began to inch forward, meaning to come up on either side of Jenny and Cabus—.

There would still have been time to turn and run—and at least Jenny, on the mount she had, could probably have beat any pursuers to the Oldham plantation. Cabus had the look of being ready to try running for it, but by now he'd already waited too long. Then, strangely, he took off his flophat, and with one hand clutching the brim held it tight against his belly, almost as if ready to bow in submission.

I touched my heels to Comanche's flanks. He lunged into the middle of the road—I had the drop on the strangers before they'd had time even to think about going for their guns.

Still no one said a word. The two bushwhackers—which they sure did look like to me—were well armed. One, a chuckle-headed fellow, had a pistol like mine in a side holster, and the other man had one stuck at a cross-draw angle in his belt. Besides, Chucklehead had a cut-off smoothbore slung behind him, and his partner was carrying in a saddle scabbard under his left leg a carbine of a kind I did not recognize, though all I could see of it was the stock, a hump of metal on the bottom of the action and a long-looping trigger guard.

Not a half a minute had passed. In that time a deadly calm took possession of me, a deadly assurance—which the two men took for hesitation, having faced men with guns before.

"Whatta you think you're up to, kid, stopping peaceable folks on the public road?"—that was Chucklehead.

I narrowed my eyes on them and stiffened my grip on the pistol. Yes, they'd seen that kind of thing too: a readiness to take life. Just one featherweight of resistance from those two and the anxiety to kill I'd carried deep in my guts since yesterday would have taken over. Two outlaws I could justify killing—and how easy it would have been to pull the trigger.

When I spoke, neither man lost any time in doing what I ordered:

"Let your reins drop, put both hands on your saddlehorns—and keep them there. First man to make a move I don't order is a dead man."

"Now—you first," I said to Chucklehead. "Get down slo-o-ow. And keep ahold of that saddlehorn."

He did.

Next I ordered the second man to dismount—his hatbrim was pulled so low over his eyes you could hardly see them—then I had the two of them step forward a couple of paces with their hands up and stand side by side at the edge of the road facing me. Cabus, at a word from me, went around past them and led their horses back behind Jenny and me. Then I made the bushwhackers step out into the middle of the road.

Separating Chucklehead from his pistol was no problem: I simply made him unbuckle the gunbelt, let it slide to the ground and step back while I dismounted to retrieve the weapon. Then I ordered him to sit down in the center of the road hugging his knees.

Hatbrim still had hopes, I could tell, that I might make a slip in taking his pistol away from him. So I enjoyed ordering him, hands still raised, to walk over to Comanche and lean way forward, arms outstretched to brace against Comanche's side. In the process the black hat got pushed back and flopped over the man's back to the ground. Comanche gave a mean nicker that I quietened with a word.

Stepping up close I said to Hatbrim, "A little signal from me and that horse'll jump aside so quick you'll smash that sneer on your face"—a sneer that was fast fading anyway— "Plus which I'd have to shoot you while you're down."

I just let him stay like that till his arms had time to get lead-heavy, till he snarled out, "All right, goddamn it! I believe you."

I reached out and relieved him of his pistol, stepped back, flicked a hand and clucked my tongue. Comanche sidled closer to Hatbrim to help him straighten up. Hatbrim stood looking at Comanche in astonishment till I motioned for him to go and sit down beside Chucklehead.

A great burden lifted from me.

Oh yes, but here I was with two bushwhackers on my hands, and what in the hell was I going to do with them?

As if she'd sensed my quandary, Jenny spoke her first words: "They may be deserters. Or Union men—." But she hushed up fast when I gave her a look—wished she hadn't said that, I guess, to judge from how rosy her face went.

I thought to myself, 'Of course such as that is what first comes to your mind. That's your daddy talking, ain't it.'

Well anyhow, one thing Jenny's words decided me on: which was that I would not turn these men over to Ticknor's troops for anything in this world. I would not deliver them into *his* hands if they were the worst renegades the devil ever spawned. Confederate deserters? I was in a position to wish they were. And far from wanting to shoot them now, I'd resolved to let them go, though I was convinced they were bushwhackers, nothing else. Even so, I could not bear to picture Ticknor marching them to the hanging tree. Why, even along with— Pap, for God's sake!

But first, the thought of that strange-looking carbine coming back to me, I stepped over to Hatbrim's horse and pulled it out of the scabbard. Funny how it looked familiar, even though I was sure I'd never seen the like of it before.

"Where'd you get this?" I said to Hatbrim.

I suppose he figured it was safer to act like a rebel, the fix he was in: "I taken it off a dead Yankee."

"Cavalry?"

"Yeah."

"How come him dead?"

No reply.

Now that I had time to handle and puzzle over this gun, I remembered: once in a while an old copy of a Dallas newspaper would come our way. In one of those I'd seen a drawing of this gun, under which ran an item: "The Spencer carbine, a new weapon of the Union cavalry, a lever-action repeater. A joke circulating in the Confederate Army says you load it on Sunday and shoot it all week."

I got down on my knees facing Hatbrim and Chucklehead, laid the cocked pistol close beside me, thumbed back the hammer of the Spencer, worked the lever—and slick as you please a brass cartridge slid into the firing chamber.

Hatbrim's voice was nervous: "You know how to handle that thing? It goes off easy."

"Bet it'll shoot straight too."

I shifted the carbine to my left hand, picked up the pistol: "Now stand up, both of you. Raise your hands above your head. March to the river through that opening there. Slo-o-ow does it."

I followed and brought them to a halt at the water's edge, facing across.

"You fellers're lucky," I said. "The river's down. You can maybe wade all the way."

"Now hold on here," Chucklehead protested. "You wouldn't want to turn a man aloose afoot in this country, would you? Without no gun nor nothing. Let us have our *horses* at least."

"Can't do that. The rightful owners'll be wanting them back. And I expect you got friends over there. If you ain't, you better make some quick. And listen, you don't realize what a favor I'm doing you. If you knowed who that girl's daddy is, and how he *lo-oves* to see people he don't care about dangling from a limb—Colonel James Ticknor, you ever heard of him?"

They had, from the scowling looks they exchanged.

I stepped back a pace: "See that little glade across the river in front of you, that runs all the way to that piece of timber yonder? You wade across the river, and you walk an arrow-line to that timber. You make a break for the brush on either side, and I'll test out the range of this Spencer."

They stood looking down at the river current like it was mad at them.

"Get!" I yelled, leveling the carbine at Hatbrim.

So into the water they plowed, striking it hip-deep and swift in a couple of places. They never looked back, and they did strictly as I'd ordered them till they reached the far timber and went out of sight.

Jenny was still perched up there in her sidesaddle. Cabus stood clutching the reins of the two captured horses and his mule, looking worried and wary. There'd be no uppity remarks out of him for a while, I could be sure. And as to that, I had Jenny and him both where they dared not speak till I gave a sign as to what to do next.

I took my time going over to Hatbrim's horse: to unbuckle the Spencer scabbard, to latch it to my own saddle. In one of Hatbrim's saddlebags I found better than a hundred rounds of the right ammunition.

—And in my mind I heard a grim voice: 'No matter what I decide about killing whoever, I've got the gun now that'll reach out and drop several men before anybody knows what's up.'

II

IN THE NEXT INSTANT, by an involuntary twist of the murderous instinct still potent in me, I pictured myself in the act of putting a bullet through Colonel Ticknor's chest; and sensing Jenny's eyes on me, I gave her a quick, guilty look, as though she might be reading my mind. But whatever else my look may have transmitted, it gave her the courage to speak, though her voice was trembling, humble:

"Thank you, Todd." Breathless: "Thank you."

My name on her lips for the first time—I could have been melted and poured into a candlemold. Still the disturbing image of Colonel Ticknor had not faded, so my own voice, shaky itself, came out gruffer that I meant it to: "How can your father allow you to ride around in these brakes with no protection but Cabus?"

"My father? My father's dead."

Now then I had my eyes on her, and could not pry them away, and with my face ablaze and my tongue tied, I must have looked—as I certainly felt—like the world's prize damfool. The angry and helpless certainty that Jenny was Colonel Ticknor's daughter had fastened on me like a devil that will not be cast out—.

"Well...Ticknor—," was as far as I got.

"Oh. No. Uncle James was—is—my father's brother."

Relief. Embarrassment. Contradiction thrown in too: good cause to be glad she was only his niece, but also to be sorry she'd have that much less influence over him.

While I was untangling my mind, Jenny broke out explaining: "You see, Todd, Colonel Oldham wanted me to wait till he felt like escorting us home, or when Bill'd be available to do it. But I just couldn't delay any longer, with Uncle James away and Aunt Mary at home by herself. And besides, the Oldham girls and I have ridden back and forth along the river so many times with just Uncle Cabus to protect us, and we never met with any danger at all—."

I found my tongue: "Just luck you didn't. Anyhow, them—bushwhackers may team up with some more and be back sooner'n we think. So we better make tracks for—your uncle's place."

I made ready to groan, expecting she'd come out with some kind of mincey, genteel stuff like 'Oh I don't want to put you to any more trouble,' but to her credit she only said, again, "Thank you, Todd." And turned me again to wax.

I'd finished stowing the extra weapons where I could on my saddle—here I was with more guns, suddenly, than I knew what to do with—and then I mounted up. Jenny couldn't've failed to hear that I hated like the devil to set foot on Colonel Ticknor's place—. Though damn it, I had to keep in mind that from now on I had to be less antagonistic toward him.

Looking to me for confirmation, Jenny said, "Should Uncle Cabus come along behind us with the other horses?"

"Yes. And we'll turn them over to somebody at your uncle's place. Probably stolen from around here anyway, is my guess."

So we headed out, but not in the hurry we wanted to, what with Cabus slowed down by the two horses unused to being led and resisting every step of the way.

"How far is it to Colonel Ticknor's?" I asked Jenny.

"Four miles, about."

As much as an hour, then, at our speed. I reined up, turned to Cabus and said: "Can you shoot a pistol?"

"I can shoot a pistol."

A doubtful look passed over Jenny's face.

"Then here," I said, handing him Hatbrim's gun. "Stick this in your belt and be ready. Just in case, you know."

"I do know."

As we rode on, I drew out the Spencer and laid it across the pommel before me, my fingers thrilling to hold it.

"Not that much cause to be afraid, probably," I assured Jenny. "But no use being unprepared either."

"I didn't look—funny, when you spoke to Uncle Cabus, because I was afraid."

"Why then?"

Her voice went low: "You giving him a gun. Please understand that he's one of the most dependable people in the world, and he *is* like an uncle to me, but you may not know."

"Oh yes, I do know. A slave's forbidden to carry a gun. I know something else, too, about who the rebels're disarming, in Milcourt for instance."

Bitter, I knew my voice to be—as I glanced across to meet a new look in Jenny's eyes: unwavering, fascinated yet perplexed. I swallowed hard. Yet: 'Be blunt,' I thought. So: "I had a musket taken away from me there yesterday, by *Captain* Dexter."

She lowered her gaze but did not turn her face away. I did.

We rode on in silence, her not knowing, I guess, what subject to risk bringing up, myself not knowing how to get into the matter uppermost in my mind.

And then, with the prime danger falling behind us, even with a rifle balanced in front of me, a change I'd never have expected came smoothly over the morning. Here I was riding along through the bright sunshine and diminishing wind with a beautiful girl. I shot glances her way often enough, poised up there as she was in that sidesaddle, wearing a riding habit the likes of which I'd never seen close up, just glimpsed at a distance back in Missouri. She had her long brunette hair coiled up on the crown of her head, some of the glints that thrilled me lost because of that, but the lovely swirl made up for it. And to top off that hair-do she had a little hat pinned on at a cocky angle. From her profile you might have called her fragile, delicate, over-protected. But when she turned her head and set her splendid eyes glowing at me, I thought deep in my heart: 'No, she's no ragdoll, nor one made out of china neither. But being from plantation folks, that's just how she's supposed to look—or thinks she is.'

Evidently she meant for me to have the next say—.

"Your folks—your mother—family. Do they live in these parts?"

'—Oh Jesus, put your foot in it again. Bet her mother's dead too.'

"I don't have any immediate family left except my mother—and I'm an only child. Our home's in Tennessee. Or was. Till Daddy died, leaving Mama and me without anyone to turn to over there. So we decided to sell our little plantation, just a farm really, and come west to

Uncle James and Aunt Mary. Mama sent me on ahead with Mammy Sarah and Uncle Cabus, meaning to follow as soon as she could sell our place, and the other negroes, and get all our affairs settled. Then all of a sudden came the war, and no demand for a little place like ours. And now Mama's sick, too, and can't travel. And how can I go to her from out here? Specially since Mammy Sarah died last year, and now there's only me and Uncle Cabus."

The tremor in her voice. Sadness. Ripe for sympathy. Now was surely the time to edge into the subject of the trials. But how to begin?

Jenny went on before I could get my thoughts in order to speak, talking to me as to some presence near at hand only half known to her, as though exploring the capacity of that presence to listen: "Just as soon as he can manage a leave, Uncle James intends to go after Mama. Then we can all be together. Our families have always been like that: so tight knit. Mama and Aunt Mary are sisters—brothers married sisters. And when I was small, before Aunt Mary and Uncle James came to Texas, he was almost like a second father to me. He and Papa had always been close. And I was with him so much while Papa was away from home. Papa traveled a great deal in his slave-trading business."

What in the name of Christ had I run up against: a girl with a slavedealer father and a slaveholder uncle now taking his place! And my own father at the mercy of their kind. And here we were dallying along remembering old times—her old times—like this was just your everyday social occasion.

The furrow between my brows must've been pretty deep.

"No. Please understand me. A slavedealer, yes. But Papa was the kindest man alive. He—he made it a point, when he could, to buy mistreated slaves, and he sold to nobody but good masters. He was even opposed to slavery, you see. And like so many people in the South, he wanted it abolished—just as soon as that could be done without disrupting the whole country."

I couldn't help it: disbelief was certainly written all over my face. A humanitarian slavetrader, almost an abolitionist? On seeing the tight-lipped smile I could not repress, Jenny bridled: "I can tell you don't believe me. And you'll say, what do I know about it anyhow? My father was a good man, I know that. And Uncle James is a good man too."

Ready to defend her uncle even before words of defense were called for: maybe because she had doubts of her own about him, certainly because she knew what my opinion was.

Already I knew I should be preparing to maneuver—for she did like me, or else she wouldn't have opened up on matters next to her heart. But I was too green at this sort of thing. What I did was erupt in spite of myself along maybe the worst course possible: "But you must have some idea of what's going on in Milcourt. You must! And of what that Uncle James of yours is doing. You must know the predicament *my* father's in. You *do* know that, don't you?"

Hesitant, suddenly. Sorrowful: "Yes Todd, I know your father's one of the men on trial."

And there went my blood again, a rush of it on hearing Jenny speak my name. Made me furious, that I was powerless to quiet my blood.

Which turned my voice loud and hard: "Don't you realize, don't you want to realize, what your Uncle James is doing! Him and his slaveholder friends. They yell conspiracy, insurrection, treason. And the men they've got locked up, meaning to hang every last one of them. Sure, they voted against secession. But all they've done since then is protest conscription and talk in favor of bringing back the Union. And so all they're really guilty of is not knuckling under to the slaveholders and keeping their mouths shut in what used to be called a free country."

'Oh, but no,' I protested to myself. 'No good going on like this—doing harm, that's all. And to a young girl, at that. Next thing you know, you'll have her in tears.'

"But Todd, it's not at all like that. Your father—all of those men—they're accused by law. It's a trial. There's a jury. If they're not guilty of conspiracy and—insurrection, why then the jury won't convict them. I'm just a girl, I know, and it's true that all I have to go on is what I hear from Uncle James and Colonel Oldham—but they're fine men, wonderful men, and they, I know—."

—Yet how could I stop now, I was in so deep: "And you believe Oldham and Ticknor agree? You can't see Colonel Oldham has serious doubts about the whole thing? And it ain't no *legal* trial. It wasn't set up legal, and they decide by majority vote, as no real jury ever does. It ain't nothing but a kangaroo—let's give it its right name: it's a lynching committee."

"No, Todd! No! That's an awful way of putting it. There's a dreadful misunderstanding somewhere."

—Oh yes, but the uncertainty was there in her voice: she'd seen, no doubt, how troubled Colonel Oldham was by the trials—and he was sure a hero of hers too, if maybe less of one than her uncle—.

I was in strange territory, but feelers I'd never known I possessed could sense this: a Jenny little known probably to herself existed beneath that long-cultivated exterior of the innocent, self-effacing young lady.

I forged on: "Jenny, just listen to this, please"—yes, she did like the sound of her name on my tongue—. "The slaveholders worked in Colonel Oldham as chairman of what they called a 'citizens' committee,' when there ain't no such thing with any legal authority, and it's *criminal* to claim there is. Then what did they get Colonel Oldham to do? Why, to appoint three men—three slaveholders—to another committee. And then how did this committee choose a so-called jury? They picked out *seven* of their slaveholder friends, and five other citizens just for a show of fairness. And they're down there in Milcourt right this minute handing out death sentences by majority vote. And to top that off, the men accused don't even have a lawyer to defend them. If you believe Colonel Oldham sees that as justice, why you pin him down the next time you see him. He'll tell you different. Leastways he did me. And he knows—and you'll see it in his eyes though he won't admit it—that he's been used and shoved aside. And the last time I saw him he was aiming to fight back—or so he said."

So there it was, all poured out, not spoonfed to her as I'd meant to do.

Yet for a little while I saw no reason to fear I'd said too much. With her head turned away, she was gazing into the distance, apparently at a loss for words. I took heart. Once it had been put to her straight like that—which naturally nobody had ever done before—she began to understand—maybe. And maybe now could not deny out of hand my description of the court. And if I'd got that far with her....

We'd picked up our pace a little, the captured horses cooperating better now. But oh Lord, when Jenny looked again in my direction, her eyes had turned brighter than ever, and I knew what that meant: tears ready to spring at the next wrong word from me. I shuddered. No, a girl's crying I did not know how to cope with. My only experience with that was how it affected Sis, and when she got ready to burst into tears, as a rule it meant she was about to be all-fired unreasonable.

Still, if I did not take the plunge now, I never would: "Jenny, back when I thought your Uncle James was your father—." Then the words seized in my throat, from an upsurge of fear that I'd broken the dam holding back the tears—.

But mercifully I was wrong. Curiosity in her look. And still sympathy, even increased sympathy.

"Yes? What?"

I looked her square in the eye: "I didn't just happen to be in the river brakes this morning. The honest truth is, I was on my way to Colonel Oldham's to find you. I had hopes you could talk to—your father, I thought then—your Uncle James, that is. Persuade him—."

But, oh my God, where to from here? Because it had not occurred to me before that I'd have to hint at least at the attempt Preacher Tillman was making to manipulate the jury, have to risk trusting her not to pass on to the wrong people what I said.

"Persuade him?" said Jenny.

"Yes. Because you see—well, here's the gist of it: I've heard on pretty good authority that at least some of the prisoners may go free. But even if they do they could be grabbed and lynched by the mob the minute they're out of sight of the courthouse. And if that's set to happen, there's only one man in this county who can stop it: Colonel Ticknor."

Her eyes went wide, resentful: "Are you trying to say he'll permit that to happen! Listen, Todd, my Uncle James is a law-abiding man. That's why he was so in favor of forming the jury. He's convinced it's legal, whether you are or not, and he'll make certain that everyone abides by the jury's decisions."

—Now what to do? How could I go any further into—into what? Into questioning her uncle's integrity, without offending her and losing the ground I'd gained?

So I kept quiet, casting around for a way to proceed and baffled in every direction, anger edging in likewise that she appeared unwilling to entertain even the smallest doubt about her uncle's intentions, when I was persuaded she did have doubts. And against my own will I was thinking, 'Yeah, sure. Like you don't owe me the favor at least of listening—seeing what I did for you an hour ago.' And I was about to go so far as to remind her of that, in some roundabout way....

But then my silence produced better results, it turned out, than any words could have. At last a tentative if indirect admission: "But yes, Todd, Uncle James is—what I mean is, others—men in charge of the militia—may try to get past him and take the law in their own hands. To warn him about that would do no harm. Is that what you mean?"

It wasn't, but I said, "Yes."

"And—you want me to speak to him about the danger."

"Yes"—if that was all I could get.

"He'll be—displeased if I do, because he's so very proud of knowing his duty and how to carry it out. But—."

It scared me out of my wits, what I knew she was about to say, yet I wanted to hear it. Because I could sense it would come close to what I'd been thinking. And I held my breath as you sometimes will when on the verge of seeing what you wish come to pass and yet fear that everything will even yet go wrong....

"But—I could—if I mention what you've done for me today, it can't fail to help. Yes, yes. If you want me to speak to him, I will."

Her gaze had been on me but veered back suddenly straight ahead, a deep blush suffusing her cheeks.

I kept my voice quiet and gentle: "If it's to do the most good, the sooner you talk to him the better. If we can, we oughta get you to town today, someway or another."

She was about to speak, I rushed on: "Jenny, I can't tell you how grateful I'll be. You may be saving not only my father but no telling how many other men from that death tree."

Then I found myself blushing as furiously as she was, both of us now conscious of the sudden nearness between us brought on by a pact, an alliance we'd stumbled our way into. And for the time being we could not meet each other's eyes.

—And so, if for no other reason than the breath-taking embarrassment of this, I was relieved that just now we came out unexpectedly into an open bottom, and there a short ways off was Colonel Ticknor's house.

Cabus sang out, "Wheee—Lord help my time. Am I glad to see that!—Marse Todd, here."

—First time he'd ever called me by name—.

I drew up and turned, to see Cabus approaching with the pistol held out to me butt first.

"Here," he said again. "They say I ain't supposed to touch one of these."

I took it. Nodded. —A person can come to more recognition in an instant than he can straighten out in a week. My eyes rested now on a different Cabus from the one who had ridiculed me just yesterday—nor was he looking at the same Todd. From most of what I'd heard about slaves, they were supposed to be natural-born cowards, which Cabus had not shown himself to be when facing the outlaws. Powerless to fight, yes. Losing the opportunity to run, yes. But cowed? I did not think so, in spite of that apparently obsequious removal of his hat. And right now, what he knew he did not have to say was in his eyes for me to see: he looked upon himself as the protector of this girl who was nursed at his wife's breast—and maybe also because of some deep gratitude to her father; and it was a protectiveness that at least for now he took to be shared with me. So the discoveries forced on both of us since yesterday were suddenly firm: for me, that a slave might be far from what hearsay reported him to be; for him, that a common farmer might also be other than he'd heard.

If I could have done it in secret—and known he'd accept—I would have handed the pistol back to him.

But nothing was private any longer. Slaves, men and women, came out from several directions. Mrs Ticknor appeared on the front porch of the big house, two girls maybe ten and twelve close behind her. And not a white man did I see yet on the place, though two or three of the male slaves looked as if they could handle about anything if they had to—and wanted to. Well then, but they had no guns.

Then one question answered itself by the arrival of three militiamen from what turned out to be their camp beyond the barn, curious to know what was up.

So then, out of all the commotion the upshot was that I turned the captured horses over to the militia, having already emptied the saddlebags. Even gave them all the guns except the Spencer. The way that militia sergeant eyed it, his hands were itching to take possession of that too. But seeing he had no justifiable reason to take it away from me—because I didn't let on but what it was mine—he had to hold off. How I wished I'd managed somehow to hide that gun in advance. The less known about me having it, the better.

As for the renegades, I just told the sergeant they got away, and about where they crossed the river, in case he felt like going after them. He didn't. Said his detachment's job was to watch over this place, and he had strict orders not to cross the river.

After that, once I'd turned Comanche over to Cabus to water and feed, I couldn't put off any longer going into Colonel Ticknor's house to join the womenfolks. Only to find Jenny running over all that had taken place, for Mrs Ticknor's benefit—all of it punctuated by repeated thanks from this lady to me. I began to feel that this was the strangest predicament I'd ever landed in: to be thanked and thanked and made over like a combination of long-lost relative and bravest man in the world—and all this from Mary Ticknor, whose husband was right now making ready to send my father to the hanging tree. I tried to cut down on the effusiveness by letting her know who I was—and only made matters worse. For that flustered her, and the more flustered she got the more she wagged her tongue—with Jenny chattering as well, and that was out of character for her.

So I fell back behind the only barricade I had: to play the big quiet male and let them talk.

Then all the rushing around to get dinner on the table softened Mary Ticknor's uneasiness some. But it made mine worse, if anything. She tore into inviting me—several times—to eat, and into apologizing for the grub and all like that. No question but I had to accept, since refusal would have been an out-and-out insult.

So we all sat down to dinner: Mrs Ticknor, Jenny, the daughters, the three militiamen and me. I sat taking all the special treatment from the two women as cool as I could. But in the foreground of my mind all the time was, This is Colonel Ticknor's grub. Just don't for God's sake choke on it. And what if he was to ride up! How could that fail to spoil everything?

—Oh but really there was no fear of that as long as he had men to hang in Milcourt!

As soon as the meal was over, the minute I considered it polite to say so, I declared I had to be moving along, letting Jenny know by looks how bad I wanted to talk with her before we parted company. She caught on, and when I'd finished my thanks and goodbyes to Mrs Ticknor and headed for the door, Jenny came along with me.

We strolled out to the corral where Comanche, having finished his oats, stood waiting. Jenny walked close beside me as I led Comanche over to the water trough for a last drink before departure.

Jenny crossed over to the other side of Comanche now.

"Is it all right for me to touch him?" she said.

"Lord yes—for you it is."

So she stood running her hand along Comanche's mane while he was snuffling the surface of the water, or swallowing in long draughts.

"He must be a wonderful horse, you seem to think so much of him." And beyond a doubt the gentleness in her voice was meant for me too.

"Best horse that ever was"—then I lowered my voice, thinking of Comanche alongside that beautiful bay of hers: "Though none too handsome."

Comanche had just deliberately lifted his head from the water trough—he understood her attention, that clown. Jenny put her arms around his jaws and kissed him lightly above the eye—then said, "Handsome is as handsome does."

While my insides did flips, I said, "Then handsome he is."

And that's all I could say, my mind otherwise a blank, and stayed so while I led Comanche back to the corral fence, where I slung the saddle on him and cinched it up.

Jenny stood leaning against the log wall of a corn crib adjacent to the corral.

Ready to mount up, I turned at last to look at her, not daring to open my mouth.

Jenny saved the situation: "Todd, I don't know, truly, whether I can do any good. But I do want to say this to you. About Uncle James"—cheeks flaming now—. "I was brought up never to criticize a family member, especially a man, to an—outsider. Yet I must say this—for you already know the bad part of it, really. Yes, Uncle James is a stubborn man with a hard temper that he can hide—for a time. And, for the better part that you don't know, he's not like he used to be. Always had that harsh streak, yes. But always kind too. The war's changed him. He'll do anything, I'm afraid he'll—stop at nothing for the sake of the Confederacy. If what I say should turn him against me, which can't be ruled out—for he'd never dream I'd be saying what I intend to—he'll just become worse than ever. So we risk seeing harm instead of good come out of it. But then, as a help, we want him to know that you saved me this morning, and that I'm speaking up for your sake. But though it may sound funny to you, we can't let him find out you *asked* me to do it. Even if I have to lie, Todd—yes, even if I have to lie, he mustn't know. That means nobody must know—."

She broke off, but she did not take her eyes away. I stood gazing at her with every nerve electrified, my heart full of her, not so much thinking as feeling what a level-headed and appealing wonder of a young woman she was.

"Oh," I said—and I really had just thought of something: "Maybe Cabus heard me ask you."

"If he did, he'll never tell."

I thought so too.

I turned to look at—I guess at my saddlehorn, and actually succeeded in mastering my voice when I said, "Let me say it again: I never can tell you how much I appreciate you trying, Jenny."

She avoided responding to that: "It'll mean thinking up an excuse to go to town, as you said. Because he won't be likely to come home, with the trials going on. I'll make one of the militia boys take me there. Today if I can—though I'm afraid that may be out of the question. Tomorrow I'll come, for sure."

Suddenly, like a blow: just as with Colonel Oldham, a promise to intercede—today—or tomorrow—.

But no! Look! And I did turn my eyes to look. There she stood: a Jenny I could hardly believe was talking about the same uncle as the one she'd so hotly defended this morning. No more of this great-man-that-never-goes-wrong business. Had him judged all along. Willing now to repudiate her whole upbringing, criticize him aloud for the first time in her life. And all for me—.

We stood in silence, lost in each other's eyes. Jenny still had on the black skirt and English boots of the riding habit. And also the white blouse that her breasts filled out in a marvel to swirl you into ecstasy—a pocket over one breast displaying a delicate lace handkerchief. The little hat was gone, her hair was uncoiled and flowing over her shoulders with all the glossiness come back: with color like a bronze light that streams unexpected some morning in the glory of autumn. And that wild-plum color high in her cheeks—so that if you thought about it for more than an instant you'd rise and float.

—It would be all right to do what came to mind, I knew. So I stepped closer and took both of Jenny's hands in mine. My lips were quivering like jelly. I clamped my teeth shut to keep them from chattering. She'd let me kiss her cheek, I knew. What I did not know was how I could ever stop at merely that. All of a sudden there were too many directions to get lost in. I saw tears now beginning to well in her eyes, then the lids brim over, and one by one the big drops roll down her cheeks—and all at once, if I could not cope with tears from any other woman, I could cope with tears from Jenny—.

One thing I knew a gentleman could do, and not at the moment risk running amok in any available direction. So I did that: I lifted one of her hands to my lips, then the other. And when my lips touched the smooth, soft, silky, white skin of Jenny's hands, they touched the first miracle I'd ever known to come down to earth.

—Whirling around half blind I vaulted onto Comanche's back, flipped the reins along his neck, and he fairly dug up the earth taking off. And even the thought, 'Sure, and you done the same thing yesterday' didn't trouble me. The little difference of today made all the difference.

When I stopped at the edge of the woods and turned to look back, Jenny was standing on the middle rail of the corral, and as I watched she drew the lace handkerchief out of her breast pocket and waved it high and fluttering—nearly like yesterday too, but again, oh how different.

I lifted my hat and waved back. Then I wheeled Comanche and we bolted away.

12

R*IDING BACK* to Milcourt that afternoon, I kept to the rises as much as possible, for although someone might try to pick me off with a shot from below, that did not equal the risk of meeting the two bushwhackers again today—maybe head-on in some draw, and with reinforcements.

I sure did like the feel of that Spencer under my left leg, with the scabbard tilted just so, where I could reach over and whip it out as easy—I imagined—as drawing a cavalry saber. And I was eager to try it out, too, as I'd soon have to do, so as to educate my eye to the sights, precious as the ammunition was: no more of it to be had, likely, between here and Fort Scott. Still I had to keep telling myself no, not to fire it here. The sound of gunshots might bring no telling who running in my direction.

Yet, when I'd ridden a good ways out on the prairie knobs, and could see for miles in every direction, I couldn't resist the temptation any longer. So I stopped Comanche and sat there spying all around for some object to shoot at. Like maybe the trunk of some lone tree, though most of the trees out here were in the draws.

Then—What? I glimpsed a movement a good distance away, across two knobs to the west. Or did I? I trained my eyes on the only object in immediate view over there—what appeared to be a clump of bushes—let my gaze drift aside now and then, blinking: in that best of ways to pick up a flicker of motion as preparation for centering on it. And before I'd scanned for long, I caught it, then squinted and squinted, because I couldn't believe what my eyes kept telling me.

That blotch of vegetation came apart slowly, making two blotches, and one of them was moving: inching and stopping, inching and stopping.

A wild cow? No. A mustang? No. I ran these questions through my head because from the size and shape of it I already knew what it must be—and yet could not be. None had been sighted this far east for a good while. But that's just what it was—as I found out when I put Comanche into a gallop to reach the next knob for a closer look. A stray buffalo. Big. An old bull for sure, driven off by younger bulls out of some herd on the high prairie.

Now Comanche had paid no great heed till this minute, when he gave his head a little toss upwards and perked his ears as if this caught his interest more than anything had in a long time. A tensing up ran from his head to his hindquarters. The wind was coming at us. No doubt about it. Comanche could maybe see but above all smell that buffalo. And the question that had gone through my mind a many a time before—whether Comanche truly had once been an Indian pony—became a conviction in a second. He must have been, and some warrior's buffalo horse to boot. And as if that wasn't enough to make me burst with pride and excitement, here I was with a Spencer carbine in my clutches.

"Comanche," I said, "I believe you. Folks told the truth about you. And here's a chance for you to go at it again, just like you used to. And proud as hell I am to be riding you."

Well, he didn't have to be told to do one thing. All he waited for was permission, which I gave him with a little flip of the reins. Then he slipped easy down off that knob into a draw and went along up it at a walk. I'd lost sight of the buffalo, screened off as he was by the tall growth along the bed of the draw. That didn't matter. Comanche knew precisely where he was, since in a little bit he swerved out of the drawbed into a joining gully. The little wind in motion drifted our way, and it was plenty for Comanche to go by.

Now he came to a halt. I looked up and down the gully: it was overhang for the most part on the side toward the buffalo, but there was a sluff a little ways ahead. To that I guided Comanche, and before us now was a notch leading at a steep grade toward where we needed to go. I slid the Spencer out of the scabbard, and then up the notch we headed. As we topped out at a slow pace, there was that old bull grazing unconcerned a hundred yards off.

Comanche froze in his tracks, waiting for me to do my part. Now then I wasn't about to disappoint both of us by shooting the animal on the spur of the moment, which would have been easy. There stood Comanche quivering all over by now, and the same anticipation went through me too. So I leaned forward along his neck, the Spencer across the saddle under my belly, and said in a hissing whisper what I'd said that day in the glade when Comanche first proved what he was made of: "Yeee-Haaa!" —And barely had time, even knowing what was in store, to brace myself to ride the wind.

Comanche bore down on that buffalo so fast we could have run right over him before he lifted his head, saw us and had time to bunch his muscles for a getaway. As Comanche wheeled aside to circle, he gave a lurch, and once he'd limbered up to run tore away fast for such a heavy beast. Comanche closed in beside him and wove along like a wolf holding off till its prey tires out.

So now came more of my part in this: to shoot the buffalo on the run. For Comanche's sake I wished I had a bow and arrow, and was expert with it. Having instead the Spencer, I thought: 'Hell, this is too easy—yeah, sure, thanks to Comanche.' As far as that went, I could simply have drawn my pistol and plugged the buffalo in the spine at the base of the neck.

Whichever I did, I saw that Comanche was in no rush to get it over with. Neither was I. So along we dashed: down the knob where we'd jumped him and through a draw, losing contact once when we had to dodge low-hanging tree limbs. But as soon as we came into the clear again, taking the slope up toward the next knob, the buffalo heaving and laboring to make it to the top, Comanche drew in next to him again, and on we thundered neck and neck.

What seemed like a long time went by, but all of it still as if in the instant of chase—in what I suddenly knew the awesomeness of a chase to be: a headiness and a swiftness of time arrested at the instant of climax.

Yet, for all that, sooner or later the chase would have to be brought to an end: at the right tick of the last minute when the buffalo was spent. When finally I sensed we were nearing that point, I made ready to cock the Spencer, rack a shell into the chamber and put an instantaneous end to the buffalo. As I was thumbing back the hammer, though, an abrupt and all-mighty twist along Comanche's back nearly hurled me out of the saddle. For while my attention was distracted the buffalo had all of a sudden stopped and whirled and charged us. Comanche was out of the way in plenty of time, but I was just barely still with him. The buffalo swooped on past, ground to a halt, wheeled on his front feet, planted them and lowered his head, this time to make a stand. Comanche waited, knowing whereas I didn't what was up. After the buffalo had stayed facing us for a short time, heaving for breath, then with a snort he leaped into another charge. All I could do was leave things to Comanche, and just when I was beginning to suspect he'd waited too long, he sprang aside like a dog, me having a hard time keeping my seat yet again. The bull forged on by us a few yards before he got his momentum under control. At first I thought he meant to swivel and charge again, but at the last second he changed his mind, plowed his hooves into the earth and took off at a dead run, Comanche trailing and catching up with him before you could breathe twice.

So on we swept once more, uphill, the buffalo tiring fast, Comanche bounding along beside him as if his hooves were spinning the hill under us.

But, delay it as long as I might—now in this second lap of the chase—the time would come, had all at once come, to kill the buffalo.

—Or not to. To listen instead to an unexpected shift in my instincts....

But then, before I could gather enough thought to deal with this new circumstance, the buffalo stopped again, just short of the crown of the slope, panting and exhausted, and turned at bay for what he appeared to take as the final onslaught. The moment for the kill had come, and now that it had I was not ready for it. To give myself time to think, I tried to head Comanche away from the buffalo, and had to battle him to do it. Once I at last got him moving and had reined him in a hundred yards away, he still resisted, straining against the bridle bit closer to disobeying me than he'd ever been before.

But still, this new thing that had entered the picture, what about it? Why shoot the buffalo? There he stood, vibrant, defiant, utterly vulnerable. To put an end to him seemed a great let-down after the delirium of the chase. Practicality came to the aid of that thought too: I had no time to skin him, and what could I do with the meat away out here? Nothing but leave it to the buzzards and the coyotes. Pap and Ma had both always said it was a sin to waste anything: which I could not get out of my mind, even though this meat would probably be too tough, anyhow, for human consumption.

—But yet there was Comanche to consider. He'd never understand, he'd never forgive me for not keeping my end of the bargain and killing the game we'd run so hard to bring to earth.

My next thought didn't satisfy me, but it was simple and that made it easier to act on. Just do this. Just think of the target practice I needed, and had been in search of when I saw the buffalo in the first place. So then let him be the target.

I dismounted, rested the carbine across the seat of the saddle, rocked back the hammer, levered a shell into the chamber, paused long enough to say: "All right, Comanche. Okay. But you'll have to be satisfied with this."

—Then just as I was drawing a bead, I thought, 'God in Heaven, suppose it was Colonel Ticknor—her Uncle James—that I was lining up these sights on.'

I shook my head and gritted my teeth to clear my mind—to attend only to the buffalo, to draw a bead again, to squeeze the trigger and absorb the shock of the explosion.

The buffalo lurched, fell to his front knees, hindquarters still upright, stretched up his head and let out a strangled bellow.

I threw another cartridge into the chamber: "One more time, Comanche. Hold your patience."

—Missed! Saw the bullet kick dust on the hillside not a foot over his back. He was farther above me than I'd judged—not aiming low enough—though square on target as to right or left.

The third shot hit home. That buffalo tumbled over like a boulder falling.

When I swung up on Comanche and turned his head toward the buffalo, he flew up that slope bursting to get at the chore he knew lay ahead of us. When I reined him in beside the carcass and got down, he went stock still, expectant.

I stood looking down at the great dead beast....

"Sorry to disappoint you, Comanche," I said finally. "Wish I could make you understand why I'm not doing what you know is supposed to come next, specially since you've showed me one thing for certain today: you're a true-blue buffalo horse, all right. And one of these days—if that day ever comes—me and you'll take off for the high plains, and run with a big herd of buffalo ahead of us every day of the world."

—And oh, for a second how glorious that shone in my heart: Comanche snaking in and out among a crashing buffalo herd, he and I working together like one animal, with an arching blue sky over us, and a flashing sun, and a cool wind to breathe—and wide open prairie vast to the world's rim....

Until this present day came back down on me like the blow of a hammer—.

"Okay, Comanche. Let's get a move on."

So I swung up and guided him away, reluctant and straining against the reins to turn back, which he kept up till a rise separated us from the dead buffalo. Then I relaxed my hold and gave him a heel touch, and we fogged out down the road toward Milcourt.

Still I kept in mind that riding into town with this Spencer would mean having it confiscated in five minutes time. In addition, I'd become uneasy about how secure the muzzleloader was where I had it stashed; and having by now remembered a stretch of brush where nobody'd stumble onto my weapons cache except by pure accident, I went out and retrieved the rifle and swung by the new spot and hid both guns well. I'd still have to chance keeping the pistol in my saddlebag. What had taken place this morning showed how bad I could need it in a hurry.

Entering town I circled and wove around so as to reach the center without passing the coffin-building site, the graveyard in the park, or the hanging tree. When I made it to the courthouse square, the sun was just going down a flaming red through a sky full of banded clouds. The longer I stayed around the square the worse the longing became—as so often before—to see Pap. But most of all, oh how wonderful it was to consider that help more certain than Colonel Oldham's was surely on the way now—and from two sources at that: Preacher Tillman and Jenny.

So my mind was all aglimmer with optimism, and as I was halfway into one of my slow rides around the square, lo and behold—I could have sworn I was dreaming—before my very eyes appeared Pap himself! Yes! Flanked by a guard on either side, he was walking across from the Dayton Building toward the courthouse.

At first an awful fear shut out the gladness—fear that he was headed over there to be tried. And even before I could get hold of myself, I'd already jumped off Comanche, left him with the reins dangling and begun elbowing my way through the crowd, calling out, "Pap! Pap! Pap!"

It was a wonder I got as far as I did before they stopped me. For one reason, Pap had veered in my direction even before he heard me—for he wasn't going to the courthouse as I'd thought, only to the outhouse. When he heard my voice, he stopped in his tracks. By now two militiamen had hold of me, but by this time, too, Pap was not ten steps away. I glanced at my captors: one of them was Dawse Mackey. I turned on him and ground out in a fury: "For Christ' sake, give us a chance to say a few words! Suppose it was your daddy, Dawse."

"I can't help it, Todd. Nobody talks to the prisoners. Colonel Ticknor's orders. What can I do only follow orders, Todd? Just understand that, please."

If he'd said 'Todd' in that pleading voice one more time, I'd have doubled up my fist and cold-cocked him. As it was, I lost my head: "If it wasn't for whining sneaks like you, Dawse Mackey, all this killing wouldn't be going on."

By then Pap had stepped a little closer on his own, because his guards had let him—one of them was Harvey Whitman, who shifted his eyes away fast when I glared at him.

In one way here was luck then more luck on its heels, because right at that time Preacher Tillman came out of the courthouse door and walked our way. As he passed by, without a pause, he said to Dawse Mackey, "Go ahead and let them talk a little." And Dawse, scared of disobeying anybody he thought to be in authority, loosened his grip on my arm, so I twisted free and took a few steps towards Pap.

Already I'd burst out with, "Pap, I'm doing what I can, I ain't been idle"—said that before Preacher Tillman was out of earshot, when he could still give me a warning look not to say too much.

Pap stood before me as calm as you please, which at first had a settling effect on me. Then there he was asking me quietly, gently, just as if he'd been away for a while on a normal trip, "Is everybody out home doing all right?"

"Yes sir, we're making it fine, considering. And...uh...I been talking to this person and that person. I saw and talked to Colonel Oldham, for one."

—But what was the good of that: offering him back the bare hope he'd offered me the night of his arrest: that Colonel Oldham would intervene. And yet so far he hadn't. It wouldn't do to let Preacher Tillman's name drop, or Jenny's, but hints I could offer: "Others besides him, too. I hear—that is to say, word's going around as how one or two more, with likely even bigger say than Colonel Oldham has, are working to put a stop to this whole affair—one or two—one or two."

Then I went to bobbing my head 'yes' like I didn't have good sense.

"Todd, I know you won't let up till you've done all you possibly can."

Scared me to death, that did: just the tone of his voice, just how different it sounded from three nights back. For oh how nearly beyond hope that voice had gone: flat, remote, saying now, "They tell me Colonel Oldham's been ailing."

—What rushed all over me then—too much like the sensation three nights ago when Pap had seemed far away in space—was that he was now like a distant ancestor, long dead yet unreachably alive. And in horror I felt relieved that the guards would prevent me from taking the couple of further steps to touch him—to find my fingertips, I was afraid, in contact with nothingness. Then yet another stab of memory: as a child touching the scaly surface of a painting of Pap's grandfather that we used to keep over the fireplace in Missouri—.

"Yes sir, he's sort of sick, but I don't see how there could be too much the matter with him."

But still he hadn't come to town as he'd sworn he would, had he? Sicker? Or, as I'd suspected, incapable of going against his own kind?

Then, at least this: no, Pap was not oblivious, indifferent. Underneath he was straining to the bursting point—I could sense it now in the tension of his body—to reach out to me in words, and no words to be had but these common ones about another man's health.

Pap still had on his Sunday suit and the white shirt he'd worn to town the day they arrested him: the stiff collar open and bent back away from his neck, the black string tie unknotted and hanging loose on his breast. Supposed to be old: the way I felt about him then, and still to this day can't escape feeling. Yet just now he looked young—in contradiction to the ancient air that still hung about him: cool clear gray eyes, red cheeks edging along dark beard, smooth tan forehead, black hair puffed out in curls covering his ears—a couple of streaks of gray—. That whole vision kept churning inside me, but at the same time losing itself in the old painting. Till I was ready to scream to bring Pap back to the present day where I stood, here in the commonplace town square—.

"Here now. Please, Todd," I heard Dawse Mackey whimpering. "That'll have to be enough, y'all. We got to move on. It's orders, I tell you."

"I spect we better break it up," Harvey Whitman put in. "Colonel Ticknor and Captain Dexter're both right over yonder. They won't like this a bit. So move on, now, before they see what's happening."

One thing did rouse a hateful chuckle from me: to see Dawse Mackey nearly shit in his pants to think Ticknor and Dexter might see him breaking orders.

As they led Pap away, he spoke over his shoulder, "You give all my love and caring to Ma and the kids. And you look after them, like I know you will."

I'd begun, I thought, to put aside the feeling that Pap had lived a long time ago, but now his words slammed me right back into it, choked me so much that I could say nothing till he was nearly out of hearing, then I called out: "Oh you bet I will. And don't you give up hope, Pap. We got *good* reason to keep on hoping. We have, sure nuff." —Then my voice left me.

I turned and left as quick as I could, running from a new recurrence of another sickening thought that dogged me: that dark figment of Pap suspended by a rope, face contorted, strangling, which only served to verify the conviction that he was gone, long gone, if not into the old picture then into the hanging tree, all but his shadow swallowed, and that left tangled in the branches of the tree. And against that, once more in a rhythm of ghastly memory, that tree was flung out in my mind as it had stood to welcome us the day we first crossed the creek into Milcourt. Now all of a sudden that tree was monstrously alive, and devouring men brought to it in sacrifice—fragments of my dream of last night rising vividly before me....

Back in the saddle before my mind truly caught up with the present, I hurried off to overtake Preacher Tillman. I need not have rushed, I soon found, for I'd no more than turned the corner into Industry Street when I saw him standing in front of Stafford's log store, gesturing for me to join him.

So I rode up and got down. That derby hat was set squarely on his head, his brows under the brim knit with determination. And he was in too much of a hurry to speak to have good news. My heart plummeted.

He said, "You may not believe I've accomplished a thing. Because you haven't been where I've been this day. Where you could know how terrible hard I've been pushing—." He sensed how disturbing his talk was—. "No. Wait. Let me explain. You see, after these last men—."

"Last men?"

"Yes. Four—let me finish—we convicted four men today. To hang. That's right. But hold on. I wrung a promise out of them, the majority. They gave me their word we'll talk—."

"Talk!"

"Hold on now. Hold on. I'm not alone in this business anymore. That's what I'm coming to. We tried a fifth man besides, you see. The majority, they convicted him too, on barely any evidence atall. And Reese Culler, he balked at that. Along with me. He stood up and declared what I've been repeating in there every day of the world: just any hint of a man being Union is enough to earn him a death sentence. Said we might as well just hang every prisoner. No need for any trials at all. So me and Reese, we argued with them till we adjourned, just now. All we could get out of them—a long ways from perfect yet, I'll be the first to admit—was that we'd have a session after supper tonight and thrash this thing out. We'll plead with them, me and Reese. Unanimous decision: I'll begin with that. And I won't get it, no. Then I'll pop the two-thirds idea on them. Reese has promised he'll pull hard with me in that. And if it comes to a showdown, we'll threaten to resign. Force their hand, don't you know—."

"Force their hand how?" I snapped. "Why can't they just let you and Reese Culler resign? That's hemming yourself in a corner, looks to me like."

"No. They won't let us resign. One man, yes, they might. But two, no. They'd be afraid the jury might fall apart, leaving the mob to storm the courthouse and hang every last man. Then Colonel Ticknor, he'd either have to squelch the mob or let it come out in the open that the slaveholders want every Union man hung by any means whatever. As they do, yes. But they want it done by these trials. Legal steps, in their eyes, you understand—."

I cut in: "I know what you mean. No need explaining."

"Yes," he said. "Now looky here, I have to be going. Ought not to be seen talking to you at all. And we're due back in the jury room right away. And I need a bite of supper mighty bad."

With that he turned and made haste down the street, armswings pronounced, more assurance in his gait than I could feel his reading of the situation warranted. Up to now his self-importance had made it simple for the slaveholders to lead him along, just for the advantage of having his name on the jury roll: led him to believe he was indispensable. But only look how little heed they had paid him today. Four more men condemned, while Tillman begged them to drop their majority rule—or claimed he had. Was that to be believed, even? And what had he gained from the slaveholders? Merely a promise to 'talk.'

All of which made me suspect that even if Reese Culler did throw in with Tillman, the slaveholders would do with one or both men what they'd done with Colonel Oldham when he'd served their purpose: cast them aside.

It was good and dark by now. Returning to the square I tied Comanche to a hitching rail and strolled around to pick up any bits of rumor I could. Still a mass of soldiers to be seen. Not as many, quite, as a day or two ago. You could better tell now who was in the mob: some of them soldiers along with the "citizens," and not just the militia but even Confederate regulars. A person could only snort at the claim that the military was here to keep order while the jury went after justice— that's how it had been put out to the public.

Then as if I didn't have enough worries already, I began to have suspicions that Colonel Ticknor might be wrong about the extent of his control over the mob, with this many soldiers already openly siding with the unruly civilians. It sent a chill through my bones to foresee that if the jury broke up, the soldiers and the fire-eaters of the populace might run rampant in one big mob, trampling Colonel Ticknor's authority as well as any other. Could be too that he knew this was possible—and by extension that the best way to get rid of the Unionists was to proceed just as now, just as Tillman had said: a mob threat Ticknor was supposedly controlling, a jury that was convicting every prisoner.

And if that was so, then how did Preacher Tillman have a ghost of a chance of breaking the pattern?

Jenny—only resource left—if any....

So night settled in, but with not much darkness to hamper, the moon lifting up enormous almost as soon as dusk had faded. How good it was now to have the moon, for it might be long into the night before the jury session broke up. And I couldn't dream of going home till then.

As time went crawling by I circulated, keeping to the shadows, and listened, staying quiet myself for the most part. I found out the names of the four men convicted today and scheduled for the hanging tree tomorrow—eight men in all condemned up to now. And I heard all kinds of talk, some of it running high against the prisoners, some of it subdued and apprehensive—and then the haunting look of the many people still who strayed around as though stone dumb—.

The longer I stayed that night the more it flashed and writhed in my head: All of them—all of us—we were crazy. We'd gone insane. Like the rest, I'd been drawn into this lunacy ruling these great clusters of people. I would suffocate, or go berserk, if I stayed here long. I wanted just to run away, just to leave this place. At once. Right now. But yet I dared not. The slim chance that Tillman might accomplish something before that madness sucked Pap into its chaos—that one slim chance held me, bound me, to this crowd.

It was near midnight, with the moon standing high and pure as butter over the Dayton Building, when the jury disbanded. At my first glimpse of Preacher Tillman coming out into the square, I hurried to accost him. But before I could cross the space between us, people collected so thick they blocked his path as well as mine. He stopped and looked around, recognizing that many of these people were family members of prisoners, though I myself was too far back for him to pick me out.

He said, "The jury's come to the conclusion to go by a two-thirds rule instead of a simple majority. From now on it'll take eight votes to convict a man, not seven like before—and I can't discuss it, I can't do that. I was told I could announce it, but no more, no more"—he was in a rush to add these last words against a rising mutter from the circle around him, for most of those present could have no notion of what such a change might signify, and so took it for a mockery. Preacher Tillman tried to move off, saw that he couldn't, set in to pumping his hands up and down, "I can't tell you any more. I have to abide by the decision of the jury. We *all* have to abide by it. Remember, remember: it's the only law we have."

He had slipped into his preacherly tone of voice, as though at any moment he might launch into a sermon on law and order. Some militia commander must have seen what was going on and sent in the squad of men that arrived now to disperse the crowd and escort Preacher Tillman out of the square.

Since I'd anticipated the worst, a deadness went over me that lasted all the while Tillman was speaking to the crowd. When he left and people began to mill once more, still I stood there limp and muddled. The first channel of my mind to recover direction reasoned that I should not seize on the particle of hope in Preacher Tillman's announcement as something great. But I couldn't prevent myself from rejoicing, slight hope or not, because this was still the only motion away from despair since this time of atrocity had begun.

Military escort or not, I could have cut through by back streets and waylaid Preacher Tillman at his house. But I decided against it. For he was right. It was dangerous for him to be seen in my company, and nothing must be done now to hinder what this first little victory might lead to. Wait and see. Wait and see.

Weakness and blankness still followed me, though, still ate at the frail joy in my heart, as I went back to Comanche and climbed in the saddle. I was in a state like convalescence; I had just will enough to turn Comanche in the direction of home and let him set his own pace.

By the time I had ridden to the edge of town, the open country coming up beyond revived me. Up yonder past the top of the sky, with not a cloud to interfere, the moon hung at its brightest. Comanche was taking the road at a good clip, but I seemed to drift along, the moonlight penetrating my eyes, my consciousness, filling me with its dazzling.

And there in the midst of the dazzling floated what did most of all to buoy me up: the image of Jenny.

13

So in this nightmare that seemed to fill not a few days but an endless time, four men had been executed and four others condemned to die. But now, according to Preacher Tillman, a change in the jury's voting procedure promised to bring the slaughter to a halt. By the time I'd ridden home that Saturday in the exhilaration of the moonlight, and had painted as bright a picture as I could for the family of what was to come—only to see little change in the bleakness of my mother's face—I was left to a sleepless night of tossing and worry.

Next morning I arrived in Milcourt early, far ahead of the time for the jury to go into session, and wandered around through the crowd that by now seemed always the same crowd, eddying constantly through the courthouse square since the day this frenzy began. It had always been a quiet gathering, but the silence that ruled when the jury convened that morning could not have been greater if the human race had lost the power of speech.

Then the unbelievable took place: in a short time the jury retried and cleared the fifth defendant from the day before. Still, nobody dared as yet to breathe a natural breath—too much fright left in us from an inevitable looking over our shoulders at recent events. But as the day wore on with one man after another freed, the faces around me did begin to relax, and the eyes to recover from the vacant stare so prevalent before. And, incredible still, for the whole of that day it was the same story, man after man declared innocent and released. The next day the same: one happy outcome succeeding another unfailingly, and even yet too strange to credit, just as the progression of tragedies had been before: the whole train of events made more incomprehensible in that guilt or innocence, thus life or death, turned on so little. But confused by events or not, relatives wasted no time in hustling the liberated men out of town, in most cases out of the region altogether.

I soon lost count of the number of men turned loose. Not that I wasn't glad to my toes to see each one set at liberty, but I couldn't keep my mind on anything for long but my breathless yearning to see Pap walk out through that courthouse door a free man. And I vowed that he too would leave Texas just as soon as I could spirit him away, even if I had to hogtie and float him across Red River—for I worried that he might actually be inclined to trust the rebels even yet.

Naturally, all that week I talked everything up to the family as looking cheerful, with even Ma brightening. When I rode home of an evening, one of the folks was bound to see me at a distance, and then they'd all troop outdoors and stand motionless on seeing me ride in and Pap not with me. Then they'd every one come rushing down to the barnlot to learn the latest while I went about tending to Comanche.

And so, on it went like that, the course of the trials. As far as I could judge, every action of the jury went circulating through the square almost as soon as it was taken, and no word came that a single man had been condemned. From that continual good news my confidence grew till one morning I woke up certain that I should lead Old Prince to town with me—from a flicker of a dream that this day would bring Pap's liberation. But I soon saw—and I held my tongue around the others—that this was no time to tempt fate on the strength of a dream.

By now the families of the prisoners were so in the habit of hearing only good news that we accepted the rumor of Colonel Oldham's suffering another spell—apparently the second one since I'd seen him—with little comment or uneasiness. I simply assumed that the first spell had prevented him from coming to town on Saturday. Not that it seemed to matter further anyhow, since it now looked certain that Preacher Tillman's maneuvering of the jury into the two-thirds procedure would wind this thing up favorably once and for all. I began to feel, with shame, that I'd misjudged Tillman. I thought it wise to go on staying away from him for the time being, so as not to arouse any suspicion of collusion, for all my great desire to find out when to expect Pap's trial—and to inquire also about another point that troubled me from time to time: what about the four men condemned during the last majority-rule session? Nothing ever came to our ears about hanging them, or any other disposition of their cases. Surely they deserved a new trial. Or was Tillman afraid to risk upsetting the delicate balance of affairs by pressing the new lenience that far?

In any case, if prohibited by my own caution from speaking with him, I could certainly look, and anytime Tillman and I happened to pass in the street, I did my utmost to spread gratitude all over my face.

Every day from the start of that week of the trials I kept a sharp lookout for Jenny, but saw no sign of her. And a terrible absence that would have been, if an appeal from her to Colonel Ticknor had been my last alternative for saving Pap. Since I had no doubt whatever that she'd done all in her power to come to Milcourt, as the days went by I became more and more anxious to know what had kept her from carrying out her promise. Late in the afternoon of the fourth day—a Wednesday—after the jury began finding men not guilty, I at last had the opportunity to learn something: I caught sight of Cabus on his mule crossing a corner of the square. I set out in pursuit, overtook him within a few blocks. When I hailed him he drew up to wait, his face lighting up when he recognized me.

"Marse Todd," he said.

—A change of tone from the other day I now noted in Cabus's handling of that term: I liked the new tone better.

"How're you, Cabus?"

"Fit as can be."

New tone or not, conflicting currents were audible in the voice behind the welcoming face. Not much of the acceptance of collaboration in protecting Jenny was there just now. Was there a return to an edge of the mockery he'd been so bold about flaunting when we first met? Or was it a shade of father-like resentment, jealousy?

—From what he was already telling me I learned this much: none of the militia men would escort Jenny to town without Colonel Ticknor's permission, and when it was sent for he would not give it. It was after hearing this, leaving Cabus to head back to the river and riding toward the square again, that I began to know just how bad I wanted to see Jenny. I caught flashes of her out of nowhere—hair streaming, eyes with their way of opening wide, lips curving into a smile: most of all how delicate and still and yet how warm and alive and strong her hands had been as they lay between my fingers, and touched my lips, that day when I'd kissed them.

And much as I tried to suppress it in the days ahead, that yearning only increased, even in the face of knowing that I must stay in town because Pap's trial might come off at any hour of any day.

But then that reason dropped away near noon on Friday. First off, the word spread that the jury was about to recess. Why? everyone wanted to know—with a sizeable bunch of men still in custody—and for how long? And when we tried to find out if the jury meant only to adjourn until the next morning, some who claimed to know said yes—and some said no. The best information afloat, after it had gone the rounds a little while, seemed to be yes, they'd reconvene tomorrow morning. Being used to good news like everybody else, I was inclined to take this recess as a favorable sign—though the suddenness of the decision did worry me.

Still, it was excuse enough for me to leap at the opportunity of seeing Jenny, and I made ready to leave town at once, with eagerness aplenty to master the chill I experienced as witness to an incident that showed the stresses behind the now smooth functioning of the jury—.

I was in the saddle about to pull out when Preacher Tillman appeared, walking along the street next to the Dayton Building. Headed directly to meet him along the board sidewalk came Matt Scanlon, a fever-pitch rebel and one of the ringleaders of the mob. Besides which, he was as tough as they come: dangerous as a sidewinder, Pap had often said about him. Now Scanlon had a pistol slung on him, while Tillman had never carried a weapon in his life, that I'd seen. Scanlon came to a halt barring Tillman's way, so he too had to stop. Scanlon thrust out one arm stiff as a poker toward the Dayton Building and blustered, "Ever man locked up in there, and ever man that's gone scotfree, knows *you're* the one that's getting them off. And *we* know it too."

Tillman stammered, trying but failing to keep his eyes off of Scanlon's holstered pistol. Finally he said hoarsely, "The whole jury decides on a defendant, Matt, not just me."

Scanlon didn't look disposed to argue the case. He swung that stiffened arm around, crooked it in front of him and began jabbing his forefinger at Tillman's face, not a foot from it: "You put this down in your *gospel*, Preacher. You may turn them loose, but that bunch of men'll answer for what they done. And that goes as well for any of the jury that's plotting to let them go."

With that he wheeled in his tracks and barged off down the sidewalk clumping his bootheels fit to make the worms underground quiver.

So now it was head for the river with a new woe to plague me, and little to ease my mind of it: that the mob might still take matters in their own hands, with no protection remaining against the Matt Scanlons and Harley Dexters except Colonel Ticknor—if he would offer it, or if he could exercise it. So reason again after all—and now more than ever—for Jenny to be in Milcourt. So I would just put some hurry into the trip, that was all, and scheme out a way to get her here, and figure on being back in town before nightfall.

Now on the way from Milcourt to Colonel Ticknor's, on a road that crossed Wolf Ridge a ways east of the Oldham road, you passed only two houses this side of the river brakes: one was the Bob Wharton place. He was away in the Confederate army, while his wife and children were still trying to live out there on the farm, with a handful of slaves, though they'd been warned often enough to move to town, what with Indian raids on the increase and bushwhackers roaming the countryside.

Just as I was coming up even with that house, where I heard people inside but noticed nobody stirring, I saw five riders topping the rise a quarter of a mile beyond the house and coming toward me: four men and a woman riding sidesaddle. I was not an instant in recognizing Jenny, and one of the men as Cabus on his mule—the other three no doubt militiamen.

My heart began bounding, ready to go wild.

But I got a grip on myself and stopped to wait. Then as soon as Jenny saw who it was and commenced waving, I dashed off up the road to meet her—charged along in an outburst of speed I just could not repress, wheeled Comanche on a tight rein and veered in beside her. Jenny sat looking on, all smiles, then as I stopped held out her hand—that hand, that hand.

"I was just riding over to see about you," I sang out, unthinking. "And I'm sure glad you finally found a way to come to town."

She gave a quick shake of the head, face instantly serious, and kept her voice low: "No. I haven't. I'm not coming to town, you see. Uncle James wouldn't let me. I'm coming to visit Jane Wharton"—but with that she darted me a look asking for no further comment just now.

As we rode on, chatting eagerly to catch up on the last few days, soon the people at the Wharton house noticed us and the place came alive, the mother and Jane and several younger children filling the front porch and gesturing for us to hurry and come on. So we struck up a trot and in no time we were pulling up in the yard. The whole family, above all Jane—a homely girl about Jenny's age—began to fall all over themselves greeting Jenny. And they made me abundantly welcome too when Jenny said merely that I was a good friend of hers. Next she thanked and dismissed the militia boys to go on back to Ticknor's, then I let Cabus take Comanche to the barn along with Jenny's horse, and the Whartons led us into the house.

Here it was, then, that Jenny and I were surrounded, and as the afternoon went along no opportunity could I discover to talk with her alone. Mrs Wharton, and Jane with her, could outdo Mrs Ticknor in chattering, not allowing Jenny herself the time to say much. As for me, I didn't even try to get a word in edgeways. But my mind was made up on one thing: after the luck I'd had in meeting up with Jenny away from the Ticknor place, I'd arrange for us to talk before I went away, if I had to stay the night after all to bring it off, more and more of a mind that Jenny's intervention with her uncle might be the only shot left of heading off the mob, and that for the moment I was more useful here than in Milcourt.

As you might guess, Jane and her mother cast around in all directions to size up the situation between Jenny and me—when, Godamighty, I didn't even know what it was myself. And included in that probing was of course taking on over me, the way a bunch of women will over a young man—and he doesn't mind it a bit. Jane and her mother kept at me to stay for supper, and also to spend the night, and that being right in my line of thinking, to confer with Jenny and just to be with Jenny, I was easy to convince. Besides, if I'd needed another excuse, while I was only too glad to get rid of the militia, I was uneasy about women and children being out here with no protection except Cabus and a couple of other unarmed slave men. Jane and her mother might be used to it, but I knew, whereas they didn't—and so did Jenny after the scrape we'd been in—how many outlaws the river bottom held, and that at no great distance from here. It was a miracle the Wharton women hadn't been molested thus far.

So it was decided, then, that I'd stay overnight, and the looks coming my way from Jenny made me especially glad of the arrangement. Ma and Sis would be concerned, naturally, but not unduly, I was hoping: I'd said that I might spend some nights in town if matters ever appeared to demand my presence there.

It was Jenny, after supper, who schemed around so we could be by ourselves, leaving the impression, I guess, that we were involved in full courting. For all at once Jane and her mother made themselves scarce, while Jenny and I drifted out to the front porch and settled down in the big swing.

For a good while we sat quiet, balancing, gently rocking. The blackest kind of a night and a sky peppered bright with stars tilted back and forth with us in a small arc, a breeze fanning up from our motion. Then a light wind rose and added itself to the night, turning gusty off and on but for all that mild and soothing. Standing a little distance from the front of the house was a big pecan tree that I'd hardly noticed until now, until the wind began to sound through its branches: first a soft hissing, then a rise in pitch to a humming, a singing, when the wind strengthened. I'd heard and welcomed them from childhood on: the tones of wind in trees I knew or trees I came upon by accident.

—But then all of a sudden I felt myself reeling beyond the cadence of the swing, encountering the new and terrible identity of trees: in the dark of night, with stars to trace its outline, this tree in shape resembled the hanging tree. With more than enough to keep my heart thumping madly just from being close to Jenny, moment by moment that terrible form threatened to engulf me, and at each of those recurring moments I felt closer to defeat, to pure terror, even in the midst of this bliss.

And then more than all, this too came down on me: the swing we rocked in—and the swing on the postoak at home—how I'd sat there a few days ago and looked up to see the rope around the limb—.

My feet acted in spite of me, stamped the porch floor and brought the swing to a standstill—.

"What is it, Todd? What's the matter?"

—But by the time she had those words out, it flooded over me: Why no. No reason now to fear that Pap would be hanged. Remember! It could be tomorrow—surely tomorrow or the next day, that the jury would hear his case and dismiss it. And we'd go home. And I'd rush him out of the state—.

But still, but still: Scanlon's threat—.

"Nothing, Jenny. I was just thinking."

I took the time to lay my arm along the back of the swing touching her shoulders before I went on: "Tell me, now. Why was it you wanted nothing said earlier about you going to Milcourt?"

—Though actually I thought I'd figured out why, but I wanted her version of it.

"Yes, let's do talk about that now, Todd. Because coming here to visit Jane is a way I thought up to get me to Milcourt, and now that you've come, it'll be very good to have your help with it."

Our heads seemed to have drawn closer together of their own accord, and the whispering we'd fallen into was not all that necessary. Only wonderful.

"Not even that I'll be needed in town, maybe, the way things have gone—or can do any good if I am there. But let's go on with it just in case, and at the very least I'll be doing Jane and Mrs Wharton a favor, bigger than they realize."

"Sure. I think I see what you mean"—while I was thinking at another level that this was not the time to bring up the mob and hint that she might be needed after all.

"Yes," said Jenny, "it's simple. Tomorrow morning I'll tell them about the bushwhackers, with you here now to back me up in it. And if that won't scare them into moving to town, I don't know what would. And I—along with you—can help them load up. And I won't have to ask Uncle James's permission. He'll have to understand me helping them. Then once in Milcourt no need for me to hurry about going back to the river. I can just go on visiting Jane, and he can't object to that either."

"That's right clever of you," I said. "And if it comes to another emergency, which I hope to God it never does, then you'll be on hand to try and work on your uncle."

Even as I spoke a current of hopelessness ran strong against my words. *If* another emergency arose, wouldn't Jenny pleading with Colonel Ticknor prove to be useless in any case, headstrong as he was. And the questioning I did my best to keep at bay: why was Ticknor permitting the jury to free so many men, when I was positive he wanted them dead? Had the jury recessed for just that reason, and were he and the mob plotting another course, of which Matt Scanlon's threat to Preacher Tillman was the first step, and when the jury resumed tomorrow, would it be another story?—Tillman and his faction to be coerced into pronouncing the prisoners guilty—. And if that didn't work, then a mob takeover....

—Jenny was talking. As soon as I picked up on her voice, it smoothed the surface of my bad run of thought, even if it left the deeper turmoil untouched.

"Oh Todd, I'm so happy this awful trouble is nearly over with. Four men've died, you say, yes, but then it's *only* four, as terrible as that sounds—because it could have been maybe a hundred."

"We'll hope it's all coming to a close, as it still looks to be," I said—

and shifted ground: "And in the meantime we'll prepare—we'll go about getting Jane and her mother out of danger."

"Yes, Todd. And I'm so grateful and relieved that you're here to help me."

By now I'd built up enough courage to do it, to take the dive into the flames. I drew Jenny over till her shoulder slipped into my armpit, and felt her head lean into the hollow of my neck. The fit was perfect, only her meeting me so ready and willing nearly frightened me out of my skin, callow kid that I was and never this near a girl so marvellous in my life. When I recovered my breath I proceeded to lose it again: tilted her chin up with my fingertips and fixed my eyes on her face—the perfect shape of it framed around by that wonderful mass of hair: that face so close to mine I could hear and feel the warm quickness of her breath—.

I closed my eyes and let my mouth sink against hers.

Knowing so little about girls, I'd always believed a kiss was something you stole. Anyway the few I'd ever had I got that way—though I expect the girls I robbed mainly pretended thievery was going on. But with Jenny there was none of that holding back. As she always had right from the start, she met me halfway. And while I suppose I thought that kissing her mouth would be like kissing her hands the other day, only more so, that's not how it was. The first touch of the skin of her lips was no miracle, for a miracle does take place in this world. But with the first tender, warm and total clinging of Jenny's lips to mine, my soul went through this world like a gale and swept beyond it. This earth slipped away behind, below, and I carried away along with her and myself the close cool darkness, the dazzle of the stars in the deep sky, a drift of scent from flowers somewhere, the singing tree, the faint teetering of the swing that just our kiss itself seemed to put into motion now—all that I rose up with in a piercing second and plunged into space as though my body had died and the life of my soul bearing the essence of all joy had caught fire to burn its way into the heavens. That burning was swift as no burning on earth could be, not even the flame that went through me when sometimes I'd lean over Comanche's neck and heel-touch him a certain way and feel his body stretch out over the earth like an arrow let loose—when I'd close my eyes and know, at one given instant, that Comanche had won the power of flight, his hooves never to touch the earth again—.

I can't recall a word that went with that first kiss; I don't think we spoke any. At some time a long while later—after a kiss, then come up for air, then a kiss again—Jenny gave me a hard close hug and whispered, "We'd better go in now, Todd."

If I'd known well enough all along that it would have to end, I'd never let myself admit it. Tighter than ever I held her, for a long kiss, but as soon as I loosened my hold a little, Jenny wriggled out of my arms and was gone into the house before I could recapture my breath, leaving me with a husky "Good night, Todd" lingering in my ears. Then I could hear her feeling her way up the dark stairs.

—I gave a push against the floor with both feet. The swing began to sweep back and forth, hard, creaking on its chains. Till that motion shot a dizziness through me, and I reached out and grabbed a porch railing to cut the swinging short. I stood up, and the dizziness gave way to a sinking, sinking. The vibrating network of stars poured out endless flashes of light, thrumming. Not only my heart but the darkness itself was throbbing so hard it hurt. The singing tree was poised to reach out and dance to its own music. And as long as I kept my eyes away from this tree, all other senses attentive, I could exclude that other one, the tree of death, from the pulsating sphere of emotions my heart occupied.

Hardly knowing where I drifted, I crept in and groped my way to the pallet on the parlor floor, which was the only spot available for me to sleep. I'd had the pallet made up by the front door, and had brought in the pistol to keep close at hand. As it happened, I was a more alert guard than I intended to be, for not much sleep did I get that night. I tossed and turned and sighed and groaned, every bit of me yearning for every bit of Jenny. I was terrified, too, of a compulsion I'd never experienced before: if I hadn't known for a fact that she was in a bedroom with Jane—.

"Whoa, fella. Whoa, whoa, whoa," I whispered to myself over and over—and groaned with it. "This is no time to bolt ahead, you blame fool, to run away with yourself."

At last I did drift into a light sleep, though I'd never have known it if I hadn't sensed the first light of day the next time I found my eyes open. Not that Jenny had ever left my consciousness in the meantime, but had been with me or near me through a feverish thrashing of dreams that pitched me all at once into the shock of waking here in the dawnlight. I wanted Jenny with such passion that I gripped the pillow close to my face and hugged the whole pallet till I nearly burst.

Then maybe having passed through a dozing moment, I found myself blinking and blinking, and then by degrees I faced up to the case that had to be, that never would be otherwise: Jenny and I must be married. But for all its certainty that thought could not outstrip those that came as a matter of course in its wake: the obstacles thrown up by the differences between her kind of people and mine.

—Though anyhow, for one stroke of luck, now we were not to suffer, it seemed, from all that would follow if her uncle had had a hand in condemning my father to death—'But wait a minute, wait a minute, damn it! It's not over yet'—For while, yes, Pap could possibly go free, then what? The Confederacy her family swore by, and the Union we swore by, the war entangling all people in violence added to violence. And then just suppose the rebels won, and each day it looked more as if they would—when the men I'd always taken to be the most level-headed had thought it impossible—a victory that would put the Colonel Ticknors in charge for good, with all the Harley Dexters crowding around to kiss ass. Then this would not be a country worth living in.

"And what? You and Jenny get married!" I muttered aloud.

Then words inside, the words of what had to be attended to first of all: 'You see it in the cards right now, don't you. Waiting won't do. Pap's gotta hightail it out of this country. Yes indeed! And that ain't all of it either, is it? The whole family's got to move on with him to a new part of the world—try to—starting the day Pap steps out of jail—."

'So Jenny and you? —Oh shut up, just shut up.'

'—Or more yet. Which new country? You think the rebels're gonna let you folks merely ride out of here—like head for California maybe, like I know some in favor of the Union did before the clampdown—.'

'And the draft. Yes, that. You can bet they'll snatch up your ass the minute this present commotion is over, if they don't do it before. And even Pap, even he ain't too old yet to be drafted....'

And on like that: mixed up, no logic in my head, troubles attacking me from every angle and no solution to be seen to any of them. Like that it went till night had finished thinning out, and dawn was about to give over to sunrise. Then I ordered myself to drop all such thoughts—but the best I could manage was to push them out to where they floated along with me as I got up slow, unbolted and opened the front door. Shapes out there had just about completed taking on their daytime presence. The wind had died down, so the tree had come to the end of its song for this night: standing huge, dark and silent, just gathering the first of the sunlight into its branches—.

With no warning I choked up, and tears rushed into my eyes. The hanging tree had loomed also into my vision. But then in a solacing instant it faded, and what followed was almost too much, striking deep and unexpectedly: a joyous assurance that the peaceful tree before my eyes could take the place of the deathly tree I'd been possessed by during these many terrible days.

14

WHEN JENNY HAD FINISHED telling her story that morning about our run-in with the bushwhackers, Mrs Wharton and Jane were fully persuaded to pick up and move into town. And fretful as I was now to head for Milcourt at once, I felt I couldn't take the risk of letting them make the trip with only the slaves to watch over them.

But then before we'd gotten up from the breakfast table came news to rend the heart out of the morning—an open revelation of the murderous power I'd glimpsed the day before in Matt Scanlon. For these past few days I'd kept up hopes that maybe the moderates were delaying action on the four men sentenced prior to the change of rules, till they could safely call for the sentences to be set aside, or else request a new trial. Whatever their intent, it had been overridden by the mob. With Matt Scanlon at their head, they had forced their way into the Dayton Building at first daylight that morning, dragged the four men out and hanged them—while the military in effect looked the other way. And what could be Colonel Ticknor's logic for permitting this? Why, easy to answer. Just letting the 'citizens' carry out sentences already imposed.

For a few interminable minutes rage and helplessness bound me to the chair where I sat sipping Mrs Wharton's hoarded coffee, surrounded by the three women. The four militia men who had brought the ghastly news stood by the door of the dining room—. As it turned out, Jenny's visit to the Wharton place had already been reported to Colonel Ticknor, and he'd sent the men to watch over her. But they couldn't very well object, under the present circumstances, to accompanying all three women to Milcourt, and so within a little while everyone was making preparations for the trip.

While still there at the breakfast table, however, when I'd had a few minutes to regain something like composure, I dared to look at Jenny for the first time, to find her already gazing steadily at me, with anguish in her eyes. I couldn't tarry here now, and there'd be no opportunity for a real parting, but she understood the strength of the look I kept on her for a brief time, and I understood the one she returned.

I rose from the table: "I'm going to town," I choked out to all of them. "You can see why."

I didn't wait for an answer from either of the Wharton women. It may have been that Jenny had already given them a sign not to speak, and her look had told me to hurry on. Nor did she follow me when I left the room.

As I was saddling Comanche, my hands trembling, who should walk up to the corral fence but Cabus, leading his roan mule in from the pasture, but seeking me out for sure.

He spoke up at once, in a new, a private way: "Mr Todd, I got something I want you to see. I ain't ever showed it to no other white man." Then out of a ragged canvas saddlebag he whipped the longest and wickedest-looking razor I'd ever seen: "I'm satisfied you think I was plumb paralyzed in front of them outlaws t'other day. You seen me take off my hat and hold it again my belly when they come in our direction, I'll bet. Well, I had this under that hat. I reckon they thought they was too good to pull guns on a young lady and one old nigger. I'd'a had time to slash one of them's jugular vein for sho', before he could draw, and give Miss Jenny time to run before the other'n got me."

I quit my saddling up, went over and leaned my forearms on the fence, facing Cabus across the top rail—it was a hard matter to keep my voice steady: "No, Cabus, I didn't judge you to be scared to death, because you didn't look like that, though I wondered why you took off your hat, and I thought the two of you should've lit out and run at once."

"You're plumb right about that. I give Miss Jenny time to say hello, and I shouldn't ought'a done that."

Cabus had put his razor away, with never an interruption to holding me in his gaze, a tight-lipped smile on his deep-wrinkled face. I had no more wish to end our conversation than he did: I just did not know what more to say to him. What held me in surprise, and admiration, was to learn that this slave was so attached to the girl I loved as to be ready to die for her—another mystery on top of the others about Cabus that had gone on contradicting one another since I'd met him, increasing my conviction that it took experience I was totally without to deal with slaves.

That inner voice of mine that has the power to speak unawares, sometimes when I need it most, put in: 'Sure. And if he had hold of that Spencer, who's to say he wouldn't be as much of a man as you are? Who's to say he ain't anyhow, even without the Spencer?'

What I got out at length to Cabus sounded lame to me: "Well, we have to take good care of her. And I'm certain sure you know that. And will do it."

"I reckon I ought to know it. Ain't I been doing it all her born days?"

I went back to saddling up, drawing the cinch tight, then swinging up.

Cabus hadn't moved a muscle. I sat sizing him up, then put in a hesitating voice words that had been gnawing at me: "Did you...owe Jenny's daddy something?"

"Just my life, that's all. My wife's too."

I looked at him steadily for a moment, I leaned over in the saddle to shake his hand, and he accepted it as any white man would have.

Then I said: "Well, Cabus, I'll see you and the women in Milcourt."

"You sho will. And you take good care of yeself."

I waved a hand and rode off.

As Comanche loped across the prairie, my mind wouldn't even turn to the crisis ahead: it ran too full of thoughts about Cabus; or rather about where to place Cabus in the greater flood of thoughts about Jenny. The whole slave business came home to me as it never had before—which was not to say with any great understanding of it. This old black man and his younger wife had sheltered their white mistress all the dangerous way from Tennessee to Texas, a task to be entrusted even to few white couples—the man allowed no weapon either, and no one aware of the hidden razor. It was simply assumed that Cabus would lay down his life for Jenny. And Jenny's mother, at least, must have known that he would have, as her husband had known before her— and never doubted that Cabus's vow of loyalty was unbreakable.

And so arose the incomprehensible situation that after the death of Jenny's father, Cabus had in effect stepped in to take his place—and not at all her Uncle James, let her or him say what they would to keep the situation socially acceptable.

—But then by now I was on the outskirts of Milcourt, with a host of other suddenly pressing problems to occupy my mind.

And yet the town was quiet, which stunned me, coming in as I had in expectation of a furor. From what I soon pieced together, the four men had been hanged in quick succession, taken then to graves already dug in the makeshift cemetery by the river—no waiting even for families to claim the bodies—and by shortly after sunrise the butchery was all over and done with.

The jury too had met early, was now in full session, though what we were to anticipate, in hope or despair, who could know? Strange, strange it was to think that while the supposed jury was acting—or had been acting—with mercy and restraint, the most brutal massacre so far had been committed without a protest. More than that, it became a great mystery as time went by just what could be occupying the jury so intensely. All morning long not a prisoner was brought across from the Dayton Building to the courthouse—yet it was known to everyone that all the prisoners left were housed in that building. What this implied was that the jury was no longer trying cases man by man but rather weighing the matter as a whole—which could mean either the best or the worst of outcomes.

Great as the suspense was, around noon I gave in to the impulse to ride off toward the east part of town—making my wide circle as usual to avoid the hanging tree—then headed for Mrs Wharton's brother's house: I could not put off any longer finding out whether Jenny and the Wharton women had arrived safe and sound.

It was a fairly large one-story house standing on a wide rough plot of ground, and had a deep verandah on two sides. As I turned in from the street I saw Cabus and one of Mrs Wharton's slaves, plus another I'd never seen before, unloading belongings out of a wagon and carrying them into the house. By the time I'd dismounted at the front gate, Jenny had spied me and come stepping sprily around a corner onto the front verandah. The way her face lit up on seeing me turned my legs to jelly as usual—left me hardly the steadiness to walk to the house.

"Here we are, Todd...." All of a sudden she remembered, and the brightness faded from her voice: "How is it down there? What're they doing?"

I dropped down on the edge of the porch, with more than one reason to be weak in the legs: "Nobody can say for certain." Then I told her about the jury being closeted all morning but trying no individual prisoners. Jenny looked at me steadily, wholly, as she so often did, pain and sorrow written on her face: "They——."

"No, I think you mean to ask—I mean, yes, I think, and several others think...they're taking up the whole matter at once. That means they could either turn all the men loose, or—the opposite."

The trouble in Jenny's features deepened. We went on gazing at one another, as she stood above me leaning on a verandah post.

Now changes could always come over Jenny so fast they left me gasping, and often I welcomed them even when I knew they were forced, as now. Anxiety all but vanished from her face; instead it was bright eyes and a warming smile—all to comfort me:

"Please come in the house, Todd, and visit a little bit with us—though the place is a mess—and drink some tea. Jane's uncle actually had some English tea in a cupboard. Jane was just starting to make it when you rode up."

Jenny had on that riding habit again—a different blouse, though, on which bands of lace ran down from the shoulders, mounded over her breasts and curved on below to the slenderness of her waist. Her breasts hung in balance like two cups filled and lifted up from the river of life. And when she spun around—knowing, oh knowing—her skirt gave a whirl and pressed for a moment over the lovely mold of her bottom. It was enough to churn up every morsel of life inside me. I stood up all but weaving and followed her inside, as yoked and mute as any ox.

When Jane and her mother found out I was going to have tea with them, they got into a flurry—a tea-party, another one of those practices I'd had precious little to do with. While Jane was arranging tablecloth and napkins and silverware and delicate china—all from the well-stocked cupboards in the kitchen—Mrs Wharton rummaged around in packing boxes and came up with tea-cakes: none too fresh-baked but a surprise anyhow, for sugar at the time was a precious commodity on the frontier. And then after the bit of time needed to ease down, I sat there enjoying myself as much as the women were: lifting and sipping out of a cup as fragile as an eggshell, nibbling tea-cakes according to my best possible manners, smiling and nodding and chuckling—offering a word now and again—while the Wharton women ran their heads off waiting on me and talking on in general like they hadn't laid eyes on me in a year's time. Jenny they didn't ask to do anything. She and I divided our time between looking at one another and at the dishes. The flashes that darted between us off and on were fervent enough to rock the foundations of the house.

Yet, even all that could not pull me far, without a rhythm of guilt pangs, over what I was supposed to be at. And the guilt built up too, for at one instant, with the teacup to my lips, I went hollow with shame and remorse. Sitting here, eh, with these plantation ladies. And no matter if I was eating my heart out over one of them, she *was still* Colonel Ticknor's niece. And if Ma or Sis could have seen me socializing here while Pap lay in prison wondering whether his neck would be the next one stuck in a hanging noose—well!

My hand set in to shaking so, that it was all I could manage to place the cup in the saucer. Jenny saw in an instant what was wrong, was on her feet the moment I was, with a deep and understanding look in her eyes, and tears barely contained.

"I do have to get back to town." And my voice shook.

By then Jane and her mother had caught on too, and came chiming in with: "Oh of course—Oh we know—Oh, we'll be so glad when this is all over with, and all the men are free"—and such words as that.

Jenny, though, stayed hushed up, caught hold of my hand and gripped it firm as I led her out onto the verandah, down the walk, out the front gate to where Comanche was tied. Just as I was putting my foot in the stirrup, anxious to escape even from Jenny, I had a sudden change of heart, whirled around and swept her to me, one arm clamped around her waist, the other her shoulders, and kissed her mouth to mouth so hard that I later discovered blood on my lips—mine? hers?

As I rode away I never looked back—for if I had so much as turned my head the tears would have brimmed over.

Then, when I'd ridden downtown and entered the square again, almost by the time I dismounted, a rumor reached me that brought one of the highest moments of elation, of joy, to come to pass during the whole of the ordeal. I did not dare at first to believe it, though it was on everyone's tongue with emphatic vows of certainty. The jury, people swore, had voted to clear and to release every man left in custody, and I couldn't resist being carried along by the talk, even though I kept telling myself not to get caught up in a whirl of good tidings that might yet prove to be a delusion. But then at last—though he never caught sight of me—I overheard Harley Dexter angrily telling another man that yes, the goddamn jury had decided to let them all off: which could leave no doubt about it—but at the same time raised the specter of what the mob might do.

Still it took great restraint to contain myself from tearing over to the

Dayton Building and pleading for Pap's immediate release—which naturally would not have done at all. But then I could carry that as a dream to be dreamt while standing up and walking: in so far, that is, as my feet touched the ground at all.

For I suppose two hours the good news kept me floating. Glimmers of schemes to flee the country—the whole family—popped irresistibly into my head, wayward schemes that best summed themselves up in an ever-returning vision, which was just new life in an old vision: the westering in the ox-wagon, the moving on from Missouri to the Cross Timbers reborn in a fresh moving on to other new lands beyond the horizon. It was exultation so far-reaching that for the time being no disturbing glimpse of Jenny's face either illuminated or darkened it....

What brought me down to earth was not serious to begin with, but at once it began complicating itself as it went. First, I heard that the jury had decreed that the prisoners would be held, even yet, until next Sunday—a week from tomorrow. And that seemed so peculiar that I took it at first to be merely the sort of crooked tale that slips out in the midst of public excitement. But then the next thing that came to my ears was just as curious, and far more troubling: confusing too, in light of all I'd heard up to now. People said the decision to drop all charges had been made in secret, and the jury had adjourned—or was about to—with the intent of making no public announcement for the whole week, but rather to reconvene Sunday week and release all the remaining prisoners by official declaration.

Secret! Why? Presumably in hopes the mob would disperse and the lynching fever subside. Yet, if secret, how could the news have spread all over town almost as soon as the decision was taken—?

The answer was not far to seek: some member of the jury, if not more than one, had leaked the news to let it spread—and for reasons likely to be among the worst.

For yes, Matt Scanlon and that whole gang—when all their probable motives one by one penetrated my heart, I shuddered, while the dreams of an hour ago fell in ruins.

'Oh no. Oh no.'

And my hunch was correct. By middle of the afternoon, a clamor for the mob to take charge and lynch the prisoners to the last man was running tumult high through the town: fed, within plain view of everyone, by Matt Scanlon, Harley Dexter and all that ilk.

For this whole time I roved around on foot, trying always to stay inconspicuous among knots of people, that constant fear of being arrested myself hovering over me. In the worst way I wanted to speak with Preacher Tillman, but he was nowhere to be located, neither in the square nor at the house he was staying in, though I dropped by there twice in search of him. Several times I saw Colonel Ticknor at a distance, as I ordinarily had seen him since the beginning of this affair. He looked and acted in command of the situation, not as yet allowing any great congregation of men before the Dayton Building. But while it still appeared that he was the man with authority and the soldiers behind him to put a lid on the turmoil and keep it there, it was also unsettling to observe a cold aloofness in his manner, as though he might at any moment arbitrarily let slip the reins on the mob. How could I not believe that he was simply playing his own game with the lives of the prisoners, seeing he'd done nothing this morning to stop the execution of the four men?

So what it came down to was that this was the time, if ever, for Jenny to make her plea. And with that decided I rushed off to the Wharton house to tell her, if possible to have Cabus bring her straight to the square. Yet, on the way, I had second thoughts. Colonel Ticknor, with all his hidebound Southern-gentleman notions, wouldn't want his young niece shoved into the midst of mob excitement. And anyway, how could she talk with him confidentially in such a public place?

So once I reached Jenny and we could discuss it, we filled out a plan I'd already begun to outline in my mind: she'd send Colonel Ticknor word by Cabus that it was urgent for her to see him, immediately. There was a lot of risk in our scheme, naturally. As yet he might not even know she'd made it to town, and could lose his temper when he found out. And then if he paid any heed to the message and came to her, when he learned what she had to say to him he might fly into a rage that would spoil any chance of persuading him. Still, as Jenny and I said to one another more than once in the course of our talk, what else was left to turn to?

—In fact Colonel Ticknor did nothing: he sent Cabus back to say she'd have to wait, that whatever she wanted couldn't be as important as what he was doing. In addition, he laid down the law: so she'd had to help the Whartons move into town, but under strict orders she was not to budge outside the Wharton house until the criminal element— that's how he put it—was brought under control.

Who did he consider to be 'the criminal element?'

—As if I didn't know!

And so now what? The one slim hope remaining was Preacher Tillman—no hope, at that, but in any case it could do no harm to talk with him. But I still could not find him, though I went about searching more openly now, since everyone seemed too wrapped up in events to be aware of my existence, as I went plodding up and down the streets and periodically rechecking the square.

What was building up now was all too evident. Little packs of men went milling here and yonder, around the square and in the side streets, every pack with some fellow among them whipping up excitement. Every once in a while they'd gather in a larger group before the Dayton Building, and still each time Ticknor's troops would move in to break them up. Before night came, though, the line so far vaguely drawn between soldiers and mob began to fade altogether: a squad of soldiers would approach a throng of men and draw around them, but then amazingly the soldiers would often break rank and join in the wild talk themselves. As stern about discipline as Colonel Ticknor was, the truth had to be that he was purposely easing up on the militia—which most of the ones he sent among the crowd were—maybe so he could claim later on that they'd overthrown his control and gone pellmell over to the mob.

So night fell, and every nerve in that square was by now stretched as tight as catgut. Up to a certain time the noise of the many voices rose louder, until, in a moment arriving out of nowhere, there came a sudden quietening down that I could not account for: it was no releasing of tension, for sure. Not until I saw people stirring at the mouth of one of the sidestreets and had wormed over near enough to see, did I begin to understand what was in the wind. All twelve of the jurymen, accompanied by Matt Scanlon and Harley Dexter, came trooping out of that sidestreet. And even yet I could not grasp what an outrage was in store. I could only suspect that silence had fallen because word had been passed to key people, and from them to the whole mob; that Dexter and Scanlon had become so powerful they had the entire jury at their beck and call—had probably been browbeating them at a meeting—which would explain why Preacher Tillman was not to be seen all afternoon.

A thought hit me, and in the next instant I put it into action: I made a dive for the courthouse door barely ahead of the line of men marching for it, expecting every second to be snatched back and manhandled out of there. And I was not, I'm sure, only because every eye was on that procession the crowd split to let pass.

Once inside, I mounted the stairs leaping like a goat, and by the time the procession began climbing behind me, I was hid in a dark cranny just outside the juryroom door. Scanlon, Dexter and the jury crowded up, opened the door, filed inside, pulled the door to after them.

Foiled, for God's sake! Unable for all my effort to see or hear. But luckily I soon found a way to remedy that, because the door was hung to open on the side next to my cranny. Making sure that no one else was to come up, nor any guard stationed inside at the foot of the stairs, I eased a crack in the doorway that if noticed might look as if the door had failed to latch when closed and had swung open a fraction. With that done, I stood by the doorjamb alert to duck back into my cranny at any sign of danger.

Harley Dexter was doing the talking, plenty audible though out of my line of vision:

"This jury's had its say, now. It's met for like ten days in a row, and has only the hanging of four traitors to show for all its doings—I don't count the other four because I know and you know the jury would've found a way to turn them loose on the public if the citizens of this county hadn't taken it on themselves to carry out your verdict for you. For most of these ten days you've been setting traitors free acoming and agoing. And this evening we the citizens of the county and the Confederate States of America have found out in spite of you gentlemen that you made it up in secret to trick us out of the justice we demand—concluded no less than you'd let ever traitor we caught go scotfree. Now you may have got in ahead of us up till today, and we can't undo every harm you've done, but let me tell you this: we're going to have what we can reach set to rights. And we'll hold *you* accountable if you try to stand in our way—and I don't believe I have to spell out what I mean by 'accountable.'

"Now then, Matt Scanlon and me have been elected to deliver this message and this request to you. Officially. First, we want to see a list of all the prisoners left. We aim to pick out the few that need killing worse'n the rest. And tomorrow we aim to hang them. And don't think for a minute you can turn us down on this. You do, and we'll collect all the citizens and storm that building over yonder and clean it out! And we won't stop putting ropes around necks till ever traitor caught has swung from that elem tree—. And we may not stop there—if you know what I mean. Let me see that list, Whit."

Whit Smith was one of the recording clerks. He must've handed Dexter the list at once, because a total silence fell. I could bear it no longer; I twisted my neck and peeked through the crack, standing as close to the door as I dared, but the angle was such that all I could see, still, was Dan Montgomery, the man they called the president of the jury, scowling and glowering in the candlelight—and looking like he for one had no quarrel with what was going on—.

Harley Dexter's voice: "We want him...and him too...and that one too—." So he must be ticking off names on the list.

I edged the crack in the doorway a inch wider; I couldn't keep from it to save my life. Then I came near fainting. Wary, hell! I felt them now, a throng of people behind me that I'd been too caught up by the scene inside the juryroom even to hear coming up the stairs. I shut my eyes and tensed up to be seized.

But no such thing happened. A quick glance around told me who most of the cluster behind me were: members of families who had relatives imprisoned. They wedged in and I could not resist them, and the door was pushed open a little at a time till it stood wide, and a dozen or more people were packed against the opening. The only precaution I'd been able to take meanwhile was to sink back into the middle of the group and crane my neck to watch over or between heads.

—Harley Dexter lifted his eyes from the sheet of paper in his hand long enough to run them over the occupants of the doorway. Then he stooped to hold the list closer to the two candles burning on a table before him and took an exaggerated pleasure in making obvious motions—quick slashes with the stub of pencil he held—to check off more names from the roster. But still not a name did he utter aloud: just "Him too" or "Yes, and him" and such like. Till he came to the bottom of the page. Then he handed the list back to Whit Smith and spoke out in a loud voice: "I reckon that'll satisfy us. Read off the names, Mr Clerk."

An age could have gone by while I stood there with my breath cut short. Yet at one and the same time I was stiff from the top to the bottom of my spine with one dire vow: if Pap's name was on that list, Harley Dexter and Matt Scanlon had no longer to live than he did.

So then Whit Smith began to read out the names, not in A-to-Z order but haphazard, how many in all I soon lost count of, perturbed as I was and straining my ears for one name only. Now every time Whit read out a name, I heard a gasp or two from those around me, or a sob smothered in some throat. Then I tried to catch up—ten names, eleven names?—while expecting always that the next name sounding in the half-dark room would be my father's. The tally reached—I thought fourteen; Whit went silent—and still Pap's name had not come to his tongue.

"That's all," he concluded in what was now a half-choked whisper, his eyes in the candlelight wide enough to pop, and roving from Dan Montgomery to Preacher Tillman to another member or two of the jury, sick of his job, helpless to understand why the jury couldn't muster one voice against this travesty, this outright lynching.

Preacher Tillman and another juror consulted each other in husky whispers, and ended by shaking their heads, just for their own benefit.

The rage and terror that before had kept my insides quaking now gave place in part to bewilderment: as to why Harley Dexter had not seized this opportunity to pronounce judgment on Pap. A ghost of a hope flitted through my mind that maybe Colonel Ticknor, knowing I'd rescued Jenny from the renegades, had decided to repay me in this fashion. But unfortunately there was a hint of a motive in Harley Dexter's look, too, one that came close to paralyzing me. All along I'd thought he hadn't seen me, that I'd drawn back out of view in time. All of a sudden I saw that it was not so. His gaze was after all in my direction, and no mistake that he had me spotted. Was it this?—that he was toying with us, luring me with Pap as bait, on the chance that he might get both of us at his mercy. And his next move increased my suspicion. He said: "Oh no, we don't say that's *all*. Just all for now. We'll confer closer tomorrow about some of the others accused."

A stillness followed. At length Dan Montgomery rose and spoke: "Do any of you jurors have an objection to raise against the sentencing of the men whose names the clerk's read?"

Tillman! Tillman! I felt the name come to my lips as in a prayer.

Not a peep out of a single man, for you could sense it in the air, if Harley Dexter's words had not already made it clear: any protest from a juror might condemn that man himself to the hanging tree.

"All right then!" Dan Montgomery slammed the tabletop with the palm of his hand. "This is to be considered as a group trial. A group trial. The fourteen men designated are herewith condemned to be hung by the neck until dead, sentence to be carried out tomorrow! And may God have mercy on their souls."

No point in waiting around for more. I squirmed through the people now close packed halfway down the stairs and didn't let up walking till I'd reached Comanche, then swung up in the saddle and made straight for home—because at least for now I had, if not the best news, anyhow news a great mercy to what I could have had to carry to Ma and Sis—if only the better news could last.

The great question now was, what would Harley Dexter do next in what was surely a cat-and-mouse game? Apparently he felt he could maneuver as he liked without interference from Colonel Ticknor, and if he didn't succeed in trapping me, now that he also had the jury cowed, he could step in whenever he wished and dictate that Pap be sent to his death.

On my way past my weapons cache I dug them up, inspected the rifle as well as I could in the dark—having decided to take it home and leave it with Ma and Sis—worked the hammer and the lever of the Spencer a few times, in case moisture had found its way into the mechanism, then rammed that gun into its saddle scabbard—.

"Tomorrow," I said to the night, "may be the day slated for all hell to break loose."

15

DEAD AS I WAS FOR SLEEP when I rode in home after midnight, I had to stay up a great deal longer, since the whole family rallied around to hear, down to the last detail, what I'd seen and heard since I last left home. Ma stirred me up a quick meal and waited on me while I sat as usual at the dining table, talking between bites, going through what had become a ritual recounting each time I returned from the outer world bearing its horrors. Telling all of it took a long time, for I held back nothing but Harley Dexter's closing threat—and steered around references to Jenny as much as I could: though not enough, I noticed, to keep Ma and Sis from perking up their ears, nor Ma from turning onto my face that wide-eyed gaze of hers, that seemed wider yet.

It was away along in the night, then, when I wound up my story, and by then my nerves were keyed so high that I'd lost any hint of sleepiness. And I'd no more than fallen silent when Ma spoke up in a slow and even voice, "So that jury's decided to let everybody go except the fourteen men they're to *hang tomorrow*"—grinding out those last two words—. "And I take it that still means they're to set the rest free this coming Sunday."

—I choked on a mouthful of cornbread, in spite of myself, began coughing and gasping—found Sis slapping me on the back, recovered my breath, finally got it out: "Yes—. Yes—."

Ma and Sis and I were the only ones up by now. Quite a while ago Montecristo and Jenk had stumbled off to bed. Scooter was long since asleep. After my answer to Ma, the room went totally quiet for the first time since I'd entered it tonight. Only all at once I heard what I knew could not be outside me: an odd noise like rustling whispers in the air. Exhaustion, exhaustion, I tried to convince myself. Then the flames of the two candles wavered and flickered, and the wick of one gave off a tiny sizzle. I flinched. And now out of the candle shadows flapping along the walls, suddenly two blacker shadows took shape, jolting the three of us seated around the dining table.

—It was Montecristo and Jenk, who'd crept in unnoticed out of the shedroom.

Montecristo said, "We been talking in yonder in bed, me'n Jenk. We wanta go with you to Milcourt tomorrow, Todd. You got the cap'm ball pistol and that Spencer carbine. I'll tote the rifle, and Jenk the sawed-off musket"—one thing I never had reported was Harley Dexter taking that musket away from me—. "Us two'll lay out in the brush till you give the signal, which you can do if they make a move again Pap. Then we'll all make a charge on them and have Pap rescued and out of there before them rebels know what hit them."

Sis jumped up and ran over and hugged them both close to her, crying like fury. Ma never made a move, but she had tears brimming in her eyes. It took all the control I could exert not to burst into tears myself—while at the same time I was marvelling at how much the tone of my voice must have conveyed: because all that I'd said outright implied that Pap was to be released next Sunday: no question. Yet even the boys picked up on the doubts I couldn't root out of my mind.

Getting my emotions in hand enough to speak, I said, "I reckon if that could possibly be done, boys, I'd rather have the two of you in the fight than any two grown men I know. But you don't realize—and nobody else could that ain't seen it with their own eyes—how many armed men the rebels have spying on any move you make." —All at once an urgency came over me to make it all clear to them. "You see, I had the same idey as you—that is, rescuing Pap—the first night he was locked up. And then a fair-size squad of men, you remember, met and decided it was no use to pitch into any rescue attempt. The situation's even worse now. Get yourself shot, that's all that'd happen—meaning the three of us'd be mowed down in no time flat. And think of it now. Where would that leave Ma and Sis and Scooter?"

—Just to see those two little fellows standing there wild-eyed and hopeless brought me lower in my mind, I thought, than I'd ever been before: how even they envisioned that unless something drastic was thought up and done, they'd never see their father alive again. Only that extreme, maybe, could have led me to conceive of what—yes, what might offer a faint light toward success—though for now I pushed it to the back of my thoughts, until I could look into it deeper the first time I was alone.

By now morning did not seem far away, with me wound so tight and blare-eyed still that I couldn't've slept a wink. On top of that, if I could actually flesh out the ghost of a plan I had in mind, I'd have to be in town before daylight. So in reality there *was* no time to mull it over. I had to leave now or let it go. So casual-like I said to Ma, "I believe I'll carry a few vittles with me today, just in case."

"Now!" Sis said. "You're leaving now?"

"I believe so."

—And thankful I was that Ma didn't resist, or ask what she could've asked: 'In case of what?'—but rather just wrapped up some cornbread, a couple of slices of sidemeat, a sliced raw onion and two boiled eggs. Then she did make a hesitating effort to get me to stretch out for an hour at least. But I just shook my head and made ready to go, filling my saddle canteen at the spring. Last of all, right as I was about to leave, on a sudden thought I went to the woodpile and picked up an axe to carry along.

From home into town that morning I had the light of the moon's last quarter to go with me—small glow that it was, even in the stark clear sky. And I arrived with barely time, before the sky began brightening for dawn, to make a half-circle in my route and wake up Thorne Maxwell at his livery stable on the north edge of town, so as to put up Comanche for the day. From there I at once hiked out on foot, with the Spencer and the axe both wrapped up tight in my slicker, the head of the axe sticking out to fool comparative strangers—counting on meeting no one else at this hour—into thinking I had nothing but tools in the bundle.

Straight down the west bank of the creek I went, even though by doing so I had to pass near the gallows tree—because that was the likeliest way to slip into the center of town without being suspected. A few other people were stirring some ways off, but I succeeded in staying clear of them, hurrying till I came to the last stopping place before the big effort itself. That place was a vacant lot catticornered from the rear of the Dayton Building. From there I spied out the situation, breathing a lot easier when I discovered that I'd remembered right.

When the Dayton Building was put up I suppose people thought a side street would soon be laid out behind it, seeing they'd included a big verandah at the rear on each of the two stories. Thus far only an alley passed this way, both verandahs out of use and stark vacant. Another thing, too, I'd had figured out correct: no guards at the back of this building.

'Here I go again,' I thought to myself—left the axe and slicker behind a scraggle of bushes, stole along the alley with the Spencer slung on my back by a piece of rope, together with the dinner package and the canteen. I crept up the dust-covered stairs, shrinking inside in dread that my form might be seen through one of the three windows I passed. No hitch though, till the only real difficulty came: snaking out over the railing of the top verandah, clinging to an eave and climbing to the sloping shingle roof of the verandah. And then, worse yet, stretching up to the rim of the parapet and scrambling over to the flat roof of the building. The metal roofing on that was tarred at the seams in bands wide enough so that you could move around as silent as a cat along them.

On the roof, crawling along to the front of the building just over the street, I stretched out on my stomach all tuckered out and addle-headed. And then be damned if I didn't quieten down so far as to drop off to sleep: dozed maybe thirty minutes before noises in the square below woke me up. Yet still I lay there confounded, sick to my soul from realizing what I must be a witness to on this day.

The plan I'd worked up I looked into again, clear now as never before but revealing more inherent dangers too. What had brought that plan into being was the suspicion—conviction, nearly—that Harley Dexter might find some dodge by which to send Pap to the hanging tree. All day long I meant to keep a watch on the square. If Pap was ever hustled out the door of the Dayton Building or the courthouse and into the death-wagon, Harley Dexter was certain to be nearby to watch him go. And Harley Dexter would forthwith die, before he could ever have the satisfaction of seeing Pap hanged. There was a hideous comfort, too, in the hollow throbbing of my bowels: that if Pap was pulled out to be executed, the look on Harley Dexter's face last night had already told me that he would be the one purely to blame, and so him alone would I have to kill—and not *her* uncle along with him.

And then, so far, the second part of my scheme looked promising too. My thought had been that with the sound of my rifle filling the whole square and reverberating between buildings—plus the great excitement sure to follow—no one could tell right away where the shot came from. In addition, I was banking on nobody suspecting that a sharpshooter could be firing from the top of the very building that served as a prison. Sooner or later, to be sure, they'd hunt out every last cranny within gunshot distance, including this one, but I felt the odds were better than even that I could climb down as I'd climbed up and be clean gone before they thought to look for me up here.

The sun rose but stayed hidden except where a flame burned here and yonder in holes torn out of the clouded sky. All vestiges of the norther were gone, a light wind rose out of the south. A warmer spell in the offing.

I dared not look over the parapet, but by luck that I took to be the first portent of success, four holes about six inches square for rain gutters opened on the courthouse side of the building. Not only could I see a fair cut of what was going on in the square if I pressed my face in close, but one of these openings I could well expect to use as a loophole for a shot.

In less than an hour after I'd made it to my lurking place, the ghastly routine of the day began. Harley Dexter, Matt Scanlon and two of their cohorts led Ramah Dye out of a doorway directly below me, the soldiers forcing everyone to give back and make way. Ramah could stand and walk with no difficulty, but his legs kept veering him this way and that of their own accord, even though the gallows-wagon was only a few yards away. Harley Dexter moved up to walk close on one side of Ramah, and Matt Scanlon on the other, and when Ramah swerved Scanlon's way he'd guide him back straight with his elbow, but when Harley Dexter had to set him right he did it with the butt of his rifle—made my flesh crawl as though he'd done that to me. Yet one gratification, along with a lacerating hurt, poured through my veins: if Harley Dexter ever fell in with Pap on such a walk today, either from the courthouse or the Dayton Building, from this very loophole I could not fail to send a fatal bullet through him.

Ramah Dye did his best to climb into the wagon on his own, but his toe slipped on the step and he not only fell, he tumbled into a heap as if every part of his body had collapsed. But then he astonished everyone by suddenly bunching his muscles and springing to his feet, actually succeeded in evading Dexter and Scanlon and ran a few steps before three soldiers grabbed him and began grappling him into the wagon, while he fought savagely—.

—From off to my right a loud wailing scream lashed out, stung me like a whip. Craning to look from a new angle of vision, I recognized Ramah Dye's daughter Rachel over there, fighting two soldiers to break through and get to her father. One of her brothers, Wendell, was there too, at one second cursing the soldiers for everything he could drag up, the next second pleading with Rachel to let him take her away. I'd never seen any person look so near to raving insane as she did. I nearly cracked my knuckles gripping the stock of my rifle.

The soldiers must have threatened to lock her up or worse, because she did settle down enough for Wendell to half lead and half carry her away out of the square.

By now Ramah Dye was in the wagon, where he flopped out on his back with all the fight gone out of him, his chest heaving—.

What?—what had I seen? I swung my gaze back toward where Rachel and Wendell had gone out of sight. Oh. A rocking chair on a front porch that jutted far out onto the street. And Preacher Tillman slumped in that chair, hunched like a man a hundred years old. Yet every now and then he gave one quick violent rock, and just as quickly arrested movement by scotching a rocker with one foot.

Till that moment it hadn't struck me to the core that this was Sunday, jarring loose in memory those Sundays with Preacher Tillman at his sermon in the pulpit. I knew then what suffering he must be undergoing to see the Lord's Day come to this....

The death-wagon was hitching away down a passage opened up by the soldiers, the people immediately flowing back close behind it, a dividing and reclosing wave that crawled out of sight past the edge of my peephole. I laid my head down in the crook of my arm and tightened my face to keep back the shivering, the weeping. On this day of any day yet I could not let myself give in to tears—not through all the stark and dreaded hours to come—nor to weakness, faintness. Yet here I was already near to passing out for the sake of Ramah Dye—and to think that he was just the first of fourteen, and the majority of them as close neighbors as he was.

So I just lay there, gone limp. If I'd had a mind to, I could have crawled over to the opposite side of the building and had a clear view of the entire route of the death-wagon, all the way to the gallows-tree. No, nothing to prevent me, if I kept my head low, from observing it all over the parapet on that side, the hanging included. Then came a sickening revulsion. I vowed I'd never look in that direction today, come what might, even if Pap—.

And then by a contradiction that I had to fend off, I wondered if I could truly hold to that vow.

So I stayed put, for what seemed like a long while, before I heard the wagon and the crowd coming back. I did look out again when noises told me the wagon was passing underneath—and didn't glance away before it was too late—before my eyes were glued to the scene: watched while Ramah's body was being laid out on a wagonsheet. Not till then did I notice that Wendell and the other Dye boy, Albert, had driven their oxcart into a corner of the square. They came over to where the body was stretched out just as four soldiers bent to pick up the wagonsheet, one at each corner. The Dye boys shoved two of the soldiers out of the way, and the other two dropped the corners they had hold of. I heard Wendell scream out, "Don't you handle him like a slaughtered hog, God damn your rebel souls!" Then he clutched his father's armpits, while Albert lifted by the legs, and together they carried the body to the cart. Rachel was nowhere to be seen—not till the oxen slowly wheeled and lifted their necks against the yoke and began to lumber away. Then from a doorway onto the porch where Preacher Tillman sat, Rachel darted out and stood at the top of the steps above the street, shaking both fists over her head at the whole squareful of people, screaming as if to burst her throat. Preacher Tillman sat petrified. And if any of that voice divided itself into words, I could not make them out: just howling and squalling and screeching so much like the cry of an animal that it speared me to the bone. Then all of a sudden she stopped, dashed out to the cart and scrambled into it, crouched and took her father's head in her arms, glared back at the crowd baring her teeth and snarling like a wolf as the cart drove out of view.

—And here I was left to witness murder and more murder—thirteen in all yet to go—oh God, for strength to watch thirteen friends driven to their execution today. And fear grew in me that I could not hold out to the end.

As time crawled by that day, it began to seem that the procession after procession from the square to the hanging tree and back would last forever and one day more. The sky cleared, to make matters worse, and the sun on the metal roof filled my hiding place with stifling heat, relieved only rarely now and again when a little wind drifted across. Every time a man was brought out of the Dayton Building, through the door squarely below me, I lay perspiring more than ever in my sweat-soaked clothing, as long as the wall at the bottom of my vision hid the man's identity. And when he came into view my jaws would slacken and my whole frame go into an uncontrollable trembling. No—oh thank God, no—once more it was not Pap. And in the midst of recognizing the next victim I felt a sting of relief, and the guilt that went with it, to see that it was Arphax Dawson, or John Crisp, or Eli Thomas—just as long as it was not Pap. What a pass to come to: that any awful discovery whatever was welcome next to the most horrible one of all. It was too much to keep under control, so as time went on I grew confused, as though losing my mind, full of hope one instant, full of despair the next, with one thought alone to sustain me: that this carnage must at length end. Yet, no. For as the number of men still to hang diminished, and Harley Dexter and Matt Scanlon swaggered on, as if confident of getting away with anything, I couldn't help believing that after the list of fourteen was exhausted, Dexter and Scanlon would go right on hanging other men for as long as they liked: or anyhow on through a few more that each one might want to get rid of—and no doubt about it, for Harley Dexter, Pap would be the first to go.

Later on I thought that if one other thing—one small action—prevented me from taking leave of my senses that day, it was this: once in a while, as Harley Dexter tramped along escorting a man to the death-wagon, pushing on ahead with his back to me, I'd draw a bead on him—keeping the gun muzzle just inside my loophole—and hold that aim till he was clear across the street—though I did take the precaution against a powerful compulsion by clutching the rifle stock a little way back from the action. I did not dare allow my thumb to creep up to that hammer, nor my finger to come near that trigger, lest I give in, throw a cartridge in the chamber and have done with it—.

So the sun climbed on to noon and then sank with unbelievable slowness toward evening. And still the fearful cadence went on: one by one the victims driven to the gallows-tree, one by one the corpses hauled back, the same impassive slave behind the same muleteam the whole day through. Toby, the slave's name was; his master was Isaac Bucknell, a lawyer. Toby looked at nothing, even though he kept his eyes on the mules or the floor of the wagon at his feet. He never glanced back at who or at what he was hauling.

Body and soul can endure only so much. By mid-afternoon, in a stupor from loss of sleep, every fiber of me beaten to a pulp by horror upon horror, I had scarcely enough alertness left for a single focus on the movements of Harley Dexter, while the last few men from last night's execution roll went to the tree and were brought back dead. While I remained aware of who the man was that walked or staggered or was dragged along between Harley Dexter and Matt Scanlon to begin his last ride, more and more I was conscious only that the victim was not Pap. As the afternoon light began to soften, and yet was a dazzling flood for me, with the sun setting in my face, I could only fear more and more that when the moment arrived I'd be incapable of recognizing even my own father—or if I did, incapable of shooting straight enough to hit Harley Dexter, not Pap.

—In your sleep sometimes you wander through a fearsome territory and there meet a family member or friend. Together you endure terrible and swift-changing events, with the air all around you full of chaos, and you helpless either to fight it off or avoid it. Then will come a transformation, the rising of another scene, with no passing of time between, and up floats a man who is the same friend or relative and yet another man altogether.

—This was the moment of half-sleeping waywardness I seized on to drag myself awake. Came the shock too of realizing I had eaten nothing all day—and a gagging at the thought of food. I couldn't recall, either, when I'd had my last drink of water. I took a few swigs from the canteen, gasping between swallows. I then concentrated every morsel of attention I had left in me on whichever man was now headed for the wagon. Carrying over from the muddle of dreams that vision of sensing two people at once in the same body, I stared at this man or that, each of whom I knew well, as though I must in seeing him for the last time draw some ardency of being out of him that I had never before known he possessed: as though I was already seeing the vibrant soul of him in existence beyond the hanging tree, and with it, still, the man in the body walking before me, away from me—. There went Wig Wernell, short and wiry and quick as a cat, forever joking, as I remembered him, then laughing in a low in-and-out panting many times funnier to listen to than the joke he'd told. Whenever he turned serious at any task, his quickness made him prompt and competent and committed. He moved like that now, as though to attend efficiently to his own execution—. There went Harry Kilborn, religious and ever serious about it, who climbed right up into the wagon as if maybe headed for preaching somewhere. I could feel in my bones, even at this distance, his assurance that he would meet the Lord in the air when the rope had flung him into eternity—. There went Wash McCready, said far and wide to be the ugliest man in the county, and joshed by one and all for it. He was rawboned and lantern-jawed, wearing his natural expression: the corners of his mouth drawn out against wrinkles in his cheeks so that, as people had always said, you couldn't decide whether he was about to laugh or cry or was just in pain. It was pitiful to the edge of hysterical laughter for a man that ugly to be hanged. There went—but no, to this day I cannot bear to go on calling up that procession of phantoms, not even this more than half a century after they were killed.

—Now when they came to man number eleven, or twelve—by that time I'd lost count—I was stunned by yet another wave of dread: if it so happened that Pap did appear below, and I killed Harley Dexter on the spot, they would interrupt Pap's hanging, wouldn't they? to look for the sniper. And if I made good my escape I would not see him die, would I?—I don't know whether I even remembered, at the time, that I'd sworn not to watch any hanging, Pap's included. Nothing was straight in my head by this time. Decisions, when they came, popped out of nowhere. This one arrived as firm and sure as it was sudden: I must watch the next hanging, either as what now seemed an essential substitute for witnessing Pap's death or, by some vague and opposite feeling, as a magical anticipation that might circumvent Pap ever being hanged.

—The wagon was now on its way to the tree; I dragged myself across to the east parapet.

The hanging tree was at such a distance that everything there took place in miniature, but, with the late sun behind me, clear as clear could be. The tiny wagon drove under the limb—the limb that reached out west, the limb balancing the trunk that tilted over the stream:

Just like a tree....

Never after that could I bear to bring the words of that hymn to mind, yet never could I resist soon enough to prevent them from coming.

Curt Locke it was this time. Alec Dunbar, once county sheriff and now the jury-appointed hangman, climbed into the wagonbed beside Curt, helped him to his feet, tied his hands behind him and offered a blindfold—which he refused—adjusted the rope around the neck—.

I got a feeling, suddenly, that I was verifying the report of the one little boy to the other, that first day—.

—Led him to the tailgate. Slung the loose end of the rope up over the limb—two tries that required. Got to the ground. Pulled the slack out of the rope. Called in two helpers to keep it taut while he wrapped it three times around the tree trunk and secured it. Signalled the driver—. Curt knew—we all knew—that if he gave a leap just as the mules jerked the wagon from under him, he might be so lucky as to have his neck snap when the limit of the rope snatched him to a halt.

The slave lashed his whip across the hindquarters of the mules. They lunged. Curt tried to jump. One foot caught on the edge of the lowered tailgate, scissored his legs apart, swung him forward and released him— he dangled, he twisted, he jerked, he fought to free his hands: it took Curt Locke a few short, eternal minutes to choke to death.

—I was puking before I knew it, puking not even having eaten for hours, a sudden violent upsurge and outspewing of all that was inside, of my very guts. Retching out of control, and gasping to calm down, fearful someone would hear me in the street below. Choking then, and clawing at the roof, in a straining to eject all to the smallest clot, crawling and leaving a thin trail of vomit behind me. By the time I was halfway across the roof I was too far gone in nausea and exhaustion even to stay on my hands and knees. I sank down prone, and almost as I did that at last the retching stopped, left off as suddenly as it had caught me. I then wrenched myself along to a clean place and flopped out loose on my belly, panting for breath, shaking as though I had a high fever.

—Well, nobody'd heard me: at least no change in voices and movement from down there to say so. Ought to have felt a great relief in that. But none. Nothing. Just dullness, helplessness. Couldn't budge. No desire to budge, even though having lost count I couldn't guess how many men remained to be executed. Soon I gathered from noises below that one more had been taken away, and then his body returned, to all of which I listened as though it was remote from any concern of mine.

It took a short and all-pervading silence to rouse me, when a spasm went through every muscle and brought me in recoil to my knees— what if I'd fallen so far behind in numbering that the fourteenth man was gone, and Pap was doomed to be the next!

But I was wrong, for hearing the disturbance of another man being brought out, I scuttled over to my loophole and recognized him as Paul Cottrell—and in that instant remembered that his was the last name Harley Dexter had read out last night. So I was confused, having counted only twelve, the other two lost to my dazed mind.

Paul was walking as steady as you please: he had a reputation for being a brave young man—and he was proving it. Now he was halfway across to the wagon. Then it happened, turning my bowels to ice. A man's voice cried out high and wrenching: "Paul!"

It came from the right, outside my frame of vision. I lay craning my neck to the limit, still not seeing, when it came again, three times: "Paul! Paul! Paul!"

And now I knew by the voice who it was: Paul's younger brother, Joe, about my age, who I knew looked up to Paul as few brothers do, or can, look up to a brother. Repressing sobs now grew so hard for me that in spite of my clenched teeth, and the hand gripping my cheeks together over my mouth, they came out in low squeaks and squeals.

"Paul!"—. Now I could see: four militiamen had surrounded Joe and thrust him against a wall, ordering him to be quiet in a low muttering of voices. He would not—.

"Paul!"

The pitch rose; he rocked his head back and forth; the frequency of the cry increased: "Paul! Paul! Paul!"

Colonel Ticknor appeared in my frame, ordered the militiamen away, must have thought less harm would come from letting Joe scream than from a scuffle in overpowering him.

Paul looked his brother's way just once, stopped unmolested to look, raised one hand high: a salute, a valediction. Joe instantly fell silent. And then, still calm, Paul walked on to the wagon. He climbed in, the wagon moved off. Joe did not follow, but once the wagon passed out of the square his voice rose again: "Paul! Paul!"

I stopped my ears with the last of the energy left in me. The world rocked. My ears rang, and the echo of that name followed me even into the dark vertiginous world where I found myself. And plugging my ears did no good, either, against that other, that also nightmare world: the wagon at length returning once more to the square with its burden.

—When I finally took my fingers out of my ears the square had fallen silent. I wriggled quickly to my loophole, I gripped the Spencer close. The sound of voices in argument rose up to me, from directly beneath, out of sight. I separated two from the four or five talking: Harley Dexter's, Colonel Ticknor's. Only one thing could they be disputing. The mob was thirsty for more blood yet. Permission was being demanded to go on with the hanging. And judging not only from the harsh voices but also from the rapid, uneasy shifting in what I could see of the crowd, it looked as if the mob might win out. For once I clung eagerly, as to the only salvation, to Colonel Ticknor's obstinate authority.

And before many minutes had passed, I knew that he had the matter in hand. His voice was brutal and commanding. He knew better than I did, until this minute, that a large segment of this mob, as in any mob, were cowards to the core and would always wilt when confronted by a man who would go any limit to assert control.

So I could know, for today at least, that it was all over with: know that inside the building beneath me—and I all but fainted now from gladness—my father still walked the floor alive.

—And only to think that beyond any doubt I owed his life to Colonel Ticknor.

16

BY NOW THE SUN had gone down and darkness was seeping in. The long day's noise fell off at such a rate that what remained hung like a silence. Soon the square was all but deserted, too, for the first time since the arrests began, as though today the town's population, gorged on blood, had slunk away to digest it. But no matter how sickening the emptiness of the square, it gave me what might be my only opportunity to make a retreat. And so stealing along, fearful at every placing of a toe, I crept to the back parapet and clambered down from the roof. And never glimpsed a soul while I was at it. Then wrapping the Spencer and the axe again in my slicker, but deciding after all against the danger of being seen on the street with this bundle, I left it hid in the bushes where the axe had been all day and strolled off, taking every precaution to appear withdrawn, preoccupied, even though every member of my body quivered from this day's burden of dread.

A short circling that seemed endless led me to the Maxwell Livery Stable where Comanche was. Once I'd paid the bill, saddled and mounted up, the compulsion I'd been fending off since I left downtown got the best of me: in spite of hell I'd drop by and visit Jenny before riding for home. For if ever I needed to see her face, surely that time was now. All those recent hours of abomination held me suspended in a void still, and nothing had come to me as a comfort on my walk back to the livery stable except an occasional mental glimpse of Jenny. That was enough, finally, to overcome my one misgiving: the likelihood of meeting Colonel Ticknor head-on in the Wharton household. Oh, but how could that be so embarrassing now?—I reasoned with myself. Look what he'd just done. Look at how thankful I must be to him. And yet, still.... No, no need to rush eagerly into gratitude. Not yet. Not till Pap was cleared and set free. So far it was too early—it would always be too early, until you saw how they worked out in practice, to comprehend Ticknor's irrational notions of justice.

And so, as you will when you've made up your mind against a strong inclination, even as all this was chasing through my thoughts, I was riding in Jenny's direction—and was not to be deterred even by noticing, as I rode near, a horse standing at the Wharton front gate that was all too likely to belong to Colonel Ticknor.

I got down and left Comanche with the reins draped over the paling fence a few feet from the other horse, swung open the yard gate, made it up the walk and the porch steps, and was approaching the front door, when—.

—Oh sure, there was Colonel Ticknor indeed, visible through the screen door, ensconced in a parlor rocking-chair, profile to me at first, then jerking up his chin with a domineering glare in my direction when he heard bootheels on the porch floor.

Too late to turn back—and well aware I was of having deliberately made it too late to turn back. I let my heels strike hard. And yet all along I was scolding myself: 'What! Afraid of him? Bluffing?'

As casually as I could, I stopped before the doorway, lifted my fist slowly and rapped on the facing—as I let fall on Colonel Ticknor what I hoped was a contained stare, in answer to that unwavering glower of his.

Jenny and Jane and Mrs Wharton were all seated in chairs near Colonel Ticknor, just out of my view till I stood directly in front of the screen-door. Jenny then bounced up and rushed over and chirped out, "Todd! I was just wondering if we'd see you today. Please come in"— spoken in an aggressively charming voice which I took to imply that she would not let me down, was ready to defy her uncle. And as I stepped inside she held out her hand in a coquettishly sociable manner. None of which got by Colonel Ticknor—nor was it intended to get by him. Made him widen his eyes—if a man can do that while scowling like a storm at the same time.

—All of that from him when maybe—I thought—he did not yet know my last name, had just seen enough to put him on guard: this boy in a homemade shirt and country suspenders holding a beat-up felt hat in his hand—this sort of kid trading smiles and long warm looks with his elegant niece.

Jenny did not falter; she just gave matters a further twist by speaking out in a low firm voice: "Uncle James, this is Todd Blair"—and I silently gave thanks that she left out any reference to me, just yet, as the one who'd saved her from the bushwhackers.

All Colonel Ticknor did was to go on sizing me up. And made no acknowledgement except for a slight bob of the head, and: "Colonel James Ticknor."

"Honored to meet you, sir." —What the hell. Anybody could mete out that gentleman-stuff without surrendering any territory.

And that gave me the jump on him, I figured. So I took the advantage. I put in with what I meant for sure to have out in the open: "Nathaniel Blair's my daddy."

His dark-skinned face turned a shade lighter—I think at the nerve of me putting it so calmly, because I sensed that yes, he already knew who I was. Then in an instant he got a grip on himself, went more rigid still, all the while scowling deeper than before. His complexion, I observed, was a little like Jenny's: which came close to driving me to open hostility.

But not so fast! Maybe it was myself I'd worked into a corner. I'd all but shoved that rightful gratitude to him out of my mind. So now what? How to get it said—or rather how to put it in my look, no more wishing to say it now than I had earlier, not knowing what was yet in store, nor what was at work in that implacable head....

Colonel Ticknor said nothing. The fact was he did have me in a fix now, and he knew it. Caused me to do a flip-flop, to speak out after all. My face took fire as I blurted out, "I hope, sir, that the men still locked up know it was you who put a stop—that is, kept the situation under control there at the last today—."

Wrong way to put it—but was there any right way?—I saw how wrong before the words were well out of my mouth; saw besides what devious channels the mind of Colonel Ticknor ran in.

"Control! Why do you mention that? Of course Captain Dexter would obey my orders."

Just like that! I came close to rapping it out: 'If *Captain* Dexter's so snappy about obeying orders, why didn't you give him some strict ones last night before he marched into the jury room?'

Only I knew too fearful well what the answer surely was to that—which was why I needn't overdo the gratitude.

Jenny had been scooting over another rocking-chair. I sat down in it facing Colonel Ticknor, but a fraction closer to the women than to him. Forcing myself as best I could to make this seem like merely a social call, I gazed around at the women with what I hoped was a natural smile, doing my best to keep the barbs out of it.

Jenny was about to speak, but I thought I'd better establish a point for Colonel Ticknor's benefit, so I drawled out to the women: "I was just fixing to ride out home, but thought I'd mosey by here and say goodnight to y'all before I got plumb out of town."

Ta, ta, ta...little social call...just friendly common folks, all of us....

Evidently that grated on Colonel Ticknor's ears worse than the gentleman-act had. Must clamp down on myself, damn it! Keep foremost in mind how ticklish my father's plight still was. Avoid riling this man with the power of life and death in his hands. Yet, there again, I had no experience, no earthly idea what to say to him. But just to sit there like a hick would not do either. Best to let this visit pass quickly, then, with a few remarks on hoping the women were getting settled and such, then take my leave—not even call Jenny aside for a few words, that eye of Colonel Ticknor's being riveted on us as it was. And I *had* achieved what I came for: a solacing look at Jenny's face.

So now I was just on the point of saying good-night when be damned if Mrs Wharton didn't swoop out of the blue with this: "Oh these last days have been so terrible! And I for one'll be thankful to Heaven when they're over and done with—. It is true, isn't it, James, that the jury has decided to free all the rest of the prisoners this coming Sunday."

Talk about a head that should never have had a tongue installed! And she saw her mistake, if too late—for not even she could miss the horrified looks on the faces of the two girls.

Colonel Ticknor's eyes had been on her as he listened, but now they shifted to me. And while I did not flinch under them, never in my life had I tried so hard to appear meek and gentle—while doubting I succeeded.

"The jury has decided that, yes."

But the tone of his voice was all too revealing: that he was flatly opposed to the decision. Meekness and gentleness, hell! how could I keep it up when I felt on hearing his voice like going for his throat—.

But still I did keep a straight face, and my lips clamped shut.

—Only Jenny could have known how to turn the tables, how to seize on Mrs Wharton's foolish remark to prod him with, put the finger on his brand of honor. Her voice was mild, and oh so becoming for a girl, but with an edge he couldn't fail to recognize: "Yes. And while I think the jury did wrong to conduct that 'group trial' last night, you did abide by their decision, just as you've said right along that you have to do, Uncle James. And I'm so thankful we have you in command, especially now, to see that their other decision's carried out. Without you that mob'd certainly take over."

I'd started out holding my breath, but by the time Jenny finished I could almost have chuckled. Those words putting it all on the table made him wince, even if he did keep that jaw of his set rigid.

He couldn't stand that corner he was in for long, though. Just had to change the subject: "Blairs. Let me see. I believe your family lives out yonder in that...Upshur Community, don't you?"

—He knew damned well we did.

"We do live out there, yes sir."

I caught myself wishing hard just then that Ma hadn't dinned it into me always to say 'sir' and 'm'am' to my elders. For I sensed what he was getting at: as much as to say 'that community's full of traitors' or the like. Instantly my stomach churned, seeing in a flash the faces of my neighbors grotesque in torture as they hung from that tree—one of them being Frank Upshur, after whose family the community was named.

Had me off guard, he thought, and Jenny with me. Leaned forward like a prosecutor: "Your father does belong to the Union League, or whatever it is, am I right?"

Jenny caught her breath in anger.

"You ask *him*," I came back, frosty.

No fazing Colonel Ticknor though. He clenched his teeth: "They *all* belong to it, the ones in jail and a great many more besides who're still at large all over the county. The Red River brakes are full of them, men out there never to be brought to trial. Free to undermine the Confederacy just as they please—. But then, as Martha says, the jury's come to a decision to let even the ones we've caught go free—."

He struck the arm of his chair with an open palm—Colonel Oldham had done likewise. Where was the distinction between the two men; and if there was none, what?— "This is a law-abiding state of the Confederacy. We'll follow what a citizens' jury decrees!"

—Not that anyone was arguing with him. But under the terrible vehemence of that voice I had to compel myself to bite back the words: 'You mean like today's bloodshed, so *legal* and all.'

But the fire he glared at me showed that he knew what was on my mind: which in turn sent him snaking around to another angle of the subject. He threw this out at me: "Even the best of citizens can only stand just so much...disloyalty. Or rather let's call it by its real name: treason."

I'd been dragged in over my head, but even yet I ought not to have undertaken it: that striking out for the other shore, "It ain't a crime, I reckon, to want to bring back the Union when they didn't vote to leave it in the first place."

Jenny darted me a warning look.

You could see how it got to him that a log-cabin kid could so brashly disagree with him: with Colonel James Ticknor, officer, planter, gentleman—this also a part of that disloyalty to the Confederacy that in his opinion showed what the world had come to—.

Colonel Ticknor then gripped his hands together in his lap and turned his eyes to stare ahead at no one, speaking also to no one when he began—making a damned speech!—in words that in a moment led him to where he appeared to forget our very presence: "The Union is over and done with. Texas is now the biggest and strongest state in the Confederate States of America—and it always will be. Texans decided this question in a free and fair election. The ones that voted the other way will have to abide by that decision. Yes, and what's more, *prove* themselves to be good Confederates. If they fail to, they're disloyal. Traitors! The men we've got in jail plotted to rise up in arms and go on a rampage slaughtering one and all. We broke them up just in time. And now what're we doing but turning them loose, and the county'll be crawling with them again. And all because of a few spineless men on that jury—."

"Uncle James!" Jenny cried out.

He came back to us, but by no means embarrassed: "All right then! The jury's decided—." Then pointing a finger at me, he snapped out, "You tell your father and the whole bunch of them this: we know they're traitors, and we'll be watching them close. Let any one of them make a slip, and he'll be jerked up before a court martial and sent to a firing squad. —And as for you, young man, I advise you to join the Confederate army at once. We've got a conscription law, as you well know, and if you don't volunteer we'll be coming after you. I'd also advise you, at the present moment, to head on back to your log cabin. My niece has better things to do than sit and talk with you. —And now! I must get back to my command."

With that he came to his feet as though worked by a spring. I kept a rein on my tongue, though I didn't budge. Mrs Wharton—bless her—more than made up for her previous mistake: "Why James! Please! Todd's more than welcome here in *my* house. And from what you say, I think you must not know what he did for Jenny!"

That hit home, all right—but aroused a response that did not even surprise me anymore: "Certainly I know it," he ground out. "Do you think anything of that sort could happen in this county without it being fully reported to me!"

Silence. But at least he did not stalk out. He might have done so, in a moment, if Jenny hadn't stepped up facing him and grabbed him by both sleeves of that Confederate uniform: "Uncle James! Todd saved me from being *raped* by a pair of bushwhackers."

He winced at her use of such an unadorned word: "Please! I understand." And turning to me, to my now gloating face that must have stung him hard, he gave a stiff dip of the head: "I'm greatly obliged to you for protecting my niece."

I bowed my neck in imitation of him, but I just couldn't let it go at that: "What the river brakes is more full of than anybody else is bushwhackers like them two." —And no picture did he require to know that I meant he ought to be using his precious command to go after outlaws rather than what he was now using it for.

Jenny sensed we could hit him straight once again before he escaped: "Uncle James, I realize you have to go, but let me say just this: some of the...men gathered around town aren't the good citizens you think they are. They'll take the law in their own hands at the slightest excuse—." Then she went too far: "Please don't allow them to do again what they did today."

Colonel Ticknor bristled: "As I told you before, my dear, the jury was fully consulted about the sentences imposed today. A group trial, as I informed you, and there is precedent for such a thing—."

That was just one time too many for me: "Consulted! Ordered by Matt Scanlon and *Captain* Dexter, you mean. I was right there, standing in the doorway, and saw it all."

I got a scathing look this time: that insolent kid again, was it? But before he could lash out, Jenny cut in, "I want you to promise me, Uncle James. Please!" Tears began running down her cheeks now—I could've sworn she brought them on deliberately— and that at least did make a crack in his shell—"I'm begging you to promise me you *won't let that happen again!*"

"All right, child. Yes! I do promise. But why do you not comprehend that you don't have to wheedle a promise out of me to do what I'm sworn to do as a military officer. The jury's made a lawful decision to free the remaining men. I'll see to it the decision's carried out. I for one can obey what the law orders me to do, whether I agree with it or not. —And that's more than some others can say."

With which he gave me the haughtiest glower yet.

For the first time tonight I had a firm enough hold on myself to draw conclusions as well as observe and react. Yes, it was just as Jenny had said the other day—which did not prevent it from being mystifying, at that: Colonel Ticknor had a wide gap in the middle of him. If talk coming from one side of the gap did not jibe with what came from the other, he never appeared to notice. To call today's lynchings the result of a 'group trial' and yet in the next breath to declare that he never veered from his sacred duty to uphold a just and reasonable law!

Crossing his arms so as to reach Jenny's hands, he unfastened them from his sleeves and lowered them gently—gently for him—and let them go. It sent creeps down my spine to see those bloody paws holding Jenny's hands; and also to hear him say to her quietly, "Good night, my dear." Then he stepped back and said, as though implementing some momentous decision, "That's that. Now I can't tarry." Then he dipped his chin to Jane and her mother—"Good night, ladies"—scooped up his cavalry hat and left—without so much as a parting glance at me.

I put it in words inside: 'He's more dangerous than I ever realized. There's a *gulf* running down the middle of that—soul.'

Jenny sank into a chair, trembling. Probably until now she'd never seen to the bottom of her uncle either, for all that she thought she had when she described him to me the other day. I stood there yearning for something to say, but nothing came. The most I could do I did: slid a chair over close beside hers and sat down.

For a couple of minutes all was quiet. Then Jane sprang up from her chair in a swirl of skirt, saying, "Mama? The coffee that's left!"

"Oh yes," said Mrs Wharton, Jane adding, "Listen, y'all. Mama and I still have a smidgen of that *real* coffee we save for special occasions. I'll run and make it up quick. What do you say to that, now!"

Jenny glanced at Jane with a quick headshake.

I spoke up, "No, no. I couldn't drink...coffee. Couldn't drink anything. My stomach...." I shook my head, and more fright came over me than when I was facing Colonel Ticknor—because what special occasion could Jane mean if not the jury's decision to free the prisoners, and how could we even hear of celebrating that when it might never come to pass!

"And anyhow" —I relaxed my voice as much as possible— "Ma and my whole family'll give me out for the night if I don't start home right away."

So then I said good night to Jane and her mother, and Jenny walked with me out to where Comanche was standing at the fence. The nearer I came to the moment of parting, alone now with Jenny in the dark, the more I felt my throat tighten over what I was resolved to say and how incapable I felt of putting it into words.

So I lifted the bridle reins from the fence and gripping them in one hand turned to face Jenny, who stood beside me, her face wondrously close in the darkness.

I said: "It'll be a week before I can breathe easy again. And what I mean is...what I want you to know is...Jenny, I may come to town some, or I may not, just depending. But if I do...well, we better not see one another. Don't get me wrong. If this was ordinary times, your uncle saying for us not to visit would make me that much more bound and determined to do it. But if I show up at this house before Pap's free, no telling how Colonel Ticknor's liable to take it."

Now that I'd let loose I'd have said the same thing in a dozen other ways if Jenny hadn't cut me short: "Oh yes, I know, Todd. You don't have to explain so. No! We can't do *anything* to tip over Uncle James's temper. We have to watch any move we make till your father's out of their hands."

Yet, for all my talk of caution, I threw it to the winds now, here in front of this house where anyone might ride by and see us. I let the reins drop, reached both arms around Jenny's waist, lowered my face to hers, and we stood there squeezed into a long kiss that left out time altogether—released me for the time being from the racking this day had put me through: those hours when the border between waking and nightmare had vanished, and agonies with no perceptible end to them had closed over me—as time might go by in hell. The feel of Jenny's body curves, the taste of her lips and tongue, the scent of her hair—the vision of her too, behind my eyelids shut tight—were the whole promise fulfilled of what I'd dreamed of in a woman without half knowing I dreamed. Here she stood tonight, yet also beyond tonight, beyond tomorrow, or next week, in the distance and nearness of an always bright and happy future—illusion though it might be—even while I realized that what made it all so nourishing to my starved soul was this day's ghastliness.

—I found my hands creeping over her back and down her body, in a sudden access of desire that sent me delirious. I pressed hard into her. She slowed me down—though in no great hurry—by grasping my hands and leading them till her hands and mine were doubled together between her belly and mine—and began to whisper, when I thought voices had stopped sounding throughout the universe, "I wish you didn't have to go, Todd darling, but we know you do. We'd better say good night now. Really we had."

It took a while for those whispers to tear me loose—and for her really to want them to. When our bodies separated, I went so dizzy I had to grip a fence paling and suck in a few deep breaths to regain my balance. Our hands would hardly unclasp at all, even when I was in the saddle and bending for a parting kiss, that lasted till I nearly toppled off—.

What finally brought us to was the distant sound of hooves. And even so, as I rode away, I turned in the saddle and waved my hat from side to side over my head. This time Jenny did not respond with any lady-like waving; she stood inside the white fence seen just from the waist up, dim as in a dream, one arm half-lifted, as in a goodbye too full of thought, too intense, for waving. Then the vague form of the rider we'd heard came into view far up the street beyond her; she disappeared, and I hurried on, then slowed for a cautious circling back to retrieve the axe and the Spencer.

As I rode home I thought, 'This is leaping too far too fast, but—.' Yet blocking my own train of thought did no good, for close on the heels of such interruption I still took the risk of creating bad luck by counting on good luck: thinking, 'The next time I see Jenny, Pap'll be a free man.'

17

THE NEXT MORNING I slept late, a rare thing for me, so the sun was well up for what promised to be a cool and cloudless day before I finally idled out of bed, my mind at first exulting in the thought that this was Monday, and so we had only until Sunday to wait to see the end of all this, and Pap at home once again. And for the early stretch of that bright morning, I was able to maintain that thrill of anticipation with no fright running cold through my blood as it had these past many days together.

After breakfast, though, one of the old aches returned: to see and hear and know anything that might be going on in Milcourt, to be present in case something did go wrong. Sitting in the doorway of the cabin pulling on my shoes, drinking fresh warm milk that Sis had just brought in from the cowlot—and wishing it was coffee—I soothed myself down some by announcing publicly: "I guess I better just stay out of town for the time being."

—That was in the main for Ma's benefit, who I knew was within hearing distance.

The clacking and whirring of the spinning wheel stopped, in a back corner of the front room, and I heard Ma's step approaching: "I didn't catch what you said, Todd."

"Oh, I say I reckon I better stay out of Milcourt for a while. I can't get in to see Pap nohow."

"I think so myself. Let all the tempers cool that can, and don't be around to stir them up, is what I say."

With that she hustled back to her spinning—but she must've sat there meditating at first, because it was a little while before I heard the clacking of the wheel again.

Then the lethargy that had kept me in bed so late and still hadn't let go entirely took control again, put me to drowsing, soon persuaded me that not only was going to town too ambitious to think of, but even ranging beyond the cabin door. So I just drooped there blinking out onto the world.

—Onto the farm, rather. And the tasks that'd been piling up during these recent hectic days began to penetrate my laziness as insistent demands. The last picking of cotton, for one thing, was yet in the field that ran down the near slope from the cabin, most of the late-maturing bolls now open—as helped along by the recent rain—a heavy speckling of white intermixed with the brown of shrivelling leaves. At least a bale of it there, cotton that with the bolls open we could lose anytime to a similar unexpected rain—cotton that would bring a good price, what with the value of Confederate money at the moment rising. Also beans dry on the stalk in the fall garden, to be gathered and winnowed. Also sweet potatoes about ready to dig. Also that newground field where I was when all this began, still to be grubbed—but that at least could wait till cold weather, when Pap—.

I pulled away from any more thoughts in that direction.

But all the while that I shied away from open expectation of Pap's homecoming, still I saw that I could do, without words, what brought equal gratification: I could put things in the order he'd wish to see them in when he came back to us. That ambition got me into motion at last. I soon had Montecristo and Jenk in the field with cottonsacks. Hearing the bustle Sis called out from the kitchen to say that as soon as she finished peeling potatoes she'd start picking too, and Ma volunteered to help after dinner. Before all else, to sort of link together what had snapped the day Pap was arrested, I went to the newground and from there walked over every field, in order to lay out what needed to be done. Then I flew in to picking cotton with the others. All that day we made good progress across the field, and the pile of cotton in the wagonshed grew, a sight so pleasant it almost consoled me against the fear of the unknown coming up at the end of the week—.

If my hope and fright for Pap could be put into actions as a substitute for worded thoughts, there was still that other absorbing concern that could not be: Jenny, Jenny, Jenny, in vision after vision multiplying in pain and beauty, went with me around the farm in an aura so powerful that I was sure it must be sometimes visible to all eyes.

Visible or not, late in the morning on Tuesday my absorption in dreams of Jenny was shattered by a thrust of unwelcome reality. I'd just gone to the barn with a sackful of cotton over my shoulder, emptied it, then walked to the spring for a cool drink. I took the gourd dipper from a nail on a sapling, lowered it into the section of oak barrel we'd sunk in the ground to catch and hold water from the finger-size stream that flowed up through a core of sand out of the hillside. As I brought the dipper to my lips, tipped it, drank my fill, I stared down into the slow eddy of cold, clear water held in its passage from earth to earth in that cylinder of rough dark wood. When thirst was slaked I turned to fling the water left in the gourd onto a bed of flowers that Sis was nourishing next to the spring. And as I turned I found Ma standing beside me, her hands bunched under her apron. A glance was sufficient to see she had something on her mind.

"You never did look up from the field," she said, "but Willun Hackett rode by here and stopped a little while ago. He went straight on home right away when he seen how busy you were."

"Who? Oh—you said Willun. What did he say? Had he been to town?"

"He just got in from town."

Why was I having to pry? "Well, did he say anything about the prisoners? Any news?"

"No. Only Colonel Ticknor run onto him. Told him a fresh company of volunteers was making up. Told him he'd better join up if he knew what was good for him."

"Why, he's too young! Even to be a ha-ha volunteer. And what about Brother? He's the age to be corralled."

"He left the country, him and four or five more about his age. Night before last."

"So the rebels figure to pick the boys up a little early, do they? Grab them before they can slip out of their clutches."

"That Confederacy needs boys to throw in front of guns. Blood. That's what the infernal Confederacy demands."

Why say it? She knew it: they'd be after me all too damned soon—even sooner if they let Pap go. Show my gratitude to my so-called country by joining up.

—But that wasn't topmost in Ma's mind right now, and she wasn't long in coming out with what was: "Willun said he was in town a'Sunday too—all day, though you didn't see him, I reckon. Said he saw you. Saw Comanche, that is, tied at that Wharton house. And besides.... Thought he saw you and Jenny Ticknor waving goodbye to one another later on, and you riding away. He was staying in town that night or he'd've caught up and been company on the way home—."

"Did, uh...did Willun just volunteer all this information?"

"He mentioned something about it. Alluded to it. Then I asked him a few questions. Why? There's not supposed to be any secret about it, is there?"

—Aw now, all this didn't even *sound* like Ma. So this must be getting to her deep—.

"Why no, no secret atall. For one thing, I had a considerable confab with Colonel Ticknor at the Wharton house."

"With Colonel Ticknor! Why, you never said a word about it."

The hurt in her voice began to make me wish I had—and had mentioned Jenny too, while I was at it. Because you could see the worst suspicion come over Ma in a flash: I was a green youngun being lured into the camp of the enemy by a pretty girl—when the chance of saving Pap's life, for all she could see, might ride on staying clear of such people—.

"You've gotta realize, Ma, that as hateful as he is to deal with, Colonel Ticknor's the only man that can see to it the prisoners're let loose like the jury decided—the only mortal standing between them and Harley Dexter invading that Dayton Building with his bunch of hellhounds to lynch every last prisoner, jury or no jury—. So yes, I tried to reason with him—or well, not exactly. He's not a man to listen to reason. You see, he swears up and down by his duty as a Confederate officer to see the decision of the jury carried out. But he can switch arguments fast—when sometimes I think he never even knows he switched. So...well, Jenny and me decided we ought to keep some extra persuading before him—her mainly, I mean. She begged and pled with him—."

"You mean you and Jenny Ticknor had that made up from sometime before? You mean you didn't go over to that Wharton house just especially and only to see Colonel Ticknor?"

—Boy, if Ma didn't have me pushed into water rising to my neck. And soon it would be sink or swim. I should've known that keeping more and more back from Ma and Sis as the complications grew—about my brush with the outlaws, about my vigil on the roof, more than all else about Jenny—oh yes, I should've known it'd all come down on me at once.

—But then suddenly an argument came to me: 'Why, hold on now. I'm nearly a grown man. What am I crawfishing for?'

Ma would not let up: "And if you two had a scheme she'd beg and plead with her father—."

"He's not her father, he's her uncle."

That silenced Ma for a second. But no longer: "With her uncle, then—to plead to save the prisoners—. Then why didn't you two realize it'd be better done between him and her, without the son of one of the prisoners being present—if he's as hateful as you say he is. To my notion he's far worse. He's a cold-blooded murderer, that's what he is. A *gentleman* that'll whip a slave to death. Or hang a poor farmer just as quick—."

"Ma! Quit it now. I don't for a second doubt he's all you say he is. The fact is, I know it. He's a fanatic. But you do have to understand the whole picture."

And be switched if it didn't sound, even to me, like I was defending him. I let my voice die out. The right words to go on with wouldn't occur to me. And I was still squirming around in search of them when Ma put in: "Picture of what, son?"

At that minute, of all things, here came Sis walking up—she'd emptied her cottonsack and also come to the spring for a drink; the two boys were still in the field, mercifully, though playing some game under a tree at the end of a row.

"Picture?" said Sis, and Ma started: too intent on looking at me to notice Sis approaching from behind her. Flustered, Ma said, "Oh, just a matter I needed to speak to Todd about. But the morning'll be gone before you know it. I better get on with the rest of dinner. And y'all go on back to the field. We got to get all that cotton in by the end of this week."

Sis looked puzzled, glanced back and forth. It crossed my mind, 'No use worming around.' But oh if there was any time when I should've held back—too late I thought it—for I'd already blurted out: "No, now. Wait. You're both here, so.... So I'll just let you in on how it all stands. I got acquainted with Jenny the first time I went to look up Colonel Oldham."

Sis paled, her eyes grew wide—.

"Next time I seen her," I said, "she was riding along where she had no business abeing, in the river brakes, with nobody but one old slave to protect her—. Now let me tell you the whole story. Two bushwhackers tried to stop her, just as I happened by. I got the drop on them and run them off—that's where I come by that Spencer. Took it away from one of them. Now you see, I thought too that old Ticknor was Jenny's daddy, and I'd already meant to ask her to put in a plea for the prisoners—for Pap anyway. And when I found out he was really her uncle, I still asked her—with better reason than I'd had before, seeing as how I'd rescued her from no telling what. So now...So now the reason Jenny come to town with that Wharton mother and daughter—well, I stopped by there Sunday night to find out if she'd spoken to Colonel Ticknor. And blamed if he wasn't there, and seen me...uh, before I could duck out of sight and leave. So anyway, Jenny put it up to him then and there to guarantee the prisoners' safety. He said.... He *said* he would."

Now then Ma wasn't part Indian for nothing. My voice, and surely the look on my face with it, would've shown any woman how matters had gone between Jenny and me: too far to head off. And to Ma that meant clamming up: she'd done her talking for the occasion, and maybe was wishing she'd brought up the subject some other time, when she could've been sure Sis wouldn't happen by. For Sis was ready to explode wanting to fly into me, held back only by recognizing it was Ma's privilege to speak first. But when she saw that Ma didn't mean to go on, she clapped out: "Jenny Ticknor! Why *I* knew she was that old devil's niece. She's from Tennessee. And her family's got a plantation bigger'n Ticknor's or Oldham's—."

"Did have. Did have. And not that big, not by a long shot."

Sis shrieked it out: "Todd! What in the name of common sense!"

"What in the name of common sense what? And who asked you to come up here and bogue into this anyhow! I was talking to Ma."

"Here now, you kids." —That appeal of Ma's to calm a quarrel between us when we were little. Sounded strange now.

Well, I didn't want a racket with Sis, but—. "Now y'all listen to me. You don't know nothing about it, neither one of you. She may be some akin to old Ticknor—."

"Some akin!" Sis mocks out. "A right smart kin, if you ask me, being his *niece*."

"Just quieten down now. Dadgone it!" I yelled out.

"Todd! Mahuldah! Y'all stop it. You hear me!"

—Well, I thought the world and all of Sis, and she did of me, and we hadn't got rubbed together the wrong way like this in years. But that scorn in her voice—downright scorn, fury, jealousy—when she spoke Jenny's name....

"Well, plague take it, Ma, if she'll just hold her blame tongue and listen—."

"Whose blame tongue! Don't you cuss me."

"It ain't cussing, dad blame it!"

"Oh Todd. Mahuldah. Please don't, please don't"

And the breaking in Ma's voice set Sis and me to glaring at one another: as much as to say, See what you caused.

Ma sank down limp on a rock next to the spring. Stepping over and sitting down beside her, I eased into talking in a smoothed-out voice that Sis didn't dare, at first, to shout down: "I want mighty bad for you two to understand what I'm about to say. Jenny can't help it she's Ticknor's niece. Can't help it either if she was brought up supposed to have nothing in her head only how to act delicate and catch her a planter husband. Then when her daddy died—."

Oh to be sure. Sis was amazingly well informed, and knew just when to lash out with it: "Her daddy was a slave-trader!"

Ma took a quick breath, aghast.

"At one time! At one time! Jenny told me all about it herself."

—How in the hell did Sis know all that, seeing she seldom went off the place. Some neighbor girl. Gossip. But had passed none of it on to Ma....

"And *that* she can't help any more'n the rest"—I kept it calm—"Brought up never to question her uncle, neither, be sure about that. But I soon learned she can see through him, and knows how to make a dent in that hard-shelled head of his, too—. And listen, Ma, you're wrong about it not being wise for her to hit him up in my presence. The more he has to pledge his *sacred* word of honor with people around, the harder he'll find it to go back on what he's vowed to do. He can talk his own self out of anything too easy: like letting the mob hang fourteen men and swearing it was legally authorized by a 'group trial.' Believe me now, both of you. If Dexter and Scanlon and all that trash start pressuring Colonel Ticknor, then Jenny may be all we've got standing between us and...the worst."

But not even the specter of Pap being hanged could prevent Sis: "And so this going against her own flesh and blood that Jenny Ticknor's doing is just out of being grateful to you for saving her from the bushwhackers?"

I meant to keep my head if I had to reach up and screw it on a few threads tighter: "Be reason enough, wouldn't it?"

"But you slither around by leading us to believe it's the only reason, don't you," Sis sneered.

I never left off meeting Sis's gaze, just tipped my head toward Ma as a warning not to quarrel. Sis flushed. Her eyes said, 'You coward! Hiding behind Ma's feelings!' And a shock of anger went through me. And then, as I was about to say more—I didn't yet know what—a strange muffling stopped up my ears, and then a moment of ringing pierced them—for I saw fragments of those appalling scenes again: the offering up of the fourteen men one at a time to the tree that stood in blood—the creaking of the wagon taking them away, the creaking of the wagon bringing their bodies back. I went faint, consciousness ebbing away, tipped out of balance even though my arms were rigid and braced pressing my ribs, hands spidered at my hips against the rock I sat on, fingertips clawing as if to dig into the gritty surface. A tremor began in my upper body and slowly descended through my feet and passed off, but a hard shaking then seized the core of my spine at the base of the neck and sent shudders down through my arms till they shook like an old man's with palsy. There before me in our yard, unrealized until this moment, stood the postoak with the swing on it—as I'd seen it days before—how many days? Would I ever in my life again be able to look at any lone tree without...?

"What is it, Todd? What's wrong?"

—Ma talking, Sis too, their voices fading out then coming loud again. Sis was standing over me, behind me, both hands stroking my temples. A black curtain drew itself across my eyes and then shuttered away, and the world clarified, while I sagged there drained of all strength. In a moment it began to flow back, as if through my emptied veins, and I could set in to protesting that it was nothing, it was nothing. The scene that had overwhelmed me I couldn't share with Ma and Sis: I still had within me intact the resolve that I'd never tell them about spending the whole day on the roof in full view of the hanging processions.

Sis now came around and sat down close on the other side of me from Ma. I took a sidelong glance at each of them, and saw tears in their eyes. Sis gave a few little sniffs that meant she was on the verge of sobbing. I myself blinked hard against the tears.

Ma it was who spoke, in a hollow voice: "Oh Lord, oh Lord, this is only Tuesday." Then she stood up, laying her hand on my shoulder for support. I ground my teeth in wrath against every rebel ever born when

I saw on looking up at Ma how much she'd aged in these recent days.

Next Sis sprang to her feet, snatched up her cottonsack and headed back to the field. Ma trudged wearily up to the cabin and disappeared inside. I heard the swivel over the fireplace screak as she swung the beanpot around to check whether the contents had boiled dry. I grabbed my own cottonsack and struck out for the field too. And when I saw Montecristo and Jenk still playing under that tree, I yelled, "Y'all boys cut that out and get back to picking cotton, or I'll come down there and make you wish you had!"

They scampered back to work. I flung out my sack to trail behind me, took two rows next to and a little behind Sis, and bending and plucking out cotton locks as I went, inched along down the field—.

The change in Ma's eyes when they fell on me after that—right from when we came to the house at dinnertime that day—was hard to single out. Love was there, as always, and sadness too: which was maybe the addition that kept her look detached from the crowding in of a mother's love, gave it a standing back and a waiting, the apprehension of not having the final say anymore, of a readiness to obedience herself even in mistrust that this son and child had put on a man's identity too quickly to be capable, now or maybe ever, of leading not following. Underneath all that, though visible, lay the heart-wrenching of forced admission that this son and child had without warning gone where she had no right to follow, into the sphere of another woman. What disturbed me most of all was the dread and suffering I could sense over that woman being who she was, but any stray hint of that pain in Ma roused me to a silent but no less fierce defense of Jenny.

As for Sis, she'd gone at the rest of the morning's work energetically, a half-scowl on her face, the wounded look in her eyes all too apparent anytime she dared to turn them on me. During the coming days she got to where she'd pout and frown openly, then whirl off out of one spot to occupy another, for no reason you could fathom. As much as I could, I stayed strictly out of her way....

Now by that noontime, concerning the farm, I'd become convinced of one thing: that with only the family working we'd never finish what we ought to by the end of the week, so as soon as I'd swallowed my hasty meal, I rose and said, "I aim to get that cotton out of the field somehow, and there's too much of it for just us. I'm going out to hunt up some hands right this evening. Soon as y'all're done eating, why hit it again. I'll be gone for an hour or two."

"What hands do you think you'll find?" Ma asked.

"Willun and the Hackett girls, most likely, and anybody else I can locate big enough to drag a cottonsack—. Now then, you boys," I said to Montecristo and Jenk. "you see how fast you can go at it. I'll pay you as much a pound as I pay the rest."

Then those two began to let out a clamor about how much money they'd make, till Ma hushed them up.

—Now at least I had judgment enough not to come right out and say what I had in mind, but then I was wondering about Sis. If I paid Montecristo and Jenk.... All I did, in fact, was turn to look at her, finally. She took me up with a vengeance: "Don't say it! *You* don't have to pay *me* to gather my daddy's cotton. Unless you're gonna pay yourself."

I just ducked my head and made for the door: "And the same thing goes for gathering the beans and digging the sweet potatoes," I threw in. "I intend to have them all out of the field before Sunday."

So I went over and hired the Hackett kids, and was lucky enough to catch several other hands from among the neighborhood boys and girls. Most of them I sent to the cottonfield, but put a few to picking the dry beans, while with a couple of helpers I flew in to digging sweet potatoes. With all the work going faster by far than I'd anticipated, late afternoon Wednesday we finished everything: sweet potatoes in the cellar, beans in the smokehouse where they could wait till a convenient time for winnowing, a good hefty bale of cotton heaped in the wagonshed.

Pap'd be mighty well pleased, proud of us....

Now I had just come down from the house to the wagonshed, after paying off the workers. For a few minutes I stood there content, looking down at the heap of cotton. Then I walked off, just straying around the outbuildings, and came up a little farther away in my drifting to the grove of timber a distance east of the cabin. I strolled on through it over to a glade at the far edge. A little way into that glade a big rock with a flat top rose out of the ground, gray and scaled over with a pale green moss. I climbed the rock and stretched out on my back, with my hands locked behind my head, and it elevated so that I could gaze far off: a pastime I'd always had a great liking for, this being one of my favorite spots for such. Away to the southwest from here was a layout that I loved with a deep yearning I could never account for. Close at hand was a low grassy swell that hid nothing important from view, just gave a nice send-off to gazing beyond: to letting my eyes roam across a dipping away of open glade and on down over the branch course past a couple of tall cottonwoods, and on up a gentle slope that had one patch of woods the right size in the right place. Beyond that the country began to roll, advancing at a good distance against the low wooded hills that make up the bulk of the Cross Timbers. At the farthest point of my view were two hills crossing at the base with a notch of horizon between. One hillside was bare save for two big cedars, the other solid timber—. Ever since I'd first seen it that notch had told me of some great and wonderful place lying beyond it, a spot never to be reached except by passing through that notch—a passage waiting to be taken some day in assurance of a glowing future—.

But now a shadow fell between my eyes and that notch, on this my first contemplation of it since Pap's arrest—a nebulous and portentous shadow to which any promise of the future was vulnerable: the frustration again of uncertainty over Pap's release. Even if it came to pass, and with all our goods once more in the oxcart we could manage to escape toward that gap in the hills, we'd be traveling as fugitives, refugees, renegades in the eyes of some: toward no wonderful country surely but into danger and privation—.

A new flash came over me. I sat up quickly. I said it aloud: "No, no. I am not. I can't just sit here and wait till Sunday. Town's not the only place where maybe something remains to be done: and something that might still make a difference. Colonel Oldham. What's happened to him? I'll go find out. See if he's worse or better. Sure, maybe his promise to help, assuming he's able to, is a need we're past now. Maybe not too...."

In that vein I went on justifying what was already clinched in purpose—. Oh, I'd steer clear of Milcourt: that was still my promise to myself. I wouldn't put temptation in my own way to swing by and see Jenny. But at the bottom of it all—and I didn't even fool myself on that score, let alone Ma and Sis—was a feverish desire simply to be moving in the direction of the place where Jenny was.

18

IT WAS APPROACHING NOON the next day by the time I'd wrapped up odds and ends connected with the last gathering of the crops—for one thing pegging down a wagonsheet over the heap of cotton to protect it till we could haul it to the gin in celebration of Pap's coming home. So I asked Ma to hurry up with dinner, which she did, and I sat down to a hasty meal before taking off for the river. All the while Ma kept giving me quizzical looks—for I'd said nothing about going anyplace, dreading to tell her and Sis, putting it off till the moment when I'd be ready to leave. When I pushed back my plate and blurted it out, both women laid down their forks as if they'd been trained to perform that act simultaneously—and both set in to voicing their objections at about the same time too. I didn't argue, just sat and let it soak in that I didn't intend to be swayed, which it soon did, and both of them fell silent. All I did then was ask them not to fret if I should happen to be gone all night, and repeated what I'd promised early that week: that I wouldn't go near Milcourt. But the look on their faces was plain enough: they were skeptical I could travel so far in Jenny's direction and yet stay away from her. Their disbelief shocked me, I must say, as did the flare-up of jealousy on Sis's face. Jealousy, for God's sake! Hurtful to me, and puzzling—naive kid that I still was, for all my recent claims to manhood. Why should Sis be jealous of Jenny? A sister jealous of a sweetheart?

Ha!—is all I can say now.

It was a relief, a comfort even, to turn my eyes from Sis to Ma, whose look was doleful and remote, as if she expected me to lie about a sweetheart, and did not blame me for doing it....

Right away I saddled Comanche and pulled out.

—Now if one other thing bore me along through those frightful weeks besides my dreaming of Jenny, it was to ride, ride, ride. In some ways, at some times, the riding was even more sustaining. For while I couldn't ponder over Jenny without being torn as much by fear and grief as by a disturbing joy, to be carried along on Comanche's back was pure exaltation. A heel touch, a cluck of the tongue, and he did the rest. At full gallop it was as if he lengthened under me. As though his hooves in reaching for purchase spun the earth beneath us. Like a perpetual outrunning of a big wind ahead of a stormcloud. Like a momentary thrusting of the war and the rebels and the lynchings behind us. Like soaring through that unique notch in the hills back when the prospect of marvels beyond it had not yet dimmed—.

Just as soon as I'd left home that morning, all of that was what I let Comanche loose to do for me, and gave him free rein to keep it up till we were less than two miles from town. At a lesser pace then, we circled wide around Milcourt, crossed the big open prairie glades north of town, skirted the hills and some flats thick with timber, came out at length on an eastward extension of Wolf Ridge a good distance downstream on Red River from where I'd been in the habit of crossing that ridge. I cut back southwest a little so as not to pass too near the Ticknor place, but then— well, I did not backtrack far enough to be out of reach of my curiosity—nor of the compulsion that soon got hold of me. So at what I judged was a bit southwest of Ticknor's place, I veered north in spite of myself, crossed over Wolf Ridge into the washes that descended to Red River, and ended up in a little open spot among thick brakes at what I estimated was near the Ticknor house—and as I did all this I shook my head at myself over and over for acting foolish.

So, anyhow, leaving Comanche tied to a snag in the shade of a big cottonwood, I stole along till I could see out to the east. And there at no great distance away were the buildings of the plantation.

—To judge from the number of horses in the corral and the trappings hanging here and yonder, a few soldiers must be around, though out of sight just now. No sign of movement at all till a slave girl stepped out of the house and stood drawing a bucket of water out of the well near the kitchen door. Then Mrs Ticknor appeared in the doorway and said something to the girl that I was too far away to pick up. The girl stopped pulling the rope long enough to listen, without turning her head, then nodded and went back to drawing water.

My eyes being so held by that little scene, I took no account at first of another movement, not till it became a drift of color at the right border of my vision. I gave that color an instant glance—meant to—and stood magnetized. For not a hundred yards away, walking along slow in a billowing of purple and white dress, was Jenny!

On pain of death I couldn't have prevented myself from doing what I did next. Not even giving myself time to think, I stepped into the open and motioned for Jenny to come to me, then jumped back out of sight.

—But then Jenny did not notice. She passed the girl drawing water, not looking at her either, and in another few seconds would've been past the line of vision along which I could expect to attract her attention. Once more, growing frantic, I stepped out of hiding and tried to signal her. This time, thank God, she did see me. Turned—picked up her pace—made a beeline for where I waited. And a long time it seemed, of heart-pounding fear that we'd be discovered, before she slipped into the thicket, and into my arms. And there we stood planted, absorbed in a kiss that snatched the two of us breathless.

Then I stood back gripping both her hands and gazed, caught up in deep longing, into her tender, wondering eyes. Only a few seconds of that before we were back in each other's arms again, cleaving tight, with Jenny touching light kisses along my neck, jaws, ears, driving me delirious. So it was a while before I could recover enough presence of mind to lead her deeper into the thicket, the fear overtaking me at last that the slave girl or someone else out there might glimpse us through the screen of brush. A little ways into the timber we came to a fallen treetrunk that I simply had to drop down on, heart racing, breath short, and pulled Jenny down beside me. Again we fell to kissing, then merely to clutching one another in silence—.

The same question was so much on each mind, when the time at length came for words, that we were about to ask it in the same breath. I saw and let Jenny speak first: "How do you happen to be here, Todd?"

"Just what I was ready to ask you, darling. My own answer is that I'm on my way to see Colonel Oldham again, see if he's sick, see—. Well, see what he *could* do if it falls out necessary to do anything. —Not that I believe it will, you see. But in case, just in case—."

That was enough said for the time being—more than enough. I pressed her to me again and we set in once more to kissing hot and heavy—. Till it nearly slipped my mind to take a moment to ask my own question: "What made you leave town, Jenny?"

She drew back and looked up at me, eyes wide and serious: "Not what, who. Uncle James made me, that's who—and you know why?"

"To get you as far as possible away from me, naturally."

"Yes, of course. And he was sly about it too—sly for him, that is. Kept on saying how worried he was about Aunt Mary—like she didn't have soldiers up here to protect her. But knowing what was behind his hinting around, I just wouldn't volunteer. Finally he asked me pointblank to go, and I was afraid it might be crossing him too far to resist."

"That was the right thing to do. We don't want him upset in the least—not till Sunday's come and gone."

We said nothing further, and in no time were so wrapped up in each other's presence that we half-consciously rose and began picking our way around thick-standing cane brakes and through dogwood thickets in Comanche's direction, without paying much heed to what we did, dawdling and kissing as we went. We hardly came to ourselves till we reached the cottonwood where I'd left Comanche—arrived there by surprise, really, as anything outside our little sphere of love and rapture would've been taken for a surprise just then.

"Oh," said Jenny, when she saw Comanche, as if she hadn't expected to find a horse here: as if in our state of being, movement over the earth by magic would've been not only credible but just a matter of course.

Comanche tossed his head in greeting. Jenny laid her hand on his neck: "Handsome is as handsome does. Remember?— But you never did tell me his name."

I could only wonder why I hadn't done that.

"Comanche."

Jenny gave me a puzzled little squint. I said, "You see, Pap bought him from a trader that claimed he was captured from the Comanches. And I guess he was, for this much I know: he's a jimdandy buffalo horse. Because we chased one down."

Jenny slipped her arms around Comanche's neck, pressed her cheek against his jaw, and soft and gentle said, "Comanche, Comanche. You carry my Todd safe wherever he has to go. And you bring him back safe to me."

That caught my breath in my throat and held it, and sent both my arms to circle her waist. She turned to wrap her arms around me and push her whole body tight against mine. I began kissing her hotly: from the forehead down over that tender face; to the eyelids, nose, lips, chintip, throat, and all along her neck. Till she bent her head forward and threw her streaming hair over my arm and shoulder. And now I kissed the nape of her neck, long and clinging. And when I finally drew my lips away, out of breath, she tossed her head upright and loosened her embrace long enough to sweep back her hair, some of it rippling over her shoulders, clouds of it settling in front to frame her face. Then those deep hazel eyes revealed by the hair tossed back fell on me with every meaning a woman's eyes can have for her lover, though instantly she bowed her head, a deep blush in her cheeks.

I guided her across into the thickest shade of the cottonwood, onto the little oval of still-green grass surrounding the trunk of it, and we sank down clenching one another—.

"The grass'll stain your dress," I whispered. I rose, stepped over and whipped my slicker and blanket from the back of the saddle. Well, but—a thought stung me. What about Comanche? Embarrassed, suddenly fumbling with the slicker and blanket, I muttered, "Just a minute—." And led Comanche into the brush and tied him out of sight. Rushed back, spread the slicker down first, then the blanket on top of that.

We lay down.

—All the taking thought in pain and dismay of the days just past went out of me in a quick lurch of time, delivering me, and Jenny with me, into a world where neither of us had ever been before. I slid my hands under the volumes of cloth that made up her skirt. Then bloomers, lacy around her legs just above the knees. A bodice tight-laced. I could only dimly know what clothes there were between me and Jenny's body, and could only fumble to handle them, awkward, and ashamed of being awkward, though it helped that she was awkward herself. And all at once shy, when it was my clothes coming off too. She buried her head in the hollow of my shoulder and began to tremble. All nude now, we clung to each other for a little while, a moment's pause blind and breathless for me in the daring of what must come next. I stroked her up and down behind, from her shoulders to the plump little bottom almost too wonderful to touch and stay sane. All of which drove me on to nuzzle a breast and take its nipple strutted hard between my lips. Then softly to slip a hand between her legs, that spread just enough to admit it. Then delirium burned up fit to shatter my heart, my whole body, my whole being. As I swung up over her, her legs spread and lifted to meet me. Pressing hard but doing my utmost to be gentle, I let myself thrust, sink, thrust, sink. She gave a sharp little cry or two, but these only led to further surrender, to a firmer pressure against me: to surround me, never to draw back. Then the spell of response one to another went into a rhythm of total absorption: to be wholly joined, immersed, then a retracting and a thrusting again, bringing another gasp from Jenny, only now in another tone. Then for endless, unmeasured moments all consciousness, and every awareness beyond consciousness, centered in the cadence of our bodies. When the culminating instant of panting release came, it was like a transformation into fire, like being wrapped in one flame with Jenny, a flame that burned us out of present existence and left us helpless and still and silent for a little space but in sure knowledge that soon we would rise up newborn, never to be the same again.

—When I was a child I used to wonder how angels felt. I used to think it must be the way their blood flowed that made them what they were. Because sometimes when I was a child my blood ran so light and swift and glowing that my body nearly soared out of this existence. And then I'd glimpse in a flash a presence like an angel hovering over my soul—who was really myself, and I knew it. For an instant that afternoon with Jenny, that childhood vision of rapture reappeared whole and vital to set my heart into a coursing of ecstasy—.

But no such ecstasy could last, soon had to fade before other powerful emotions that began to surge as we lay back side by side. And as the vestiges of angel flight dimmed, the dread and joy of the fearful present filled the channels of my being once again, and now with a power more difficult to comprehend than ever. In the space of a few minutes we had become man and woman who with a deep bond of love between us could stand up and walk across a world meant to belong to us. —But did not. A world denied us because lost in dread, even though suffused with joy. I shut my eyes tight against that dread, turned and again drew Jenny into close clinging, found a voice hardly my own to speak in a hoarse whisper, "Jenny, I love you, I love you, I love you."

—Yet those very words were pursued by terror, and in defense against the terror, desire welled up powerful, irresistible, till my breath caught then exploded out of me.

Feeling me gasp, Jenny lifted her head, anxious. Her movement touched off a shock that ran through my body and left me dizzy, as though whirling on a tilting surface where I lay. I struggled to my knees, wrapped my head in my arms till equilibrium came back, Jenny all the while clutching me in fear.

"It's all right, everything's all right," I whispered, and lay down again, taking her in my arms. For the time being desire had sunk to a simple wish to hold her tight, to be warm and still. In that state we subsided into absolute stillness. I petted her, rubbing tenderly up and down her silky back—whispering—murmuring: no words, little coaxing sounds. She drew one profound breath, then another, and another, and snuggled her face into the hollow of my shoulder. Time went out of mind.

—Till all at once, the dread still at the core of me communicated to her, she pulled her head away and sought out my eyes, tears forming in hers and gathering on the rim of the lids. Her face before me went into a haze, into a new field of vision where all outlines were shaped by the tears in my own eyes. An urgency to speak came over me; a knowledge too that speaking now was like reaching for meanings that words had never had before—like creating what they were to mean as they started in my throat—.

"We have to be together," I murmured. "I never want to leave you."

"Yes, Todd, yes. Never. Always." She bit her lip and trembled. My whole body quivered in response.

—No way back now, and none desired, from speaking on: "When all this is over with—after Sunday—next week—we'll find a way."

"We'll find a way, yes. It'll be hard, awful hard. They'll never understand, but we'll find a way."

"They'll have to understand. We'll make them understand."

No need for words to phrase who or what we meant—we already knew: and drew our breath in fear that even the naming of who or what stood in our way might confound the world we hoped for.

Jenny began shaking her head, tiny whimpers sounding in her throat. But never taking her eyes off me. And the tears now came trickling down.

I choked back my own tears: "If we have to we'll run off. We'll gather up what we can and head out for the nearest gap in the hills. We'll do it. We'll just do it."

—Yet crying out and kicking against the barriers before us could not make them fall. As I knew. As I knew.

Jenny came chiming in, "We just have, we just have to"—and repeated that till she broke into racking sobs. Yet still she gazed at me, never faltering.

It went all over me then how little we were saying, or could say—

and how much less we might be able to do. The many obstacles that divided us—the what and the who—made defeat seem inevitable. Which only went to wrench from my throat in wonderful tormenting words: "Marry me, Jenny precious. Will you marry me? Be my wife. Jenny, Jenny. I'll die if we don't get married."

"Oh yes, Todd. Yes, yes. I'm yours, yours."

—Uttered in anguish, all our vowing words, exposed to abuse by every human cruelty, by any mockery of event—those best of all words with their fresh meaning in our private, new-created universe. With those and all our other powerful words of bliss in peril from the dark times ahead, I struggled to surpass them by clutching Jenny hard again, turning us till she was under me and sliding deep and tender into her once more, our bodies soon moving in full and mutual possession.

After a long while, again as if outside of time, we began to return to this world, grew still, lay clinging to one another as if always to be united—.

—At first I didn't, I could not, or would not, take in the sound I heard: as of a voice somewhere in the distance. A voice. A woman's voice, it might be. Yes, it was a woman's voice. Several times the straining shrillness of it went past me through the air, before it penetrated—before I lifted my head and perked my ears, struggling to regain this world. Though even then I could not summon up alarm, for alarm still seemed impossible in the present, to belong only to the past or the dreaded future, a future against which I wanted to scream out the command to be delayed forever.

—As yet, with her face against my chest and a mass of hair covering her ears as well as half my body, Jenny had heard nothing. It was agony to think of warning her, letting her hear, bringing this day to an end, to feel crashing down on us the future that I was still in an inward frenzy to postpone.

—That voice was calling, "Jenny!" and then again, "Jenny"—closer but still far out beyond the edge of the brakes.

I had to begin, mildly, gently: "Listen, my darling. But don't be scared. No, please don't be. But do listen. I hear a voice. It must be your aunt calling you, but she's a long ways off."

Jenny had sat up as I started to speak, as I went on speaking in hope that the rest of my words would soothe her down, ward off the fright that came over her at once, that she could barely contain.

—And so there it was. The end of one day that at this peak of bliss and tribulation descended like the end of all days.

Jenny didn't panic, though. And already, as she hurriedly but smoothly got into her clothes, it all but rang out between us: the understanding, the pact of secret love ready for any deceit or craftiness to keep itself concealed from the world.

"Yes," said Jenny, in a loving, wily voice. "It's Aunt Mary. Oh, she won't venture in here, but I do have to go home right away. She'll send out a search party of soldiers if I don't show up soon."

—At that second came another voice, loud but also distant: "Miss Jenny. Miss Jenny."

"Cabus!" said Jenny, wrenching on the last of her clothes. "And he *will* come in here."

Yet when she was all dressed we took long enough for two deep kisses.

I said, "I don't know just how soon I'll see you again, Jenny precious, but it'll be the first minute I can."

"Oh yes, I know."

—Then she was gone, before I could warn her not to bolt straight out of these thickets: a warning she had no need of, for when I first heard her voice in answering the calls, it came from down near the riverbed, so that when she emerged in view she'd be many yards north of a straight path in to our meeting place. Soon after, the tone of all three voices told me Jenny was with her aunt and Cabus, the aunt's voice scolding but nearly hysterical with relief, Cabus going into spells of sudden loud laughter and whoopings of gladness.

—Silence now, absolute silence. Not an insect, not a bird. I lay on my back, still naked, a profound protest inside me against shutting out the last of this magnificent day by putting on clothes. And yet, tense and pulsing as every fiber of me was, strange to say I dropped off to sleep, into oblivion that might have lasted for hours if the sun sliding west had not sent a dazzle through a pinpoint hole in the canopy of cottonwood leaves to pierce my eyes.

—I was jarred awake, still to lie blinking for long seconds wondering where I was. Then in a rush my mind caught up with this world.

Yet not the whole of the world, not until I had turned over and risen to my knees. Then a sensation went through me that my conscious mind had difficulty overtaking: and when it did found me staring wildly at a handful of withering leaves among the green mass high up near where the sunlight had pricked through. Then once again, as on the night last week of the thunderstorm, I was wrenched into a state of being where for a stricken instant any tree—this tree above me—was an embodiment of the death tree. Only now that sense of fate was anguished by the anticipation of fall in that patch of shrivelling leaves, by this reminder that like these before their time, all leaves must soon dwindle and die: a dying of the year like no other, since none like this had ever transpired in my blood before, nor ever would in like manner again—.

—Now in our part of Texas the first killing frost, the true autumn, might occur anytime between early October and mid-December, ordinarily arriving behind the first powerful norther: the setting in of winter that the norther last week had failed to bring, in spite of the force of its arrival. That would have been no reason for troubling, except that the circumstances of today, delirious happiness and all, touched everything with a foreboding strangeness. As though that norther, in failing to usher in cold weather after advance signs of radical change, announced that the massacre, this eerie turn in the affairs of men, had twisted the seasons out of their natural course—. And then in the next instant—had division by instants been possible—a full image of the hanging tree barren of leaves flared up as a mass of stark branches enmeshing the ghosts of the men who had died on it. And how could I believe, carried away as I was now, that my father could escape joining them? For here was this familiar yet mysterious delay of autumn, forcing itself on me as a premonition of death. With an uncontrollable quaking in my soul I knew that from now till Sunday I'd be in terror that the first blight of winter would arrive before my father could be freed: decreeing the end of his life as well as the dying of the year—cold to wilt the leaves, to strip the limbs, and by fate dire and unfathomed to pluck my father out of this life.

Nor was that all. The unleashing of passion with Jenny was now haunted by a dark guilt: only to think that I'd surrendered to wild pleasure while my father lay in the valley of the shadow of death. Not even the knowledge that I'd been caught up helpless into that passion could diminish the guilt, not even the suspicion that all things including this passion were ruled by a universal injustice all the more horrifying for being inevitable: a diabolic, indifferent urge for the perpetuation of generations, a passion that required the death of my father in the operation of its natural and merciless law.

I struggled to my feet, shivering though not cold, fleeing such thoughts, and hastily dressed, forcing myself into routine motion, going to where Comanche was tied, methodically replacing the slicker and blanket behind the saddle, then mounting and putting him into an easy amble toward the river.

The afternoon was advancing swiftly toward evening, but I still had plenty of time to cover the distance to Colonel Oldham's before dusk.

Better to have been more alert, I soon discovered, for as I rode unwarily into the wagonroad by the river, I saw a rider coming along it, not far off on my right. He'd seen me first.

—But no fear. It was just Cabus mounted on his mule.

I pulled up and tried to appear casual—no other way out of it. And as Cabus approached, I called out nonchalantly, "Out for a ride, Cabus?"

"Yes—as you might say."

"If you're headed for the Oldham place, so am I."

"I'm not what you'd call headed for Colonel Oldham's, no."

He drew up beside me, kept his gaze on me for a little before he looked away. Neither of us spoke now till he came out with, "No, I guess you could say I was sorta looking for you."

"And I could only say that's surprising."

"So you could."

I left the next move up to him, as we sat facing one another, his eyes back on me now, Comanche and the mule a couple of yards apart. Cabus then shifted his gaze a fraction, again, this time toward the horizon where the sun was measuring the last hour of daytime. He might've been involved in the measuring, for any of him that appeared to be left in my company, or for any visible intention to speak before sundown.

Finally I got enough of it: "Well, I reckon I'll be moving along. You may not be going anywhere in particular, but I am."

All at once Cabus came out of his musing: "If'n it's no objection, I do believe I'll ride along with you."

"None atall."

We moved on then, stirrup to stirrup, Cabus's eyes still on the task of conducting the sun down: my task too now, for we both watched it closely. Then Cabus ended his part of that operation abruptly, broaching a subject meant to go its roundabout way to some other: "Gonna be harder times coming up than any we ever seen yet."

"Who'd know that better'n me?"

"Lemme tell you I'm hoping as hard as I can to see yore daddy and the rest of them men turned aloose."

"I'm sure you are. And I appreciate it."

"Letting them go free'll end one pack of troubles. But it'll turn aloose another'n, as I reckon you know. But what I first got to say's this: I done clean changed my mind about you since the first time I seen you. Thing is...listen, if I hadn't by now concluded you was man enough to take it straight, I wouldn't say to you what I aim to. I had you pegged, you see, as belonging to that sort of white folks I don't think much of—."

"I know. White trash. The ones that slaves look down on."

Cabus nodded. "That's right. Peculiar, ain't it. Course everbody's gotta have *somebody* to look down on."

"Does seem like it. And white trash, yes. Plenty of them around. And in this war some are floating all the way to the top."

Cabus nodded again, then: "But to come to the main thing. Any way you look at it, Miss Jenny's gonna have burdens to bear. Heavy ones."

—So of course he knew: knew at any rate that Jenny and I had met today. The evidence had been in her eyes, no doubt, when she came out of the brakes. I recalled hearing that distant whooping laughter of his. Not much ever got by Cabus—.

But I wasn't about to discuss the subject of Jenny, and Cabus didn't seem to be expecting any comment from me—.

"Again I'm banking you're a man that won't take offense when I say this: I just wish you'd go your own way and leave Miss Jenny strictly alone—. But then I'm pretty sure, too, that you won't listen to me. Nor nobody else black or white, in that respect."

And when that brought no response from me either, Cabus gave a deep sigh: "Course you won't. So let me put in this much more, and then I'll shut up. I'm just only one old slave, but, as I think you already know, if Miss Jenny ever calls on me for help in anything she's convinced is the best for herself—whe'er I think so or not—I'll go the limit to help her. Course I reckon you know it can't amount to much, my help. And I reckon you know, too, that if I fall down in Colonel Ticknor's eyes, I'll be in as bad a shape as your daddy is—or *was*, let's pray to say."

No, I hadn't been prepared for that: seeing that I would refuse to give up Jenny, Cabus stood ready to help us, for her sake, well aware that if Colonel Ticknor found out, his position, even his life, might be at stake. But then it was just the kind of loyalty he had shown before.

"I appreciate that." —My voice cracked as the words came—. "And though I have no idea what I can do for *you* in return, if the time ever comes when I can, I hope I can repay you."

Pause. Silence. And more silence.

Then Cabus: "That young lady's about all I got left in this old world."

Something else needed to be said. I searched for it, tried: "A whole lot of folks say slavery's bound to end, whichever side wins the war. Maybe then I——."

"Freedom!" Cabus couldn't help the mocking, the bitterness in his voice. "I wouldn't know what use to put it to if I had it. Too old and wore out. My wife's dead, and a powerful lot younger'n me she was. All we ever had's one child, still-born. Just as well. If she'da been quick-born justa been *sold*——. Miss Jenny ever tell you she's exactly the same age as that child. My wife nursed Miss Jenny when our baby born dead. Save her own mammy the trouble, don't you know——." The mocking deepened, but with a sudden gentle turn: "Though in this here case, I'm powerful glad my wife was there to nurse her."

The sunset clouds were catching fire. Suddenly Cabus tightened his reins— "Whoa"—at the same time scowling at the sun touching the horizon. I halted too.

Abrupt again, Cabus said, "I better be getting on back. You look after yourself. For Miss Jenny's sake."

"I'll do that. And you do the same."

He only bobbed his head, with a tight smile on his lips, and turned the mule and rode off.

I sat till the western sky swallowed the last rim of the sun. Still no need to hurry. I could count on being at Colonel Oldham's well before dark.

19

AS I WENT ALONG the narrow road by the river, trying to put thoughts of Cabus aside and mull over the best approach to Colonel Oldham, I became more and more uneasy that whatever condition I found him in, and whatever my words, this visit would imply a rebuke of him for not having done more to halt the trials. Still, since the trials had been halted, maybe I could leave the impression that I was grateful for his general good influence, and was paying a visit with that in mind as well as a concern for his health. More than all else I grew afraid of what might happen if his son was at home. Neither of us, I knew, could hide our mutual hostility, which would be even worse than before if Bill Oldham sensed anything about Jenny and me, what with every probability that jealousy would be added to our other antipathies. On that score my greatest worry was the Oldham girls, for if either one of them should happen to bring up Jenny's name, I couldn't fail to blush all over myself—a dead giveaway.

Still I stayed with my decision to go on, and in the twilight I reached the spot where I'd first laid eyes on the Oldham plantation, all of which looked the same as on that day such a short time ago—and yet different: as though years and not days had gone by, as though the eyes I saw with now had matured—or aged—faster than time could pass.

Today also, as I entered the yard, a fierce onset of dogs. Only now, so far, no Bill Oldham to challenge me, and it was a slave boy instead of Cabus who came running out to take Comanche. Colonel Oldham did not come to the door, either, but the older girl, Millie, did. And I was glad—because for one thing this gave me an opportunity to get some of my blushing over with. She was all smiles, greeting me with looks that showed she was aware of the attraction between Jenny and me, and broke out in a gushing voice: "Oh goodness, Todd, it's you! Come in! And come through this way. You want to see Daddy, I'm sure. He's resting in the parlor—. Daddy, it's Todd, Todd Blair, to see you."

"Tell him to step in"— Colonel Oldham's voice came faint but cordial from the room beyond.

By now I was already feeling more at ease with Millie, though my cheeks tingled. And along with my letting go a little, the gist if not the particulars of the secret between Jenny and me must have emerged all too plain on my face. So now it was Millie who blushed hotly—but still her gaze hung softly on my face.

As I came into the room Colonel Oldham rose stiffly from the sofa where he'd been lying and offered a friendly hand—the old firmness of grip was still there, though he couldn't hide the quiver in it. A slave woman standing nearby picked up a rocker from a corner of the room, brought it over and placed it facing the one Colonel Oldham now sank into—.

So here I was sitting down to engage in something like the old conversation again. The colonel's brows were drawn in embarrassment—anyhow uncertainty—but with no indication that he was ready to offer excuses or apologies. I wanted to save him such as that anyway. I'd learned—oh how much I'd learned since our first talk—and I wanted above all to make him comfortable:

"They tell me you've been pretty sick, sir. That's one reason I came."

"That's right. I have. I'm some better now though. And I'm obliged to you for your visit."

"The latest news is brought to you all the time, I'm sure. So you know that Sunday's supposed to see the wind-up of the whole business in Milcourt—all the men're to be turned aloose."

"I know it, yes. And I think I know too what your other reason is for dropping by: wondering what my part's been in all this, if anything. Am I right?"

I was ready for him: "Oh, no sir. I don't have to be assured you did all you could, even being laid up and all, and not able to get to Milcourt to tend to it in person—. No, the other thing I came for is to say I'm grateful. To thank you."

Actually, as far as I knew, he'd had but little to do with stopping the trials; but if somehow he had, my devious way of saying 'thanks' would give him an opportunity to say how much without any great flap.

What I found was that he'd hedge: "Well, fact of business, my health didn't permit me to do much"—but he made that sound like undue modesty, which I let my silence approve of.

It came to me clear now just where and how I had to lead him, but with a light touch, so as not to make a slip: "I spoke with Colonel Ticknor just after the last hangings. No need for him to assure me, but he did assure me, that he'll carry out the jury's instructions to the letter."

"Certainly he will. As he has right along. However wrong the jury may have been."

Yet there was too much the tone of one military officer defending another in his voice: nearly like Ticknor he sounded. I kept a poker face. How could he be so emphatic? 'What about that group trial?' I was hot to say. But then oh, of course, he could always blame that on the jury, and no doubt would.

I said, "Oh, I know,"—knew what?—"I'm happy to have Colonel Ticknor in command right now. No doubt about his ability to put down certain elements if it comes to that." —Really? I thought—. "And you know, I expect, which element I'm referring to."

He did, his look implied.

Then I nearly said too much: "Harley Dexter'd love to be judge and jury over them all. *Captain* Dexter, don't you know."

No, that wouldn't do. Colonel Oldham, I knew, would hold Dexter as scum, though he'd never say so to me; and he didn't relish seeing a tenant farmer a captain. Yet he appeared to suspect that I was casting a slur on the Confederate army. So I shut up.

And we weren't getting far as yet toward where I wanted him to go. The only real encouragement up to now was that Colonel Oldham didn't seem to be as sick as I was afraid he might be. But that just meant—well, what? We'd have to see.

All Colonel Oldham did now for a bit was gaze off into the distance. Then, "The best any of us can hope for in all this is to maintain a good conscience. What I've done I've done in that spirit. And I'll stick by that to the end."

—Now he did have me wondering. Was it guilt he felt about having taken a big hand in forming the jury in the first place? Because when most men—but a southern gentleman especially—took pride aloud in the robustness of their conscience, that usually meant it was hurting them—oh I was learning, all right. 'Now hold steady, hold steady,' I thought. 'The way he sounds, he couldn't know the whole truth about that "group trial," could he? Or if he does know, then he's a downright hypocrite, and I can stop wasting my time in *any* appeal to him.'

All right. Yes, I'd spring it on him. But wait, wait, wait. Not yet.

—Whichever one of us began it, presently we were both rocking in our chairs. And saying nothing. Finding things too quiet, I guess, Millie glanced into the room. Then so did Mrs Oldham, bringing me to my feet to pay my respects.

After that the two women left us alone for a long while.

So now it got to seeming that I'd have to be the one to make conversation, if there was to be any. And there had to be, because more than ever now I wanted my visit to look as if it had a greater purpose than any I'd expressed, and to make him think that in due course I'd come to that. But for the time being I just sat there, stymied, with any remark that occurred to me tending toward immediate reference to that 'group trial' that Colonel Oldham so far had passed over as smooth as Colonel Ticknor had, displaying what appeared to be just as great a knack as Ticknor's for talking out of both sides of his mouth. And yet I couldn't feel this was the case with him.

After casting around for something to say for a time, and then noticing that Colonel Oldham had dozed off, I was about to stand up, just to arouse him, when Mrs Oldham appeared in a doorway again and walked briskly over to her husband:

"John, are you feeling bad? You're so quiet."

Colonel Oldham was jarred awake: "Me? Why, I'm fine, Lizzie. A few things on my mind, that's all."

All courtesy as usual, Mrs Oldham said to me pleasant and friendly, "Won't you stay for supper—I'm sorry, I've forgotten your first name."

"Todd, ma'm. Todd Blair."

"The 'Blair' part I guessed the minute I saw you the first time you came. You have the family eyes."

That was startling, disconcerting: that a comparative stranger like Mrs. Oldham could spot at once those eyes we'd actually inherited from Ma's side of the family, the Bracketts; it was embarrassing, too, because I'd always thought such eyes were too large and clear for a man to be proud of—.

"No'm," I said, "I've got to be heading on home in a little while. It'll be away into the night before—."

Now why the hell had I said that? With nothing yet accomplished.

"Go home without your supper! Why, you can't do anything of the kind!" she protested.

"What's this?" Colonel Oldham broke in. "Go home? No, no. Don't hurry off. Besides, I've been studying about something. You spend the night, and—you and I might ride to Milcourt together in the morning."

Now that really jolted me. So he really had been thinking hard. Not dozing. Just his eyes closed.

"No, John," his wife cried out. "You're not able to get on a horse yet. The doctor said so just yesterday." And she gave me a sharp glance, as if I'd been persuading him.

"I've known that doctor to be wrong as many times as right," said Colonel Oldham. "And don't look at this young man like he talked me into it. He hasn't even brought it up. Seeing him's done me good, though, I can tell you that. Puts me in mind I ought to show up in Milcourt to see this thing brought to a close, since I had the big hand in starting it."

"John! John! Yesterday you were flat on your back with another spell. How can you know when they'll come on! How can you dream of riding a horse!"

"I reckon there's buggies, if the case demands it. But no, I don't need even that. I feel better than I have in a long time, and I suppose I'm the best judge of how I feel. Take it for decided, Lizzie. I'm riding to Milcourt with Todd tomorrow morning. And while we're making decisions, pick up that medicine over there and throw it in the river. It's working against me—. Now you'll stay all night, and keep me company tomorrow, won't you, Todd?"

While this went on I'd gone breathless, with a hollow heart. Too good to be true, I was afraid. To ride into town with Colonel Oldham! To see the look on Colonel Ticknor's face, and Harley Dexter's. To rest assured that no mob—no commander—nobody!—would dare to lift a finger to interfere with the release of the prisoners. And already my mind was running on ahead: how to get Colonel Oldham put up in the Wharton house, keep him in town till Sunday even if he should begin feeling worse, assure that he'd be on hand when Pap was set free—and while we were at it, even keep Pap under Colonel Oldham's protection till I could whisk him away, out of Texas—. Yes, and I'd even join their damned rebel army to bring about Pap's escape, if that was what it took. There'd always be the possibility of desertion as soon as I came within reach of Union territory.

So with all of that throbbing inside me, I rushed in to answer, "Yes sir. I'll be more'n glad to go with you. I'll be honored."

—Mrs Oldham just turned her eyes sadly away, but the tightness of her lips made it plain she hadn't said her last word on this subject—.

Then Colonel Oldham settled another worry of mine unasked: "Because if you don't go with me, there'll be nobody to ride along but a nigger. Bill couldn't stay away from his company any longer. Left yesterday."

Even that in my favor. That detestable Bill out of the way.

From there on the evening couldn't have run any smoother. This time a meal with the Oldham family was full of ease and pleasure. Colonel and Mrs Oldham treated me like a welcome guest. She fussed over me. He sat straight and proud, though never stiff, at the head of the table, and continually spoke to me as an equal. Far from being frightened by Millie and Connie, this time I so enjoyed being near them, and talking back and forth while their eyes glowed and their cheeks went rosy warm, that at times I was exultant. Those two girls looked so lovely and delicious I wanted to hug them both. It was amazing how this day of total intimacy with Jenny had made me capable of thrilling at the presence of other pretty girls. Amazing too how thoroughly and naturally they caught the magnetism and responded to it—Millie in particular, while Connie struggled in defiant determination, as she had on the other occasion, to be as much of a grown woman as her sister.

Yet I couldn't fend off the twinges that came now and again over what Ma and Sis might be thinking, worrying that I hadn't yet come home—or picturing what they'd think, how appalled they'd be, if they knew where and with whom I was spending the night. And if they could know about Jenny and me—great God, it was beyond imagining!

Mrs Oldham sensed at least one part of my concern. As we were waiting for dessert to come in from the kitchen, she said, "I hope your family won't be uneasy about you not coming home tonight." And the guilt grew, and the enjoyment went out of the moment. —Easy to conclude, though, that while the edge of anxiety in her voice might be a token for me, it was chiefly directed to her husband. No, she hadn't given up on keeping him at home tomorrow. But it did seem now, besides, that she might be nourishing a hope I'd convince myself yet to leave tonight—sorry no doubt she'd asked me to stay—for without me Colonel Oldham, with no one but a slave to accompany him to

Milcourt, might be coaxed into giving up the trip.

"No'm. That is, yes'm. They may be a little worried. But then I've been away all night before, these terrible times."

"Oh well, yes," said the colonel heartily. "Selfish like, that never crossed my mind. I'll send a slave down there as soon as it's daylight, to let them know. You just tell him where he's supposed to go."

"Oh! No sir. That won't be at all necessary. I'm pretty sure to see some neighbor in town who'll be passing that way. Or if not, please. It won't matter a bit. As I say, they're used to it."

Colonel Oldham had apparently missed the horrified look that must've crossed my face, but his wife hadn't, though I made every attempt to squelch it, disgusted that I'd given myself away—. But oh, I could just imagine it: a slave riding up to the cabin, likely enough putting on a lordly air before these poor whites, announcing to Ma and Sis something like, 'Marse Todd's staying with Colonel Oldham, m'am.' And when he'd gone Ma and Sis sitting there in silent conviction that Jenny was behind it, and that because of a pretty face I was being hogtied and dragged over to the planter faction.

Well, the niceties of the supper and its conversation still went on afterwards during the parlor visiting, until I could almost relax, though in the midst of it all there would come a gnawing from time to time that I must not allow myself to be lulled into believing this was all that it seemed: an easy sociability with a kindly parental couple, two pretty girls shown off by a glowing lamplight, myself the young man unexpectedly arrived from a distance with an air of adventure about him and the natural claim of a stranger and guest on their hospitality. Yet none of this bland surface could hide the brutal fact that Colonel Oldham and his kind were responsible for Pap's imprisonment: an arbitrary power with an irresponsible military force and a mob to back it up.

The night was still young when we all went to bed, though I was glad of the opportunity for some much-needed rest. I had a big room to myself in the northeast corner of the second floor, with big windows looking out on the river from one angle, on outbuildings and the road going east from another. Only I was afraid to gaze out much along that road: it wasn't far to Jenny in that direction. I lay there with my face snuggled into the fresh-smelling pillow and burned with such imaginings of her that I felt close to sailing through the window toward her. What I did soar into when least expected was a deep sleep tumbling with dreams: naked, wonderful, tormenting dreams. When after a long time I was drawn away from those dreams by some hidden force, I found myself in a whirling confusion and then experienced a sudden penetration of consciousness—. It was just coming dawn and the first birds had set in down by the river. A cardinal. There he was. Listen. Then a mockingbird turning the air to song.

All of a sudden full awareness of what a terrible and a great day this was to be—and a greater one day after tomorrow. Oh, let there be no slip, when even the slightest one could spell disaster.

First thing I heard in the household when I'd dressed and was tiptoeing downstairs past the Oldham's bedroom, making for the concealment of the barn to take a leak, was Mrs Oldham's low and tireless-sounding voice urging her husband not to undertake the trip to Milcourt. I heard nothing out of him, but I was relieved to hear from her tone that she was making no headway.

When I got back to the house, everybody was up and active. Breakfast I dreaded, seeing it would be Mrs Oldham's last opportunity to dissuade the Colonel, and I was nervous she'd take the last recourse of trying to manipulate me to get her way.

Millie and Connie were so pleasing to look at, with their fresh dresses and bright hair ribbons and shy good-mornings, that my heart swelled and flooded. I remembered, and was ashamed, that I'd once called them, if only to myself, Colonel Oldham's frilly daughters.

We were well into the meal and as yet Mrs Oldham had said nothing, but from the looks she shot the Colonel now and again I knew he'd promised her to question me further about any possible emergency in town.

When he saw he could delay it no longer, he spoke up: "Could I ask you, Todd, about your talk with Colonel Ticknor?"

"Yes sir, of course."

"Excuse me if I misunderstood, but my impression was that you...no, I won't say have some doubts about Colonel Ticknor's ability to command in a critical situation—. You said, I believe, just the opposite. But that he...might be subject to undue persuasion from some of the private citizens. As I say, pardon me if I'm wrong."

Well now, precisely what he was getting at was longer in dawning on me than it should have been. I hadn't said a word that could've left such an impression; in fact I recalled making every effort to avoid it. But my inkling that Colonel Oldham had a suspicion from another source that something might go awry was still with me: that maybe he was putting a false face on the savage facts of the latest hangings but truly did not know the whole story. It was when I thought of who must have brought him a report—his son Bill—that I—.

Ah, here was my chance. I plunged in:

"I have a question for you, sir. What were you told about that so-called 'group trial?'"

"Why, that the jury singled out a number of men they believed to be the deepest into this thing, heard arguments enmasse, let some go and condemned the rest. As I've told you, I think that was a flagrant violation of their rights. Colonel Ticknor didn't think so, obviously, or he'd've stopped the proceedings. Nothing can be done about that now—except to see that it doesn't happen again. I sent Colonel Ticknor word by Bill, as he went that way to join his outfit, to be sure it does not happen again—even though it couldn't anyhow, because the jury's *decreed* that the remaining prisoners're to be set free day after tomorrow."

"Well, Colonel Oldham, that's just what I was afraid of. What happened in that courtroom was not the way you heard it. Your son couldn't've known because he wasn't there"—a good way around saying the sonofabitch would've lied about it anyhow—"but I was. I was present during the whole thing."

So I began and told him all of it from start to finish, and as I talked his agitation grew to such a pitch that I toned down my words all I could and still not gloss over anything. His eyebrows seemed to grow bushier above the storm of rage in his eyes. As I'd seen him do before, he gripped the arms of his chair as though for purchase to spring at somebody's throat. I knew, with pity, what was coming home to him, never to be deniable again: that he had beyond question been a mere tool for the hotheads, and that his own son had been the messenger to keep him in the dark.

The women all sat thunderstruck, terrified.

When I finished, a little space of silence weighed heavy on us all. Then Colonel Oldham's hands convulsed upward, he slammed one palm onto an arm of his chair—a loud spat—then reached out and clawed at my knee so sudden and tight that I almost leaped out of my chair.

"All right, by God! They put me in charge of this to start out with: the leading citizens and the whole lot did. Then by God, I'm still in charge! Till they throw me out of office, if they think they're big enough to do that. Yes! I'm striking out for Milcourt this morning, you bet your life I am. And I'll see to it the rest of this confounded affair is brought to a peaceful end—with the charges dropped against every man."

So all Mrs Oldham did after that was help the colonel get ready to go. On leaving I made a big show to myself and everybody else of kissing their hands when I said goodbye to Millie and Connie—and Mrs Oldham gave me the same privilege. I had a new liking for this family now—for Colonel Oldham most of all. It was triumphant to know that we could ride away together with assurance on both sides that we had before us the joint task of restoring justice and order to a community in chaos, in full confidence that we could achieve it—.

Colonel Oldham was riding a splendid bay gelding. I'd long since gotten over, and had turned into secret pride, how rough and rumpled Comanche looked beside almost any good-looking saddlehorse, let alone one like the colonel's magnificent mount. At first I thought that poor comparison was the thing on the colonel's mind as he kept casting looks at Comanche. He even seemed to be amused. I was glad to see him feeling so much better, from all appearances, which was such a welcome turn that I was willing for him to think what he liked of Comanche.

But his thoughts were on a different tack: "First one and another have told me, although he certainly doesn't look it, that your horse is one of the finest in the county."

"Why yes. He is. You can't imagine how smart he is. I was always told he was a Comanche pony, and here a while back I proved it...."

So I set in and told him about the escapade with the buffalo. I'd never before seen delight on Colonel Oldham's face. But now there it was, increasing, my story absorbing him as he listened, that story warming us greatly to one another.

So the colonel and I rode on at a leisurely pace through one of those fall mornings that stand among your best moments of being alive: air still and cool and clear; sun burnishing the sky, still low in the east—of that color telling you the sun was beginning to age for winter, though not as yet overtaken by the cold. And then the ravels of mist creeping along the river bottom timber here and yonder. Shreds of vapor like that had always seemed to me to carry a message I didn't even need to decipher to know the great meaning of—.

A sudden desire rose in me to put this morning wonder into words for Colonel Oldham's sake. But no words could I summon up that wouldn't have embarrassed me—and probably have been lost, I thought, on him. I'd discovered long since that most adults paid no such attention as mine to the natural world around them. I was about to manage, at least: 'Fall sure is coming late this year. Looks like the pretty weather never aims to come to an end.' —Till I was struck dumb by a gushing of that terror I'd suffered yesterday in considering this very thing.

Then to my astonishment he said it himself: "We're sure having a late fall this year. Some of the oldtimers, like my grandma, used to say a late fall meant a good crop another year. Don't know that I ever saw it work out just that way. But then never the other way either. Yet maybe it's still a good sign. I hope so. Because for next year we could sure use some better times—and not only for the weather and the crops either."

From there on the choice of direction in the talk should be his, I felt, although with the subject that arose I was soon wishing I'd headed it off.

"Well, I have strong hopes," he said. "Myself, I feel good about the future. This war can't go on too much longer. We've whipped the Yankees now at about every turn, so I don't see how they can fail to get enough of it soon—. Let's be frank about this, Todd. You and your father feel loyal to the Union. Yes, and I want you to know I admire your courage. But you're still Southerners, still Texans. And I have faith that with you and the others like you, when all's said and done, being a Southerner and a Texan'll come first. Now I hope, my boy, that I'm not rubbing anything in, only applying salve to a sore spot. My hope and my belief is that before long the Yankees'll leave us alone, and we'll all be friendly neighbors again around here, and all of us pulling together to make the Confederate States of America amount to something—. You're wondering, I see, why I say all this now—and I can see it irritates you too. But I'm saying it in hopes you'll bring it to mind when the time comes to let bygones be bygones and start the healing of the wounds. We'll need fine young men like you to do it. At my age all I can do is pass on a few words of advice that I think will help—."

I'd set my jaw, swallowed, scowled—in short, anything to hold back the anger: which did begin to cool, though, as I saw his intention more clearly. Yet I just couldn't come up with an answer. Till at last—and hesitantly—I said: "Well sir, one thing for sure. Neither Pap nor myself nor anybody involved'll have cause to hold a grudge against you, however the war may come out. Pap's often said he has a high regard for you, and it's plain now he knew what he was talking about."

Colonel Oldham reached over and laid his hand on my shoulder: "You tell him I appreciate that."

Along we went, then, holding to the road toward the Ticknor place, still a ways from where the road branched and one fork led south toward Milcourt. The shorter horseback trail I generally took I didn't mention, not wanting to subject Colonel Oldham to any more saddle roughness than necessary. But then shortly before we came to the head of even that trail he said, "There's a short cut right through here. Let's take it." And he veered off into what looked like solid brush. But it wasn't. A trail new to me did run through, the brush scraping your legs as you went, a trail nobody could've kept to unless familiar with every twist. Single file we went, for about a quarter of a mile, when the thickets abruptly left off and we found ourselves in one of those clear little glades you run across here and yonder along Red River, a little ways out from the streambed.

Now directly ahead of us partway across the glade was a knoll, beyond which the ground levelled out again but right away rose into a grassy slope that came to a sudden end against a narrow band of thick timber, past one border of which you could see a brushy watercourse snaking away upward between bald slopes that merged into the knobs mounting toward Wolf Ridge.

Colonel Oldham reined in his gelding. I rode up beside him. The sun was heating up the glade. His breath was quick. He took off his hat, wiped his forehead with a large white handkerchief. I grew uneasy to see him sweating so much, afraid a chill might strike next.

—That's when I first saw them: just as the colonel was stuffing the handkerchief in a hip pocket. They saw us at about the same time. They halted in their tracks: three men just emerging from the band of timber. Colonel Oldham, following my eyes, saw them.

I said, "I wonder who that is"—and softly I let my hand creep around the butt of my pistol, which I now had stuck in my belt, and glanced instinctively at the Spencer in its saddle scabbard.

"Nobody I recognize from here," said the colonel. "Though wait. I believe I have seen that sorrel before"—I was surprised at how trusting he sounded, a long way from how I felt.

We sat and waited for them to make the first move—and they did likewise by us.

—Why, oh why hadn't I carried the Spencer upright before me along the trail, then for sure I'd've been sitting here now with it lying across the saddle, primed for action.

"Well, let's just ride over and see," said the colonel impatiently.

"I don't think we better do that. Let them come to us. Or better still, let's whirl and make a dash for the brush. We'll make it before they can unlimber a rifle, and it's out of pistol range."

"Aw, can't be much harm in them, I don't think" said the colonel. "Not since they're coming from Milcourt direction, and not out of the brakes where bushwhackers'd likely be."

And before I could stop him he'd flicked his quirt across the gelding's withers and was moving on. I dropped in beside him—at a time like that you don't want any man to get an idea you're a coward.

Soon we'd ridden to where the hump in the glade lay between us and them. I was bursting to say it, yet it stuck in my throat: 'Let's run!'—all the more so in that up to the time the knoll hid them from us, those men hadn't budged—just letting us come within a sure range, maybe.

We rode on. At the point where we topped the knoll we were a hundred and fifty yards or so from the men. Then two simultaneous motions: Colonel Oldham lifting a hand to wave, one man there bringing to his shoulder a rifle he'd made ready while we were behind the knoll—. I can see that man to this day, branded in my memory.

I swung Comanche into the gelding, to make him skitter: no matter which of us the man had in his sights, any sudden movement by our horses could easily spoil his aim. In that split second I noted too that he was firing a muzzle-loader, and that neither of the other men had a gun out.

From the thousand times I've thought it over since, I've come to the conclusion again and again that the rifle report burst out at the same second when Comanche's shoulder clashed against that of the gelding, and my right leg knocked hard against Colonel Oldham's left. If the gelding had been as clever and agile as Comanche, the two horses could almost have wheeled as one. But the gelding's long legs got tangled; he stumbled, and fought to stay upright. For all that, still it was only a matter of seconds before we'd turned and gone back to where we had the summit of the knoll between us and the bushwhackers. But oh God, from appearances it was all to no avail. The man had not missed. Colonel Oldham was slumped in the saddle. I snatched the gelding's reins; I leaped off Comanche; I reached out to grab Colonel Oldham, to keep him from drooping further. But a poor hold was all I could get on him. He toppled; he slid through my arms to the ground. The ball had struck him squarely in the chest; the blood oozed and trickled.

—No time to check further. If I wasn't too late already. I whipped out the Spencer, flattened on the ground, scuttled on knees and elbows to where I could see over. The three men had decided not to advance, had disappeared into the edge of the woods, but I caught a movement between two trees. I let loose at it: Pow! Again: Pow! Wanted them to think we were both firing, since it was improbable they'd know I had a repeating rifle.

Colonel Oldham lay still and silent behind me. No motion in the timber either.

—Oh, but that pow! pow! went through me bone and blood, like the pounding of a second heart. I'd waited these many days—and waited—hogtied by circumstances at every turn from fighting back. Scheme and chase around and worry, worry, worry. Now I could shoot—cock the hammer, rack in a shell, pull the trigger, at an enemy out there.

I waited, finger on the trigger, itching for any kind of a shadow to fire at. Let those three men over there be the targets to fulfill at last the aiming in frustration I'd done all that day of the hangings. Let those three men over there stand for every sonofabitch who'd lifted his hand against my father, and my neighbors, and me, while at the same time I dealt vengeance for what they'd done to Colonel Oldham—real targets answering to real causes now, not just one mangy old buffalo—.

But the hard choice at hand soon pushed all that aside: how could I give Colonel Oldham the urgent attention he needed—still no sound from him. No reason to assume he was dead though—yet how could I tend to him and keep watch for the attackers at the same time, especially if they meant to wait us out?

—Yes, it was worth the try, precious as my ammunition was. If they were lying in wait, it must be they couldn't see any sign of me, for they hadn't fired. I did it—pow! pow! pow!—the shots placed in a line across the wood's edge.

It worked. Made them think there'd been more men behind us, that they were outnumbered. In a minute I saw all of them cautiously leading their horses into the brush of a draw on the other side of the woods: caught glimpses of them mounting, then picking their way through the brush in the opposite direction, probably thinking they were out of my line of vision.

Pow! Pow! Pow! And my heart sang to the rhythm. How close I came, or whether I scored a hit, I never knew. All three men bent low in the saddle as they left the brush and tore out at a dead run, weaving along a slope onto the knobs, in the direction of Milcourt.

—Neither did I ever know who they were. None of them resembled the bushwhackers I'd met up with earlier—.

Springing up I rushed back to Colonel Oldham and knelt beside him. Sprawled in his own bloodflow, he was as white in the face as the highest cloud, and already had that far-off, inscrutable look of the dead. Still I pressed my ear close to the blood stickiness of his chest, felt earnestly for a pulse, put my ear almost against the half-open mouth and the nose.

No doubt whatever: he was dead.

As yet the body was warm enough to be flexible. By straining and straining I could lift and handle it. The gelding turned out to be too skittish to control, so I had to wrestle the body onto Comanche's back. He sagged his hindquarters to make it easier for me—just as he'd done on other occasions when I was loading a deer carcass.

The road back to Colonel Oldham's was ten times longer than it had been this morning, as I rode the gelding along at a slow pace, leading Comanche close behind. Though maybe I was wishing the road could be even longer, never-ending, or would lead toward another part of the world, like across the river into a different kind of a land. Up to that time I'd never dreaded a thing more—not the dread of every day since Pap's arrest, not the awaited moment of seeing the next victim emerge to begin his walk to the death-wagon that day of the hangings. The mere thought of what lay immediately ahead chilled me body and soul. The very thought of riding up to those three women with their husband and father slung a corpse across the back of my horse—.

20

STILL IN ALL, premonitions tingled through me that more sinister troubles lay in wait than the bringing home of Colonel Oldham's body. No way it could fail: the rebel hotheads, above all Bill Oldham, would jump to the conclusion that I'd either killed Colonel Oldham myself or else led him into a trap. Yet at the moment I couldn't dwell on an intuition of fateful days ahead, my mind already brimful with the dread of delivering the gruesome burden on Comanche's back.

—To this day I can call back every particular, every word, of that long half-hour at the Oldham plantation. No sooner had I ridden into the yard, to the usual chorus of barking dogs, than a burly slave came striding out—a man I'd never seen before. Froze in his tracks, but not for long. Taking it all in after his own fashion, he gave a sharp whistle that brought two more muscular slaves hurrying out. Before I could give orders—meaning to raise a strong voice to dampen a potential panic—these three men converged and took charge of the body, cut me off from it, wouldn't allow me to touch it. And to my infuriated amazement the burly slave snapped, "Get out'n the way, white trash."

Of course I couldn't take him up on that here and now—as he was well aware—but in the frustrated rage that went all over me, if I could have, I'd've whipped out my pistol and killed him on the spot.

Little time I had, though, to be occupied even with that, for in less than a minute word of what had happened blazed through the household, and the screaming and wailing erupted—among the slave women, as it turned out, since when Mrs Oldham, Millie and Connie appeared on the front porch, only Connie was whimpering, Mrs Oldham and Millie still too stupefied to react.

Then, panting and trembling but in control of herself, Mrs Oldham said, "Bring him into the parlor. And send somebody to town for the doctor on the fastest horse we've got."

I had no heart to say that a doctor would be useless; and neither, I was glad to see, did the slaves. I just stood biding my time at the foot of the front steps, while the slaves were maneuvering the body through the front door. The mourning inside the house had risen to pandemonium, with Millie and Connie drawn by now into the wild grief of the blacks, both of them shrieking and crowding against the slaves in an attempt to hover over the body, until Mrs Oldham ordered them aside. Her own response to the situation was to turn stony-faced with determination, and as she also was about to follow the body into the living room, the burly slave murmured a few words to her that she seemed not even to hear.

—I could not bear to keep quiet any longer. I stepped up to the porch to catch her before she disappeared into the house and began abruptly: "Three men came riding out of the brakes—."

But why go on? Maybe my words were lost in the commotion, or unregarded like the slave's. Anyhow at this moment nothing, it seemed, could penetrate the intensity of Mrs Oldham's concentration on her husband's corpse. Oblivious to everything, she pushed in close behind the others through the doorway.

Suddenly too weak in the legs to stand, I sat down on the porch steps. I'd wait—I'd have to—at the risk of my own safety. The militia at the Ticknor place would be notified in a flash, and soon they'd be hurrying this way. I ought to beat the news to Milcourt, also, to be the first to carry it to Colonel Ticknor. And if I left this instant I could still outrun any other messenger.

But instead I sat, till the outbursts inside had settled a little, till I judged I might succeed in calling Mrs Oldham aside and getting a few words of the truth across to her. So I rose and walked in, stopped in surprise to see that they must've taken the body on to another room, and left Mrs Oldham standing alone in the middle of the parlor between the two rocking chairs where Colonel Oldham and I had conversed yesterday—or better say a century ago.

Hearing my steps, she turned her eyes on me—they told me she now knew that he was dead—and said simply, "Todd"—not in welcome, not in hostility, but as if to someone she was expected to know but required only to identify by name.

I said, "Could I have a word with you, ma'm? Out on the porch"—because if Millie or Connie should happen in now, it would tear me apart.

She walked behind me toward the door, silent, obedient. And kept the same gait when I stood aside to let her precede me. Once through the door she came to an abrupt halt, cast down her eyes as if the world at large was overwhelming, and leaned against the door-facing, rigid and distracted—.

"Three men came riding out of the brakes. Colonel Oldham thought he recognized one of the horses. I'm satisfied he did. Some horse stolen hereabouts—." It seemed of the utmost importance that I be terse and exact: I'd be called on for an account any number of times, and one telling must never contradict another—. "As we rode toward them, one levelled on Colonel Oldham with a rifle and shot him. I was able to get us both behind higher ground and fire back, but they got away. Bushwhackers. None of them—."

Not a thing I said appeared to interest her. At least listening now, yes, but remotely. Yet what really stopped my words at that second was not her indifference, it was a click in my mind, and the word 'Lie!' And then a rapid fumbling for what that lie might achieve, one that could roll right off my tongue: that one of the men, or two? were the same bushwhackers I'd rescued Jenny from. Who would ever know...?

"None of them was any Union men I know, and I think I know all the Union men around here. Bushwhackers. Nothing else."

Oh, it wasn't squeamishness that kept the lie stuck in my throat. I'd have uttered any falsehood without one qualm to save Pap's life. It was the outside possibility that I'd be caught in the lie, and that might spell disaster.

I shifted ground: "Oh how I wish I'd never've come up here. Then he wouldn't've been going to town with me, only to be ambushed."

—I thought this hint that she'd been right all along might shake her. But no, no visible effect from this either. Still just that concentrated listening, as if to pick up a significant sound from a great distance, her gaze still on the floor.

"And I'll have to say something more, m'am. I have to say what I don't want to: that is, what's apt to take place now. And it may outdo all the trouble so far. Colonel Oldham's friends'll be out for blood, and a many a man may die as a result. Union men, you understand."

With that she finally lifted her eyes, a first light of comprehension in them. Now—.

"Your son'll be here, as fast as he can travel. And uh...I ask you please to hear me out, and to pass this on to him. That I had nothing to do with Colonel Oldham's murder. I say this because he's bound to believe I'm implicated—."

"Implicated! *You!*" All attention now. Shocked. And a flood of warmth rushed into my heart: that it hadn't even crossed her mind to suspect me.

"Yes'm. Your slaves think so already."

"My slaves? Duff?"

"The real big one, if that's Duff. He never put it in so many words, but yes."

Suddenly she saw the need for authority over the slaves. She stood looking dazed, resolute as ever and yet indecisive. And I could sense the shadow of habit in her thought: John'll have to handle this. My husband—.

A twitching of the shoulders. A little gasp: "My son William'll soon be here to control the slaves." —She went red. Deeper water yet she was in, she saw. Her voice rose: "But Todd, why on earth would William blame you? Why, John was on his way to Milcourt to help your father! How could you possibly want him dead?"

"I'm just afraid nobody'll stop to reason that out, at a time like this. Over and over people don't. And if they don't lay it onto me direct, well, they'll accuse runaway Union men, and that'll give some of them a chance to say I led him into a trap the Union men had laid for him."

She was about to protest, a pained look on her face. Then she glanced away, flushed, realizing who I meant by "they," and even at this pass unwilling to deny what she knew to be her own son's nature.

She squared her shoulders, met my gaze again: "I promise you this, Todd. I'll make every effort I can to convince him otherwise."

My voice would tremble, I knew it, yet with her I didn't mind: "Mrs Oldham, no words can say how grateful I am to know you believe me."

"But it's *obvious* you're not guilty."

If ever I wanted to get on my knees and thank somebody, it was right then. I just stepped forward and held out my hand, hoping only that she'd offer hers and I could kiss it. But she brushed the hand aside, caught me in a close hug, driving me dizzy, with barely enough presence of mind left to squeeze her just as tight. And I'd simply have to escape as soon as she let me go, or I'd bawl for sure. And so the instant her arms relaxed I worked free and made for the porch steps, calling back, "I can't stay a minute longer. One chance in a hundred I can still beat the news to Milcourt—if the militia don't nab me on the way."

"God bless you, Todd. God bless you." Then a sudden eruption of sobbing that I rushed even faster to escape—.

In the dash for Milcourt that day I'm certain Comanche broke his own record—and I almost ruined everything at that, by forgetting until just a pulsebeat before it was too late to hide the Spencer in a handy place before I rode in.

But it was all in vain, to have lathered Comanche so: the news had arrived ahead of me, and had swept through the town like a prairie fire—later on I learned that Duff had sent a slave to the Ticknor place the moment he caught sight of me coming in with Colonel Oldham's body on Comanche's back. If I'd stayed at the Oldham place ten minutes longer a militia detachment would've overtaken me.

The mob and its onlookers, I found, had thinned out considerably over the past few days, and so there were not enough men around—yet—to gather in big crowds. But plenty still to keep up a constant turmoil in the vicinity of the courthouse. Right away I learned why: the jury, several military officers, and the leaders of the so-called citizens' group—whose vigilance had not slackened during the week gone by—were convened in the courthouse. And of course Colonel Ticknor must be among them. But since it was right at noontime, the meeting would probably adjourn soon, long enough for every man to have a bite of dinner.

In any event, for me it was wise to avoid the square, so I rode to an out-of-the-way place on Colonel Ticknor's probable route to the Wharton home, and waited. And before long he did come riding by, hastily. I followed, a good ways back, figuring it was best to accost him in the house itself. Having witnesses present, especially women, might tone him down.

So as soon as he'd gone inside I rode up, draped Comanche's reins over the paling fence as usual, walked up to the front door, knocked. Mrs Wharton came to see who it was, turning pale and scared when she found out, but all the same she rushed to ask me into the parlor. Colonel Ticknor must have heard our voices, for he came to the doorway of the dining room—they'd been waiting expressly for him and were on the verge of sitting down to dinner. He threw me a killing glare, and in two strides he was nearly in my face: "*You* were the only one with him when he was shot, weren't you? Led him—no, I won't say that yet. But he was shot by your Union men, in *your* presence. It's all over town. Deny it, if you will!"

"I'll deny it. That's just wild talk, Colonel Ticknor. But yes, I was the only one with him. We come up unexpectedly on three men in the river brakes, and as we rode toward them, one of them upped his rifle and shot Colonel Oldham dead. But a bushwhacker, that's what he was, him and his partners. Because listen, sir, I know every Union man in this county, and I'll take my oath anywhere before anybody there wasn't a Union man among them."

—But oh that temptation, again, that I was in a hair's breadth of giving in to: to declare that the killer was one of the renegades from last week.

"Of course you'd swear it!" he thundered. "Of course you would! Why wouldn't you lie to save their hides—and yours. You must think I'm easy fooled, fellow. Bushwhackers hold you up to rob you. This assassin had no such motive. Rest assured he recognized Colonel Oldham. Why didn't he shoot you! Hah, why not? It all points to a *Union* man. Whether you know it or not—and I strongly suspect you do—even your own report verifies it was a Union man, because it's an obvious lie."

Nothing I could do but stand there and take it: from this wild-eyed, rapid-talking maniac caught up in the spell of his own words, all of which made perfect sense to him. To think that this must be the sort of talk that'd gone on among several at this morning's meeting—.

"But please understand, sir. Yes, I was the cause of Colonel Oldham deciding to come to town this morning. But he was coming to help along the very thing the Union men want: the freeing of the prisoners—for me the freeing of my father. Why in God's name then would I lead Colonel Oldham into an ambush?"

"I haven't yet specifically charged you with leading him into ambush. Not *specifically*. Though for that matter, tell me this: Why did you persuade him to come to Milcourt anyhow, sick as he was? The prisoners were already scheduled to be released on Sunday."

—Couldn't say right out 'He wanted to make sure you'd uphold the jury's verdict'—"He wanted to be here to see it all wound up peaceful, that's why. And let me tell you, little persuading I did. If you don't believe me, ask Mrs Oldham, and Millie and Connie. Anyway, how could a kid like me have that much sway over Colonel Oldham?"

"Your part in it—*for the time being*—is all beside the point anyhow. So go on home and stay there—we'll know where to find you when we want you—. Mrs Wharton, m'am, I beg your pardon, but may we please have a bite now. I have to be getting back to town right at once. The meeting's to reconvene very soon."

—It was a jolt of surprise that he'd dismissed me. What I thought I'd seen building in his mind was to jerk me up before the assembly of rebels and try to break my story, wring a confession out of me. That he had no such intention led me to suspect that a decision was already formed in his mind, a decision that he had every intention of imposing on the rest when the meeting reconvened.

"Oh yes, yes of course," said Mrs Wharton, and hurried toward the dining room—but stopped in the doorway and turned to me: "But Todd, you stay for dinner too, won't you."

—Colonel Ticknor had stepped aside to let me pass out the front door. The lady's words brought rage, disgust, to his face. I almost expected him to snarl—.

A sudden great desire to stay, to see Colonel Ticknor squirm—not that easy to kick me aside, huh?—made me give him a firm, cold look. All that kept me from accepting the invitation was knowing that my presence would only increase the wrath he could take out on the prisoners—.

"No m'am"—I never took my eyes off his face—"I'm much obliged to you, but I've got to be getting home."

Throwing back at me the same kind of blazing glare I'd gotten from him often in the past few minutes, Colonel Ticknor turned on his heel and clumped into the dining room. —Jane, I now saw for the first time, was standing in this room, on the far side: good judgment on her part not to be seen acting friendly toward me.

So I gestured quickly to her, and to Mrs Wharton, in what was meant to be a silent farewell, gave both of them a low bow, turned and left.

With no satisfaction to be had from Colonel Ticknor—though at least I was for now out of his clutches—one more alternative occurred to me as I was mounting up: to catch Preacher Tillman before he went to the afternoon meeting. So I loped over to the house where he'd been staying—and found he'd just left, headed, I was told, for another house nearby. I followed his trail then not just to that house but also to another he'd gone to, only to learn there that he was now on his way to the courthouse. And so I never tracked him down, since by the time I reached the square the big meeting was in session again. I was mortally disappointed, because then and later I was haunted by the feeling that if only I could've laid the case before Preacher Tillman, however briefly, matters might've taken a different course.

—On dragged the afternoon, while I stayed out of the thick of things in sidestreets, till about an hour before sundown, when the meeting broke up—after a lot of hassling, I learned—and the word, the crushing word, reached us all: last week's jury decision to free the prisoners had been thrown out, and every man in custody was to be tried all over again. The new charge: accessories to murder.

Of course I'd known all along that something of this sort was almost certain to develop, and thought I'd prepared myself for it. But no, the shock of it nearly felled me. All of a sudden the prop of beating down my fears by counting the days till Pap's release was jerked out from under me, and there was no other support to reach for. Here I stood in the middle of nowhere with nothing left to hope for, nothing left except to stare ahead along a road leading over the brink of oblivion.

Again that day, as from time to time throughout the horror, my mind took refuge in witnessing these frightful events as passing in a dream. As if I and all the others involved were dreaming. The men gone on had dreamed their death. Ma and Sis and Montecristo and Jenk and Scooter and myself—we were bereft of Pap as a child will dream his father is lost: a terror of absence with yet the anticipation of a joyful end in the father's return on waking up. And Colonel Oldham falling dead at my very elbow, and lying in the spreading pool of blood at my feet—a dream. The ghastly pallor of his face, the awful touch of arms and legs dead but delaying to relinquish the last warmth of life—how could that be other than a dream? And Jenny—how could I have spent that hour of passion and glory with her, in that green place under the cottonwood tree, in other than a dream? —One little turn of one second, and, as with dreams, the waking up would come, and we'd all be snatched back to where we were beforetimes. As we emerged from the bloody chaos of the dream, the last sight to fade and regain its original brightness would be the hanging tree: every limb, every leaf, every invisible vein of sap, every hidden root would lose the stain and tint of blood and return to their condition of the day when we first forded the stream and passed under the shadow of that wondrous tree. And all that held us back from thrashing across the last border of dream was that we all, the living and the dead, must awaken at one and the same time. Nobody could leave the dream behind till we all consented at once to surrender it: all those who killed and all those who had crossed into death and all those in agony between. —And as that dream hung on and on, I came to move in a trance of assurance that it was my task to wake everyone up. As events went on into the lengthening doom of failure, I could barely keep myself from screaming at the top of my voice, day or night, into the face of everyone I met: Wake up! Wake up! Wake up!

That Friday afternoon—late it was now—I turned Comanche's head for home with a tremor in my guts that I couldn't control, and a weakness with it that I was afraid would wring me dry before I reached home, leave me with not even a voice to tell what I must tell. Vaguely, as I began winding through streets, I realized, as a matter of little importance, that I'd gone empty all day. Close on that thought came a repudiation of arriving home with supper as my first need. So in revulsion also against any other food, still I turned back and went by the one hotel in Milcourt. Supper was just finishing there, nothing left to set before me but a couple of slices of fried ham, with red-eye gravy for the cold biscuits, a little dab of lukewarm beans, and some muddy stuff they said was coffee but left a taste in your mouth like brassy water. After I'd finished choking down what I could and started again for home, I found the quivering far down in my guts still with me. In addition, now, I had to struggle with the urge to puke and the nearness of losing control of my bowels.

Night had set in when I came out of the last strip of timber between me and the cabin. I reined up and sat hesitating: dreading, dreading. Not that I could see much: dark shapes of the cabin and barn and the well-known trees. Candleshine gave the window facing me a dim wavering of light, and once when the door opened and closed I caught a glimpse of dancing firelight.

At the barn I unsaddled—slow—gave Comanche his oats, made sure a water trough in the corner of the lot had been filled that day. As I walked on up to the cabin, no one on the place yet knew that I'd come home—.

"Hello in there, y'all"—and I couldn't for the life of me make my voice sound like myself.

Sis it was who flung open the cabin door, who stood back waiting, anguish draining her face when she saw mine, and in her very body movements as she stepped back to let me in. I stood filling the doorway—. No. Not here. I must be inside, the door closed on the family, before I could open my mouth. Luckily it was only a couple of steps to the dining table, where I could lean, or I would have staggered. I said then in a hoarse, quiet voice—not my own voice even yet: "Colonel Oldham was shot and killed by some renegade, while me and him was riding along through the river brakes this morning."

Now the sight of me had been enough to stop the whole family rigid in whatever attitude they held when I walked in. In dead quiet they waited, and waited still, seeing that what I'd said was not all there was to be told. My breath grabbed up so short that I had to flop down in a chair.

Ma was sitting, hands poised and motionless, at the spinning wheel. She now broke the silence before I could, in a matter-of-fact voice that sent fear coursing through my body: "Now then today's Friday, I believe." And when no one else spoke she looked around, questioning: "Today's Friday? Friday? Will you answer me, somebody."

"It is," said Sis. "Hush."

I was thinking, let these words of mine be just as calm, just as steady as hers, like the commonest announcement—and I almost succeeded: "What they aim to do—Ticknor, and Dexter, and that *jury*, and all that rebel set—is they aim to put the prisoners on trial again—."

Sis's calmness vanished. She screeched out, "Why, they've been cleared, promised they could go home Sunday! What is it now? What could it be? They've been locked up under guard. How could they've had any hand in killing Colonel Oldham?"

"Accessories to murder: that's the charge. *Some* Union man shot Colonel Oldham, they *think*—which is all the proof people like them need. And what any one Union man does, they say, every Union man is accountable for."

—It seemed to me that my voice had to penetrate masses of cotton to reach my own ears.

Ma sat with her hands in her lap, palms up, fingers spread—sat there looking from one palm to the other, a gesture she'd picked up—oh God—from Pap, years ago: "Today's Friday, you say? Then day after tomorrow's Sunday. That's the day he'll come home."

Sis screamed out: "For the love of God, Ma, quit saying today's Friday!"

Unheeding, Ma said in a sudden change of tone, low but full of pain:

"Or the day of reckoning. Any day's the day of reckoning, if Colonel Ticknor decides it is. The powers of the earth."

Ma stared at Sis, then at me, wide-eyed, wild-eyed, nevertheless a gentle smile on her face, which faded suddenly: "Oh no. The day of reckoning? That's not come. Don't tell me it has. Not Colonel Ticknor—not Jefferson Davis—nobody but the Lord holds the day of judgment in his hand. The day of judgment is the Day of the Lord. On that day he'll bring *them* to trial—. Savior! Savior! Lord Jesus, judge of us all. Savior! Savior!"

Her shrieks ran through the cabin and turned my guts to ice. Then it dropped quiet, almost to a whisper: "Savior, savior..." on and on, her eyes back to searching her palms, head shifting this way and that, as if to say, No! No! No!

—How we ever lived through that night, I can't say. The baby hadn't woke up through all this, the boys hadn't let out a peep from where they sat scrooched up in a corner, though shrinking back in terror from Ma's outcry. When she'd muttered herself silent, and we all sat without a further word, Montecristo and Jenk actually dropped off to sleep, and when Ma noticed, she stood up and led them off to bed, then came back to sink again in her chair by the spinning wheel. Sis was at the dining table, head lying on folded arms. I sprawled and sagged in a chair till I found myself on the floor marvelling at how I got there. Then I went not to sleep but into a paralyzed waking. Things were going on outside me, countless rampant things taking place inside an invisible danger that gripped the world. One time the curtain of that danger drew back a small space and revealed two candles burned down to nubs that fed the last of the flames. Once a figure I thought to be my mother passed between me and the gleam of the fire, then blotted it out as she bent over it, than stepped away to reveal a leaping blaze, then retreated back, back, down, into shadows, as the dazzle of firelight filled my eyes. I thought I clawed my hands to seize at the floor, but still my fingers stayed locked stiff. Then the paralysis let me go, not for me to awaken but for the dream to close in. The Day of Reckoning. The Day of Reckoning. I didn't hear the words, I just saw what those words turned the world into. In some place close at hand the world was set to come to an end. I was desperate to locate that spot, for if I did I could prevent the end of the world. I wandered not in fire but with fire all around me. I passed myriads of people, or they passed by me, none of them aware that the world was coming to an end, while I was wild to tell them, and speaking, speaking, but putting nothing across. I could sense death, annihilation.

And yet, no! The others *were* aware, after all, but unbelieving, mocking. I saw Colonel Oldham slumping in the saddle, smeared, flowing yet crusted with blood, while I tried frantically to hold him up, while he went on sinking, sinking, slipping through my arms. —But no! he was not acting this out as true dying, rather as a ghastly pretense, a game: mocking also, playing the corpse and laughing in scorn at my stricken seriousness. And then! hearing the shots I'd fired, seeing a figure lurch and tumble from a horse—and that was also Colonel Oldham over there lurching and tumbling. —Besides, the Spencer was coming to pieces in my hands, and I couldn't make it fit back together. I saw the hanging tree, in glimpses far off through the flames, and I couldn't tell whether the tree itself was on fire—I couldn't tell whether Pap himself was at the tree, and I was to meet him there—and now and then it was as though the end of the world lay where the hanging tree was—oh to find, to reach, that place of the end. I had to, ahead of all the rest, for I alone would know what to do to put a stop to the end of the world. Yet as I rushed on to come to it, it always evaded me, turned out to be always in some other distance. Till.... Why, I too was at last infected with the mockery of the people passing, passing—all in play, all in play. And in horror every hope faded: any hope that in this game of apocalypse the pretending dead could stand up and be alive, all neighbors back at peace, the flames all put out, the hanging tree once more the great tree planted by the water—*I shall not be moved*—the tree welcoming all who came.

—Or again, the Day of Reckoning, the Day of Reckoning: the great and dreadful Day of the Lord. No longer did it matter whether I found the end-of-the-world place, nothing could halt what was coming to pass. The whole world would be gathered at the burning tree of judgment, the whole world coming upon it when they least expected to, from there to be cast into eternal flames and darkness, with great weeping and gnashing of teeth.

21

It was still pitch-dark when I came awake, struggling up from the sprawl I was in to sit cross-legged on the floor and let the world reel for a minute or two. I was alone. During the night sometime Ma and Sis had crept off to bed. So as not to awaken anyone too soon, I groped my way to the warm hearth and collapsed there, still addled, during a black stretch of time when it seemed I'd never gather the strength to perform the simple act of standing up and feeling my way to the door. Once I did accomplish that, and stepped outside into the chill air, the morning star flashing low in the east sent a pang through me like a message foretelling the ordeal of this day.

Daylight was still a good ways off, so trudging along to the smokehouse I fumbled around for the lantern and the tin box of matches beside it that we kept on a shelf. When I moved on, still in the dark, to the barnlot, lucky for me the oxen were lying close at hand, dim shapes at the edge of the woods. I lit the lantern then, and went about yoking the oxen to the wagon, in order to be ready for an early start to Milcourt.

For all my caution Ma must've heard me, or seen the lanternlight, since by the time I'd finished hitching up and was walking back to the cabin, smoke was rising from the chimney to drift as a smudge against the stars, and I could smell the preparation of breakfast.

Inside. To receive another thrust of fright on seeing Ma as she went about the cooking: her steps and the reaching of her hands through the feeble light of two candles—slow, deliberate—as if these familiar tasks were a shelter from panic, ruin. And now Sis appeared out of the dimness, hair rumpled, face drawn, and took up in silence her part of the routine. Like any other morning except for Ma's methodical fending off of chaos and the utter silence.

—No, not to touch either of them. No, any touch could shatter the fragile confines of the monstrous grief pent up inside us.

Just as we were sitting down to breakfast, the others all awake and with us now, I came to a decision I'd toyed with since starting to yoke the oxen: how to conceal the Spencer. —I'd retrieved it on leaving Milcourt the evening before and stowed it in the barn for the night. So excusing myself I went outdoors, and loading an old toolchest onto the back of the wagon I laid the gun in the bottom, wrapped in a ragged saddleblanket, and buried it under an axe, a shovel, and a bunch of other tools.

From the handling of that shovel I quivered and quaked all the way back to the house. And as I hurried in to the breakfast table, Ma glanced up as if recalled from a far-off place and murmured, "What did you forget?"—the first words out of anyone today.

"Just an item." Then I lowered my head over my plate.

By the time we'd eaten and gathered up what we needed for the trip and come outside, the morning star was glittering high up, but as yet with no streaks of dawn under it. The first of these glowed up in filaments of cloud while we were on our way to the Hackett place to drop off the three boys—and all but had to hogtie Montecristo and Jenk to make them stay. Then from there on toward Milcourt the pace of the oxen was like crawling for me, after all the ripping around the countryside I'd done of late on Comanche.

About halfway in, it came daylight, but even so I slowed us down further by taking a lower crossing on Walnut Creek, not daring to approach the town along the main way, past the hanging tree.

So the sun was up a ways when we struck the first outlying cabins, and from where we drove into Houston Street on downtown, it held a broken stream of people going sluggish to and fro.

—A glimpse of my dream last night came and went like lightning.

And here likewise no one spoke, again as if breaking silence with another living soul might crush all human defenses. And seeing who we were, many people moved aside to let us pass, whether out of deference or fear of contact wasn't easy to say. As far as I had strength to notice, most of those wandering the street belonged to the now shaken but still hesitant citizens impotent between factions. And as far as I could tell, we were the first of the prisoners' families to appear in town today.

But then soon, as if aroused by the warmth of the sun, stray talk did begin among the passersby, and by the time we reached the square I could endure to hear the gist of several remarks exchanged along our path: the jury was supposed to be going into session immediately.

And so they did. Colonel Ticknor had soldiers lined up solid on both sides of Industry Street, and down it, single file, came the jurors, their faces no less pale and grave than if they themselves had been marching to the tree. Preacher Tillman's legs quivered visibly as he lifted and placed his feet, his face rigid as stone, however, under the neat-set half-sphere and circle of his derby hat.

Then came my first electrifying shock of that day: Reese Culler and Isaac McGraw were no longer among the jurors, but in their place Richard Goss and Carlton Dawes, deep-dyed rebels both of them. No wonder Tillman's legs trembled, and he walked like a prisoner himself, which in effect he was, as the only level-headed moderate left in the midst of the hot-heads. Surely all cases would be lost now, were lost already.

Later on I pieced together what had occurred: Reese Culler and Isaac McGraw had simply not appeared that morning, had taken to the brush themselves to escape the clutches of the hotheads. That gang, to be sure, had two of their own stamp ready and itching to step into the empty places—oh, of course they'd been "alternates" all along.

We'd pulled up next to Ballinger's log store on the northeast corner of the square, in plain view of the courthouse front and the Dayton Building across the way. Ma and I sat elevated on the spring-seat, Sis crouching on the wagon floor close behind, her face squeezed in between Ma's elbow and mine, staring ahead—that was a fine way Sis had discovered for the three of us to be close together without great risk of breaking down. But I did take a chance on one more outreach: I gripped Ma's hand in mine, brought it to my knee and kept it there.

Now my eyes insisted on seeing and absorbing in near delirium all there was in view, in desperate readiness, as I clung to a last faint hope: that I might see a quirk in events to put me in reach of some saving move, some instant when I could seize the Spencer and open fire. And yet deep down I knew I was deceiving myself—. And another expectation besides, all too natural even in this lunatic whirl of events: as the only witness to the killing of Colonel Oldham, how could I not be called to testify?

—The first thing I'd expected was a transfer of prisoners from the Dayton Building over to the courthouse, while in fact they'd all been herded late last night into the top floor of the courthouse as a precaution against any attempt at lynching. But then the mob, swollen and seething since the murder of Colonel Oldham, had nevertheless gathered to storm the courthouse and drag the prisoners out to kill them. And Colonel Ticknor, for all his brags about law and order, had been reluctant to step in and quell the riot. To my amazement I found out that Wint Crigley, whom I had down as the most cringing of cowards, had stood them off in the courthouse doorway, swearing they'd have to shoot him to lay hands on a single prisoner. And they would have too—if I knew Harley Dexter and Matt Scanlon—if Colonel Ticknor hadn't in the end ordered them off, and they didn't dare defy him.

People here close to the center of events gave us a wide berth, and not much doubt now that they were afraid to be associated with us. That too had become bitter to swallow. Then, not long after, the first audible crisis ripped the tension. The families of other prisoners, coming in openly now on foot, in wagons and buggies, on horseback, arrived ignorant of the new turn in affairs, had come to town prepared to take home a free man—only to discover that the few previous days of sanity had been a delusion passing over this corner of the earth and vanishing, with stark madness the common course once again. A great many people remained for a time stricken where they stood, on hearing the awful news. Now and again I heard wrenching sobs, a wail, a scream. What got to me as much as anything else was to see men and boys, a few women, one lone girl, aimlessly leading around horses that I was certain no living man would burden that day.

And so for a long while the courthouse stood closed up and quiet, circled by a heavy guard of soldiers, and around them the members of the mob prowling. Soon I fell to looking hard for some communion besides mere recognition in one or another of the families of the doomed men. I longed for all of us to rush together, congregate, with a harmony like the pressure of Sis's cheek on my elbow—. Which was why a spasm went through me when Sis, at the same instant, spoke out in a loud voice that pierced the square: "We ought to be united, all of us, with one accord!" And that came to my ears as perfect, that shred of the Bible verse that relates how on the Day of Pentecost the apostles were all with one accord in one place—perfect because it brought a little comfort to know that somewhere in the world and time there'd been an opposite to the murderous discord reigning here and now.

Still no one among the families of the men on trial made a move to assemble, although many looked Sis's way with gratitude in their faces, as if her words alone had linked us.

Finally, with an hour or more gone by, the courthouse door opened by degrees and out stepped a scrawny man with a floppy hat clutched to his breast. Josiah Snell. He stood there just outside the doorway looking around as if he'd been planted down in a strange country. Till a soldier standing next to him spoke, and flung out a motion for him to move on. About then I heard a strained yell from the opposite side of the square: "Papa! Papa! Over here. Thisaway. Here I am."

That oldest Snell boy it was, mounted on one horse and holding the reins of another, waving an arm frantically. Coming back to himself, Josiah Snell tottered, then went toward the boy at a stiff-legged run. The son got down and helped his father onto the spare horse, remounted and broke a path through the crowd, and hardly had they left the square before you could see a cloud of dust rising behind them.

Ma and Sis and I shot wondering but stricken glances at each other. So then some of the prisoners were being let go, and that raised such a storm of questions in my mind—who and why and how —that the breath went out of me. I caught it back hard, yet I dared not say a word, and neither did Ma nor Sis. So Lord, Lord, Lord, the waiting, the anticipation, would now be worse than ever, even in the midst of a strain of reviving hope, especially if they should happen to go on setting other men besides Pap free. And in less than the next hour that's what they did. Old Man Perce Williams was the next to come hobbling out. Great God Almighty! I hadn't even heard he was locked up. Old and crippled as he was, the rebels must've gone beyond the limit to discover "treason" in such as him.

Then after Perce Williams every once in a while another man would be released, and my heart nearly failed at each swinging out of the courthouse door. I began saying their names over to myself, to memorize them, and to divert my thoughts from a worse channel. Then a little later Sis commenced doing the same thing aloud, with me wishing she wouldn't but without the heart to tell her to hush: "Coop Moran"— "Yance Naylor"—and so on.

From the time when the door closed behind an acquitted man until it opened again for another, the courthouse might have been a vacant building from anything you could grasp of what was going on inside.

And a remarkable silence now reigned over the people packed into the square so tight they could hardly budge, a silence as prevalent between-times as at the moment of a prisoner's release: more so even, because when another man came out into the light a faint hum of recognition stirred through the crowd, and occasionally an ecstatic cry from a family member rent the hush of the square.

By noon I'd counted sixteen men set free. At the best I could estimate, twice that number must still be in custody and going through trial. And to judge from the lengthy delays between releases, the jury must be condemning several of them in the meantime. Surely, surely, I now argued on and on to myself, if anything other than bald vengeance prevailed in the courtroom, Pap must have as much reason as anyone else to expect acquital.

Now then certainly Ma would never fail to keep us fed, end of the world or not, even let it be only the cold fried ham and dried-out cornbread she held out to me—and when I shook my head made me take it. So I accepted and ate it, not because I was hungry but because at this moment I wouldn't for the world have crossed her in anything. A little later she lifted a waterjug out of the dinner basket and passed it to me, then I handed it on to Sis, and she back to Ma. Like an offering we shared that drink of cool water.

And then a different sort of shifting among the crowd caught my attention, and I looked around to see soldiers carrying food and water into the courthouse: enough, from the looks of it, to feed the jury and the prisoners as well. No recess to the trials then, which pointed to an intention to get them all over with today. And following a longer pause than before, the liberation of more men, one by one, resumed.

About the middle of the afternoon, having been quiet but in apparent control up to now, without warning Ma collapsed. No sign, no sound, just a slumping to the wagonbed floor as though every bone in her body had turned to rubber. I grabbed her the instant before her head struck the wagonbox, then Sis and I scooted her as gently as we could to the back and stretched her out on an old quilt we'd brought along. Limp as a ragdoll. As though her life had ebbed away in secret to a thin remainder of consciousness. Her eyes stared wide open at the sky. When I spoke to try and rouse her, she began shaking her head, and wouldn't stop till I took it softly between my hands and held it still.

A look between Sis and me was sufficient for an understanding that we must remain close together, so she climbed up into the spring-seat with me, and now we divided our watching between the courthouse door and Ma lying behind us.

As another man, Giles Bostick, left the courthouse, Sis asked abruptly, "How many turned aloose do you count?"

"Twenty-eight."

"That's what I make it."

—No need to inquire where, oh God where, matters stood with the others. Twenty? Yes, or maybe more.

At long last it turned late in the day. Although we attempted to rouse her from time to time, Ma stayed in her suspense beyond communication. And then, all at once, the waiting was over. Dan Montgomery, the so-called president of the jury, came out onto the rocks steps of the courthouse and announced at the top of his voice, his words reverberating through the square: "The following men were the original instigators of that evil conspiracy calling itself the Union League, and therefore caused the murder of Colonel John Oldham, and so are as guilty as the man who pulled the trigger. They've been convicted as accessories to murder, and have been sentenced to hang by the neck until dead, executions commencing at sunup tomorrow. And may God have mercy on their souls."

No wonder they needed no witness. Why, just decide who the leaders were and pronounce sentence.

He began to read off the names from a paper in his hands. Pap's was the fourth one down the list. It reached Ma's ears, for her limbs contracted, she twisted to one side, she drew up her knees, hugged them, buried her face against them, lay there rolled up like a ball. I held ready to reach out and support Sis, but she didn't falter, or look my way. Her face was set firm. Even in profile I could see the blazing defiance in her eyes. And her voice was so contained it startled me: "We've got to manage to get in to see him."

The same thought had been tugging at my mind, with me holding it back till the time to say it seemed right.

I nodded hard: "Let me try to catch Preacher Tillman—. No, on second thought... Wait. Just hold on—."

Colonel Ticknor was the one I meant to head for. But why mention that to Sis. Even at a time like this, Jenny and attendant complications would pop into her mind first thing.

But then before I'd climbed out of the wagon and gone twenty steps, I ran head-on into Harley Dexter, who maybe had even seen me first and stepped over to block my way. All the practice I'd had by now at cold and deadly control stood me in good stead: "My mother and sister and me are requesting to see Pap for one last time."

"We done made it a rule that ain't but one family member allowed in for a last talk. Y'all'll have to decide on which one."

Just then Colonel Ticknor happened to walk by. "That's correct," he threw out with one stern look at me, and passed on. Harley Dexter gave a little sneer by way of dismissing me and followed Colonel Ticknor into the mass of people.

When I'd made my way back, before I could open my mouth, Sis said, "I seen you talk to both of them. Wha'd they say?"

I had to gasp before I could force it out of my throat: "They say one of us is all they'll let in, the low-down bastards."

Not even a twitch of response from Ma. Sis's body convulsed, she sprang to the ground: "They can't do that! How can they do that! I'll get on my knees and beg them. Ma can't go in there alone."

I shook my head. "Beg them? Harley Dexter'd laugh in your face. Ticknor'd stand there like a ramrod—if he said anything he'd maybe lecture you on minding your betters."

—Ma sat bolt upright: "What is it you're talking about? Tell me what I heard you talking about."

Sis let me be the one to say it, and I choked it out without turning my head in Ma's direction, "One... One person. That's all they'll allow in to see Pap."

Then I did lift my head to look at Ma, the burning of unshed tears in my eyes. Her eyes rested on me for a moment, then drifted away to the sky in the west, where the sun gave out a clear mellowing a little above the horizon. Ma raised her hands slow, as if in a trance, bent her elbows and unpinned the bun of hair at the nape of her neck, letting it fall along her shoulders. As low as she was crouched, the hair came rippling down to touch the floor. She swung her head to stare at vacant space, away from the sun, away from us, enthralled by the great distance, and crooned, "No, no, I'm not going. He's not dying. He's not here. He's gone far off. He's gone where he can come back from. If I saw him he'd be *here*. And he could *never* come back from *here*."

Cold shivers nearly got the best of me. There she was again, the Indian woman, upholding by her voice alone the life of her warrior in death struggle on a remote prairie, willing his return.

Then Ma gathered strands of hair in each fist and pulled her head down to hide it in her lap, and fell silent again.

It was a few seconds before I could wrest my eyes in Sis's direction, on which I found her looking steadily at me, waiting, patient, then: "You're not doubting I could go in there alone to see him, are you?"

"I'm not doubting it."

So now we held one another's gaze. The square, or the world, could've drained itself empty of people, only Sis and me left, Ma and Pap taken far away from us too, with any means of achieving their return lost forever. My eyes misted over, and Sis's brimmed with tears, until she dabbed them away with the edge of her shawl, peremptorily, as though furious with her eyes for turning weak.

Now really I already knew what the choice would have to be, but better, I felt, for Sis to make it. And she knew too, and took only a minute more to put it in words: "You're the oldest, and you're a son. It's you he'll want to tell how to take care of the family."

All I could do was nod my head.

But then beyond any exercise of will my chest began to heave, and with it a racing of the heart, and I stood helpless a little while, fighting for control of my breath. And still Sis waited in patience, which soon aided me in getting hold of myself, to turn shakily away. Now it was Sis who nodded, and I walked away toward the courthouse door.

Now I'd said nothing about it, and if it failed I never would, but I was determined to make one last appeal to Colonel Ticknor, though as yet how I might do that without Sis knowing was not clear to me, since her eyes would be glued on me wherever I went if still in view from the wagon. To make matters worse in every sense, I'd no more than left the wagon when I discovered that even one person getting in to see a condemned man would take time, since you had to wait your turn, and during the time Sis and I had delayed, a line had formed. That turned out to be an advantage, however, for the line stretched back around the corner of the courthouse, ending out of sight of the wagon. So as soon as I had the building between Sis and me, not yet taking a place in the line, I searched around for Colonel Ticknor but saw him nowhere, and when my eye lit on that boy of Will Judd's, I went over and accosted him, and trying my best to subdue the fire in my eyes and to keep my voice level, I said, "Do you know where Colonel Ticknor is?"

Still ashamed maybe about our run-in concerning Comanche, he answered warily, "I believe he went inside the courthouse a little bit ago."

"Can I count on you to do me one favor? Can you take him a message?"

He wanted bad enough to refuse, but my eyes wouldn't let him—.

"All right. It may get me in trouble, now, but all right."

"Then go tell him this: *Todd Blair is asking to see you; he says to please remember about Jenny*. Just the words I've said, now, not any more nor less." Then I repeated them.

"Yes. All right. I understand."

He wasn't long in coming back, not with a spoken answer but holding out to me a folded slip of paper. I thanked him and left, and a few yards away I stopped and read: YOU DID YOUR DUTY AS A MAN. I MUST DO MY DUTY FOR MY COUNTRY. SEE THAT YOU DO THE SAME.

I wadded up the paper and pitched it away. A madman, as Jenny had said, gone insane for his cause.

All that was left to do now was fall in with the fifteen or twenty waiting their turn before the courthouse door, mostly grim-faced men, a few women as resolute as Sis about keeping calm. And now that I had nothing to occupy me except wait, I couldn't shut out the sound of the grieving that broke out in waves over the square now and again. I'd been present at the weeping and wailing of funerals often enough; the closest to this was ten funerals going on at once. Beyond that, even. Knots of people would gather, restraints of earlier in the day gone now, voices rising and falling from moaning to screaming. Some women alone, or two or three holding onto one another, wandered among the crowd sobbing and shrieking. The onlookers there out of curiosity, the soldiers, even some of the mob, were hard-troubled in the eyes and white in the face with pity. The sun was going down on all this in a deep gold sky, so close to flames low in the west that my dream of last night could've been rising before my eyes. And often enough the mourning heightened to a pitch that taunted my soul as the mad laughing had in my dream. And of all the emotions that had lacerated me these past days, this one was just now the most frightening of all: that the line between laughter and crying might vanish from the world on this day of judgment. And if, in addition, the hanging tree had covered the sky between me and sundown I would've taken that as inevitable.

When it was finally my turn, night had come on dark. And when I stepped into that narrow little room lit by three candles, Pap was already there, seated near one of the candles, looking just as he had—

I realized with a jolt—that first night of this damnable time, when I'd seen him big and shaggy-black-bearded and seeming a long way off. I wanted now to leap across the room and catch him before he receded farther away. Instead I went up to him slow, and he stood up. We stopped about a yard apart, Pap looking as resolved as I was to maintain control. Then noticing another chair in the corner of the room, I brought it over, and just as if we'd agreed beforehand, I sat down facing him, our knees not quite touching.

"You know it all, then." Pap's voice was tired but unshaken.

"Yes we do. And...we made it up for me to come, not Ma nor Sis. Ma...."

"Yes?"

"Ma's...so broken up she...."

"You and Mahuldah made the right choice."

"Pap...." I began, and couldn't go on.

"Go ahead, son." But when I didn't, still couldn't, my voice lost, Pap took up from there, "Yes I know. Everything needs to be said, and no way to say any of it. And still I've gone over a whole lot the last couple of days. You see, I feared this verdict from the time I heard about Colonel Oldham being killed. Because I was one of the early members of the league, and they turned out saying in court just what I was afraid they would. Once they'd assumed it was a runaway member of the league that done the killing—took it for a fact though nobody knows the facts—why the next step was easy for them: anybody responsible for creating the league to be held responsible for what any member'd done. The ones they let go had joined up later on: tricked into joining, that was their out—.

"Anyhow—no. No, I'm not ready to die. But seeing that's what's to be, I can make ready. I can face it, I can accept it. You haven't, I know, because that's impossible. Accepting that you're about to die can't be shared by somebody else, just like nobody else can die for you. That sounds hard, I know, and don't tell Ma and Mahuldah that right away—though when you judge the time's right you can. Only one thing I have to add to that. Tell them now, and you see that it goes on my tombstone: 'Prepare to die, prepare to live. I pray we'll meet in a better world'."

"All right, Pap," was still all the voice I could find.

"Taking good care of the family, you'll do that without me having to ask you. It's only just if you have the chance to do it. You know already, I magine, what's in store for you—."

"I do." I began to burn, and I could speak—. "They'll try to force me into the rebel army."

"Yes, they will. And do you know what else? I hate to tell you but it's worse not to. The rumor is, they mean to confiscate the property of us *traitors*."

"Confiscate? Seize our place?"

"You see, the U.S. passed a law to take the property of anybody disloyal to the Union, and so the rebels turned right around and done the same thing. But let me tell you what—time's getting short. Cousin Graham Blair, that lives down yonder close to Dallas, I want you to get in touch with him, have him ready to take in Ma and the children if need be. And you—you'll have to take to the woods—how I hate to say it—among the bushwhackers and all."

"That I'd already meant to do. Cousin Graham, yes, if the family can take shelter with him, I'll do more than take to the brush. The rebels'll find it hard to drag me into their army, or keep me there if they do. What I'll do's go north. And I'll be back. I'll be back when the U.S. Army comes to take this country again. And if any rebels grab our land while I'm gone, they'll regret it when I come home."

"Well, so many decisions'll be up to you, Todd. And I won't put the burden of promises on you—only for one, and not a promise at that, just a reminder to think long and hard about...well, revenge. You may swear to kill the ones responsible. In your place I'd feel the same. But think, and think well. Not to forgive. No, never that. But killing starts feuds, and feuds always lead to killing back and forth till both sides are wiped out, and nobody wins. As I say, think about that long and hard—."

All at once a rapping at the door—I jumped as if a mechanism had been tripped in me. And a voice: "I'm afraid time's up."

It was the voice that brought me to my feet: "Pap! Pap!" I squalled out. He was standing now too, and we threw our arms around each other. I was sobbing like a baby, and couldn't stop. Pap let out one bellow, then choked back another, but I could feel his tears flooding down my neck as he kissed me hard on the cheek for the only time I remembered since I truly was a baby. We stood locked together. I heard the door open. I screamed, "Get out of here!"

The door closed softly. Yet someone would be back. And soon. I kept Pap hugged as tight as before, and kissed his stiff-bearded cheek. Then we staggered apart, still gripping each other's hands. Looking as deep into his eyes as I could in the candlelight, not trusting myself to say a word, yet I was about to when Pap spoke up: "I do have...one request. I want to be—I want you to make my grave on our own land."

It was like a blow on the top of my head. It was not only the thought of a grave for Pap, the finality: it was remembering the desecration of the makeshift graves along the river bank; it was the desperation of knowing that the land Pap claimed for a resting place might fall into enemy hands before the clods of the mound crumbled, into the hands of his murderers themselves.

The fury of that drove me to speak: "I promise you this much, Pap. While I live, and if I have to give my life for it, our land, the land your grave'll be on, will never stay in the possession of any enemy for long."

So yes—as maybe Pap never intended—it was in a sense a promise of revenge. He may even have been thinking better of what he'd said— but then came that rapping again—.

I got out a hoarse whisper that grated in my throat: "Goodbye, Pap"—and I whirled around and made for the door and reached it just as it opened before the scared and staring face of Wint Crigley. Then, as he all but leaped back to let me out, the voice of Pap followed me, firm and deep: "You're a man now, son. God be with you."

I knew I'd never forget the sound of that voice, nor the words.

I was nearly back to the wagon before I began in a hurry to sort out just how much of what we'd said I couldn't yet pass on to the womenfolks: the danger of the Confederate army descending on me, the threat of our land being confiscated, Pap's counsel about revenge, and even his preparedness to die that he'd asked me not to repeat as yet.

When I'd told Sis what I could, she understood well enough I was holding back, but she didn't press me for more. Ma appeared just not to be listening, lying on the wagon floor much as she had been earlier.

So the night deepened then, hovering black and endless, and the three of us bedded down in the wagon, with snatches of sleep and twisted, swift-running dreams for me, and no better I was sure for Sis. Now and then Ma started up out of delirium, with wild and unintelligible sounds, or often "No, no, no, no."

Daylight arrived, and then the sun: a lucid sky above us, a soft fall breeze around us. The town woke up from its half-sleep to a nightmare beyond any the dark of night could've sent. And even yet, though having gone through day after day of the hangings, I had to strain out of a stupor to grasp what the purpose was of soldiers moving about, onlookers gathering, mob members striding around, huddles of people set apart, like Ma and Sis and me.

The same wagon as always, driven by the same slave, soon came onto the scene, and the death processions began. Around noon it was when Pap's time came. Up to that moment I hadn't been able to face the decision whether or not to follow him to the hanging tree. Sis cut into any further hesitation: "I've got to go with him. Maybe not you. But I do."

Sis's words reached into my clenched soul like a soothing touch. Truly now I had someone to share with me the most torturing hour of them all. Then as by one impulse we glanced at Ma again, to see no change. I got down from beside Sis, I stepped to the back of the wagon, without forethought, to lay my hand on Ma's shoulder. I think I was not even surprised when that contact sent her to writhing and thrashing, and wailing to split my ears and tear the heart out of me. Then just as suddenly she went dumb and stiff.

On his walk to the death wagon Pap glanced around, but as he gave no sign of recognition we were sure he hadn't picked us out of the crowd. As he climbed up and sat crouched in the wagonbed, Sis got down, stood gazing at Ma with me. In a moment she said, her voice low and gentle, "You stay with her, Todd. I'll go with Pap," and set off without waiting for an answer: none was necessary, only that my heart brimmed again with love for Sis, and my agony diminished that I could not walk behind Pap on his last ride.

So I watched the procession withdraw and for the moment lost Sis in the crowd. Ma cried out just once and subsided into a steady moaning. Just then I felt the touch of a light hand on my elbow, and darted a look around to discover young Mrs Ellery Smith standing there, a lady whose heart I'd had occasion to bless on the first day of all this. And she was saying, "I'll take care of her, Todd. You go with them."

"Oh thank you, Hannah, thank you," I was still saying as I rushed blindly away, shoving through the crowd to overtake the procession, to catch up with Sis, who was hurrying along herself. When I fell in beside her, we never exchanged a word, only a look, and with the two of us making way, we pushed in soon right up to the rear guard of soldiers, though all we could see of Pap, between shifting bodies, was his back, bent forward as though his head must be bowed in his hands.

The wagon stopped maybe fifty yards short of the hanging tree, and the soldiers fanned out to draw a tight circle around it. Sis and I made to the right, still hugging the moving line of soldiers, working our way along till we came to a point where we felt sure Pap could see us when he stood up.

And then, for some reason, a delay: activity of four men near the tree—handling ropes. I took a quick look then glanced away. Yet, if I couldn't steady my eyes in that direction now, I warned myself, what would I do when—. I looked back at the men with the ropes, watched them steadily.

Sis said, "I've got to be where he can see me, all the way to the last. It can't be: for him to die with nobody but strangers around him, and strangers' eyes on him."

Yes, strangers, though he knew every man who went about the task of executing him.

Then I noticed that Sis had levelled a searching look at me, and was saying, "Can you stand still? I don't mean *stand* it, I mean stand still. Stand and do nothing but watch while it happens?"

So well did I know what she meant that I felt not a twinge of resentment—.

"I can."

"I mean, because suffering to the last breath is all a woman can do. A man can *act*. So bide your time. Wait till you can kill them all."

As defense against Sis's sudden consuming thirst for revenge, I tried to keep before me what Pap's state of mind had been on that. My only answer was to lead us into a gap left when a couple of men moved aside. No doubt about it that Pap could see us from here.

Sis threw her bonnet off and let it dangle on her back. Pap had risen to his feet. I raised my hat, Pap lifted a slow hand, then let it drop as though it was heavy.

—Sis was right. By no means was I sure that I could stand by unmoving and see my father murdered. All that kept me rooted in that spot, or from going berserk, was a look from Pap now and again in our direction, though after the first limp wave he made no other gesture. It was a help besides to take all of it in one step at a time. I listened attentively to the crunch of the wagon wheels in the dirt as it drove to the tree, a powdery dust rising behind them, and in larger clouds as riders and people afoot approached and packed in a circle around the ring of soldiers. The slave driving the wagon reined in the mules, and the sun glanced on their rumps until they passed into the shade of the tree. Pap stood up, ignoring the hands of the soldiers reaching out on either side to assist him. A man—yes, Alec Dunbar—climbed up briskly into the wagonbed behind Pap, said, "Put your hands behind you, now," and when Pap did, tied them with a rawhide thong. A breeze, tiny as an insect's wing, brushed my ear. In the quiet I heard the air stir in the leaves of the tree, saw it carry a few of them away. Now another slave swung a rope out from a hook on the tree trunk. I peered at every foot of that rope, from the deep groove where it rode on the giant westward-reaching limb to the noose-end. I bit my tongue, brought blood, thoughtless till that second that my tongue was between my teeth. I let go of it just in time to keep from biting it deeper, for I now saw blood on the dangling end of the rope—likely a spurting from some man's nose as he had choked. It was this: that they'd hang my father with a bloody rope, that set a fury to boiling inside me.... And now Alec Dunbar did up a well-made noose— showing off his skill before the crowd, no less—slipped it over Pap's head, drew it snug, got out of the wagon, let down the tailgate, motioned for Pap to step to the edge of the wagonfloor. The slave driving tensed up, took all the slack out of the lines, lifted his long whip. Dunbar stepped back. The ring of soldiers expanded against the crowd, and all went still, as if time had stopped.

A stranger standing close nudged me to take off my hat, like all the other men around me. A second earlier, or a second later, I might've throttled him. But in the miracle of that second Pap looked straight and steady at me, eyes wild but fixed, and I was near enough that I caught from them a deep blue fire that would always yearn to leap across the gulf between us. I took off my hat, clutched it in both hands, bit down hard on the brim of it.

"H'ya!" yelled the slave, along with a neat swipe of the whip that grazed the rump of both mules. They dug in their hooves and lunged ahead—.

That instant my eyes turned away of their own accord—the difference between me and Sis, for hers did not. I might indeed have run amok if I'd seen Pap's features wrench horribly as he strangled to death. I could barely contain myself given the sounds alone, though I didn't dare stop my ears. Then I found my eyes on the tremble and sway of the tree limb above. Beyond that, time went blank....

But for all the years since then, as I said at the start, I've pictured my father as falling, falling, and I wonder if I really did extend my hands to catch him, as I've so often done in my dreams, or if I was still crushing my hat in both hands and biting the brim to keep from gnashing my teeth—as I watched the tremble and sway of the tree limb....

Another unfading vision stays with me from that day. What I saw when my glance shifted from above, still not to Pap's body, but falling across the circle, out beyond the thickest of the crowd, sent a shock through me like a cross current to the rest of my suffering. That sight and the quivering of the giant limb with it tore my heart loose and swept it away through the terrible world holding us prisoner to where maybe that world came to the frontier of—what? If not of hope at least of a pause, an arrest, on the emptiness of the future—.

It was Ma my glance fell on. She must've driven the wagon down here herself. For there she was, standing on the springseat with Hannah Smith sitting beside her embracing the calves of her legs to steady her: perched unmoving, gazing firm and straight, hands folded at the waist, hair drawn back in a bun again, eyes boring directly ahead above us all, boring straight at Pap's body on the death tree.

22

WITH PAP'S BODY wound in a blanket, we left Milcourt so late in the day it was well into the night when we reached home. By lanternlight I built a plank coffin out of an old feedbox, that being the only lumber we had. Right in the wagonbed where it lay, Ma and Sis bathed Pap's body as best they could and dressed him again in his same Sunday suit. By the time we finished and had laid the body in the coffin, it was close to dawn. The face of the earth and the sky holding a few scuds of cloud near the lightening east were restless with a fitful and shifting wind.

Off to the north of the cabin, across one oval of the wide glade and near the boundary of our land, a grassy rise slanted up from a spring branch and leveled off to end in a mott of postoaks sheltering the open crown of the rise. On a smooth and grassy spot near the trees we buried Pap, in a grave that Willun Hackett and a few more neighbors helped me dig, with a slab of sandrock at each end to mark it till we got around to putting up a tombstone with the inscription Pap had requested: Sis only nodded, and Ma not even that, when I repeated to them his words for an epitaph.

Even before we'd finished with digging the grave, threatening weather arrived, soon developing into a cutting norther, with a sky heavy and dark, and as I stood in the bottom of the grave tossing out the last shovelfuls, wisps of snow came feathering into my face. All of us were chilled to the bone by the time we got through with the burying, shortly before dusk: all of it done in grim silence, no preacher to be had in the neighborhood—nothing more to be said in any case, and the time of the first bitter weeping now past.

Sometime that night after we'd gone to bed, more snow fell, spreading a light blanket and waking us up to a white world the next morning. Not thick enough to mound over Pap's grave, though, but just to scatter white patches over the clods of raw yellow clay we'd covered him with. That was the last sight I carried away with me when I went to the grave the day after the burial. And I didn't tarry beside it, though it was the last visit I expected to make for a long time to come.

—So now, after the whole county'd gone through convulsions, the trials and the hangings were over with. Forty-four men had lost their lives, forty-two hanged and two shot down, I heard, while running to escape—. That was the number people repeated, anyhow, but I knew of and heard about other men never seen in the county again, and it wasn't likely they'd all got away to Union territory, but rather that some had been waylaid by the rebels and their bodies disposed of no telling where. A great deal of this was passed on to me by Willun Hackett, for I didn't dare to be seen in town myself. I had him do another errand, too, that would have been difficult without him. I had him locate the mail-carrier that went between Milcourt and the next town to the south once a week. By luck Willun caught him the day he was leaving on his round and gave him a letter I'd written with Ma's cooperation to Cousin Graham Blair. From that next town south another carrier took up the route on to Dallas. So if all went well—which often enough in those troublous times it did not—my letter would reach Cousin Graham in about a week.

A full council with Ma and Sis couldn't be put off any longer. I laid it out to them, what Pap had advised, and because it was his advice, they offered no protest to abandoning the place and taking refuge with Cousin Graham as long as necessary, and they both sat dazed when I brought it up that the rebels might take possession of the place. —I still couldn't quite believe that, myself: that after murdering a man, the rebels'd take away his widow's only means of livelihood. But then again, by now any persecution imaginable appeared to be possible. I went ahead to mention one idea that I'd come up with myself to soften the blow that might fall. I said if seizure was attempted, maybe Cousin Graham could head it off. He was a constable in his county, and he passed for a secessionist, though actually he stayed as clear of it all as he could and got along well enough, having the respect he did as a trusted lawman. He had every reason not to take sides any more than was absolutely essential. Nobody outside the family knew it, but he had one boy in the Confederate and one in the Union army, and in secret he was tormented day and night they'd meet on the battlefield.

Tears came streaming down Ma's face for the first time since we'd buried Pap, and Sis hid her face in her apron, when I brought up the other tough matter: that for me it was either be dragged away from home by Confederate conscription or make a run for the North, and that which choice to make was not even in question. This they knew as well as I did, and so once again our portion was to suffer and go on suffering.

So first off, and I wasted no time about it, I hunted out a safe place in the woods to lie hiding till Cousin Graham could come after the family. I found my place the second day after we'd put Pap underground, and by then the weather had moderated and the wind had swung around to the south. My hideout was about a mile through the woods from the cabin, with no trail leading in that direction: a cave way up on a rocky knoll, down among boulders and altogether out of sight unless you stumbled on it. I began at once to hide there all during daylight hours: no fire, just quilts to wrap up in, creeping home only at night and not staying long even so.

Long hours I had, then, of not knowing what to do with myself, and these made harder to bear by all the dashing around and troubling and wrestling with the world I'd gone through these few weeks past. I'd never been a whittler, but I became one now, carving out little woodblock puzzles and crude horses and such, and gave them to Sis for Scooter to play with. And while I was at that I delved and delved in my mind for what I ought to have as plans when the time arrived to take off north. Yet how could I come up with much, really? when I had only the faintest idea of what lay ahead of me. Ma once suggested I might go to her brother's, in central Missouri, the one that had inherited the family plantation. Maybe I could try that, I said. What I didn't say, though Ma must've suspected it as much as I did, was that I couldn't see a big slaveholder taking in a man running from the Confederate army, close kinfolks or not.

But, really, the whittling and the pretending to look ahead came closer to being a dodge than anything else: not to let my mind run on Pap's death—and on Jenny, Jenny, Jenny. Still, I'd catch myself flying off into daydreams, longing to see Jenny and scheming how I could, my whole body and soul remembering her, all my thoughts and visions uneasy that we'd be kept apart forever. Or suppose nothing else stood in our way other than what her uncle had done. I had full faith the two of us could overcome that, but it was foolish to think that anyone else in either family could. All this ran in circles through me, the daydreams often not to be separated from the fantasy of dreams that came edging in when I'd drop off to sleep in the twilight of my cave. And even when under the waking control of my mind, no sooner would Jenny and her uncle come to me in the same thought than my grief for Pap would erupt and nearly run away with me. But then the strangest of all, though maybe in the end the best turning of my imagination, was at first the scariest. My sorrow over Pap would hit and work itself through, then hit again. I was free to cry here underground, and I did. Sometimes during one of these spells I'd get the feeling he was close at hand, and that gave me a fright—not that his ghost would do me harm, yet still it was terrible beyond description to have my dead father and my living self occupying the same space at the same time. Once, falling asleep at the height of such a moment, I was plunged into a deep dream where suddenly Pap shouted my name from a corner of the cave, and I whirled, and there he stood facing me, more alive than when he was alive—because he was dead.

And then the going down into and the coming up out of the cave: descent, ascent, just that passage in itself. From dreading it early on, I soon came to love it—or rather to be held by it in fascinated awe: the dread and the love or awe thudding in the same heartbeat. Because this entering and leaving the cave seemed to mean that I was in a tomb myself: just as Pap was—as the Lord had once been—I too biding time till the resurrection, and as though my own at least was at hand. This last, this ancient act beginning in despair and ending in victory, brought a glimmer of solace in contradiction to the fright of my dead father's presence: as if having Pa and the Lord with me could bring me one day out of this cave to stay, and into a new life—.

The anticipated ten days went by, and still no word from Cousin Graham. Which worried me sore. How not to worry, given the tragic direction everything appeared to take for us in those days. And sure enough, when I stole in home on the tenth night, Sis was waiting farther than usual into the edge of the timber beyond the barn.

"They come here looking for you today," were the first words out of her mouth.

"Which ones?"

"Carlton Dawes. And a man we couldn't place, a militia sergeant."

"Surprised it wasn't Harley Dexter, but I'm satisfied he sent them, if Colonel Ticknor didn't." Harley Dexter had been put in charge of rounding up the men dodging conscription, Willun Hackett had told me.

"Wha'd you tell them?" I asked, though I knew already, because we'd made it up what to say in that case.

"I said you'd gone to Arkansas to see about a place, because we plan to sell out and leave the country."

For one thing, I'd thought if selling out was brought up, we might hear some word about the confiscation. But Carlton Dawes hadn't mentioned it.

"And their answer was," Sis went on, "that when you got back, for you to report to the military here right at once, that you're up to be drafted. So I just said, 'All right. He'll be back in two weeks or so.'"

For all that, I wasn't about to relax, because they might not be so easily fooled. It would pay, in fact, to be more on guard than ever. But then, to my great relief, when I met Sis the next evening after dark, it looked like I wouldn't be held up much longer. A letter had come from Cousin Graham promising to be here inside of a few days. So I went back to anticipating mightily that escape was near at hand.

But now I hadn't been in the cave that night for more than a couple of hours, and had just gone off to sleep, when I woke up breathless and certain that I'd heard a stir through the woods not far off. And I had, for when I crawled to the mouth of the cave to listen, and when the noise came closer, I could make out that it was a big animal or two. Could be deer, maybe, could be somebody's horses or cows running loose. Whatever it was, there were two of them, I decided, and in a little bit I heard them split and go separate ways around the base of my knob. By then it sounded too much like a pair of horseback riders conducting a search not to be just that.

But still I crept out the next evening close to sundown, taking a longer circuit and extra precaution, to the place of meeting Sis at the woods' edge. I led her over to the barn, where we talked a short time in whispers, and I was greatly encouraged to learn that word had just come from Cousin Graham: that he was in Milcourt and would be out to our place by the next day.

Now what I ought to have done was leave immediately, for we'd already decided that Cousin Graham and I were not to come face to face—since as a Confederate lawman he should by rights put me under arrest, and the best way out of that was for him just not to lay eyes on me. And so knowing now that he was here and ready to take charge, I could light out when I felt like it. Still, and against my better judgment, I decided to hang around for one more day—because how did I know, I argued to myself, but what a slip in the plans to protect the family could develop even yet. So when I left to go back to my cave, we had it understood that I'd pull out as soon as dark came tomorrow. In the meanwhile I decided it was best not to let on to Sis that I suspected searchers in the area; I just took my daily supply of grub and water and went pussyfooting back to my cave.

—Out of the whole tally of days from that time, not a one of them ever to be forgotten, still there are two in particular stamped in my memory as if the sun rose and set on them just yesterday: one naturally being the day when Pap was hanged, and the other the day when I waited for Cousin Graham to come.

During my time of concealment I'd had Sis keep Comanche in the barnlot all fed and watered and ready to throw a saddle on at a moment's notice—could be that Carlton Dawes had taken notice of this when he came looking for me, and said nothing. So more reason than ever to be wary.

I put in the daylight hours down in the cave as usual, and heard nothing, and all the while a warm gladness built up in my blood that this was to be the last day of skulking underground. A little before sundown I sneaked out and inched along toward the barn to be close at hand for a quick getaway just as soon as it grew dark and Sis came to tell me that Cousin Graham had arrived and had matters in hand—of course I couldn't overlook, either, that some of the local hotheads might have learned he was in Milcourt, and horned in to come out here with him.

But then be damned if—well, all I can say is that from being careful I'd gradually become what I can only call too careful, and here's how. When time had grown heavy on my hands in the cave, I'd ease the burden by checking the cap-and-ball pistol and the Spencer down to the finest point: manipulating the actions, oiling, polishing. And then another thing. Often my mind would fix itself on the question of how many rounds of Spencer ammunition I had left, and how to take care of it—because what my mind was really centered on was that these cartridges were my only hope of salvation in reaching Union territory—each cartridge a power for freedom that I could sit and fondle and exult over. I'd brought an oily rag from the cabin to keep each cartridge case wiped slick and bright, counting them like a hoard as I rubbed and handled them. But then my thoughts would at times stray and I'd forget the number as I cleaned, and in the end have to go back and recount. At least three or four times I went through that process during my days in the cave, my whole supply, including those from the magazine tube, finally laid out in neat rows on a little flat place in the cave floor.

But lo and behold, here I was now on my way to the corral, had said good-bye to the cave I thought forever, when a strange feeling came over me that I'd failed to pick up a few cartridges from the floor after the last tally. The doubt was so strong, foolish though I knew it to be, that I got down on my knees then and there in a leafbed under a big postoak, pulled the tube out of the stock, laid the gun on the ground in front of me pointed diagonally to the left, took off my hat and placed it on the ground between me and the gun, emptied my ammunition pouch and the magazine into it. The crown of my hat was heaping full of the shining cartridges.

I began counting....

Now that's just how bad a fix I was in when a scuffing of leaves startled me, and I jerked my head erect to see—Harley Dexter standing not thirty feet away with his rifle levelled at me from the hip.

A deadly stillness. Harley's eyes stood out beyond what I'd ever seen before. Pap's face came before me with a startling clarity, in the death throes that I hadn't even seen. If I must die in the next instant, I'd die as he had, unflinching to the end.

A twisted sneer took possession of Harley's face: "Just afingering his ammanition, is he? Little Todd Blair about to jack off on his playpurties."

Fear went calm in a rage that steeled my nerves, gave me back the power to think: to consider Harley's brutal glee in having me at his mercy and how he meant to enjoy it a while, taunt me, bait me. As yet he hadn't even ordered me to hand over the Spencer. He just stood there so proud of his cleverness in finding me that he was about to piss all over himself. Also, he just had to brag about it:

"I knowed you wasn't gone to no Arkansas. Knowed your slut of a sister'd be lying. Knowed you'd be cringing around here in the woods someplace. So I concluded I'd just come out and run you down and take you in by myself. Do what two men I sent after you couldn't do."

I kept as still as a post, saying to myself, 'Watch'—because a man so wound up in boasting about his great talents is apt to be blind to vital details in what's going on around him.

Now he took to eyeing the Spencer. "I've heerd about that thing laying there. Seen a picture of it. Load it on Sunday and shoot it all week, they say. Caught you redhanded with it, didn't I. And who'd have access to Yankee arms only a goddamned spy. Eh? Tell me you ain't as big a traitor as your fucking old daddy was! And that Yankee shit-pipe is gonna get you swung on that same elem limb we swung him from."

All at once he let out an explosive laugh: my silence was getting to him. But he went on: "I guess you think I don't know how that shit-pipe works, eh? Well, I do. And anyhow you ain't got no shells in it, so it's just a piece of junk iron."

A pause. Then he took up a new thought: "You oughtn't to made them slurring remarks about Old Chief, you know it."

—That was his rifle, Old Chief. What did he mean? I couldn't recall making any such remarks, but then I decided it must've been something I'd said then forgot about one time when a bunch of men in the community were testing their marksmanship and I beat him in the rifle-shooting contest. Seeing now how he'd carried the grudge, and how it burned him up that I had a weapon maybe better than his, I began beating my brains for a way to make his burning even worse, maybe delay what he was surely up to: deal out all the torment he could before killing me right here in the woods. The mob had broken up, the jury had disbanded, and guilt over what had happened was already running strong, I'd heard. So if Harley took me to Milcourt I might not end up on that hanging tree after all.

All this was in a tumult through my mind when I said, "It ain't no shit-pipe when it's got shells in it. It's plumb accurate." I was trying to weaken my voice, which took little enough effort, frightened out of my skin as I was. Then I deliberately puckered up to cry as I stared down at the cartridges in my hat and a couple in my hand, and the magazine tube lying on the ground beside me: looking I hoped like I was ready to break down because so little space lay between my hands and a chance to live.

Harley chortled so hard his gun wavered. Then he said, squinting like he was thinking hard. "Why I'll tell you what. Accurate, is it? Here. Pick up that magazine tube. Go ahead. Put the shells back in it. I just might give a piece of yankee-loving scum like you a chance to beat a rebel at shooting—just see which one of us is left for buzzard vittles."

I put on a look of the greatest surprise, acted like I was stricken stiff. "Go on. Do what I tell you."

Slowly I went at it, picked up the magazine tube and fed the shells back in till it was full. Once finished with that, I crouched there waiting, staring with a lost look at the magazine in my hand and the gun on the ground—which still didn't take much pretending.

"And so now what're you gonna do?" Harley gloated.

I had my speech ready, though humble and shaky it came out: "Well, I still don't see how you're gonna make this a shooting match between a Union man and a rebel."

"Confederate, to you."

"Confederate."

Harley was enjoying himself too much to say anything right at once. I decided on a risk: "We could do it thisaway. I could take all the shells back out but one, then put the magazine in place and after that throw the one shell in the chamber—holding it aside of course so there'd be no way I could shoot before you dropped me. Then lean the gun against this tree right here. Then you could lean yore gun against that tree beside you. Then when you give the word we could each one go for his gun. Be a matter of which one could grab and shoot the fastest."

Harley let out a snarl—just as I'd figured, even one little advantage my gun had over his in such a fight was enough to make him furious: "Yaah sure. Think you're purty smart, don't you. Yore gun's shorter'n Old Chief. You might line it up faster."

I did my best to look like I'd been found out. Harley began snickering, standing there scheming—you could see it on his face—how he could taunt me some more. Hard to tell, though, whether he'd go on in the direction I wanted him to, but that ghost of a chance was all I had: to mock him enough to tempt him into the kind of a contest I wanted, yet leading him to believe he had the advantage—knowing him to be too much of a coward, in fact, to give me anything like an even break. If I could just get that Spencer into my hands—.

—Because one thing Harley plainly hadn't suspected. He could see the Spencer lying before me with the hammer down, so he took it for granted, in his damfool way of thinking that any snap judgment of his was bound to be correct, that the gun was unloaded. But it wasn't. I'd left a shell in the chamber with the hammer let down easy on it and started counting from there. As a rule I didn't carry the Spencer around like that: too dangerous. But tonight I'd taken the risk out of concern that greater dangers than ever might be lurking in the woods between the cave and the barn.

So if Harley had let me stand up and turn aside to lever a shell into the chamber, I would have been standing close enough to that post oak to leap behind it. A good chance he'd miss, caught off guard like that. Or even if he hit me in the shoulder or the side, I might be able to stay on my feet long enough to kill him, left at my mercy as he'd be with an empty rifle.

But no, Harley came up with another way: "Tell you what. Now you do ever bit of moving just like I say. Or else. Stand up"—I did—"Now pick up that gun and hold it in your left hand. Take that tube in your right'un. All right. Now I'll uncock Old Chief. And set him down again this tree. And then we'll see just how fast you are. Because what you're gonna do is shove the tube in the stock, then get your shell in the chamber and ready to shoot while I'm picking up Old Chief, cocking him, aiming and pulling the trigger."

"Why, that ain't fair!" I screeched like a kid that's been outfoxed. "I can't do all of that while you're making yore move!"

"Oh, I don't know about that." He sounded his haughtiest. "That's a better gamble than a sonofabitching traitor deserves. So all right, that's it. Start doing it."

Well, I tried to act like I was about to draw my last breath: stood there clutching the Spencer by the forestock with the butt close to my right hand holding the magazine. Smug but at the same time red in the face and breathing quick, Harley let down the hammer of his rifle and leaned it against the tree trunk next to him.

"Yore ass is gonna be cold in the ground by tomorrow." And he snickered once.

Then, though it all took place in seconds, each tiny movement flashed alive of its own accord, and I still shake at times from how blinding bright each of those motions can be to live over again—. I let the tube drop to the ground. I grabbed for the hammer. I thumbed it back. And Harley's face went from red to pale as if his blood had drained out of him. His lips stretched open. His jaw went set. His left hand snatched up his rifle. He swung and raised it—and I saw matters were not going my way as smooth as I'd thought they would. Harley was fast. He was ready to shoot quicker than it seemed possible. And all that while I was cocking, aiming and pulling the trigger. And my gun went off no more than a second before his did. I don't know—I guess I must have hesitated for an instant—or maybe I dropped my pretense too quick, my look revealing to him before I'd even let the magazine fall that a cartridge had been in the chamber of the Spencer all along—. I don't know. I know the last look on Harley's face, because I saw it never to forget it: the look of a man who realizes too late that he's been so thoughtless as to throw his life away. And I know Harley's rifle never quit swinging to go off, till it wobbled and went out of my sight. I know Harley flopped and hit the ground. I know I fell about the time he did, the world pitching around me....

I lay there on the leafbed knowing I was stunned, and was twisted onto my left side, and unable to do anything about these distortions of mind and body. Blood was welling out from some place and trickling along my right cheek: into my sagging mouth, into my nostrils, strangling me nearly when I caught my breath. Yet still I could nothing about any of it. Not till I finally discovered I could raise my right hand to explore: along my forehead, to the right side of my skull, delicately on down to my ear—. The rifle ball had nicked a chunk out of my right earlobe. And now it came to me also that, for the time being anyhow, I was deaf in the right ear, and the left one was pressed into the dead leaves: so that's why the world was so quiet.

I began telling myself: 'Now you can get up. You know you can. Come on. Get up. Get up!'

But it was still a while after that, when I took full account that the sun had gone down and twilight had set in, that I raised my trembling body from the ground. The first thing I saw was Harley—I hadn't exactly forgot about him while I was on the ground; it was just that he seemed so far away as not to matter. I realized now with belly-clenching suddenness how near he was: body lying twisted too, the barrel of Old Chief clutched in his left hand, the right one flung out almost touching the trigger guard, as if that hand had hardly moved from it when he toppled. His head was cradled against the forestock, one leg thrown forward and one back, in a posture of charging, of hurling himself forward, had he been standing. For an instant he looked so poised, so life-like, that I started scrambling around for the magazine tube, in real fear that he'd jump to his feet and carry out that charge—. Till I thought, 'But of course he can't shoot. His rifle's empty.' And a split second after that, struggling to my knees, I saw that he was dead.

While I set in to stanching my bleeding ear with a strip off of my shirt-tail, my mind was rushing on: Had Harley come out here alone? He'd said so, but nothing was certain in that. Surely if others had accompanied him, they'd be here by now. But then yes, it made sense that he'd come alone, meaning to kill me if he found me. No witnesses about. Or wait—they could be setting an ambush at the cabin—. But then however that might be, I didn't see what else I could do but gather up and push on.

So I did, weak and quivery for the first little ways, but that passed off, though it left me with a pain throbbing in my wounded ear, and that ringing deafness. Approaching the barn with great stealth, I finally got down and crawled to a brushpile where I could peek out at the barn and cabin. Off to my right a few yards, well back into the woods, I saw Sis standing, holding Comanche by the reins, saddled and ready. Nothing suspicious in what I could see: if they'd forced her out there as a lure, she couldn't've been standing so naturally. No point in taking a risk, though. We'd made it up I was to do an owlhoot for a signal, though right then I was scared to venture even that. While I was searching my brain for some other sign, Comanche sensed me and gave his head a little toss. Sis understood.

"Come on out, Todd," she whispered. "It's all clear."

Walking up to her I asked, "Anybody been here?" Comanche nuzzled my shoulder.

"No. But I heard two shots go off nearly together nor far from here. One of them must've been you."

"One of them was, the first one. The second one was too late for the other guy." Then I let the idea sink in before adding, "I just killed Harley Dexter."

Sis sucked in a breath between her teeth and let it out easy. Then she waited for me to speak. But I didn't; I wanted words from her. Even fearing what they'd be, I wanted them.

Her voice was rasping: "That's one accounted for."

As I well knew: vengeance always on her mind—uncomplicated for her, though not for me. In any case, no good talking about it—or for now thinking about it either.

I stood keeping my head turned so she couldn't see my wound in the dark. The ear had stopped bleeding and I'd gotten rid of the bandage, but what would I do if it flowed again, for instance when she'd be hugging me goodbye—.

"Cousin Graham get here?"

"He's at the house. Told me not to call him out unless you absolutely have to see him."

"I don't. You just tell him I'll be forever obliged to him for taking care of y'all. And that someday I'll find a way to make it up to him."

"I'll tell him."

"I can't tarry, Sis. As you realize. And no time for goodbyes neither. All I can say is, I'm going north. Somewhere up there. Maybe Fort Gibson. Around there I'll strike the Union army. Don't worry but what I'll get there. And don't worry but I'll be back, neither. And the Union army with me. And when that time comes"—I had to leave her at least this much consolation—"that'll be the day of reckoning for the rest of the murdering sonsabitches that hung Pap—."

But I couldn't keep on in that vein, for what it might lead Sis to come out with next: "I don't have to tell you not to breathe a word to nobody about nothing—I mean nobody but Ma of course. And push for Cousin Graham to get y'all out of here tomorrow. It won't do to stick around here till I'm supposed to be back from Arkansas—."

"What about old Dexter's body?"

"I'll...dispose of it. Best for you not to know how. And his horse, I'll take care of that too."

It was worrying me bad, for sure, what'd happen if the rebels found that body. No question but they'd mark me out for the killer. They'd drag Sis and Ma into it right off, too, and could be even Cousin Graham, lawman or not. If it could just be hid and stay hid for a while after the family left for Dallas, maybe the law in Milcourt wouldn't try to bring them back—. No telling. Anyhow, the more time between now and when they might question Sis, the better she'd be able to face up to them. Damned little they'd get out of her anyway—.

It was a hard matter to say goodbye, even though both of us knew how dangerous lingering could be. And then that complication of keeping as sharp a girl as Sis from discovering I was hurt. She acted nearly too quick for me. Knowing it was time to part, she grabbed me around the waist and nearly hugged the breath out of me, with her face pressed tight in the hollow of my neck—luckily on the left side. She didn't make a sound, but I could feel her tears soaking into my shirt collar—'Blood on one side, tears on the other,' I thought. For two or three whole minutes we stood gripped and silent like that. Till I said softly, "I'll be back, Sister."

"I know you will, Brother. I'll pray you will."

How long ago it seemed, now, since that day a few weeks back when we'd first used our childhood names from once upon a time.

"Nobody ever had a sister as fine as you are." My voice broke. Sis caught her breath in one quick sob: "Todd, Todd, my dear, dear brother." Then I kissed her temple and pushed her gently away. But she would not draw back till she'd planted a long kiss on my left cheek and almost broke my hand in a last squeeze, kissing it hard.

I turned away, holstered the Spencer, hitched up the pistol on my belt, felt for the blanket, canteen and saddlebags, hung the knapsack I'd always carried to the cave on a thong next to a saddlebag—I did all that more carefully, more lingeringly, than I had to, or should have. Sis stood motionless. I mounted up.

As I was about to turn Comanche's head, Sis blurted out, "Colonel Ticknor, he's the one that's the most to blame. He's high up on the list."

I hesitated long enough to say, "I ain't forgot none of it."

"It'll be a hard choice for you." She said it knowing I'd catch what she meant—and also as if there could be no question about which choice I had to make.

"Such as that's for later on," was all I could come up with.

Then I swung Comanche's head and rode off.

Now then I'd already thought of how I could assure that nobody'd find Harley's body for a few days at least. So I rode back to where I'd left him lying: found his horse too; it whinnied as Comanche and I passed closeby. I got Harley's corpse across Comanche's back—not trusting how his horse might react—and started off, picking my way as well as I could back to the mouth of my cave. Then I unloaded the body and dragged it the last few yards, and struggled around over the rockpile to the place where I could roll it down to the cave floor. Then I pushed it into a remote corner. I took the saddle off Harley's horse and laid it with his other gear beside him. I balanced Old Chief across his chest.

Next question was what to do with the horse. Shooting him wouldn't do. Even if I could coax him into the cave to do that, there wasn't enough room in there to really conceal the carcass. Besides which, the noise of another shot was asking for trouble. No alternative. I'd have to lead him a good ways and then decide what to do.

I rolled a big rock over the mouth of the cave. I stood back and gazed for a bit. I felt like laughing—or screaming. I now first discovered that my teeth were chattering and my flesh crawling from head to toe. It wasn't regret that I'd killed him. No, it was like too much joy, to such a degree that the power of revenge accomplished terrified me. But that was soon offset by a sight flashing through my head that nearly set me afire: I saw Pap lying in his tomb over yonder, and Harley in his here— too close, too close, and on Pap's land at that. How I wished I could see this enemy corpse hauled away, to some other grave: anywhere, just so long as it was far off.

Now that great temptation to laugh or scream I could not get rid of altogether without saying something. When I first opened my mouth all that would come out of it was a kind of embittered chuckling. Then I got command of myself and after a few seconds spoke the only words that seemed fitting: "You ain't welcome, Harley, but I have the satisfaction of knowing you hate to be here as much as I hate to have you. So you and Old Chief just wait here till somebody comes after you."

I mounted up and reined Comanche around, and leading the other horse, we set off on our long journey.

23

DAYLIGHT WAS A LONG TIME in bringing that night to a close. In the moonlit dimness I followed the trail through the timber toward Jeb Grantley's place—as I'd done the night when we failed to organize a rescue—and near there I turned and made for Red River. A short way from the brakes, on a bald rise, as I was about to release Harley Dexter's horse and whip him away toward Milcourt, I thought better of it. If he found his way home, as he was almost sure to do, then no matter which direction he came from, an all-out search was sure to follow. So face it, the only hope I had of keeping Harley's disappearance a mystery for a while was to shoot his horse—though God, how I hated to do it.

But all right. I led him deep into the brakes, dismounted, tied Comanche just in case he tried to follow me—for I sure didn't want him to witness this—took the other horse into the brush, and stopped.

The dark mass of the animal loomed before me, under a moon hanging low in the west. I thought—and blurted it out: "Belong to a sonofabitch all your life, and then, if you could know it, meet a worse one at the end."

It was enough to shut out further thought in that direction. Then, remembering that a pistol ball might fail to kill him at once—felt the least I could do was minimize his suffering. Though as I was lifting the Spencer, suddenly it came to mind: 'What if you was to run out of shells over yonder, and this was the last one, and could maybe save your life?'

I pulled the trigger.

—Now the hours of that night crawling the slowest were those when

I put my mind to the last and most serious problem of all: how to see Jenny before fleeing the country. To begin with, I had no way of knowing where she was. Much as I hated to entertain the idea, the most likely place to find her was—at Colonel Ticknor's. So an attempt to see her could mean walking straight into the arms of the people I'd been hiding from: sure, and maybe just in time for them to find Harley Dexter's body, in spite of my precautions, and string me up in short order. On the other hand, it wasn't to be ruled out that she'd be at the Wharton house in town. So? That was nearly as risky as the other: too public a place to get in and out of unnoticed, all the more so since the rebels might be on the watchout for me, not believing I was in Arkansas.

During this time Comanche and I wove around and came to the riverbank, cut off in every direction it seemed except to cross the stream and be on our way. I got off and lay down wrapped in my blanket in a brushy draw next to a lush spot where I tethered Comanche to graze. I lay with the dwindling glow of the moon filling my wide-open eyes while my thoughts ran on unresting.

Then, thinking I'd only blinked, I twitched awake as the leading rim of the sun burned up out of a ridge to the east. Comanche was standing close beside me, head drooped in a nap but coming awake the second after I stirred.

So now what? was still all I could get my mind around. I got up, took a piss, stretched and yawned quite a bit, then keeping low in the draw I went along till it joined another one where a trickle of water ran over clean sand. I drank deep, topped off my canteen, dug out a basin in the sand for Comanche to drink from. Next I ate the last of the cornbread and bacon Sis had furnished me with. And wondered and wondered. And while I did so, sat and scanned the country in view along the opposite shore of the river. Once across I'd have only—only!— bushwhackers and Indians to reckon with. Death a possibility over there, a certainty over here: if the rebels got me in their clutches and found Harley's corpse.

But still I couldn't pull myself away from Texas, not just yet: better said, away from Jenny. So after a spell of indecision that seemed longer than it was, I sprang up and went into action: went snaking down into the river thickets afoot, skirted the channel downstream till I reached the foot of a heavy-timbered hill from which I thought Colonel Ticknor's place might be in sight. Climbing the hill, hoping I was screened from below by the timber, I came at last to a rock outcropping that did give me the right view. With an old spyglass I had, till the sun was hot overhead, I watched and watched. Caught sight of some militia men, then of Mrs Ticknor, then of the colonel himself riding off west with two of the militiamen, toward Colonel Oldham's. Every once in a while I saw a slave or two moving around. No glimpse of Jenny. But no reason to conclude, either, that she wasn't there, just because I didn't see her outdoors.

Anyhow, I'd best assume she wasn't there. And so I went back to Comanche, and was bursting with such agitation by now that I began backtracking for Milcourt, spent the remainder of the afternoon cutting back and forth over the ground between the town and the river, taking advantage of all the cover that could be found. The last couple of miles of any route going into town ran right over a prairie ridge it'd be senseless to cross before dark. So I waited—wishing with all my might to be without the brilliant moon—before I rode the balance of the way to Milcourt. And at that I stopped about a mile out, staked Comanche in a thicket, and carrying just the pistol in my belt, started along the creek that the hanging tree stood on farther down, and that also ran close to the Wharton house some distance above the fatal tree.

As I went along, of necessity slowly, my worst concern got to be that I'd waited too long into the night, that I'd find the house dark, with all gone to bed, when I came to the place. And then when I'd crept up as near as I dared, I decided that really was the case, for no light could I make out in the whole house. And though I had in mind the danger of arousing a dog, still I'd have to take the risk to find out for certain whether anyone was still up. Creeping a little closer, in view now of what I took to be the parlor windows, I made out that somebody in there was astir, from the flickering and shadows of dim candlelight—one candle only, it must be. But then, after all, what good did my discovery do me, not knowing who was there, and anyhow having no way to signal from this distance. As I hunkered there against the obscurity of the creek vegetation, indecisive, racking my brain, the more I thought about it—remembering I'd never seen a dog at the Wharton farm nor here in town either, the more I was of a mind to run another risk. So I did. I crawled under the railfence separating the creek bank from the grounds of the house and slithered along till I was a few feet from one of the windows, rose up partway, saw Jane Wharton sitting on a low stool before a dresser, brushing her long hair—so this wasn't the parlor, as I'd thought, but Jane's room. I was mortified thinking all at once of myself as a window-peeper, but by now it was certainly too late to turn back over a scruple. Scratching around on the ground, then, till I found a tiny pebble, I tossed it at the window glass—and I saw Jane start when it hit. Then I waited, scarcely able to breathe. Jane slipped into a robe lying beside her on a chair, then sat waiting, apparently not frightened, only expectant. In a minute I pitched another pebble, that landed on the sill, and this time Jane hesitated no longer—I watched as the obscurity swallowed her figure, saw her glide as a pale shape through the kitchen door and across the back porch.

"Over here," I whispered, and as she hung back: "Jane. It's Todd."

Then she came out to where I stood a few feet back in the darkness, whispering, "Keep on talking low. I'm pretty sure Mama's awake."

Taking her by the hand I led her down to the railfence, but still whispered, "So Jenny's not here, then." And I dreaded to hear the answer.

"No. She *was* here, for a couple of days. But she went back to her Uncle James's day before yesterday."

—Inside the Ticknor house then, all the time I'd watched this morning. I groaned.

"But listen," said Jane, "she's coming over to the farm tomorrow, to meet me there, to help me pack the last things we're bringing to town."

For a second my heart leaped, but then: "For how long though? Y'all coming back to Milcourt before the day's over?"

"Yes. I'm afraid we are."

Again I groaned.

Now we both stood thinking. Jane, easy to tell, would do all she could to bring Jenny and me together—which for sure Jenny had schemed with her to do if I should happen to show up anyplace.

After a little while I said, "Any way you could think of to keep y'all there overnight"—thinking 'no' as I spoke. Why would they do that when the danger of being out there, especially at night, was what had driven them away in the first place?

"Just a second. Let me think," said Jane. "Maybe. Yes, maybe. See, three or four of the militia men'll be out there with us, to escort us back to town. Suppose I—we—just slow up the packing—or pretend to lose something—and not find it till it's too late in the day to travel. Then we'd just have to wait till morning. Nobody then'd ever know the real reason behind the delay—though I'll mention to Mama not to worry about us, that I'm not sure I can get everything together and be back here by sundown. Why yes, of course we can do that."

Then she went over each step once more. It was good to see how carefully, and yet how quickly, she'd planned it. Good at womanly deception she certainly must be, when a real need for it arose.

"I don't see why it won't work, Todd. Do you see any hitch?"

I didn't, and said so. I wanted to chuckle over what a smart woman'll do: think up a slick scheme herself, then ask a man, like she wants his stamp on it. No, I hadn't a doubt in the world that in a circumstance like this she and Jenny could handle her mama, and the militia, and Colonel Ticknor besides.

I squeezed both of Jane's hands in mine: "I better be going now. Tell Jenny I'll sneak in when I'm sure the militia boys're sound asleep. And don't worry about me getting past them——. Oh—and we have to arrange where Jenny'll be waiting in the house"——. I just could not bring myself to say 'which bedroom?'

Jane caught her breath: a young girl, a virgin for sure, certain she was about to drop being a lady for a little while: "She'll be in——. No, she won't. She'll be—in my room. I'll sleep in Mama's room——. Wait. What am I thinking? I'll have her wait on the front porch."

I couldn't see Jane blushing, of course, but I could tell she was, from the embarrassment in her voice, and my face too was burning near a fever.

"All right, Jane. You're a marvel. And I'm grateful to you from the bottom of my heart."

A quick answer: "It's for Jenny I'm doing it. Or all right—yes—for you too—because—oh, because of how you've acted through all this horrible time—Jenny's told me."

'And what'll you think?' I wondered, 'and what'll Jenny think, if it comes to be known I shot Harley Dexter and threw his body in a cave? Blood on my hands——.'

Which didn't keep me from feeling light-hearted as I left Jane. Which made me careless, though, neglecting as I did to keep as sharp an eye out as before and almost blundering into somebody's yard a ways up the creek. Roused a big dog that, lucky for me, stayed on the porch and barked. But the commotion brought out a man that shouted "Who is it?" and let off a shotgun blast into the air. I'd already scampered my fastest into the brush and was out of range when he fired a second shot in my direction, spattering tree-branches behind me.

For the rest of that night, in a hiding place not far from the Wharton farm, I slept like a baby, even with my hunger pangs.

But the good sleep didn't make the next day any shorter, and the closer the sun came to going down, the slower it sank. Right now my impatience was worse than my hunger, because that I could fend off, till it was safe to shoot game, with the Indian stuff known as 'cold flour': corn pounded fine with a little sugar mixed in, to be stirred up in water a handful or two for each meal.

And so finally, when I thought it never would, the time came to go. With my route well fixed in mind from studying the lay of the land through my spyglass during the day, I rode Comanche to the nearest practical spot, tied him in a ravine, crept the rest of the way on foot. The log barn with its big lot came up on my right, fifty yards or so from the house. In the lot the shapes of horses occasionally shifted around, and after seeing one blotch stir on the ground outside the lot, I judged the militia men all to be bundled down for the night. I then circled to the left, and moving like a stalker made it past the big pecan tree, singing tonight with insects as lively as it had the night when Jenny and I hugged and kissed in the swing on the porch. Looking up from the ground often I finally stole to where I could distinguish a pale form unearthly still in that same porch swing. It had to be Jenny, but even yet I wouldn't trust my eyes. So I got down on my belly and wriggled ahead with only dead grass under me. And when at length the shape in the swing rocked a tiny bit, and lifted one hand to smooth a tress of hair hanging down her shoulder, I knew for sure it was Jenny herself.

I called her name softly, but even at that she jumped. But then she stood up and waited for me slip up the porch steps to reach her, and did not move a muscle. With my heart hammering and my breath held, I reached out my arms, and she stepped into them, fresh and soft in her delicate lace nightgown. Our lips met hard. I recovered my breath just short of suffocating, then lost it again on realizing the shape of Jenny's breasts pushed cuddling against my chest—into my rough clothes, that all at once I was ashamed of. I doubt I'd've had the presence of mind, now, to get us in off the porch and out of sight. But Jenny did, leading me to the front door, and in, and up the stairs as silently and smoothly as if we'd been a pair of ghosts. Once we were inside the bedroom door, she closed it and stood still all tensed up and waiting. All but frantic now, I began to get out of my clothes, and the second I was naked I lifted Jenny's nightgown and slipped it off over her head. Then I swooped her nude body up in my arms and carried her gently to the bed, keeping my pulse just under detonation, where we slid in between the lovely fresh sheets and lowered our heads together into the soft and frilly pillows. My hands could not be everywhere at once, but they wandered trying to be, and all the while I was covering her face with kisses in one instant, and in the next instant she was covering mine. Our throbbing and groping and gasping together rose higher till we came close to going wild. —And then the instant when she arched up to meet me, and I entered her—and a new stage of wildness began, a wildness that rose and fell and carried us to a private world inside the night around us, into a spell where in great joy it seemed that Jenny's bloodstream and mine flowed through one and the same body. And then I passed beyond that region too, like a plunge into dying itself, but in a delirium resting assured I'd soon be back to life, beating with more vitality than ever.

And out in the night, all this while, the singing tree kept up its song.

—Time that was not quite time went by as we lay there, now still and now moving, in possession of one another in either case, knowing we could not let the night go by without talking—and must be long in talking too—yet still holding back from opening our mouths for words. For when we began to talk, I knew with a deep-coursing terror now and then, that the end of the night would come only too soon.

—Until later on, lulled into a wonder of fatigue, I dozed off: till a sudden impulse brought me awake, and made me say, softly and urgently, "Jenny."

"Yes, Todd."

"Tonight can't last much longer. I have to say all this, and get it said before daylight. I can't stay in Texas any longer, and I don't have to tell you why. And what's behind us, no use talking about it. We have to look at what lays ahead. I love you, and I'll go on loving you till my final breath." Jenny clung to me tight then but didn't try to kiss me, let me go on speaking: "I want nothing in this world more than for us to be married. Will you marry me, Jenny?"

"Yes, Todd, yes. Forever."

And now we had to kiss, long and fierce, almost to the point of taking each other again. But what I had to say couldn't wait, or we might not ever get it all said in time: "So we're married then. Married in our own eyes. That'll keep us strong till I get back. And oh, I wish I could say how long that'll be."

"It won't matter—not really—how long it is."

"Just keep believing I *will* be back. It may be a year, it may be two, it may be longer. But the day'll come when you see me riding up."

"I'll dream about the day you'll come back and I'll make ready for it." Then her voice broke in sobs.

Now there it was: the first stage of all I'd dreaded putting into words had passed between us as naturally as if the words had been born of themselves and never had to be sought. But not so for the hundred other things needing to be said—and little time left to say them, even if the words had been at hand: about her uncle and the others in her family—Cabus included; maybe my family too, considering the many griefs that might bring Jenny and them into contact between now and the day when I meant to come home again. All of that was too complex even to make a beginning.

—Then steadying her voice Jenny saved me the effort on one score at least: "Todd, I belong to you now, you and yours. If Uncle James sends out a search for you, I'll scheme up ways to send him astray. If he undertakes—if he or any of them undertake to seize your land, I'll scheme there too. I may not be able to stop *anything*, but if there's a way short of giving my life—or even that—I'll do it."

Again I had to hold her close and caress her tenderly. All at once tears sprang into my eyes, and hers became tear-drenched too. We just couldn't allow time for tears, though, and so I was soon telling her vital things that came to my mind in a rush of words: where Ma and Sis were now, and to write them and Cousin Graham the minute any move was made toward confiscation. I was longing to let Ma and Sis know that Jenny and I were as good as man and wife: I could have scribbled a note and left it for Jenny to mail, I could have instructed her to tell them. I was longing for Ma's hurt over my involvement with Jenny to be cured, and for Jenny and Sis to be friends. But none of that could be in these times, and just an attempt to bring it about might mean Colonel Ticknor's learning enough to cause Jenny more tribulation than she'd already have to endure.

The final love-making of that night we both knew well to be the last for what would seem an eternity. Beyond the deep joy of it we both ended in tears once more, but then even these farewell tears had to be stifled, since the night was nearly gone. The moon and the morning star were my signals—I'd become so used to going by them that I could tell nearly to the minute on any certain night how far off sunup was. So now I had to get out of bed and put on my clothes, pausing to kiss Jenny every other second. At last we went creeping down the stairs and out onto the porch by the swing. We took our last long kiss on the porch steps, with the song from the tree sweeping past our ears, while I brimmed over with gladness to have the voice of that tree to carry with me. What it gave me above all else was a faith that I'd come back to Jenny.

Before I was even out of the yard, with an upsurge of glow in the east already dimming the morning star, I heard a couple of the militia men up and talking. I lit out as fast as I could go without making too much noise. And when I made it to where Comanche was staked out, I had him saddled and was on my way in no time. The draw with the trickling stream was as far as I went that day though, where I stayed the whole day through, eking along as best I could on cold flour. Twice during those hours I saw deer come down to drink a little way upstream. It was all I could do, as starved as I felt, to hold off from shooting one. But this much I could look forward to. When the sun went down and dark set in, I'd be free to leave: nothing further to hold me in this part of the world.

That night, then, with great caution, I forded the river near the place where I'd run the outlaws back across. Once on the other bank, in territory new to me, I let Comanche pick our way, only kept him headed toward the North Star, because no question but I could trust him to weave safely through the brush and the brakes till we came out to where the open ridges set in. And so he did. And although I'd meant to stop a little piece from the river, everything ahead being so strange to me, still I didn't, because Comanche was willing to plod along as much as the moon-filled darkness allowed, and so on at that pace we went, and even at that before the night ended we'd put a big stretch of country between us and Texas.

When dawn came I saw that our route was taking us along a high bald ridge above a timbered draw. Seeing a movement, hearing a noise, I pulled up short and sat still. Then a lone deer came out in the open just below, and soon three others behind it. I drew out the Spencer and we eased off down the slope, Comanche knowing as always what to do. The deer saw us but did not bolt, stood frozen, heads lifted, too curious to sense the danger, and having no breeze for a scent to warn them. I succeeded in creeping close enough to use the pistol, dropped a half-grown doe. The rest of the herd bolted away.

Soon I had a fire going, and meat to cook. Not only was I hungry for that meat, I was hungry besides to celebrate with a feast, to celebrate my escape. So a feast was what I made of it. And when I finished I lay down and slept for a couple of hours, resolved from here on out to travel by daylight. Bushwhackers, Indians: after all I'd been through I could not work up the fear to be troubled by the thought of them. Further, I wouldn't stumble on anyone by surprise in the daytime. I was well-armed—much better than anybody else was likely to be—and I was certain Comanche could run off and leave any horse in Indian Territory.

And so, with the sun standing high, we went to the top of a low grassy mountain lying north of us. From up here, miles behind us, over layers of ridges timbered or bare, I could see where the country bottomed out in a dark and distant band along Red River. Over there beyond, the hazy slopes of Texas stretched out of sight. As a child I'd crossed that river into a land of hope which in a few short years had become a land of despair: had brought death to my father, made refugees of my family, banished me, and now threatened to disinherit us all. For the time being, and for who knew how long, that land of promise had been transformed into enemy territory. But this I vowed. I swore it in the depths of my soul. That one day I'd be back to claim what was mine: my land, my mother, my sister and brothers—most of all, my wife.

I swung Comanche's head around, I bent over his neck—caught up in recollection of the day when I rode him full tilt across the glade, in recollection also of unleashing him in pursuit of the buffalo—and now, as then, I yelled out at the top of my voice, "Yeee-haaa!"

Comanche tore out north as if he'd kicked the earth out of the way behind us.

24

OH YES, north I went: on that long hard journey of flight and seeking, of exile and return. To this day I wonder how I ever survived it, when any quirk in events through a hundred occasions of grave risk and narrow escape could have ended my life.

That moment of urging Comanche into a gallop of deliverance could not last any great distance. Pulling up soon and resting him for a little while, I then rode on at a deliberate pace, my confidence waning as I pondered how to evade ruthless white men and hostile Indians across the two hundred miles or more that separated me from Union territory. Alone, with no advantage over attackers except Comanche's speed and the surprise I could count on from the Spencer, the odds against me were staggering. All I could do was forge on trusting to luck and stay alert to every sight and sound.

Through that first day on the trail I saw no one. When night came on chilly, I built a small fire deep in a ravine to warm myself and cook some of the deer meat I had left. Then throwing dirt over the coals, I moved up to a slope where Comanche could graze, and shivered through a restless night wrapped in my blanket. Here was another troubling prospect too: for how long could I count on weather even this favorable, traveling north as I was with winter coming on and only one thin blanket to keep me warm?

At sunrise, afraid to chance the smoke of another fire, I warily approached a nearby spring, watered Comanche, stirred up a handful of cold flour for myself, then set out for the day—soon to meet with an experience that would haunt me for the whole time of my exile.

—Topping a rise, I saw a rider coming toward me from the north. I drew up, and with no hiding place at hand unlimbered the Spencer and sat waiting. On he came, but for all I could tell oblivious of me, in fact of all his surroundings. I watched closely as he drew near: body rigid and tensed forward, face thrust out and eyes riveted ahead, he rode along as if drawn by some intention so all-absorbing that he could have passed by me ten yards away unaware of my existence. Fascinated by this strange behavior, I was slow to realize that I knew him: of course, Joe Cottrell—who on the day when his brother Paul was hanged had cried out that name again and again in a spine-chilling voice.

I hailed him: "Joe!"

He halted and turned his stare on me, but he gave no sign of recognition.

"You just come from over there?" he said.

"Milcourt? Yeah. Where you coming from?"

No response to that, but: "I'm headed for Milcourt to kill Ticknor."

So that was what had happened: Joe's grief had driven him out of his mind. To be guarded with him, then. But what to say?

I was still searching when Joe added, "I'm the man chosen to do it. It's *my* duty. Nobody else's. Is he in Milcourt?"

"As far as I know, he is—either there or at home. But listen, Joe—listen now. This is Todd Blair. Remember me? Listen, why not wait? Wait till he's less cautious than he'll be now. The time'll come. Just wait—."

Joe shook his head violently: "It can't wait! Every minute he lives is red with blood. It's got Paul's blood all over it. *They* tried to get me to wait too."

"They? Who?"

"Them. Back there." He snapped one arm aloft and jabbed a thumb backward over his shoulder. "They tied me up last night to keep me from going back. But I worked aloose and give them the slip." —With that he broke out in a wild neighing laugh that gave me a clutching in the midriff.

I had to say it—though what good would it do? "Joe, please listen to me. Please. Now's not the time. They'll kill you. Come on north with me. We'll come back together, and the Union army with us. Then we'll make Ticknor pay all right—and the rest of the bastards too. But it's foolish right now. It's throwing your life away—."

"Oh no. No, no, no." Again he shook his head vehemently. "Oh, and don't think I'd call you a coward, Todd"—so he did know me—"or blame you because you had a rifle and didn't shoot him down. Oh no. You wasn't supposed to. It's me, I'm the man chosen to do it. And don't look for me to come north till Ticknor's dead."

Joe went silent, his eyes again boring into space toward the southern horizon. An instant later, while I groped further for words—certain though I was that none could reach him—he caught his lower lip between his teeth and released it. As a drop of blood formed there, he threw back his head and opened his mouth wide. Then that outcry—that same outcry as on the day of his brother's hanging: "Paul! Paul!" Then as if listening, and staring: "Yes! I'm coming. I will! I see you! Go ahead! Lead me! Lead me!" And slashing the tips of the reins back and forth across his horse's withers, he forced it into a killing run in the direction of Red River.

For I don't know how long I sat stunned, shuddering at that voice like a wailing come back from the grave. And as Joe Cottrell flogged his horse on toward the river, that cry kept on piercing my ears till distance carried it away.

—Joe Cottrell was never seen again. What happened to him no one who knew ever told. Many people thought he'd met up with some of the fire-brands before reaching Milcourt, and as he was too demented to keep secret what he was on his way to do, they killed him and got rid of the body—.

As soon as I'd recovered a little I rode on, at a quickened pace now. The people ahead that Joe Cottrell had mentioned must be friends, since he'd been with them.

They were. A few miles on north I came across over forty people: men, a few women, even children, for the most part families of the hanged men, or men the jury'd set free. They'd made up a fugitive band and slipped across the river a couple of nights before.

Now that was the first of many turns of good luck for me. Numerous enough to discourage attack from Indians or renegades, with a skilled frontiersman by the name of Gibbs as our leader, we made the trek across Indian Territory without any great mishap, arriving in two weeks' time at Fort Gibson. There we dispersed. I went on to Fort Scott, eager to enlist in the Union cavalry, and I did so at once.

—Now after that it was two years of riding companion to death and destruction, and as if by miracle coming through unscathed, Comanche along with me—which is another story, remaining for all its havoc distinct from that enthralled existence in the ordeal of slaughter and glory in Milcourt. One protection against brute facts in those late years of the war was that nothing I did, including the slaughter of men in battle, ever touched me as reality: all of it done in a state of suspension where, oblivious to the present, I thought only of how to endure lone exile in anticipation of triumphant return to Milcourt: to Jenny, to my family, to revenge.

Yet always the question hovered: revenge how? on what terms? Any thought of killing Colonel Ticknor seared me through with a vision of Jenny's loving image turned on me as accuser. On the heels of that thought another would sneak in, tainted by the disgrace of shirking: a vague and guilty hope that Joe Cottrell had avenged us both already by doing away with Ticknor. The only actual revenge I'd taken came to mind, too, often in the midst of death-dealing in warfare: the image of Harley Dexter rigid and lifeless in a posture of attack. And of all things, by some mysterious twist I was sometimes filled with irrational remorse that I'd taken his life—remorse entangled with the regret that I'd buried him so near my father's grave, and also with a new and strange sense of fellowship created between us by the sharing of that cave: a tomb for him, for me a place of symbolic death and resurrection. In all this, besides, was a half-conscious purpose that I did not well understand till much later: the killing of Harley Dexter epitomized for me the long chain of carnage it initiated and by some distortion of conscience relieved me of the responsibility for taking lives in combat. Yet, if a normal sense of right and wrong was ever restored, how could this absolution prevail then? If I shuddered during my banishment at the thought of having shot a prime and original bastard like Harley Dexter on homeground, in self-defense at that, when I was freed from the moral anarchy of the battlefield to go home, how could I ever in my native region kill a single one of my father's other executioners?

In time a new train of thought opened a way out of this dilemma. I found myself holding the town of Milcourt as a whole accountable for the blood which, in Joe Cottrell's indelible image, had stained each minute gone by since it was shed. What I kept on seeing was the many citizens who during the reign of terror had gone on conducting private affairs as though nothing out of the ordinary was taking place—and so by their silence gave consent to the monstrous events unfolding around them. The remaining question was, how to bring retribution down on this multitude that possessed no single face? The answer came to me like an inspiration. Why, to destroy the city! Devastation! And simultaneously there came to me a vision constantly with me after that, in the charging and falling back of cavalry raids: an abiding vision of Milcourt in flames, of myself in ultimate onslaught putting a torch to every building of that place, above all to its supposed center of justice, the courthouse, till the town from end to end would be wrapped in a blaze to consume every morsel of it to ashes. And mercifully it was a vision that concealed in the flames of buildings any sight of a human face or of a human body destroyed.

Strangely, wondrously, in my vision one physical element of the town was spared from the annihilation. Within and before the flames engulfing Milcourt stood the hanging tree, whole and unsinged. Let all the town built by humans and defiled by humans go up in holocaust. But the laws of my imagining would not permit the burning of the death tree. Not made by man, it could not be corrupted by man. On the contrary, desecration of that tree by the lynchers had raised it to holiness, created an altar of sacrifice to be revered just this side of worship, idolatry.

While the gruesome conflict dragged on, and as a seasoned veteran I became a scout, my ears were always open for any rumor of an invasion of Texas across Red River. One day late in the war, summoned to headquarters, I found other scouts assembling: about twenty we came to, all Texans in exile, all itching to wrest Texas from Confederate hands. We received orders to go down and spy out defenses along Red River, in the very region of Milcourt—and no one had to tell us that our expedition was a prelude to invasion.

Although we set out at once, we met with long delays: encounters with guerrillas and bushwhackers, skirmishes with the Comanches and Kiowas. Weeks passed before we reached the river, where our first stealthy reconnoitering on the Texas side gave us all the intelligence we'd ever need: General Lee had surrendered a month ago.

Even so, we decided to mount a little invasion of our own. We rode boldly into Milcourt, and what a solace it was to our long sense of grievance to see the fright on the faces of the inhabitants. We looked hard-bitten enough to be bushwhackers—which if true would've been fearful indeed, with the Confederacy fallen apart and Federal authority not yet re-established on the frontier. But then the captain made our identity known to a few, and as word spread every gathering of onlookers we approached stood petrified for a different reason.

When we'd had enough of humbling the rebels, we headed back to wait across the river to join a larger occupying force. As I was the only man in the troop from Milcourt, and in agony for news of Jenny, on our way out of town we rode by the Wharton house. I'd no more than thrown my reins across the paling fence when Jane saw me and came running out. Even from a distance the look on her face warned of disaster. As we hugged each other she sobbed it out. Jenny was dead. She died giving birth to our child. The boy died with her.

None of the men spoke to me as we trailed back across Wolf Ridge toward the river, but they rode along around me in close formation.

After a few days of wariness and a further visit to Milcourt, we found that all at once nobody seemed to care who we were or what we did. The war was over, the country full of returning soldiers, and any battered veteran looked like any other. So we simply disbanded and each man struck out for home. No great distance for me, but my struggle against grief for Jenny, in ignorance still of the fate of Ma, Sis, Montecristo, Jenk and Scooter during my absence, was hardship enough. So much so that it didn't even surprise me to feel yesterday's ambition—my long-nourished dream of fiery vengeance against Milcourt—crowded into the past by the sudden and absolute difference of the present. War fantasies all those schemes had been, and now there was no more war: yesterday's act of combat daring was transformed overnight into a crime.

But what about the hangings? A crime surely in war or peace. Into what scheme of setting things right was I to fit them now? Was the whole atrocity merely to be shoved aside and forgotten? And if so, how could I ever consent to do nothing but endure it? How could I forego revenge, allow it also to be absorbed by this sudden new order of life for which I was not prepared?

At least for now, though, with pressing decisions called for on vital matters, I could avoid being preoccupied by thoughts of justice through revenge. I had all I could do, once free of the army, to rush around setting the cabin in order, acquiring a wagon and muleteam, heading out to Dallas to bring the family home. When I got there and found them all safe, the reunion was glorious, though we did have to wait for Scooter to recover from the whooping cough before setting out for home—.

Re-establishing the rounds of life consumed every waking hour for months—so that still the inner cry for justice could be suppressed from day to day. One nagging uneasiness stayed with me: that Sis would begin urging me on to swift revenge. I could have saved myself the worry. Sis had matured while I was away. She was soon to be married to a fellow she met while staying at Cousin Graham's. She was all tender sympathy, too, when she learned of the tragic end to my love for Jenny. When she mentioned the hangings now, it was only to reproach the local officials for not punishing the instigators.

At first action against these men seemed likely. Already when I left Milcourt for Dallas to rejoin the family, the commander of the occupying Union force had begun an inquiry into the lynchings: brief hearings that made no headway because participants on both sides of the issue were afraid to testify.

Later on we had further brief hopes for justice, when civil government was restored and there was talk of a grand jury to investigate the hangings. Nothing but talk ever came of it, and even if those official words had evolved into deeds, few were left within the jurisdiction of local courts: few to indict, few to vindicate, for all but a handful of those involved had migrated to new territory, perpetrators and survivors of victims alike.

What then? The only vengeance remaining on earth was mine. But more than ever the thought of demanding blood clashed with a warborn repulsion against killing concealed from myself all the while by an elaborate image of Harley Dexter as scapegoat. Moreover, who was within my reach to render an eye for an eye and a tooth for a tooth? Colonel Ticknor had died for the lost cause at the head of his troops in a late engagement of the war. Matt Scanlon stayed on in the Cross Timbers—though I never understood why. I saw him at a distance from time to time. He walked like a man obsessed by fear for his life. I could never have found the heart to kill him. His fright mounted to incurable terror before he died of a stroke a few years after the war.

So then my only vengeance—or justice—lay with the still undiscovered bones of Harley Dexter in a rocky cave. Being near that spot once more, with war gone from the world, in course of time I had another change of heart, coming to wonder why I'd ever regretted killing him. Instead, I now felt entitled to the consolation of that sacrifice performed by my own hand: and that the worst of the lynchers, in paying for my father's blood with his own, had in a sense died for his cohorts as well, and even expiated the crime the whole town was guilty of for allowing the massacre to take place. Let that, I concluded at last, be sufficient to keep me at peace with the bones of my father. The pain of having Harley Dexter's tomb on our land in sacrilegious proximity to my father's grave also eased away. This seeming flaw in the nature of things could now at last be fitted without disruption into the new pattern of existence.

But then the hanging tree, what of that?—the one component of Milcourt preserved in my wartime vision of holocaust. On first coming home I could not bear to go near it; and could not, at that point, confront the difficulty of how to live near Milcourt and yet keep out of sight of that tree. Then, while I was away in Dallas, events took a sudden turn that did away with any such concern.

Even before the end of the war the hanging tree had begun to arouse a dangerous range of emotions among the townspeople: awe, dread, wrath, in some a perverse pride, and with it all a growing superstition. Some broke off twigs for keepsakes. Some at night came with hatchets to chop off and save bark or little wedges of the trunk. So early one morning the Union commander threw a ring of guards around the tree and put a crew of soldiers to work with saws and axes. For three days, I was told, it went on: the tree was felled; the stump and roots dug out; trunk, branches, stump and roots cut up into small blocks; all these piled in the cavity of the stump; a great bonfire set. Then the commander had the soil plowed up and levelled over the ashes.

Stunned though I was to learn that the tree had been destroyed in my absence, as if a holy place had been desecrated, yet in time I came to feel, if still regretful, also thankful. Life lived as well as it can be in a community had best go on with the ashes of the past underground or scattered on the wind: let new trees spring up where old trees have become an encumbrance to the earth.

The end of the story, then.... And soon what must be the end of it all for me. Every day I belong less to the world I breathe in: less to a family increasingly distant in relationship, less to the small community of Milcourt, less to the vast community of the world. As a vestige of a nation-making upheaval, I am almost a legend while I live; as a man wasted by age, a burden to this generation, existing in the loneliness of legend on the solicitude of others, which in spite of its best intentions suggests that I have outlived my time. If I am still of this earth, it is the earth as history and the earth as dust. Often when I lie waking in the night my body and spirit together beg the earth to open and admit me to the past and to dust—.

Still, in the next instant may come an involuntary refusal of oblivion, and my heart ignites with yearning for a new life: to relive that season of radiance and anguish from the day when we first came to the Cross Timbers to the day when I fled into exile. Fragments of that life return as gleaming as visions of immortality, as if I could live them over in cycles through eternity. But then the darkening, the torment inseparable from the rapture: the ever-returning vision of Pap falling, falling through the branches of the hanging tree, the sun standing still overhead, while I reach out impotent to arrest his fall. Then with dread and pity my heart rebels: I realize that I cannot long to recreate the marvel of that life without simultaneous consent to seeing my father subjected to a hideous death. I cannot endure the presence of this dilemma for long, and yet I know that again and again I will reach the same impasse.

But now and then I experience a rarity among those moments. My blood courses to a deeper conviction that I need not after all shut my eyes to the immolation of my father in order to value the brightest splendor of existence: that indeed life of this intensity cannot exist without acceptance of the immolation; and on the verge of delirium I discover in myself the ability to reconcile the contradiction of such acceptance. It may be that this endeavor comes to no more than pitting my will against the inexorable laws of circumstance, never to be actualized in time, yet in these rare moments I glimpse a silence outside time where I have the power to offer up myself in my father's place. It comes to me as a great consolation, this ever-potential surrender of my own life, this willingness to submit to vicarious sacrifice. This and this alone, in brevity but in mightiness, inspires in me consent to a boundless universe where the father and the son must each be willing to yield up life in perpetual sacrifice to redeem the other.

Brief and fleeting as they are—these intervals of balanced impulse appeasing death in life—under their potency I embrace again the miracle of return to a pristine Cross Timbers and to the enchanted scenes of my young life renewed. If, in time and space reborn, I could pass under the great elm tree entering Milcourt in the ox wagon, as we did on that first day, I would go. If I could ride under a night sky cursing the fate that brought us to Texas—if I could wait in the moonlight for valiant men to gather and march to my father's rescue, I would go. If I must live again the death of Colonel Oldham, must kill and bury Harley Dexter—must walk behind my father to the death tree, or even take his place—yes, I would go. If I could rescue Jenny from the outlaws—make love with her under the cottonwood, hold her in that last night of poignancy and farewell—yes, if through all this, in tribulation and in glory, I could race along on Comanche from the first "Yeee-haaa" of riding him hard through the glade to the last "Yeee-haaa" of going north, the flight of liberation into exile and eventual homecoming, I would go.

Oh yes, I would go.

Books by L. D. CLARK

Other Texas Fiction

The Dove Tree
(Doubleday, 1961)
Is This Naomi? and Other Stories
(Confluence Press, 1979)
The Fifth Wind
(Confluence Press, 1981)
A Charge of Angels
(Confluence Press, 1987)

Other Works

Dark Night of the Body
(University of Texas Press, 1964)
The Minoan Distance: The Symbolism of Travel in D. H. Lawrence
(University of Arizona Press, 1980)
Civil War Recollections of James Lemuel Clark, edited by L. D. Clark
(Texas A&M University Press, 1984)
The Plumed Serpent, by D. H. Lawrence, edited by L. D. Clark
(Cambridge University Press, 1987)

©1992 LaVerne Harrell Clark

L.D. CLARK grew up on a farm in the Cross Timbers of Texas. He is the author of three novels and a book of short stories and has won a PEN Syndicated Fiction Award. Holding a Ph.D from Columbia University, he has also pursued a career in scholarship, with three books on D.H. Lawrence to his credit. Now Professor Emeritus of English at the University of Arizona, he lives in Tucson with his wife, LaVerne Harrell Clark, writer and photographer.